SWEET DECEIT

⁓⌇⁓

SWEET DECEIT

A gripping legal thriller

BY

CHARLES RICHARD

THE CHOIR PRESS

Copyright © 2024 Charles Richard

All rights reserved. No part of this publication may be reproduced or transmitted in any form or by any means, electronic or mechanical including photocopying, recording or any information storage or retrieval system, without prior permission in writing from the publishers.

The right of Charles Richard to be identified as the author of this work has been asserted by him in accordance with the Copyright, Designs and Patents Act 1988

First published in the United Kingdom in 2024 by
The Choir Press

ISBN 978-1-78963-472-3

Important Notice: This is a work of fiction. Names, characters, businesses, places, events and incidents herein are the product of the author's imagination or used in a fictitious manner. Any resemblance to any persons or to any corporate entity wherever incorporated or to any actual event or publication is purely coincidental.

To Sophia and Piers, whose love and friendship fed the seed from which this Book germinated

And my thanks to the Editors of 'What Doctors Don't Tell You', whose articles on Sweetener products originally created that seed

And also to Patrick for some helpful steers, and to Sophia who provided the catalyst for the Epilogue

England

It was past daffodil time in Dorset. The ice crystals sparkling in the dawn's frosty harr caught the first rays of sunlight that rose above the distant hilltop beyond the valley below. It was a brief but fleeting display of nature's magic, which began to dissolve as swiftly as it had first appeared, bringing into focus the view across the valley, accompanied by the dawn's celebratory chorus of songbirds that ushered in the day to come.

The mellifluous symphony was disturbed by the throaty rumble of an old V8 engine, slowly chugging its way out of the woodland. The vehicle responsible for such cacophony was an early version of Land Rover's pioneering off-road model which, like its ancestors, was once the hallmark of that brand's unrivalled versatility and reliability. The growl of its engine was for decades every bit a feature of the British countryside as was the harsh craw of the rooks. But its brothers in arms have slowly succumbed to the wasting effects of time and use (more often abuse) and the emergence of modern rivals.

This particular chariot was an early version of the Discovery, whose equally weather-beaten driver has pulled up alongside the edge of the large copse, where the first bluebells were ready to emerge on the south-facing clearing. His seasoned eyes were checking for any tell-tale signs of fresh predation by vermin. He was a guardian of this land, and one of the countryside's devoted conservationists, having traded the modesty of his salary for the freedom and lifestyle that come with his duties as the head gamekeeper of the Piddle Valley Estate in South Dorset.

His name was Charles Poore, or Charlie to those close to him. As befits a keeper, his ruddy features advertised long years in his vocation. Whilst the majority of his fifty-odd years of labour might have extracted their toll on his body, his eyes remained as sharp as the birds of prey and other predators from which he protected the birdlife. At this time of year, his concern was for the songbirds rather than any reared species. He had counted at least two breeding pairs of wood warblers and a pair of willow tits on his visit here earlier in the week. He listened out for their distinctive calls, and fancied he heard the warbler's call near where he's last seen it. He kept his small binoculars in his jacket for occasions such as this.

Bless 'em, he thought. But those beauties were no match for those evil magpies, of which he and his team had tried to cleanse these woods. There was no sound of them today, but they were a sly breed. So, he kept his powerful air-rifle with its zeroed scope and his trusty twelve-bore in the back of his 'Landy,' as the lads called it, lest he should spy one of these devils on his routine patrols.

He tarried a while to survey the valley opposite, and his eyes quickly took in the scene below. The cattle had yet to emerge from the milking sheds, whence they would return to the fields higher up the valley. Given the late rains this spring, they had still not been allowed to meander down into the valley, where they could feed amidst the lush meadows t'other side of the river from which the estate took its name. Their delayed appearance told the keeper that Joey Roberts, the cowhand, had arranged yet another of his nocturnal rendezvous, and had been late to rise. That did not surprise him. That young man couldn't keep his pecker under control, and was a damned nuisance.

His gaze moved across to the fields above the meadows, their newly ploughed furrows awaiting planting with wheat and barley seeds, and beyond to the fences which he and his underkeepers would help to repair later that month. Further down and set amongst those fields, at the end of a dirt track, was an old stone barn. It was a deserted, abandoned relic from a previous century, whose roof timbers and slates had sagged over the decades, much like the fortunes of the estate.

The keeper could never understand why in times past the family had not converted that barn into a 'holiday let' or a home for the owner's younger sister, especially now that the estate had been passed to the only son, Jamie, not many years back. But there was no chance of that now. Jamie had decreed that the place was 'off limits' and was not to be touched by anyone.

There had been a time when it used to be one of the favourite spots for the village lads when they would go a-courting. But not any more. None of the farmhands were allowed to use it. Jamie had bolted all the doors, and padlocked the lane leading up to the old oak doors, and the windows were out of reach.

That had all happened since Jamie had parted with that comely brunette with the alluring blue eyes and the soft Virginian accent, or 'the southern belle' as she had become known amongst the locals. Lovely lass, she were. Truth, whenever she was here, she made a point of coming over to chat with him when there was a spare moment. She had that kind of magic that, to his eyes, just drew a man. And, what's more, she had made him laugh. Aye, that had been her gift. He smiled at the thought.

It was no secret that Jamie's heart was broke when they had parted, and so no one questioned his orders to stay away from the place. It was as though Jamie had preserved it as a shrine to his lost love. He never gave any reason, and the keeper was careful to avoid the issue during his meetings with him. And even these had become more formal, and less frequent than in former times.

Any rate, Jamie was much liked and admired, and therefore his wishes – nay, this was one of his few commands – were respected. Well, at least by most in the village and around these parts. He strongly suspected that Joey, much as he liked him, had found a way in through the window at the back, for he'd seen his car parked up on the road more than once at the bottom of that lane.

But Charlie could not help thinking that the old barn, now so near to collapse, was the place where Jamie's heart had been incarcerated ever since that lass had left his side.

He shook his head. He and his good wife had been married these past forty years, and he considered himself fortunate on account of that. His earnest wish was that the young man would find new love. Some hope, he thought. Given the man's present humour, there seemed little prospect of that happening this side of the coming maypole.

He could hardly bear to look Jamie in the eyes these days. He certainly hadn't seen him smile all last year. Why, the fellow used to be one of the tidiest shots in the county. Loved the sport, he did, but hadn't been out with a gun since that time.

It couldn't be more than a six-month. The keeper would never forget that day. Jamie had as good as cut him dead when he had asked about her. Just: 'We shan't be seeing her again on the estate; it's over between us.'

Curt as that, he was.

And when the keeper had begun to offer commiserations, Jamie had interrupted him with – and it was so unlike him – 'I'd prefer if we didn't discuss it.'

Sharp as that, again. Jamie had never spoken to him like that before, and the matter had been off limits ever since.

Ah well, there it was. There's naught as queer as folk, he thought. He had been taught that as a young child, and had seen it proved true many times in his life. Cupid's arrow had sunk deep, and had penetrated the man's very soul, which now felt the loss all the more acutely.

Now what remained of that young man's scarred soul lay behind locks and chains, gathering cobwebs and dust, discarded beside stale hay bales within that desolate stone monument on the opposite side of the valley. And within it lay whatever else Jamie had packed into crates, and had padlocked inside that dungeon.

Whether time would heal those wounds was anyone's guess, but the remedy seemed to lie beyond the poor soul's reach for now.

Chapter One

London. Hilary term has long passed, and the Easter term is well underway, and the recent Easter weekend is memorable only on account of its foul weather. And this being England, the warm weather has delayed its arrival until the short vacation has passed, and the nation is once again at labour.

There are few cities whose streets and tall buildings can trap their fumes more efficiently and effectively than this ancient conurbation, despite the new green tariffs intended to discourage combustible engines.

And just so as to ensure that our cup of joy overflows and our discomfort is maximised, an oppressive, heat-induced haze has been visited on the metropolis, one more typical of the capitals of Central Europe. It ensures that the lungs of London's inhabitants inhale generous helpings of toxic pollutants, seemingly forever suspended in the fug, albeit marginally reduced following the local mayor's latest reforms.

Our story takes us west of Christopher Wren's Restoration masterpiece at St Paul's, and we journey down Ludgate Hill, then up Fleet Street, and along the Strand. We halt outside the Royal Courts of Justice (or the 'RCJ' to use their common acronym within the legal profession), a Victorian monument intended to convey the might and right of justice. We venture inside and submit to the indignity of security checks.

Now we stop to gaze at and admire the huge, marbled atrium with its vaulted ceiling. A visitor absorbing its dimensions for the first time cannot fail to be impressed. But to the seasoned lawyers who tread these marbled floors, this building constitutes an arid and airless inconvenience. Almost without exception, it is wholly unsuited to the requirements of modern legal practice. It is a place of last resort. So much so that such fresh air as might otherwise flow within the capital seems to know this, for it avoids the few apertures in the structure that are capable of providing ventilation, and which the court staff have taken the trouble to open.

We are directed to Courts 35 to 37, outside which the atrium is no exception. It is a dark and gloomy place. Assembled around its benches and tables are groups of litigants. Some impart or digest last-minute instructions. Others seek to thrash out the terms of a 'deal' before the court usher calls their case in to be presented to the judge who will hear urgent applications. Other groups have already been heard by the court, and are now seeking to agree the form of order which the judge will be asked to approve.

One is struck by the fact that the features of very few of the protagonists, even those who have notionally 'won,' exhibit complete satisfaction at the outcome of their proceedings in court. This might strike an objective observer as odd, because most laymen will naturally assume that there are only winners and losers in this business. But the reality is often rather different.

Such is modern-day civil litigation.

Some groups comprise the dark-suited lawyers alone. Others include both clients and their lawyers. The two species of client and lawyer are easily distinguished, partly by their attire (there are no wigs or gowns in this court), but primarily by the inner confidence in the surroundings, if not the circumstances, which is evident in one and clearly absent in the other.

The heat haze has exacerbated the stifling conditions that have long been a feature of normal working life in the High Court in London. And those conditions are especially acute in the dark and stuffy atrium outside Court 37. This is one of a handful of courts located in a separate wing a short distance from the original Victorian building. It is accessed along stone corridors and through stiff, oak doors – almost impossible for anyone encumbered by multiple bundles of papers to negotiate alone.

Yet it is within these courts that judges will typically hear pre-trial (or 'interim') applications 'in chambers,' meaning that these are private hearings, and that the public and the press are excluded.

It is in this intimidating arena that an elegant brunette stands alone amidst what appears to be a sea of confusion. She is here against her will, as is evident from her demeanour, and especially the expression of apprehension that she wears.

True, that would not be unusual in itself. Like so many lay participants, she has brought her own peculiar history to the occasion, yet she hopes and prays that her 'case' (and she has come to accept that term) will be preferred to that of the opposition. Hence the anxiety, for like so many other litigants before her, she brings a factual scenario that is genuinely stranger than fiction.

But, we sense that there is something special about this particular victim. We cannot put a finger on it, but feel a sense of vulnerability, of hurt, yet also something else. Could it be something approaching defiance, wrath, vengeance even? If so, one asks, how has she managed to supress those sentiments so as to create an impression of innocence, indeed one bordering on naivety?

Let us interrogate the drama a tad further.

Her name is Catriona Symonds. At five foot nine, she might be considered tall for a woman, but that may be on account of her refined pose. That she is beautiful is not in doubt, yet her clothes do not flaunt that beauty as they could. Instead, she has chosen to dress elegantly, even conservatively. The latter quality is no doubt a reflection of her respect both for her current predicament and for the legal process, and confirms the care and prudence with which she has prepared herself for this ordeal.

One is struck by a purity about her person, one not easy to fathom from a brief encounter. It is in part manifested by her modest carriage, which might at first glance appear not so much assured as diffident. But only at a first glance, because caution suggests that such a prejudice might just as easily be created by her striking features which, together with her long legs, mark her out as special. These, together with her natural poise, create an impression of an athlete of Amazonian qualities.

However, you might think differently if you knew that, whilst some have found these properties so alluring, at least one other has been quick to exploit them. We shall no doubt revert to that aspect in due course.

Why? Because a closer inspection reveals that there is nothing of the hunter about her. Instead, there is something about her that speaks of predation; of trust that has been abused. And that is no doubt why her features betray an absence of self-confidence.

Instead, they convey uncertainty, anxiety even.

But that, you say, is surely to be expected given her current circumstances.

True, that might be one explanation, but perhaps that is not a complete answer. It is partly because of who she is, and of how she looks, that she is here, now.

But more of that anon.

At her comparatively young age of twenty-five, she has limited direct experience of the affairs of commerce, and less still of the law and its mysterious procedures. As a solitary figure in these daunting surroundings, she looks particularly isolated. She is clearly nervous. The stress of the occasion is evident in her eyes, and by the way that she from time to time unconsciously holds the corners of her lips between her teeth.

In other circumstances her face would normally radiate charm, especially when she smiles, enough to illuminate a ballroom.

But there are no smiles today.

Not here.

Not now.

This contest is deadly serious.

She is dressed in white, deliberately. She might be a defendant in these proceedings, but she does not see herself in any way culpable. On the contrary, she regards herself as occupying the moral high ground. So much so that, over these past few days, she has almost bizarrely come to welcome the allegations that have been made against her; and not least because it has provided her and her co-defendants with the opportunity to carry the fight to her opponents.

The purpose of the hearing was originally to determine whether orders that were made against her and her co-defendants over a week previously should be continued, or whether these should be varied or discharged. It is a common procedure in cases of this sort for those to whom the austere surroundings of the High Court appear familiar, even on what has become a close and humid morning. A separate application by the defendants is also now in play.

But we digress. There is time enough for all that.

This woman has intended to portray herself as an innocent victim. Given her round blue eyes and fair complexion, in conjunction with her demure attire, she has certainly achieved that effect.

But hold. Is it entirely right to describe the surroundings – as austere and unpleasant as they might be to a stranger – as altogether unfamiliar to the young lady whom we now survey? That might be correct in a literal sense, for this is certainly the first occasion on which she has been physically present here. But are we altogether correct to describe the overall experience as being unfamiliar – at any rate to her? In this respect we must register some doubt.

How so? One need only look to her friendship and subsequent love affair with the man upon whom she has come to depend. Many are the times that he has trodden these marbled corridors and contested – as he now contests – with his opponents the direction in which the proceedings should be taken forward. And frequent are the times that he has consulted – as he is about to consult – with his client in this and other law courts across the land.

Indeed, at this very moment he turns to look at the young woman that has caught our attention outside the doors of this court.

And there's the clue: a smile, warm and affectionate, but of necessity brief, followed by a nod of assurance that all is properly in hand.

Ah, you surmise, so the relationship is rather more than that of counsel and client? Well, you'd be right to do so.

That said, it cannot be denied that the imminent confrontation before the judge who will soon preside over proceedings behind the glass-panelled doors is evidently intimidating to our fine young woman. Perhaps it is less so to her co-defendants, whose trade often involves such confrontation. However, that is not the full story.

Over these past seven days (but especially during the last two days), this young woman has been able to experience and digest vicariously the complex mechanics of litigation in the civil (as opposed to the criminal) courts through the time that she has spent with the young man whose eye she has just caught. The present crisis will no doubt prove a proper test of their relationship, and you would be forgiven for asking whether it has blossomed, or faltered, as a consequence of it.

Time enough for that.

What you really want to know is what it is that has caused the presence here today of this figure of beauty, and how she has allowed herself to become entangled in the legal process.

Those questions are entirely fair. The answers to them involve a short journey back in time, which we must needs make in order to trace the origins of this particular encounter, and to comprehend the events which are about to enfold.

Chapter 2

London, England

Covent Garden in London is home to the Royal Opera. Tradition dictates that this modest theatre should be the capital's answer to the grandeur in which other European and American cities stage their operas and ballets. However, in contrast to some of its rivals on the Continent, it does not feed a national appetite for the ultimate musical experience. Instead, it has become one of the playgrounds of the commercial elite. Unlike other elitist playgrounds such as Royal Ascot, Wimbledon and Henley, it boasts one distinguishing feature, namely culture. It is a place where the barons of industry come to impress either their clients and, when occasion demands, the grey and deadly men from the City institutions who control their fortunes. A place not so much now of tiaras and wing collars, but of pin-striped cloth and silk. As always, the privilege is secured by a hefty ransom. For the equivalent cost of a single ticket in the front row of the stalls, an ordinary mortal could afford to fly an entire family to Continental Europe.

But, as chief executive officer of one of the UK's largest pharmaceutical giants, Robert McBride is no ordinary mortal. He leads a business that stretches from the supply of aspirin to research into the next generation of wonder drugs. The distribution network which his company controls is every bit as efficient as those through which class A narcotics are supplied via the Afghan and Albanian militias to the street pushers of Europe's inner cities and towns, with the consequent devastation that is visited on their communities. The difference is that his production and supply chains are not only legal, but are actively promoted by central governments throughout the world, despite increasing warnings that the sort of products which his company purveys might be causing serious damage to each nation's health.

These same warnings had begun many years ago as barely audible whispers from disparate fringe groups, but in recent years have become ever more vociferous. The danger to his business, which he dared not concede in public, is that these warnings now issued from people who commanded growing influence. They are now starting to be taken ously not just by the media and the informed professional classes, bu a rising percentage of the population.

Despite this, McBride publicly created the illusion that his mission was ultimately to benefit the many. In reality, his role was to enhance the wealth of his shareholders, which in turn helped to inflate the salaries of his employees. In so doing, he was entitled to and did enjoy the incidental byproducts of all his hard work in the form of his lavish salary and bonuses, together with the other perks that he drew from the company.

He is a thick-set man of ample girth, such that he had fully expected to find that his seat was uncomfortable, at least during the time that he was likely to be conscious during the performance. His close-cropped hair is in that transient phase between grey and white, and betrays an age significantly in advance of fifty. The harsh contours of his face, and especially the hard lines around his eyes and mouth, were nature's reward for the ruthless energies with which he had stoked the turbines of his company's commerce on both sides of the Atlantic and elsewhere for the better part of three decades. But it was his eyes, as sharp as those of a lean tiger, that could transfix any vulnerable prey upon whom he focussed his attention. They were dark green, as though harking back to an ancient Indian ancestry, whose warriors were well accustomed to collecting the scalps of their victims. And McBride had lost count of the trophies that had been surrendered by the butchered and vanquished corporate victims who had failed to yield to his demands.

These features, borne as they were atop his corpulent frame, would have revealed to the casual observer that he was not a man to be trifled with. However, those with experience of doing business with him had learnt, sometimes at their cost, that one did not observe him casually. Instead, they instinctively learnt or were advised to observe him keenly at all times, and certainly never to turn their corporate back on him. Those that failed to obey their instinct or to heed that advice usually paid dearly for the mistake. McBride did not make a habit of taking prisoners.

He had kept his parentage and background a dark secret, just as he had concealed his early life as a highly effective purveyor of narcotics. This had accounted for the relatively swift accumulation of capital which he had subsequently used to buy a very substantial shareholding in the company via several carefully disguised Cayman Island entities.

Having 'gone legit,' as he had since prided himself, the voting rights afforded to him through these offshore proxies had in due course caused the expulsion of the previous CEO and his elevation to that post. He had retained several of his contacts in the criminal underworld, whose resourcefulness he had exploited in the past as and when occasion had demanded.

He and his wife were the guests of the managers of the group company's pension fund, the wealth of which had steadily increased in line with the company's profits. The firm had performed well in exchange for a handsome fee, some of which was now being returned in the form of this hospitality. His wife had pushed him into accepting the invitation. Being virtually tone deaf, opera was not a medium of which he was especially fond. However, her friends had all told her that this season's new production of Verdi's *Rigoletto* was a definite 'must see,' and it was one of the few perks from his job that she got to enjoy, and actually did enjoy. Hence, they had duly presented themselves in the foyer of the Royal Opera House earlier that evening.

Having already over-indulged in the incessant supply of champagne that his generous hosts had provided, he truly hoped that, rather than having to endure the opera under sufferance, he could doze through most of the performance. Even now his mind cogitated over the intelligence that he had received the previous weekend of a proposed 'merger' with one of his rivals (which he translated as a potential takeover bid). That development was existentially important to him, and rendered the 'tragedy' that was playing out in front of him wholly trivial.

He had stayed awake long enough to witness the scene in which the hunchback, bearing the title role, was dramatically cursed by an old man, apparently a noble, whose daughter had been ravished by Rigoletto's boss, the Duke of Padua. He had slept through the entirety of the next scene.

He counted that as a result.

When he was awakened by the applause at the interval, he reckoned that was enough for one night. He duly got properly stuck in to further bottles of 'fizz' that conveniently became available as the sets were changed backstage.

Thereafter, instead of participating in the amiable discussion initiated by his host's wife, his attention had wandered, as it habitually did on these occasions; he was scanning the lavish bar for competitors and clients.

McBride's attention was brought back to the conversation from which he had excluded himself. His wife was tracing the imminent denouement of the opera at the conclusion of the final act, although his immediate interest lay in the prospect of dinner, which he knew would be available. He had little sympathy for the hunchbacked jester around whom the opera revolved. This geek had apparently insinuated himself into the favour of his duke, who had allowed him to mock his contemporaries, and was consequently loathed by them to the extent that they had plotted retribution against him. The character reminded him of his own commercial development director, who was forever seeking to ingratiate himself with him, but whose resourcefulness McBride truly admired and had taken every opportunity to exploit.

'Spin-doctoring' might be the current vogue, but when successfully harnessed it was a very useful tool. This was especially true in his field, where the success of his entire industry depended on maintaining a 'status quo,' or 'stasis,' whereby his trade dominated those of its rivals, but whose pre-eminence might be found to be suspect if it were ever to be successfully challenged.

It fell to the likes of him, and his fellow executives, to ensure that no gauntlet could be cast in a public arena which might cause the dominance of his 'merchandising' to fall into serious doubt amongst his customers.

And foremost amongst these customers he knew to be the government departments around the world, whose enormous – and ever-increasing – budgets filled the coffers of his shareholders.

It was a delicate balance at the best of times, and one that was tested almost every month. Which was why he needed the spin doctors to weave their mystery, to sow the seeds of his trade's 'security' into the bosom of every household. He needed every mother to turn to the chemicals which his industry purveyed, rather than any earthly remedy, in order to cure any ailment from which his company persuaded them that their 'loved ones' must be suffering.

The very recent success of his company's vaccine sales – despite the absence of proper tests and the usual regulatory strictures – was testament to the extent to which his industry had hoodwinked governments across the world. And the profit had been unimaginable. It had run to the tens of billions. All on account of a fear campaign instigated by his industry, but propagated by governments worldwide.

He redirected his attention. The conversation had switched to the reasons why the elderly noble, the father of the ravished young maiden, had laid his curse on the petrified Rigoletto. He cared not a jot. Sure, it was a curse, but in modern commerce, as no doubt when Verdi had first scored this story to music, this was an everyday nuisance.

As the applause erupted, he was one of the first to his feet.

*

London's docklands on the other side of the capital have been redeveloped over the past fifty years. They host not only banks and professionals, but also some of the printing presses that churn out Britain's daily broadsheets. As the opera resumes in Bow Lane, one of those presses is preparing to run, and an electronic version is simultaneously being created. They will both in turn present a front page that is designed to catch and hold the attention of readers, and it will surely create a storm when it hits the laptops, screens and newspaper stands in the early hours.

So it is that 'the fourth estate' readies itself to do battle with modern capitalism, exposing in the process the latter's ugly and avaricious properties. It is a risk, potentially even a high risk, but it is one that the editor and his proprietor have decided to take. They sense a new appetite amongst the public for this sort of revelation.

The lawyers had combed through the small print, long frowns cautioning with the usual caveats: was this genuine whistle-blowing? Would the documents be trusted as authentic and not fabricated by their mole as a means of self-aggrandisement? Had they thought about the reaction of the industry that the article was targeting, because this would likely 'go viral' across the internet and other media? And many more.

The editor and the lead journalist, Ken Baxter, were seasoned warriors, and had been through many such battles before. The documents – and they were assured that there were many more – had come from within the target, both in hard copy and electronically, and they had grilled their mole to the point of exhaustion.

As scoops went, this was a humdinger! The documents revealed what many had long suspected, namely that the UK's biggest pharmaceutical company, AlphaOm, had been playing a very nasty game. They had created a brand of sweetener which the company had knowingly vested with a propensity to accelerate diabetes. At the same time, they had marketed an insulin product that was deliberately targeted at the symptoms that the company's sweetener had induced. And AlphaOm had brought both products to the market by conning the relevant authorities with some highly dubious test results.

This was going to run and run.

So it was that the editorial board had been able to give the necessary assurances to the experienced law firm and had eventually pacified them; and the proprietor in turn had given the nod.

Hence the presses had begun to role.

Time for a drink.

*

Waking again, McBride reluctantly brought his attention back to the stage, greatly relieved to realise that the final act was reaching its conclusion.

Rigoletto, the hunchback, was bending over to collect what he believed to be the body of the Bad Guy, apparently the duke, having hired a hitman to eliminate him in revenge for the fact that the duke had ravished Rigoletto's daughter. But Rigoletto had been duped by the assassin, who had found a substitute in the form of none other than Rigoletto's daughter, whose own implausible infatuation with the duke had rashly led her to sacrifice herself in order to spare his life.

Thus it was that, in the final moments of the opera, the hunchback was now confronted with the body of his own dying daughter. As she had died in his arms, he had blamed his fate on the curse from the old man whom he had ridiculed, rather than hold himself to account.

At least that part of the plot was reasonably close to real life, thought McBride.

As they rose to leave after the applause, his host, adopting his quintessentially English mannerisms, described Rigoletto as being 'altogether a complete toad'. McBride rather liked that expression. As far he was concerned, the toad was getting what was coming to him. That's what you get for biting the hand that feeds you, he thought.

In the real world, McBride would not tolerate any form of insubordination, of which treason was the most extreme form. Seen from his perspective, if the duke was turning in a good performance for his kingdom, that was all that mattered. And if he got his kicks from knocking off other folk's wives and daughters, that was entirely his business. If the profits and stock values were staying on the upward trend, then in his book the guy could do no wrong, and it was right and proper that he had got a reprieve.

However, McBride knew better than to give voice to such an opinion, being in no doubt that the consensus amongst those close to him would first castigate the duke for his lechery, sympathise with the girl's naivety and then grieve for her lost innocence and untimely death.

His instincts were vindicated by a quick glance around him, which duly revealed that tissues had been applied to damp eyes after the daughter had finally croaked.

He mentally shook his head. In his world, this was an everyday reality.

Now at last they were on their way to dinner, which was for him the high point of a rather low evening. Good wholesome food was a subject dear to his heart, as long as it involved plenty of red meat, cooked to his own fastidious tastes.

His host, Patrick Fraser, led them past the magistrates courts in Bow Street.

'Say, Pat, what's that building?' asked McBride.

'That's London primary magistrates court. It's where the "bad guys" of commerce get taken to after they've had their collars felt.'

'Sorry, collars felt?'

'Ah yes, it's how we rather quaintly describe the act of being arrested,'

'Is that a fact!'

'So,' continued Patrick, 'your views on the performance?'

'There are several morals to that story, Pat,' he began, carefully avoiding a response which might involve him in commenting upon the quality of either the voices, the music, or the set, lest he be challenged.

'The first is that, if you want something important done properly, make sure that you either do it, or that you supervise it, yourself. Second, "vengeance is a dish best eaten cold", as the old saying goes. Third, don't open hostilities unless you can be sure of the result, or at least of overwhelming odds in your favour.'

As an afterthought he added: 'Actually, there's a fourth, I reckon. Never underestimate the irrationality of women's love and its capacity to surprise.'

Satisfied, he turned to his host, and asked: 'Your thoughts?'

'Nicely put,' his host diplomatically concurred. 'I had thought that you were going to amuse me with one of your more acerbic comments.'

'What, me be cynical? Perish the thought, Pat, as you Brits like to say!'

Fraser pondered for a moment.

'I think that many in the audience, our wives included, will have pointed to the injustice of the heroine's death as yet another example of the consequences which invariably follow when men revert to aggression to settle their differences.'

'A fair point, and I wouldn't disagree that most of the fault lies with the father in turning to the hired gun in the first place,' agreed McBride politely. 'But history – especially this island's history – is full of examples of powerful women who have resorted to violence. There's Maggie Thatcher, for a start.'

'Always a good example to throw in.'

'And, as our politicians on both sides of the pond keep reminding us, Pat, there will always be some unfortunate casualties of war in the event of hostilities.'

'Steady on, Robert, I'm not at all sure that our women would take kindly to the heroine being described merely as "collateral damage". That phrase has rather exhausted its currency in the light of recent events in the Gulf and Syria.'

'Let's not go there, Pat.'

They had caught up with their wives as they reached the restaurant.

'What's this that I hear about the heroine being described as collateral damage,' said Patrick's wife, Mary, over her shoulder.

She was a striking woman in her mid-thirties, with short, skilfully styled brown hair surrounding an intelligent face. Her tailored black skirt and jacket suggested that she hailed from the professional classes, as was indeed the case. She was a litigation partner in one of the 'magic circle' law firms based in the City of London, which had to date resisted the lemming-like migratory path eastwards towards the docklands.

'Not guilty,' replied McBride, holding open the door for her. 'But we were debating the moral lessons to be learnt from the opera. Let's continue once we've got ourselves installed inside.'

Patrick returned to the subject as they were being shown to their table.

'So, the issue before this house is whether the daughter was primarily the author of her own misfortune by offering to sacrifice herself in exchange for the duke, or whether she was purely the innocent victim of the feud between the two men.'

Mary was quick to harness her terrier-like properties that she had developed in her career as a solicitor, and seized on the arguments.

'On a point of order, I protest that the question misses the central point,' she corrected. 'The girl would never have been forced to make that choice if her father had not created her dilemma for her by engaging the killer. He could have turned the other cheek, but chose not to do so. Also, his daughter would never have been kidnapped by the duke's sycophantic henchmen and delivered to be ravished by the duke if the father had been more considerate to his peers. And, what is more, she was a child, whereas all the others were grown men.'

'Well, that lays it on the line,' said McBride. 'If you act nasty and turn to violence, then don't complain if innocent people get hurt.'

'So, it's all Dad's fault, then,' quipped Patrick. 'You don't think that the duke gets off too easily?'

'Of course he does,' said Mary. 'But that merely reflects the fact that the guilty are seldom punished for their sins, or certainly not before any earthly tribunal. But it doesn't excuse the conduct of the father.'

'I'd go along with that,' said Patricia McBride, joining in for the first time. 'The whole point of the story is that the duke gets clean away, despite his treatment of the young girl, who we know is certainly not the first of his conquests. Surely, it's just another example of the old saying, you know, what goes around comes around. That's why the story has the hunchback, Rigoletto, reaping the rewards of his own retaliation. Meanwhile his daughter becomes the innocent victim of the vendetta. The story is just as relevant today as it must have been back when the opera was written.'

'I'll second that,' agreed Mary. 'I imagine that life in certain countries where there is no rule of law, and where the state controls the media via their secret police, must be very similar to the portrayal that we have just witnessed.'

'Even so,' said McBride's wife, 'I guess that the main difference is that, if the same thing happened today in the States, there would be a bunch of attorneys who would gladly take the case against the duke, or his dukedom – is that what you call it? – on behalf of the heroine's estate. You'd be talking big bucks in damages.'

'Even if the principal beneficiary of the estate was the father?' asked Mary.

'Now you're getting technical,' she parried.

'Only because you've chosen as an example a country where the rule of law dominates and there is a very free press.'

'But, going back to Patrick's point,' intervened McBride, 'there's no escaping the ugly fact that collateral damage is an inevitable consequence of war. And the guys that press the button just have to be able to sleep in their beds in the knowledge that innocent people have died as a direct result of their actions. The way they usually come to justify it to themselves is that the "greater good" has been served. The trouble is that sometimes they're the only ones who convince themselves what that greater good might be, assuming that it actually does exist.'

'Quite. You know, I've often wondered,' said Mary, regarding him quizzically, 'whether there might not be occasions when the leaders of industry have had to make not similar decisions in their careers.'

The question caught him off-guard.

'How so?' he parried.

'Well,' she clarified for him, 'there's not a businessman that I know that has not had to take some very harsh decisions which will inevitably impact on others less fortunate than himself or herself.'

It took him a moment to recreate the veneer with which he maintained the polished exterior of his status.

'Speaking just for myself, I'll plead the Fifth,' he replied, in as jovial a tone as he could muster.

'Seriously?'

'No, not seriously. It's an interesting thought,' he replied carefully, 'but ultimately probably an academic one. The honest answer is that I don't know, but I should think that it's very unlikely that any CEO in the West would ever risk making a decision that would involve taking lives, whether innocent or otherwise. My guess is that a Russian tycoon wouldn't have the same restraints.'

Patrick chuckled his acknowledgement.

'Actually,' she replied, 'I wasn't thinking of that. I had more in mind decisions which could reasonably be expected to have a devastating impact on innocent people's lives, for example a living death such as bankruptcy.'

He was ready for that.

'Philosophers have argued for centuries about the moral culpability for the consequences of one's actions, whether foreseen or unforeseen. It all comes down to the issue of intent, and what you lawyers call the chain of causation. Taken to its logical conclusion, every time that a company introduces a successful new product, it has the potential to knock a rival's product off the shelf. In doing so, the company might force its competitor into Chapter 11 – or what you call over here insolvency – in just the same way as it might do each time it collects an unpaid debt from a customer. You would know more about it than me, but my understanding is that the law does not impose liability in those cases, at least in the absence of bad faith. The question is, where do you draw the line? We could be here all night discussing the morals of being a successful entrepreneur.'

'And let's not forget, Mary,' Patrick cautioned, 'that Robert is our guest here tonight, and he's not on trial.'

'And I'm sure he'll be the first to warn me if I'm overstepping the mark, darling husband. I just happen to find this a very interesting subject.'

'As should we all,' McBride agreed, with forked tongue. 'Perhaps Mary and I should draft a code of ethics for big business?'

'Now you're just teasing,' she complained.

'Surely not!'

'But seriously, Robert,' she persisted, 'if you felt that your company's policy was likely to result in someone's death, whether innocent or otherwise, surely you wouldn't hesitate to change the policy.'

'I've never been in such a position, and very much doubt that I ever shall be. There's always the risk that some crazy nut could threaten to top himself unless I agree to take my best-selling product off the market. If that were to happen, then I regret that I wouldn't fall for it. The nut would just have to swing, and I doubt that the share price would drop if my decision became public. That's just the way of the world. Sorry about that.'

'OK, put it another way,' she continued. 'Would you feel any moral obligation, or would Patrick and his friends advise you, to resign if a person was killed as a direct – as opposed to indirect – result of your actions?'

'Tough one that,' McBride answered. 'I think it would depend on all the circumstances. Where would your firm be on that, Patrick?'

Fraser frowned for a second, and then opted for neutral ground.

'When the question is put in a vacuum like that, without any underlying facts, it's almost impossible to express any meaningful view. I'm not trying to duck the point, but I'm not sure how far we can get on the current premise.'

'All right. I'll give you an example, taken from real life,' Mary insisted. 'A key witness in a big lawsuit gets cold feet just before he's due to give evidence on behalf of the claimant. He tells the claimant that he's decided that he can't face the prospect of testifying against his former employers, who are on the other side. The senior barrister for the claimant calls a conference with his client. He tells him that, without the evidence of the key witness, the claim will fail. The chief exec of the claimant applies pressure on the witness – I think you'd call it turning the heat on him, and tells him personally that he's got no alternative other than to show up. He gets his solicitors to serve the guy with a formal subpoena to appear in court the next day. Just before the trial opens, the claimant and the lawyers get a phone call from the guy's family to tell them that the witness had killed himself. So, if you were the claimant's chief exec, would you resign.'

'Jeez, Mary, that's an awful story,' commented McBride. 'And you're telling us that it was for real?'

'As true as I'm stood here, as the farmers say where I come from.'

'Whether I decided to resign or not,' he pondered, 'I'd have to live with the fact that I had caused a man to take his own life. Even though I was just doing my job, that would be a terrible burden to have to bear.'

'What happened to the chief exec in real life?' asked McBride's wife.

'Well, you won't be surprised to learn that he didn't do the decent thing. Once the story got out, he stayed on as chief exec for quite a while, although he was crossed off several Christmas card lists. Oddly enough he wasn't criticised for putting pressure on the witness. What did for him was the fact that the high-profile case collapsed and his company was left with a huge bill for legal costs. The shareholders were not best pleased. After that the knives were out, and it was just a matter of time. He was also attacked for his decision to expose the company to such a risk when the whole case relied on the evidence of a turncoat.

One can speculate as to whether he jumped or was pushed, but in the end he resigned.'

'And what about the lawyers?' asked McBride.

'I happened to know the queen's counsel – that's the senior barrister – very well. He was profoundly affected by the whole affair. He was so upset that he considered retiring as a QC, but was talked out of it by his colleagues and his wife. But he did eventually go to the bench rather sooner than had been expected.'

'The bench? Sorry, what's that?' asked McBride.

'Forgive me, Robert. That's an old English expression meaning that he became a High Court judge.'

'Got you, I should have figured that out for myself,' he said with a shake of his head. 'Right, so he gets to sit on the bench?'

'Just so.'

Then he added: 'And the other attorneys?'

'The partner in charge of the case merely shrugged the whole thing off as being just one of those things that happen in litigation. He had skin thicker than a rhino, but he lost most of his legal team who had worked on the case.'

'And did that team by any chance include you, Mary?'

'How very perceptive of you, Robert,' she complimented him. 'Yes, it did. I had worked on the case with him, and resigned from the firm and joined another in whose ethics I could have rather more confidence. And I have no regrets.'

'Neither do they, by all accounts,' said her husband, 'since they made you a partner shortly after you joined.'

'Well, I'll drink to that, and from what I hear from the guys in your corporate department, you're a damn good litigator at that,' said McBride.

'Thank you, Robert. I never refuse a compliment.'

'Speaking of drinks,' interrupted Patrick, using the opportunity to change the subject, 'let's order our meal before it gets too late.'

The proposal met with unanimous approval.

Despite the lateness of the hour, they each managed two courses of excellent Italian fare, washed down with first an 'impertinent' Pinot Grigio followed by an unusual – and organic – Primitivo from one of the lesser-known estates in Puglia. Such was their good humour that none of them frowned at Patrick when his 'portable office' (as Mary described it) alerted him to an urgent message.

After a suitable interval, he excused himself from the table. He was gone only a few minutes, but when he returned he wore a frown.

Having ascertained that none of them wanted to accept the challenge of another course, he politely suggested that the women might like to take the opportunity to freshen up while he ordered some coffee and herbal teas and sorted the bill.

Mary took the hint, and the two women retired.

Patrick turned to his client, his expression suddenly deadly serious.

'Sorry to spoil the evening,' he said, immediately capturing McBride's attention, 'but I think we have a problem.'

'Don't tell me. Those hyenas in Zurich are making a full bid.'

'No, but this news won't help unless you get it sorted before it goes much further,' Patrick replied.

'Doesn't sound good, Pat?'

'Well. I'm told that there's an article coming out in one of the leading broadsheets in the morning which contains some seriously damaging allegations against the company. It's just the kind of story you need to avoid right at this particular moment. I don't have a good enough signal down here to open my electronic copy of this rag. So, we can either read the article on the net at your place or we can get to one of the early morning newsagents. There's a few around here. You and I can take stock of things from then on.'

'Hell, you know that I hate to read detailed stuff on my phone. The text and font size give me such a headache. Have you got your driver with you tonight?' asked McBride

'Very much so,' Patrick replied. 'I was expecting to give you a lift to your house. It's on our way.'

'Thanks, we'd certainly appreciate that. Meanwhile, I'd better start making a few phone calls, beginning with my marketing director. It's his job to ensure that the media are kept onside so that this sort of stuff doesn't get into the papers.'

'Do you have a preferred firm of litigation lawyers? Or perhaps you adopt the trend followed by most of the other big companies, in that you spread your work around the magic circle firms so as to conflict them from acting against you?'

'I've no particular policy on that score,' McBride replied, 'and I'd generally go with the advice of my legal director. You're not suggesting that we call the lawyers onto the case right this minute, are you?'

'No, I'm assuming that it is too late to do anything about tomorrow morning's edition – or perhaps I should say today's edition – but you might be able to kill the story before close of play tomorrow – that is today – if you give the lawyers a head start.'

'Well, the only litigation lawyer that I'd be able to get hold of at this time of night has just been sat beside me at dinner right here in this place. Are you suggesting that I use Mary's firm?' asked McBride.

'I'm not making any suggestion as to which firm you should instruct, Robert. That's got to be your call. What I am saying is that, in my experience, the sooner the lawyers get their hands on the raw material, the more chance they're likely to have of getting you a result in the short term.'

'Fine. We'll see how things stand once I've spoken to my legal director, assuming that I can get the idle fart out of bed. Mind you, if you saw his wife, you'd realise that he's got little incentive to get into it! So he might still be up.'

Patrick let the remark pass without comment.

'You're welcome to use the car in order to make your calls,' he offered. 'It's somewhat more secure than a restaurant.'

'Thanks. It could be a long night!'

Chapter 3

The term 'commercial development' or 'CD' is a relatively recent euphemism. In common parlance, the term 'marketing' would be more familiar, especially to the 'grey pound' who regard it as an unmerited title. They would regard it as having been bestowed upon those who otherwise have nothing of value to contribute to a viable business, thereby creating an importance which is both undeserved and wholly illusory. To them, the modern spin doctors of each industry have propagated the notion that they actually make a real contribution to their business. What is worse, they have persuaded boards of directors around the globe that they, the spin doctors, have become indispensable.

So it is that many consider it a real sadness that the spin doctors have convinced themselves of their own worth, and point to the fact that, as they see it, no real qualification is necessary in order to secure a role in the department. By 'real' they mean something other than an ability to subvert the English language into meaningless sound bites, and a propensity to talk, interminably and usually without invitation.

However, the reality is very different. A successful marketing campaign has the ability to propel a product or enterprise into a world-beating phenomenon, and those who manage those campaigns harness emoluments beyond the reach of most mortals. That is why most companies, and more recently partnerships and small businesses, have persuaded themselves of the necessity for such a resource, and few chief executives would have the courage to dispense with it. Many have even elevated into main board directors their heads of commercial development.

In fact, such is the status of the CD directors or managers that questions are frequently asked (sometimes within and sometimes without a private forum) as to whether the tail has begun to wag the dog.

Such a situation obtains at AlphaOm, where that very question has indeed been asked. And the subject which is on the tongues of several of its directors – and many of its employees – is whether the head of CD has been promoted to a position which is far beyond his ability. True, he pioneered the hugely successful change of the company's name so as to promote the myth that it could purvey (if not produce) pharmaceutical products across the board, literally from alpha to omega, from the beginning of production to the end-user in that lucrative market

His name is Chuck Thompson, or 'CT' as he prefers to be called. Or, when he is sending his chummy emails around the company, just to remind all and sundry of his importance, he likes to use the epithet 'CT of CD'.

As the head of commercial development at AlphaOm, he attracts vitriol in substantially greater measure than he does praise, and even that is seldom fulsome. He has closely cropped hair, a small moustache and a short goatee beard. His narrow eyes have a snake-like quality, as does his tongue, both physically and metaphorically. Many of his colleagues at work have compared him to a viper.

His unofficial soubriquet is 'the Python', and it is well-deserved. It has been earned in part because of the annoying habit that one is forced to observe in his presence of his tongue darting out of his mouth at frequent intervals. But only in part. The other part of his nickname is also apt to capture his uncanny ability to entrance members of the female species into sharing first his company, and then his bed.

CT despises the journalists who are forever circling AlphaOm like the sharks he knows them to be, waiting for the merest sniff of blood. Yet it is his job to court them and to feed them the material which he wants them to print. Those whom he has taken into his confidence are the first to be given the big stories, the 'scoops' in respect of new developments, and potential breakthroughs into new remedies.

Yet here he was, smoozing up to the media with his usual charm, dropping hints to the chosen few of the great progress the company was making on its new products. Small morsels, with the odd false trail set for those who have yet to conform to the code by which he expected them to behave.

All strictly off the record, of course.

He was currently State-side, attending a rather tedious but necessary conference in New York. His eye had caught one of his new trainees, a pretty young thing with long brown hair. Just his sort. He had been grooming her over these past few weeks, and this was the first of these conferences that he had asked her to attend with him. She had jumped at the chance to be able to eat at the top table, or perhaps to catch the golden crumbs that she hoped would be dropped beneath it, courtesy of his influence and seniority within the company. And she was performing her well-rehearsed part perfectly.

She was perhaps not as striking as his last conquest. That had ended in tears, and for the first time not on his terms, but on hers. He still felt aggrieved at the notion that she had determined that their 'affair', as he liked to call it, must end. Never before had he been jilted quite so abruptly. But he had taken his revenge. He was especially proud of that particular assassination.

But his mind was wandering. Stay focussed, he reminded himself as he slowly eased himself through the crowded floor of the conference hall towards his latest prey. He needed to ensure that she did not make any other plans for what was left of that evening.

He noticed that a 'missed call' from his chief exec showed up on his mobile. He toyed with the idea of responding to it there and then, but the prospect of closing in for what he hoped would be 'the kill' somehow had the edge over what he assumed would be another round of corporate politics.

He let the call go unanswered.

*

Patrick Fraser had despatched his driver to one of the newsagents in Soho so that he could collect copies of the early morning edition of *The Daily Chronicle*. He settled the restaurant bill, reflecting afterwards that he had not even checked it. By the time that he and their respective wives were ready to leave, McBride was already into his third phone call in the back seat of the car. His copy of the offending broadsheet was beside him when the others joined him.

He ended the call as they got into the car.

'Right, well at least I've got hold of my director of internal affairs. She's called Barbara Spooner. She'll have to run with this for the time being, and frankly she's the right person for this. She'd make the KGB look like amateurs. My head of legal is not answering his calls, and my head of PR is away on some conference back over the pond, so they're not gonna be any use to us until the morning, which means that we shall lose half a day unless we go with what we've got.'

Patrick acquiesced with a nod.

'You're right, Patrick, we can't afford that kind of delay. Not with stuff like this all over the front pages. Which means that we need a team on it tonight.'

He turned to look Mary in the eyes.

'Barbara tells me that we've used your litigation department in the past, and that you guys have performed well, but she's not familiar with your name.'

'Perhaps I should have told you that I still use my maiden name in my profession,' she informed him. 'It's Mary Fellowes.'

'Apologies. I gave your name as Fraser. I told Barbara that we'd all been having dinner together. Now I want you to give it to me straight, Mary, because I'll come right to the point.'

He jabbed the newspaper as he spoke.

'This paper has published a story about my company, saying that we've been guilty of deceiving the public with products marketed by separate divisions of the Group. They are also saying that we're involved in some kind of anti-trust move, along with a bunch of other companies, to squash the competition from any of the so-called alternative medicines that are out there. That's a load of bull for a start, if you'll forgive the language. I can tell you right now that we've absolutely nothing to fear from a bunch of old druids trying to peddle their herbs as a cure for every known disease. There'll always be plenty of weirdos out there on the fringe, but if I have anything to do with it – and believe me I do – that's where they'll stay.'

He realised that he was digressing.

'My apologies, Mary. From what I've read so far, what really gets me is that this paper has quoted from documents that belong to us but that have been leaked by some pseudo-whistleblower bearing a grudge. The way I see it, documents that belong to my company are my company's property, and, as far as I'm concerned, they are confidential. Either way, the paper certainly didn't get them by asking us, and we sure as hell wouldn't have given them copies if they had. This is theft, pure and simple. Call it industrial espionage or sabotage – I don't care what name you give it – I want it taken care of.'

He brandished the paper as he spoke.

'So, straight up, Mary. Is this the sort of case that your firm could deliver on? Could you get a stop put on this baloney?'

Mary remained calm and returned his steady gaze.

'First, Robert, I haven't even read the article. Second, I'm ready to take your word that there's no substance to it, although my immediate view is that you should not even put that issue on the table. Third, your best point seems to me, subject to seeing the relevant material, that the paper has misused the company's confidential information. If, as you say, the documents are confidential and have been obtained unlawfully, then there is a good chance that a court will order the paper to return them and to desist from any further articles which might rely on that material or any information which is contained within them or derived from them. Finally, I'd need to run the usual conflict searches, although I'm reasonably sure that we don't act for the paper. But, in a nutshell: yes, Robert. We can deliver.'

'That's what I wanted to hear.'

'I should add a note of caution, though,' she added.

'Why does that not surprise me,' retorted McBride. 'I've yet to meet a lawyer who doesn't qualify every bit of advice he gives.'

He had looked at Fraser as he said this, but he returned his attention to Mary when she retorted: 'Except that in this case it's a "she". Sorry about that,' she began.

'That's never been a problem in my company before,' he parried, 'and I'm not about to make this an exception.'

He gave her one of his looks that he reserved for board meetings, before adding: 'Just so that there's no misunderstanding.'

'No misunderstanding at all,' she said, as she continued with her caveat.

'Before you instruct us to go charging off to court, I should want to be satisfied that you and your board of directors have reflected on the potential downside. I'm sure that you've seen numerous examples of stories which have hit the headlines for a day, or even a week, only to disappear into oblivion once the public are no longer interested in the subject. So, this could all die a death by the end of next week, and the public will probably have forgotten all about it by next month. Once the appropriate denials have been issued, and assuming that the paper hasn't got anything else up its sleeve, then this could all be a rather tiresome flash in the pan which will soon become a distant memory.'

'It could,' agreed McBride, 'but it might not. And even a week of this sort of bad publicity is the last thing we need right now.'

'True,' she replied. 'All I'm saying is that you need to reflect on this.'

He considered her for a moment.

'So, assuming we have a week of hell, at least – is that the downside you were referring to? Because if it's the upside I'd like to know what the downside is – how much worse does it get?'

She considered his question for a moment.

'It's a potential downside,' she answered. 'In order to obtain an injunction against the paper, the company would have to commence proceedings. We would obviously want any such proceedings to be conducted in private session, and not in open court. Either way, sometimes facts can come out in the course of those proceedings which turn out to be highly damaging to the claimant, who then wishes that he's never gone to court in the first place.'

'Explain, if you would.'

'So, take that beefburger company, for example, almost a household name. They did untold damage to the value of their business by bringing a libel suit against two relative paupers who had paraded outside one of their shops for a few days with a poster which tried to tell the world nasty things about the company and the contents of its products. The case back-fired horribly, even though the company won it in principle, and we all got to learn about the awful stuff that goes into the burgers that the company sold. You would certainly not want to end up in a similar position.'

McBride pondered that advice briefly.

'But the alternative,' he reminded her, 'as you yourself accept, is that we give the paper a free hit for at least a week, and allow them to make use of our confidential material, even though there's probably nothing behind the stuff they've printed.'

Mary shook her head in response.

'I'm not advising you to take that course, Robert. I'm just inviting you to consider whether there are potential pitfalls which you and your shareholders would ultimately prefer that the company avoided.'

Fraser deemed it politic to intervene at this stage.

'If the majority of the shareholders are true to form, and we know most of them, they would be mighty disappointed if the company took no action to restrain the unlawful misuse of its confidential documents. Speaking for myself,' he added, 'it seems to me that you're damned if you don't do anything, but you run the risk of being damned if you do. By that I mean that we shan't know until we're much further down the line whether you're at risk of being damned because you have done something about it. I agree that we're potentially between a rock and a hard place, but I doubt whether the company's got any choice in the matter. And if it's going to act at all, it has to act fast.'

'And that's where the commercial decision lies for you and your board,' cautioned Mary. 'You've no doubt heard the old adage: "act in haste, repent at leisure". Well, it's part of my job to remind my clients of the principle.'

McBride nodded in agreement.

'I've been reminded of that – what did you call it, an adage? – in the past. But,' he posed, looking Mary directly in the eyes, 'I assume that we'll have the morning to consider this? I doubt you'll be ready to go to court before noon?'

'At the very earliest,' Mary agreed. 'It's more likely to be some time in the afternoon by the time we've got our application together.'

She reflected for a moment.

'You see, what's niggling me is this.' She considered it the right time to drop this into the discussion. 'My firm does a fair bit of this sort of thing, almost always acting for a claimant against one of the papers. Our experience is that, almost invariably, the journalist cultivates a mole who is usually a past or serving employee in the claimant's company. Having got the preliminary evidence, what they then try to do is to persuade the mole to provide them with the company's internal documents which will back up what he or she has told them. If and when they're really confident that they've got enough, then they'll run the story without seeking any comment from the company, thereby putting it on notice of what's coming. If they haven't got enough, then they'll water down the initial story into something less dramatic and try to set a trap for the company and get a few quotes from one of its unsuspecting officers.'

'Sounds familiar,' observed Fraser.

'But, by the sound of it,' Mary continued, 'in this case the paper has gone straight for the big story. Am I right?'

'I guess,' agreed McBride. 'None of my directors have alerted me to this, so I assume that none of them have been approached for a comment.'

'Which inevitably makes me ask myself,' Mary continued, 'what else have they got, or what are they holding back, that they're reasonably sure you don't know about? Could they have got themselves a mole with top level inside knowledge?'

McBride smiled at her.

'I think we're gonna get along just fine, Mary. That's exactly what I've told Barbara to find out by the morning. She's rounding up her team for an early morning start right at this very moment.'

'Excellent,' she congratulated him. 'Because if we can find out who the mole is, we can begin to tilt the chessboard back to level, and ultimately in your favour.'

'AlphaOm's a huge company though,' observed Fraser. 'The search for the mole could take quite some time.'

'Maybe,' she replied, 'but I'm sure that Robert and I don't need to tell Barbara how to do her job. If she's as good as Robert says she is, she'll start with the list of those employees who have recently left the company, and continue with those who either have a disciplinary record or whose career with the company has for some reason dropped off the escalator. That's usually a good way to begin.'

McBride looked at her admiringly, and reached into a pocket to extract one of his business cards, on which he wrote down his private line and that of Barbara Spooner. The car had pulled up in their street. While his wife gave the driver directions to their house, he made arrangements with Mary so that in the morning she could speak to the team that was being assembled overnight.

As the car pulled away, Mary began the unenviable task of summoning her team for a 7 a.m. conference in the office later that morning. It was time for them to really earn their six-figure salaries.

*

As Mary Fellowes' team of able assistant solicitors were assembling for their dawn conference later that morning, and slowly coagulated into the well-trained pack of hunting hounds of which she was justly proud, Barbara Spooner was preparing to address her own meeting at AlphaOm's offices. She had been there since 5 a.m. that morning. Those whom she deemed suitable to attend her meeting were drawn exclusively from her own department. She was not yet ready to draw into her confidence any of the lower species who inhabited what she regarded as the company's Legal Department.

Barbara Spooner's presence at the table commanded instant respect, which was duly forthcoming. She insisted on being addressed by her full name. She would only permit the use of her childhood appellation of 'Babs' by express invitation, which she persuaded herself was extended exclusively to her friends. However, few wished to admit to that status, and even fewer had it bestowed upon them. Fewer still aspired to it.

She was universally reviled throughout the company. But none dared to incur her displeasure, or to question the ruthless efficiency with which she discharged her duties. To be singled out for criticism by her was to be avoided at all costs, at least if one intended to progress within the company.

In formal parlance, she was referred to as the director of the Office of Internal Affairs. Behind her back, her department had acquired the appellation of either 'the Gestapo' or 'the KGB,' depending on the case. Meanwhile, she was herself generally referred to as the 'Mamba,' or 'the Black Mamba' to use her full title. It was considered to be a suitably apt description of her snake-like properties, including her poisonous tongue, and the colour of her hair which her ancestors had bequeathed her, and which she routinely replicated in her attire.

She had at one time acquired the appellation of 'the Black Widow'. This was thought to capture both the lethal venom which she was able to direct at those unfortunate to cross her, and also the intricate web which she had woven within the company, reaching as far as the chief executive. However, that title had not lasted long. In the way that these things happen, it had been pointed out that this title implied that a man had once been fool enough first to court, and then marry her, before finding release in death. By general consensus, it was agreed that such a scenario was wholly implausible. Hence the unanimous approval of the reptilian label.

Her thin black hair, prematurely greying but regularly dyed, was pulled tightly into a bun at the back of her head, as was her custom. The purpose, no doubt, was to ensure that the narrow, mirthless eyes, which were devoid of any warmth, were afforded a clear field of vision. However, it also gave the appearance that her eyebrows had been stretched back over her forehead, a result not unlike that of an ageing American heiress who has over-indulged in plastic surgery in her quest for eternal youth.

Beneath the pointed nose were thin, taut lips, their only moisture provided by the crimson lipstick which had been applied with calculated caution. The combined effect was to produce a cross between a 'Cruella de Vil' imitation (minus the long cigarette holder) and a worn-out mask which had survived the previous year's Halloween.

Each of the persons in attendance that morning had been purposefully selected by her on their particular merit, some for their painstaking dedication to detail, others for their ability to detect and report even the smallest misdemeanour. The result was an investigative team which would have been the envy of the Spanish Inquisition, if not Walsingham's secret service under the sixteenth-century Queen Elizabeth I.

That team now hung on her every word as she outlined the strategy which she was certain would be endorsed by the main board later that day.

On the table before them, alongside the printed text of the article which had appeared in that morning's edition of *The Daily Chronicle*, lay copies of the documents to which reference had been made by the paper. Some members of the team were charged with making a detailed schedule of each such document, its known or assumed provenance and the identities of the employees who were likely to have had access to it in previous years.

That task was delegated to the lower ranks.

Others in her team took responsibility for preparing a shortlist of the employees whose identities matched the three categories which had been suggested by Mary Fellowes. All well and good, but the compilation of that list was dependent upon the arrival of the staff in the company's Human Resources Department.

She herself had undertaken to be responsible for liaison with the Legal Department, and for co-ordinating the company's policy as agreed at board level. The results of these various exercises would be collated within the next two hours that morning.

Spooner turned to a prematurely balding man on her right, whose smooth crown still gleamed with perspiration after his marathon bicycle ride to the office in response to her summons.

'Good morning, all. Just so that you know, the chief executive is all over this, so it is our number one priority. Understood?'

Heads duly nodded in acknowledgement.

'We're going to need clearance from the company's compliance officer to access the email accounts of each of the shortlisted employees. Dick, I want you to be responsible for that. Also, I want you to set up an

IT programme which will be able to match any of those employees with the names of people who had access to these documents. That's a priority. Understood?'

'I'm already on the case, ma'am,' he acknowledged.

'Let's be under no illusions, everyone. We're fighting against the clock. We need results and we need them fast.'

She watched them nod obediently.

'Good. We'll reconvene again at ten. Let's do it.'

*

Shortly after the conference at internal affairs had adjourned, the gamekeeper heard his mobile ringing from inside his vehicle for the second time. Sensing that it might be important, he left his two underkeepers to carry on with their work, and went to check the device.

He saw a missed call from Jamie. An early start for him, he observed.

Assuming that the call was to announce that their scheduled meeting was to be cancelled yet again, he pressed the feature to return the call.

Jamie answered at the second ring.

'Ah, Charlie. Thanks for returning my call. Did you listen to my message?'

'Not yet, Jamie. I thought I should call straight away, knowing as you'd rung twice. You know what I'm like'

'Very good. Yes, absolutely right. I was just wondering if we might be able to bring our meeting forward by a day. I've had a call from some old chums who want to book up some days with us. Something about getting me out and about again. They're good sorts, and I'd like to oblige them.'

'That's fine, Jamie. Let me speak with Richard first. Are there any times that you had in mind?'

'I had hoped to make it tomorrow afternoon, Friday that is, but something's come up. Is there any chance that we could meet on Saturday afternoon instead; the later the better for me, if that would work. Can you run that past Richard and get back to me. Otherwise, it'll have to be Monday afternoon some time.'

'Right. I'll get on with it just now.'

'Okay. Bye for now.'

Well, there's a thing, thought the keeper. Just when I was convinced that he'd lost all interest in the shoot, I get a call like that out of the blue.

What was that line from that song in the 60s.

Ah yes. '... Goes to show you never can tell.'

Now, that was proper music.

*

The breakthrough came considerably faster than any of Spooner's team had expected. The company's IT Department had established that almost all of the documents which had been cited by the article in *The Daily Chronicle* had either been processed within or had passed through the company's Commercial Development Department, or 'CD' as it was known. This fact alone significantly narrowed the search. The company's records showed that several of the documents had been drafted as a joint effort between CD and at least one other department. Also, some of the key documents appeared on their face to have been copied to employees in other departments, including in particular the PA to the director of sales.

Human Resources, or 'HR' to use its common acronym, reported that there had been one significant departure from CD in the past nine months. The individual was a young woman in her mid-twenties who was widely believed to have worked with and reported to the director of CD, and who could therefore have been expected to have had access to the relevant documents.

What was more telling was that her company email account recorded that she had exchanged at least one email with none other than a journalist at *The Daily Chronicle*. Admittedly, this was only circumstantial evidence, but this particular journalist had been the author of the article in the very same newspaper.

Spooner did not believe in coincidences. If two events appeared on their face to have been connected, there had to be a rational explanation.

Circumstantial such new evidence might be, it was good enough for Spooner as a primary lead. The forensic IT people were working on recreating the texts of the various emails, together with a schedule of any outgoing phone calls from the girl's desk. The latter was a long shot, but worth the effort.

The girl's name was Catherine Symonds. Her HR record revealed that she had been progressing well within the company, and appeared to have made a good impression on the director of CD, judging by her annual appraisals. However, the record of her exit interview with HR had revealed an alarming level of discontent with both the strategy and the ethics of the company. More ominous still was her statement that her reasons for leaving were both professional and personal, and that she would need to consider further what action to take in respect of them.

A note on the file from the director of HR recorded a concern that there might be more to this than met the eye, and that it should not come as a surprise if they were to hear from the girl again. A request to the director of CD to shed possible light on the reasons for the girl's departure had yet to produce any helpful response, nor indeed so far as the Mamba was aware any response at all.

No surprises there, thought Spooner. She knew the CD director of old. In her book, whilst Chuck (how she loathed that appellation) Thompson might be regarded as a wily old fox by the company at large, she had him down as a lascivious predator. It wouldn't surprise her in the least if he had helped himself to something more than the girl's overtime outside her normal working hours.

She disliked mysteries, especially when they arose in the course of one her department's investigations. She made a note to ensure that one of her team spoke with Thompson on his return to the office.

Meanwhile, Spooner had just put down the phone following a conversation with the partner in the law firm with which she had been ordered by the chief to liaise. She was impressed with the woman's efficiency, having been told by her of the provisional arrangements that had already been made. These included a conference with leading counsel later than morning – either by videocon or by telecon – and an urgent hearing before a High Court judge in the afternoon.

She had been told that what they lacked, and what Spooner was confident she would now be able to deliver, was the evidence which would show that the documents cited by the paper (1) were not in the public domain, (2) were confidential, and (3) had been unlawfully obtained. The first two boxes had been relatively easy to tick. The third represented a very significant challenge, but she had assured the lawyer that the full resources of her department, namely the Office of Internal Affairs, were employed on this very issue even as they spoke.

Shortly before ten, Spooner made the short walk from her office to the door to the IAD's bespoke meeting room, which she had declared to be their 'Major Incident Room'. Her staff were waiting for her in the corridor, and followed her in after she had unlocked the door. None of them was late.

She greeted them with her habitual smile, which was as short lived as it was warm, the eyes immediately commanding attention.

'David, thank you for the email. I noted that it has been circulated to the whole team, and I therefore assume you have all read it.'

This was intended as a statement rather than as a question, but heads were nevertheless nodded in dutiful acknowledgement.

'There are two points which I want us to deal with right now. First, are we satisfied that we should be focusing solely on the Symonds girl? Second, assuming we are on the right lead, where are we on connecting the girl to the documents which were used by the paper?'

She glared at the two juniors to whom she had delegated this impossible task.

When neither responded, she added, 'I see these as the two main priorities, and I suggest that we take them in that order, unless anyone wishes to comment on these or to suggest others?'

Although this last sentence was couched in the form of a question, it was received – as she had intended – as an instruction. Nevertheless, as was her custom, Spooner permitted a brief interval in her opening remarks so that any audible dissent could be voiced by any member of her team.

When none was forthcoming, she continued:

'So, David, can you please give us an update.'

She had addressed her command to a clean-shaven, balding man dressed in a white shirt with a light-blue tie. David King had worked for Spooner for some ten years, and was one of the department's longest serving members. He duly opened a folder of documents on the table, whilst his colleague beside him clicked the keypad of the laptop which they had brought into the meeting, engaging the overhead screen at the opposite end of the room to Spooner's throne.

'We've done a trawl of all the other potential suspects, but so far as we can tell none of them has had any contact with the newspaper – unlike Symonds – and we are reasonably sure that none of them would have had the same level of direct access to the documents used by the paper as she did. It's early days still, I know, but Maria and I are as close as we can be to certain that we're right to be focusing on her. We both strongly recommend that we should continue to do so.'

Spooner nodded slowly, letting the meeting absorb the impact of what had been said.

'Does anyone here either disagree with that analysis or have information which we should all know about before we commit?' Spooner asked.

She acknowledged the shaking of heads in response.

'OK. That was the easy part,' she continued. 'So where do we stand on the documents and the connection with the girl?'

There was little doubt around the table that her question had been directed at David again, and the others were content to let him answer.

'OK, this is what we've come up with so far,' he began. 'We've checked Symonds' email account here at the company. Don't worry,' he added quickly, 'we received clearance from the compliance officer before we ran the searches. We struck gold almost straight away. We've found emails going between her and the journalist, but none of these had any attachments.'

'Not promising,' quipped the Mamba.

'So far, we don't have a definite trace showing the documents going from her to the paper. But we're working on that with IT. But what we have found – or rather IT have recreated – is her diary going back over the past twelve months. And this is where it gets interesting. Or at least we think so.'

'In your own time, David,' Spooner prompted him, in her icily sarcastic tone, 'but today would be nice.'

'Yeah, well. What we found,' he replied, restraining his enthusiasm, 'is the date when she first arranged to meet with Ken Baxter. That's the journalist at *The Daily Chronicle*. She actually put his name and his phone number in her diary. What's more, shortly before she left the company, she deleted the entry in her diary for that meeting.'

He paused for dramatic effect.

'Well now, David, you have been busy,' applauded his boss, in what passed with her for congratulations. 'I'm glad that I gave you this particular task. And is there anything else that you're keeping from us?'

'Not a lot,' he continued with a satisfied grin. 'Only that we've found a whole series of appointments in her office diary with the abbreviations

"KB" in them. And there were several in the weeks before she handed in her notice. Oh yes, and each of them was deleted from the diary just before she went.'

A rare smile from the Mamba.

'If I didn't know you better, David,' she remarked, with one of her pencilled eyebrows demurely elevated, 'I could be forgiven for thinking that you and Maria were rather pleased with yourselves.'

She curtailed any response and, as though rotating on a ball-bearing, turned her attention to the other participants.

'That's very useful material. We need to get it to the lawyers within the hour. I shall need statements from each person who has been involved in the audit trail of these emails and diary entries. I want them in draft form – and I mean draft so that the lawyers can play with the words – on my desk before eleven. David, I want a report of all that you and Maria have discovered, just as you've described it, on my desk in the next thirty minutes.'

There was an audible gulp as the two unfortunates gathered up their papers and prepared to leave the meeting.

'Has Symonds' employment contract been sent through to the lawyers as I instructed?' she asked.

The question was directed at her PA.

'Yes, Miss Spooner,' came the required response.

This met with a nod of acknowledgement.

'And who has been chasing up the issues which arise out of the HR report?' she demanded.

Spooner's eyes narrowed as one of the junior members of the team raised his hand nervously. She fixed the young man in her sights.

'I shall assume that you've read the exit interview with Symonds. I want you to focus on that,' commanded Spooner. 'You'll need to work with Maria, since she has the connection to the IT angle. I need to know what the girl's "personal reasons" were for leaving. I want a progress report on my desk by noon.'

There was a heavy silence as the team readied themselves for the immediate task ahead of them.

'We're on track. The next meeting will be at noon, unless I email you all to the contrary.'

A brief pause.

'Let's go. And remember. The chief is on our back!'

*

No sooner had Spooner adjourned the team meeting than her assistant, Maria Lutherson, had immediately dedicated herself to the two principal tasks which had been delegated to her. She set about her commission with the passion of a zealot and the doggedness of a trained terrier. Nothing less was to be expected of her, for it was on account of these particular qualities that she had been recruited by Spooner.

Maria's ancestors had not been at the front of the queue when fate had seen fit to distribute what might have passed in others for physical beauty. Indeed, the less tangible mysteries of feminine charm appeared also to have eluded them. Maria had in turn duly inherited what the more charitable amongst her contemporaries had described as 'plainness', a feature which in itself should not have presented a challenge.

The female species is usually adept at discovering new ways to overcome such handicaps. And Maria would probably acknowledge that she had been slow to adapt her own appearance into something more agreeable than a grumpy frown. Indeed, she'd been adept at taming her wiry, mousy-coloured hair, which of late she had allowed to grow unchecked.

But here's the thing. When she considered herself to be on 'office time' – which typically occupied the majority of her waking hours – she contained her ample mane by the simple expedient of imitating her boss. The difference was that, in her case, she utilised a variety of combs and pins, the combination of which might be thought capable of tethering a small herd of goats. Meanwhile, both her eyes and eyebrows were concealed behind thick, black-rimmed glasses.

Maria had found her true vocation as a result of her interview with the director, or 'Ms Spooner' as she preferred to address her in fawning subservience. Her subsequent employment in the Office of Internal Affairs had provided her with the opportunity to realise her full potential as an efficient if officious servant, and she relished every moment of it. Having modelled herself on her boss, her consequent unpopularity and loneliness within the company was only ameliorated by the approval (and occasional praise) which she received at regular intervals from the director.

Maria persuaded herself that she was regarded by the director as her deputy in all but name, and whilst others might have deemed it prudent to keep such an opinion to themselves, she chose not to follow that route. Whilst she was prone to give voice to her opinion, the general consensus was that, on the subject of succession planning, she represented a vociferous and ardent minority of one.

The first item on Maria's agenda that afternoon was to return the call from one of the junior members of the IT Department with whom she had been liaising shortly before the meeting that morning. The two of them had revelled in the opportunity to act the part of a sleuth in search of the missing link in the jigsaw which the director and her team had been trying to piece together. That had occurred in the short interval which had elapsed since they had all been summoned to the office in the early hours of dawn.

She eased the extendable microphone closer to her mouth, and spoke into it with the *sotto voce* whisper of a conspirator.

'Tim?'

'Speaking. Is that you, Maria?' came the response.

'Yes. Look, Tim, I'm sorry I couldn't call you back straight away, but I had to attend the team meeting that I told you about with my boss. I'm really grateful to you for the time you're putting in on this. I know that you had a very early start, and that you've been giving this the same priority as we have.'

'No worries,' replied the voice with an assuring sincerity. 'But I think we need to meet up. And I mean urgently. I've found something here that you just have to see. I think it could be what you're looking for.'

Maria sought to disguise the excitement in her voice as she replied.

'Does anyone else know about this yet in my department?' she asked, almost casually.

'No one else besides you, although of course you won't know what it is until I show you. And it might be nothing at all. But, I need to know if I'm on the right tracks here, and that I've not been wasting my time.'

Maria was tempted briefly to defer the immediate tasks which had been assigned to her by her boss in return for the chance of delivering the vital evidence into the admiring arms of her idol. She imagined the praise which would be heaped on her by the director as reward for pursuing this particular initiative, if she were to succeed in bringing home the goods. However, even as she considered whether she might be able both to complete each of her two assigned tasks and meet up with her fellow foxhound within the time available, she knew that she dared not risk the consequences. As much as she coveted the director's approbation, the all too real alternative of a reprimand which would follow in the event of her failure was too awful to contemplate.

'I'd really love to come over right now,' she replied, with obvious regret, 'but I've got to finish off a couple of important reports that my boss needs to get to the lawyers within the next hour. Can we meet up after that? We'd be looking at around twelve-thirty or a bit later. I'd come to you, of course.'

'Sure, I'll be here, but I won't chase this up any further until you've had a look and told me that we're definitely on to something.'

'Understood. I was just thinking,' Maria posed, 'that I might be able to get my boss to re-assign my jobs if you were able to give me some idea over the phone of what it is that you've found that's so, you know, hot. Unless, of course, it really is something that you need to show me in person ...'

'No, it's not that,' replied Tim. 'It's just that we've been running some further tests on the documents which we were looking at here, you know, the ones on your list that you told me the paper had used. Anyway, we think that this girl in the marketing department may have sent them, or at least some of them, from a different email account. You know, one of the private ones.'

Maria could hardly believe her ears.

'You've got to be kidding me! You've traced them already?'

'Hey, don't get too excited,' Tim sought to caution her. 'We've only run a few tests so far, obviously, but it does look as though some of those documents, and possibly others, could have been attached to emails.'

This was potential dynamite as far as Maria was concerned.

'And were they sent by Symonds?' Maria probed.

'We're not sure yet,' Tim replied, 'and they could be internal messages, of course. That's why we're not really in a position to tell you much more than this. We're about to start the full audit trail on them now. By that I mean the trail of the list of documents which you asked us to concentrate on. We're assuming that, for the time being, we don't need to focus on the other ones that we think she might have sent.'

Maria did a quick double take.

After a moment, she took in the import of what she had just been told.

'Sorry, Tim. Did you say "other ones" just then?'

'Yeah, but these are not ones that are on your list. These are some which Paul came across – he sits beside me here – he came across them when he ran a check on the documents that the girl had worked on or retrieved during her last six months. He ran a global search on that whole population. That was before he refined it to cover just the documents on your list. Anyway, before he refined the search, he noticed that some of the documents – that is the ones not on your list – had been attached to emails, and that her PC had been used.'

Maria had been expecting something like this, albeit not quite so quickly, because her boss had suspected that the documents which the paper had used in the article were probably only the tip of the iceberg.

'What sort of documents are these?' she asked.

'Sorry, Maria, I haven't looked at any of them yet, and we didn't want to waste time on them in case they turned out to be irrelevant. But it's one of the reasons that I wanted to meet up. I need you to look at them so that you can tell us whether you want us to focus on them.'

Maria cursed inwardly. Maybe she should go straight to the director with this now, she thought. But she knew the answer even before she had entertained the thought. No, this would have to wait just for the moment. She'd speak with David and get him to run off the report for their boss by himself. That would take some of the pressure off, but she'd still need to complete her statement by the noon deadline. Time was marching on, and being late with the director was not an option.

'Look, Tim, I'll come across to you just as soon as I can get these reports out to my boss, I promise.'

'OK, cool, I know what your boss is like about deadlines. We've all been there with her. But we do need to get a thumbs up from your lot as to whether we should continue to chase this lead. As you know, our resources here are already at full stretch on the IT upgrade that we're about to migrate across the company.'

'Believe me, Tim, I do appreciate the efforts that you and your team are all making. Everything is urgent right now, but I'm not the one who gets to say which is more urgent than the next.'

'Ah yes, the old moaning mushroom. Just keep on piling on the stuff and make sure that we never see any daylight: "Our's not to reason why", and all that. The gripe of the common man.'

'What's that?' asked Maria.

'Never mind right now. I'll explain when we meet up. Give me a shout as soon as you're free, and we'll pull up the search on the screen here.'

'OK, and thanks again.'

*

The young man who had been charged with the task of interrogating the HR issues that had been flagged up following Catherine Symonds' exit interview was Roger Smith. He was one of the newer recruits to the Internal Affairs Department, but had brought with him sufficient experience of the ways of the world.

He had interviewed the records of personnel in both the Commercial Development and Human Resources Departments in order to gain an understanding of the background to her departure. None of them had been able to shed any light on the 'personal reasons' that Symonds had cited as part of her motive for leaving. That said, it was common knowledge that she had accompanied the head of CD on a number of external conferences; and that the boss had an eye for a pretty girl; and that Symonds had been very attractive. The latter fact was circumstantial only, but it was also highly relevant.

In addition, it was reported that she had been well liked; had made few if any enemies within the company, and had received excellent appraisals. In all, she appeared to have been an ideal employee.

On the matter of ethics, Roger had discovered that Symonds had prepared a paper that she had circulated to her boss and to the head of sales suggesting that the company should be the first to promote the inclusion of complementary therapy and medication so that these could be marketed alongside the company's other products. The paper had been well researched; it was well reasoned; and it carried its message with conviction, advocating that if the company did not do this, then one of its competitors would in time do so, and reap the profit.

Alas, the initiative had been short lived. The paper had never progressed beyond an item at the bottom of an agenda in a routine marketing meeting between Sales and CD. In short it had been spiked. What is more, she had complained that the company was at fault in its decision to attack alternative medicines and therapies such as homeopathy and reflexology, and to do so in concert with others in the industry. She had apparently been quite outspoken on the issue at one of the internal meetings of her department shortly before she terminated her employment.

However, none of those interviewed was able to shed any light on how Symonds, if it was indeed her, had gained access to the documents that had been cited in the article by *The Chronicle* that morning. That was very much a mystery.

In short, it was apparent that she was dissatisfied with the company as a whole, and in particular its ethics, but had otherwise appeared content in her place of work. And Roger was unable to point to any motive that might have caused Symonds to wish harm on the company by releasing what were clearly confidential documents to a newspaper and thereby exposing alleged wrongdoing.

Roger ended his report to the Mamba by cautioning that it would be wise for the company to obtain advice on whether Symonds' actions could properly constitute whistle-blowing if the documents proved to be genuine – as to which he offered no view.

*

The offices of Pointer Raymond, solicitors, are located close to the Holborn Viaduct in the City. Noon found Mary Fellowes and her team in a conference room with both junior and senior counsel. Each of those present had before them on the table a dossier which had been emailed through to Mary's PA some ninety minutes previously from the Office of Internal Affairs of AlphaOm. Its contents had been examined with such care as the exigencies of the moment had permitted. Those exigencies had required that the greatly respected presence of Mr Alain Gaitsland QC should remove its posterior from the familiar if modest comfort of his chambers in the Inner Temple, close to the Royal Courts of Justice in the Strand, and that he succumb to the indignity of a meeting in the offices of his instructing solicitors. Feathers suitably unruffled, and pride intact, he had presented himself at these plush offices of Mary's firm, whose atrium would have accommodated most of the rooms occupied by his chambers.

Mr Gaitsland hailed from 'the old school', as his colleagues (he had few friends) were wont to remark. If he had ever been 'young', they surmised, referencing Mr Tulkinghorn, it must surely have been before the invention of the combustion engine. His thin frame and gaunt face gave him a slightly cadaverous appearance, which his tailors in Chancery Lane – chosen not for their skill with needle and thread but for their proximity to his chambers following a recommendation from his former head of chambers – had done little to improve. He adjusted first the cufflinks on his left sleeve and then his papers on the conference table before him as he prepared to discuss the merits of the matter before him with the others in the meeting.

'In the very short time that I have had to consider the issues,' he began, 'there seems to me at the very least to be a strong arguable case – which is the relevant test – that the documents on which *The Daily Chronicle* has relied in their article are the property of, and are therefore *prima facie* the confidential property of, AlphaOm.'

He looked up from his papers.

'I assume that's how I should pronounce it?' he asked Mary.

'That's fine,' she replied, slightly irritated by such a pedantic question.

'I'm obliged,' he continued, with a cursory nod. 'Once we have established that central fact, then the burden will fall upon the newspaper to show one of three things: first, that the documents were at the relevant time in the public domain; alternatively, that the paper came into possession of those documents by lawful means. On the evidence that I have seen, it appears highly doubtful that the paper can readily prove either of these matters, and I note that it does not so assert in the article itself.'

He paused to allow the assembled throng to make a note of his words.

'Which brings me to the third test. That is that, notwithstanding the confidential nature of the documents, and the fact that the newspaper cannot show that it had lawfully come into possession of the documents at the time of publication, it is nevertheless in the public interest that these documents should be disclosed. The threshold for passing this test is set deliberately high, and the article contains nothing that would on its face justify continued use of the documents by the newspaper.

'In those circumstances, it appears to me that AlphaOm is entitled to an order from the court restraining and preventing the paper from making use of the documents which the company can show are confidential to it. Further, the *balance of convenience*, which is the final test which the court will apply when deciding whether to grant an application for an interim order, clearly favours placing a hold on further publication. There is no great urgency in this story coming out now, even if it were true, which I am instructed we can assure the court it is not. Therefore, the *status quo* which obtained prior to the story being published should be maintained. And that, in my opinion, is how the court is likely to view the matter.'

'But,' he continued, 'there are also other relevant factors.'

Having created such a dramatic interval, he used it with a practised art to turn the pages in the file in front of him.

'We have this morning been shown a report prepared by members of the company's Internal Affairs Department, or IAD, which provides circumstantial evidence of the means whereby the confidential documents, or at least copies thereof, came into the possession of the paper, and were thereafter unlawfully used by, it. This report is further supported by draft witness statements from certain of AlphaOm's employees, most notably in the company's IT and IA departments.'

He pointed to the bundle on the table in front of him.

'In the short time that we have had to read these drafts, it seems to us that this is helpful evidence, so far as it goes, which is likely to improve the company's case considerably once it is properly presented. In particular, the evidence points strongly to the source of the documents as being Miss Catriona Symonds. She was until recently employed by AlphaOm as an assistant manager in its Commercial Development Department, where she reported directly to the director of that department.'

'I hesitate to interrupt, Alain,' queried Mary, 'but could you just explain what you mean when you said that the evidence was helpful, but only "so far as it goes". The client will need this explained.'

'As it happens, I and my learnt junior, Richard, were going to deal with this in a moment,' Gaitsland replied, 'but since you've asked the question, and it seems convenient to deal with it now, I'd be happy to oblige.'

He glanced down at his notes before continuing.

'Some of the evidence in these statements is, in its current form, inadmissible for the simple reason that it amounts to what we call "second hand hearsay". By this we mean that the maker of the statement, whom I shall call Witness A, seeks to give evidence that he has been told by Witness B about what Witness B has been told or shown by Witness C.

It's an easy enough mistake to make, especially when time is short and when the statements have not been prepared under the supervision of lawyers.'

He instinctively considered it prudent to add that last qualification so that it would not be thought that he had intended any criticism to be directed at his instructing solicitors. No point in biting the hand that fed him, he mused to himself.

But this particular 'hand', as he should have known, was a stickler for detail, and insisted that he should sing for his supper.

'Just so that we're clear on this, Alain,' she insisted, 'and for the benefit of the clients to whom I'll have to communicate your views, what precisely is it that you need us to do with this evidence?'

Gaitsland restrained a sigh as he adjusted the papers in front of him.

'I apologise in advance if what I say sounds as though I'm giving you and your colleagues a lecture on the rules of evidence, which I'm sure that you don't need. However,' he continued, 'in order to be admissible in a court of law as witness testimony, we must provide the court with evidence from one of two sources. First, we can produce a statement from Witness C directly. That is the most desirable method. Alternatively, we can produce a statement from Witness B which gives evidence about what he or she, that is Witness B, has been told or shown by Witness C. There are a number of instances where this occurs in the draft statements. It is most obvious in the evidence of the two IAD investigators, and especially that of Miss Maria Lutherson, who it appears is going to be one of our principal witnesses in support of any application we may be instructed to make. She covers in her statement the IT audit trial through which the documents used by the paper have been traced.'

At this point he turned his attention exclusively to Mary.

'As I understand are my current instructions from AlphaOm,' he said, 'we intend to make Catriona Symonds a defendant in the proceedings which your firm is instructed to instigate. Therefore, the current deficiencies in this evidence will need to be rectified if we are to have a real prospect of resisting the likely, but not inevitable, application to set aside any interim orders which the court might be persuaded to make.'

Having directed his advice to Mary, he turned to address the younger barrister beside him, fixing him with one of his authoritative frowns over his half-moon glasses:

'Richard, I want you to take Mary's team through the evidence and show them what needs to be changed, and where. That's a priority.'

The young man acknowledged the command, which he added to the list of the other duties that he would be required to perform.

But Mary Fellowes was not one to be so easily satisfied.

'I'm still not clear,' she said, pursuing the point, 'whether your point is solely one of form, or whether your concerns go to the substance of the evidence. Can you just clarify that for us?'

This time a flicker of irritation appeared briefly on Gaitsland's brow, which he did his best to conceal. He was unused to being interrupted in mid-flow, even by some of the junior judges.

'Gladly,' he answered, as politely as he could. 'I've just dealt with the issue of form, so let me turn to the substance of the evidence, with which I was about to deal.'

He allowed himself a sip of water before clearing his throat, and then for the second time neatly re-adjusted the papers on the table in front of him, glancing at his cufflinks to satisfy himself that they were aligned at the right angle.

'The main thrust of the evidence which we have discovered covers three principal points. First, it identifies the origin of the documents from which the paper has quoted extensively in its article. By origin, I mean the author or co-authors of the documents. Second, it records the fact that Miss Symonds had access to all or most of these documents. Thirdly, it demonstrates that, in the period leading up to her departure from the company, she had arranged to meet with the journalist who appears to have written the article for the paper. It does not show that Miss Symonds actually met the journalist, but it is suspicious that each of the entries in her diary which had scheduled the various meetings was deleted from the diary very shortly before she left the company.'

He waited briefly until Mary's team had finished their note of his advice.

'I shall now address the substantive "lacuna" or deficiencies in the evidence.'

Another sip of water.

'The team from IAD are to be congratulated for the wealth of material which they have produced in such a short time. However, what is absent from all this material is any hard evidence that Miss Symonds communicated with or met with the journalist or caused any of the documents to be provided to him. Our evidence is, at best, circumstantial, but that is only to be expected at this early stage in the company's investigations. Should evidence emerge that Miss Symonds was indeed responsible for causing the confidential documents to be furnished directly or indirectly to the journalist or to any other agent of the paper, that would remove any doubt as to her role in this affair. Such conduct would also have been in clear breach of the duties of confidentiality which Miss Symonds owed to the company, both under the express terms and conditions of her employment contract, and also as implied under the Common Law. It is therefore my strong view that this is the area where the company should now focus its investigations.'

He smiled again at Mary, as if to emphasise that he and his junior had given careful consideration to these issues.

'I should add one point for completeness, although I'm sure, Mary, that you have already advised or will shortly advise the company on it. This concerns the company's duty to give full and frank disclosure to the court when making an application of this sort without any notice to any of the proposed defendants. The effect of that duty is as follows. Should the investigations reveal any evidence which casts reasonable doubt on the assertion that Miss Symonds was the source within AlphaOm which the newspaper exploited in order to obtain the confidential documents, we must disclose this forthwith to the court. Likewise, should we come across evidence upon which we might later wish to rely in order to make good that assertion, the company has a duty to disclose it forthwith. Alternatively, if we discover evidence that detracts from our case, but could reasonably be said to support the assertions made by the newspaper, which I should add would include Miss Symonds' motives for providing the documents, then we must also disclose this.'

A further pause for dramatic effect.

'I need hardly remind you of the consequences for AlphaOm should it fail to discharge its duty of disclosure.'

This was now Mary's turf.

'Thank you, Alain, that won't be necessary,' she said. 'We shall be covering those points in our advice to the clients, together with your very helpful summary of the evidential position. But just to close on this issue, how much detail do we need to give to the court at this stage – even in draft – as to the state of our investigations?'

She gritted her teeth as the papers were re-shuffled one further time. That habit was beginning to grate on her.

'At this stage,' he answered, 'the court will want as full an account as we can put together of what we have been able to find out about how the documents came into the possession of the paper. This account should give the gist of what our evidence will be, and by whom it will be given. It will not need to comprise at this stage the actual statements, although we can expect to be ordered to produce these within two days. In addition, the court will want to see direct evidence from the company to the effect that it had not authorised the release of its confidential documents by Miss Symonds to the newspaper or otherwise into the public domain. I suggest that this should come from a member of the company's main board of directors.'

He glanced at his junior, who nodded his agreement.

'Given the time restraints' he concluded, 'I would not have a problem with Miss Lutherson remaining as one of the principal witnesses in support of the application, especially since she is the author of the report regarding the investigation. She at least will be able to speak with some authority.'

'Very well,' Mary acknowledged. 'It shall be done. We'll have that ready in draft for you to approve by two. Since we're all here, can we just consider the matter of logistics for a moment?'

She looked to her senior associate on her team.

'Tim, before we decide who and when will be finalising our evidence in support of our application, can you remind us where we are on a judge for this afternoon, and the various deadlines.'

Her associate flicked back a few pages in his notebook before answering:

'We've spoken to the court. They can lay on a judge at 4.00 pm in Court 37 – that's the Queen's Bench Applications Court. They need our evidence by email by 3.00 at the latest, even in draft form.' Then he added: 'It looks as if we'll get Mr Justice Hunters.'

Mary looked across at Gaitsland for any sign of recognition, which was duly forthcoming.

'Yes, I've appeared before him,' he said. 'He's a sensible chap; had a decent general practice at the Bar. Should be good for us.'

'That's reassuring to know,' Mary commented. 'We've got plenty to do here in order to prepare the application. We've lined up an independent supervising solicitor who will explain the court order to the newspaper, the journalist and the girl, and we've also identified an IT expert who will be able to interrogate any PCs, laptops or mobiles which we find at Symonds' flat or at the house of the journalist.'

'We now know where she lives, and we're having the girl's flat watched to make sure she's still there.'

One of Barbara's assistants tapped her on her arm, and whispered into her ear something to do with the means by which the company had acquired the knowledge of Catriona's new residence.

Barbara waived his concern aside.

'We've also confirmed that the independent solicitors will be present to supervise the searches of the residential premises of the girl, and of the journalist and the paper's head office.'

'Good,' noted Gaitsland. 'Meanwhile, I shall be looking over the current draft of the application which has been prepared. The court will not require the company to produce a full statement of case at this early stage. But it will need a short skeleton argument in support. I'll work on this with Richard over the next hour or so.'

'You're welcome to use this office,' said Mary. 'I'm having some lunch sent up for you. Let's meet up again at two here.'

She delegated instructions to a junior in her team before turning once again to address her leading counsel.

'Alain, could I ask you and Richard to attend a brief videocon with the clients in order to summarise the substance of your advice. The main board is meeting as we speak, and they want to be patched through to us here in order to hear your views and to give us the formal go-ahead.'

Gaitsland's brow furrowed briefly. He had not understood that he would be required to repeat his advice directly to the board, but assumed that this would be conveyed to them by Mary. However, he was the hired gun, and was long used to restraining himself from displaying his irritation. But he was not best pleased to discover that, in effect, he had just been asked to perform a dress-rehearsal of his advice for the benefit of Mary's team. He considered that it was demeaning of him for Mary to have used this conference as a 'dry run' in order to 'vet' his views, or perhaps even to cause him to refine them so that they could now be presented in the best possible light to her clients. Nevertheless, he accepted that this was what he had been engaged to do, and in truth the rehearsal with his solicitors had not been unhelpful.

He therefore prepared himself for a second conference, although this one was to be conducted through a medium which he disliked intensely. Like most lawyers, he liked to be able to 'eyeball' his clients so that he could watch their body language, which normally told him much more than any spoken word.

Nevertheless, he who pays the piper calls the tune, he thought to himself, as he collected his papers together.

Chapter 4

Chuck Thompson checked his emails using his handheld 'virtual office' from the hotel, where he had fortuitously travelled to in order to address an international conference on a subject which he purported to keep dear to his heart, namely the merits of successful branding of a business. In reality, he couldn't give a fig, but such is his art that none have yet exposed the mendacity which lies at the centre of all he says and does, both in his private life and in his role at AlphaOm.

As he scanned the email from his co-director, he observed to himself that his absence from the office at this precise moment was both highly convenient and also a necessary expediency. He would be able to defer any imminent return to London until the weekend, and would meanwhile duck the increasingly hysterical flow of messages from the office through a combination of spontaneous ingenuity and dextrous spin. These were, of course, the very tools of his trade. And the hardworking folk in legal would have neither the balls nor the impertinence to question the priorities with which he discharged the heavy burden of his office, which currently took the form of a glass of wine and plateful of meat from the buffet. He had kept their heads down by composing what were to become carefully prepared statements from the chief executive and the head of research in response to what CT anticipated would be an insatiable thirst for gossip from the media. All part of a day's work.

As he set his mind to composing another work of fiction, his screen announced that he had been sent another urgent email from that persistent terrier from legal who kept asking him for a statement concerning Catherine, or 'Kitty' as he used to call her, much to her irritation. He smiled at the memory of that particular conquest. He had enjoyed both the hunt and the spoils of the kill. But it had ended as so many of them do, with Kitty finally deciding that she had to escape from the web into which he had led her, but not before he had subjugated her, moulded her into a toy with which he could play out his own perverted games. And not before, he smiled to himself, he had awoken in her desires of which she had been deliciously ignorant until their affair.

He scanned the mail again from Ted Fisher. It was timed in the early hours of this morning, and was marked urgent. As had the previous two messages. That mongrel had the cheek to demand a full account of the material to which Kitty had access during her time in his department.

Bollocks to that, he said to himself. The email suggested that if he did not provide such an account, the post-mortem into this whole business would inevitably become more penetrating. Too bloody right they would, he thought. He smiled at his own pun, but he certainly didn't want them going there.

No. They would get the standard spin from him. He would limit this to the role that she had been recruited to perform in the department, her inadequate performance (at least in that capacity) and the mutual parting of ways following her poor annual appraisal earlier this year. In the meantime, he would need to start covering his tracks, but at the same time try to work out how she – he assumed it was her – had managed to provide hard and soft copies of all those documents to the paper.

Something was not right here.

CT was on first name terms with the journalist, Ken Baxter. He made a mental note that he needed to have words with him. Meanwhile, he would check to see if he had included him in any of his most recent briefings. As a rule he felt that it was safe to assume that Baxter was sufficiently 'on-message' that he would have tipped off his department that the newspaper was going to run this kind of story about the company.

CT frowned as began to draft his reply to Fisher's email. Maybe he was getting complacent. He reminded himself that, in his position at the top of the slippery pole that was his trade, he could not trust anyone. Especially not those hyenas in the press.

He proposed to Fisher that they should arrange to meet upon his return to London. He was not due back in town on Saturday morning, so any time on Monday or Tuesday would be convenient.

More importantly, it would give him time to check his files over the weekend.

*

Maria made her way down to the floor where the IT Department was housed, having confirmed to Tim that she was now ready to resume where they had left off earlier that day. She had told her boss just enough about the promising lead which her contacts in IT had uncovered and which she was pursuing to ensure that she had received the director's blessing to follow this up. She wanted this to be a surprise, a rare triumph for her in what had hitherto been what Spooner would regard as a thorough, reliable but otherwise uninspired performance of her duties. Maria wanted to carry the laurels that would follow her triumphant parade of new material which she hoped would see her elevated yet further in the esteem of her role-model.

The lads in IT looked up as they beheld the bizarre figure making its way down the corridor formed by the banks of PC terminals around them. Nothing had quite prepared them for this phenomenon clad in black, which was unlike anything either of them had experienced before. In contrast to their T-shirts and jeans, which comprised the hallmark attire of all self-respecting IT personnel, Maria's costume took their idea of 'dressing up' (as opposed to down) to a new level.

'Shit, man,' whispered Paul to his neighbour, possibly louder than had intended, 'she even dresses like the fucking Gestapo.'

'Take it easy on her, Paul,' Tim responded, 'she's probably just doing her job. Everyone who works for that Mamba has to dress up. You know that.'

'Maybe. But just make sure you don't give her your mobile number. She'll probably turn out to be another bunny-boiler!'

He tried to ignore his neighbour's giggles as he put up his hand to attract her attention so that he could direct her across to their console.

'Hi, are you Maria?' he asked as she approached,

He tried looking directly at her, but was overwhelmed by the thick lenses of her glasses, which obscured much of her face. His first impressions had not been improved by a closer inspection.

'Take a seat,' he invited her, pulling over one of the chairs from the empty console beside them.

'Thanks. Yes, I'm Maria. You must be Tim, yeah?'

'Yep. Welcome to IT,' he said, 'although perhaps I should say welcome back, since you've probably been here before.'

'Once or twice, yes, but this is the first time that I've been able to work closely with you guys. And, in case I forget, thanks again for your help. My boss will really appreciate it.'

'Well, that's what we're here for, or at least part of it. And to be honest, we've had quite a bit of fun chasing this up. It's always good to produce a result like this, even if it has screwed up our week.'

True to her character, she wasted no time in getting straight down to basics.

'Talking of results, can you show me what you've been able to put together on this for me so far?'

By way of an answer, he turned to his screen and pulled up a document which he and Paul had been working on.

'OK. This is a table showing the dates on which various documents have been sent from this office by mail. We know this by checking the properties of these documents. What we don't know, but we're working on, is from which terminal and from which email account they were sent. But we have kind of stumbled on a new lead.'

'Go on,' she urged.

'We ran a search against all the emails which had been sent from the office account used by Symonds – that's the email address that she was provided by the company. We discovered that quite a few were copied by her to what we guess must be her own private email account. It's not one that she's ever told us about.'

'What, you mean like Hotmail or Yahoo or something like that,' she asked. 'But you have to go on to the internet to use those don't you?'

'Yes, but whoever set up the company system here had thought about that. You see, the way our system works is that any communication leaving this office electronically all goes through the same hosting processor, and especially any to which there has been attached a document which has been either generated or processed in this office. That means that, as long as you know roughly where to look, and in this case that means the email account which was used to send the communication, then in theory we should be able to retrieve a copy, together with the attachment.'

She considered that for a moment.

'But that could take an age, surely. We must send thousands of mails from here every day. Where does all this get stored?'

'The servers monitoring our exit portal here get backed up at least six times every day, and the data is stored in servers located in a cloud off-site. We can access these from here. Now that we think we know the email account that she probably used, we can do a search against her private emails. We might even be able to get into her private account itself, although after this period of time she may have trashed most of these.'

'Well, we know that she deleted data from her office diary, so should we assume that she did the same with her office and private emails?'

'That has to be a real possibility, if not a likelihood.'

'So, aren't you likely to have more luck checking our own backup servers for any data sent from her private email account, and checking for any data sent to that email address from her office email account here?'

'That's what we reckon,' he said. 'We just need you to give us the thumbs up and we'll make a start. We'll need to compose the search request first, which could take a bit of time. But we might have something for you by this evening. That's assuming that someone else here doesn't get there first, because Paul reckons that one of your colleagues might already be on to this.'

Paul shot him a frown, as if to indicate that he had said too much, but it was enough to alert Maria to the risk inherent in any further delay, namely the risk that her moment of glory could be snatched from her grasp.

That would be too much, and she could feel in her bones that the email search which Tim proposed was going to produce results.

'Sorry, what's that?'

Tim paused a second before responding.

'Ah, well, here's the thing, Maria. One of the gems that we have retrieved from her private email account is her new address.'

Maria lost a breath.

'Sorry, say that again.'

'Yeah, we thought you'd like that. We know where she's living right now.'

This latest intelligence forced her hand.

'Then do it,' she decided. 'You have my authority.'

'Ah yes,' he said glancing across at his neighbour, 'and whilst we're on that subject, and since we'll be dealing with her private and personal mails, we'll need that authority in writing before we start.'

Now she hesitated. Did she have that authority? Of course she did, she told herself. Her boss had told her to do whatever was necessary to get a result.

'OK,' she said impetuously, 'you give me the email account that you want to access, and I'll send you the necessary authority from my department.'

'Consider it done,' he said with obvious relief. 'The details will be on your email by the time you've walked back to your desk.'

They arranged to talk later that afternoon as soon as Tim was ready to give her a progress report so that she could brief the director. With that, and having repeated her thanks to her dynamic IT duo, as she saw them, for their efforts on behalf of the company, Maria returned to the familiar territory of her department.

She briefly checked in on David to update him on her progress and to exchange interim reports, but deftly omitted all reference to her private initiative other than to confirm that she was following up various leads with IT. By the time that she had settled herself back at her desk, her terminal had already received the email from Tim requesting authority to run the trace on Symonds' personal emails. She printed off a copy, and composed a draft reply which conferred the required approval.

Armed with both the request and her draft reply, she walked the short distance down the corridor to the director's suite. Her intention, in line with both her training and her instinct, was to follow Tim's example and cover her own posterior by securing formal approval of the actions which she was about to set in train. To that end, she duly presented herself before the director's two PAs. (The Mamba prided herself on the necessity for two PAs, together with a secretary, so as to achieve equal parity with the chief, and so that this trio could form a mini-cabal which would screen her from unwelcome interruptions. 'Open door' was not her policy.) However, Maria was curtly informed by one of them that the director was still in a board meeting, and was scheduled to attend another urgent meeting as soon as the former was concluded, such that she was unlikely to return to her office any time soon.

As she retired once again to her desk, Maria considered the dilemma which had been presented to her, the like of which she had yet to experience in her short career with the company. Should she postpone or abandon this promising initiative until she had been able to obtain the necessary blessing from her protector and mentor, which she had assumed would be forthcoming. Only now did she begin to harbour serious doubts. Was she being over-confident? Could she count on the support of her boss if she were forced to seek approval retrospectively? On the other hand, would she not equally be criticised if she were to prevent the hounds from following the scent for the time being, given the fertile potential for such a rich harvest of evidence that the proposed venture offered? Whilst her training cautioned in favour of the former, her ambition to win the laurels of victory on behalf of her boss, and thereby augment her own status within the department, urged her to set caution to the wind.

She considered her options if she were to follow the latter course. If the soil proved to be barren, then no one need learn that the seed had been sown, and she persuaded herself that any furrows that had been ploughed could swiftly be levelled by an electronic rake. On the other hand, if the venture were to bear fruit, then she could always seek the retrospective authority which would ratify whatever technical misdemeanours might have been committed in the process. Quite how such ratification would operate she was unsure, but she could meet that hurdle when it arose, if indeed it ever did.

Worse still was the prospect of a rebuke from her role-model that might follow her failure to act on information that might have otherwise delivered crucial results.

She pondered a further alternative. She could take someone else in her department into her confidence, such as David, and seek his or her advice. But that would involve alerting him to the leads which she would claim that she was following (the reality being that she would be instructing Tim to follow). Also, Tim – or rather his colleague – had already let slip that someone else in her department, which she assumed must be David, had already begun to make enquiries regarding the girl's email accounts.

No, she decided that she couldn't run the risk that she would be sharing, worse still handing over, this pot of gold on a plate to a rival within her own department.

One final alternative, which was perhaps the safest course, would be to go direct to the company's compliance officer in the Legal Department. The trouble with that was that it was notoriously cumbersome, and involved filling out one of those tiresome compliance and data protection requests, which would involve repeating the exercise which they had already undertaken that morning. That would waste another two hours at least, which could easily jeopardise her prospects of being the first to unearth the missing links in the chain of evidence which was in the process of being assembled by her department and the lawyers in support of the company's case.

No, she decided that this was a call which she was going to make. At the age of thirty, she considered herself to have reached a stage in her career where she could now make this sort of decision by herself. Moreover, she was not about to deny herself such a golden opportunity for self-advancement.

She therefore returned to her desk and, without further delay, sent the required email to Tim authorising the electronic search of Cat Symonds' personal emails, using her 'nomme de plume' of Assistant Director of Internal Affairs. She gave as her reason the fact that there was a reasonable prospect that some of those emails had attached copies of confidential documents which were the property of the company, and that it was both lawful and necessary to procure the return of these documents by all means reasonably at the disposal of the company.

She had drafted so many of these in the past that, when she pressed the 'send' key, she did not trouble to consider the question of her own authority.

*

'So, let's cut to the chase, Alain,' boomed the voice of McBride around the boardroom. 'What you're telling us is that, as regards these confidential documents, which we reckon we can show have been unlawfully obtained by the paper, we're looking at a shoe-in, as we like to say where I come from. It should be an open and shut number. But as regards the girl, what's her name, Simons or something, we may not have enough on her yet to nail her for leaking the documents to the paper. That's if we take it to the wire – or trial, as you say. In the meantime, we've probably got enough to obtain an order from the court to order her computer and flat to be searched. Does that just about sum it up?'

A mile or so away in High Holborn, the set of papers whose neat appearance could hardly have been improved were once again fastidiously tidied so that each of the corners were perfectly aligned. A passing bat would have detected a restrained gnashing of teeth from the other side of the conference table as Mr Alain Gaitsland QC performed his habitual ritual as he readied himself to respond.

'As I've explained, and as you are aware, we have only had a very short time in which to consider the issues,' Alain replied. 'However, on the evidence which has been assembled by the company, it is our opinion that we have a reasonable prospect of persuading the court that the company has at the very least a strong arguable case – and that is the relevant test which the court will apply at this stage – that it will succeed in proving three things at trial.

'First, that the documents on which *The Daily Chronicle* has relied in their recent article are the confidential property of, AlphaOm. Second, that the newspaper is unlikely to be able to discharge the burden of showing that the documents were at all material times in the public domain, or, alternatively, that the paper came into possession of those documents by lawful means. I have already noted that the paper does not so assert in the article itself. And thirdly that there is no other reason why the company's confidential property should be used by the newspaper, and the injunction thus granted. In those circumstances, it is our opinion that AlphaOm will be able to establish a *prima facie* case that is entitled to an order from the court restraining and preventing the paper from making use of the documents which the company can show are confidential to it. That is, however, only part of the answer.

'The next and final test which the court will apply when deciding whether or not to grant an application for an interim order in a case such as this is the balance of convenience test. In essence, this involves weighing the respective detriment which will be suffered by either side if the injunction were to be granted. In our opinion, the court will decide that the balance clearly favours placing a hold on further publication. I doubt whether the paper can show that there is any great urgency in this story coming out now, even if it were true, which I am instructed we can assure the court it is not. Therefore, I think it likely that the court will reach the view that the *status quo* which obtained prior to the story being published should be restored and maintained.'

'Get to the point.'

'Well, that is the answer to your first point. As regards the claim against Miss Symonds personally, the position is less clear. However, given the strong circumstantial evidence linking her to the journalist at the paper, and the steps apparently taken by her to cover her tracks before she left your employment, it is my view that there are sufficient grounds on which to persuade the court to grant the sort of search orders which we would be seeking. So, in a nutshell, whilst the matter is not open and shut, as you put it, we consider that the company has a reasonable prospect of obtaining the orders that we are seeking.

'However,' he continued, before McBride could interrupt, 'the proof will be in the pudding when we get before the judge. It will all turn on the view he takes on the evidence, but what I think will tilt the odds further in your favour will be your proposed statement to the effect that the company has not misled either the relevant national authorities or the public at large with regard to any of its sweetening products or its remedies or treatments for diabetes. The court will want to be satisfied that you do not believe that your company has any commercial motive for undertaking the sort of orchestrated campaign of deceit which the paper alleges that you have done. I've discussed this with Mary, and my view is that your proposed statement will be very helpful evidence.'

As if on cue, and in response to Gaitsland's implicit invitation, Mary intervened at this stage to add her views.

'As you will recall, Robert, this is the point that I was discussing with you last night. It is the only point on which I'm nervous about the application. My concern is to ensure that such evidence should not become an unnecessary hostage to fortune, or raise a possibility that it could expose the company to the sort of nightmare which McDonald's stumbled into with its libel claim about the source of its meat. Personally, I would prefer that you do not go there, but Alain's view is that we may not be able to obtain the injunction without it. I have to defer to him on that score, since he has more experience than me in these delicate forensic balances. I just want to be sure that you and your board have considered all the risks, and therefore the potential downside which might follow if . . .'

'As far as my board is concerned,' interrupted McBride, 'the worst downside for us right now would be to be seen by the market to be doing nothing about this story in the press. If my evidence is what it takes to swing the odds in our favour, and that's what we're being told by the expert, then we go ahead and use it.'

And then, as an afterthought, he added: 'And anyway, even if the company's PR machine has taken a free hit at the quacks who question our products – and I'm not saying it has, mind you – that bunch of airheads are never going to be serious opposition for us. And since when has it been illegal to dump on the competition? It's a regular event in the motor industry, and the minnows in our pool who peddle their organic nonsense often have a go at bigger fish like us. We just make sure that we use our clout to shut them up. It's called business. They're an irrelevant voice way out there on the internet – which, by the way, we do our best to silence. Anyway, that's where they're going to stay. They're never going to be taken seriously.'

There was a silence from the Holborn end of the video conference.

'Yes, well, thank you for that,' said Gaitsland eventually. 'As I've said, I consider it prudent to include in our evidence a statement which records the absence of any commercial motive for a co-ordinated campaign of the sort which has been alleged against the company. However, I'm not sure that the second part of what you've just said is the sort of line we should be taking at this stage. It's very much an argument of last resort, and if we're forced to retreat to the extent that we have to fall back on that reasoning, such as it is, then I think we shall definitely need to reconsider our position.'

'All the more reason, don't you think,' observed Mary, 'for omitting any reference at all to the motive point.'

'I'm not so sure,' said Gaitsland. 'I've given you my views, but I shall quite understand if you prefer not to follow my advice.'

McBride tried to interpret the sign language that accompanied Alain Gaitsland's response, but the deadpan features on the screen in front of him were giving nothing away.

McBride had had enough of this pussyfooting around. He did not get to become one of the lions of his industry by wimping out of tough decisions like this. And, privately, he was adept at playing the selective memory game, so if anything did emerge which might point the finger at himself, he would just do a 'Reagan' and say that he had never read the document at the time.

Decision time.

'No.' McBride made up his mind. 'If Alain's view is that we improve the odds in our favour by using the bit about the absence of motive, then we use it. Forget the rest. I was just getting it off my chest anyway, and I agree that once we get down to an argument about justification then that's probably something which you lawyers will have to argue about before the judge.'

Time to close it up, he decided.

'Right, we're running short of time,' he snapped. 'Thank you both for your advice, and thank you, Alain, for coming over from your offices, or chambers I think you call them. I hope that we haven't inconvenienced you. No doubt you'll tell me or Mary if anything you've heard today or over the next few days causes you to change your mind on the advice you've given us.'

'Happy to oblige,' came the stiff reply.

McBride looked around at his board of directors, eyeing each one in turn.

'Right, folks, you've heard it from the horse's mouth. Adrian and Mary need our decision. Does any one of you disagree with the resolution that they should be instructed to make the application to the High Court this afternoon, naming as proposed defendants the paper, the girl and the journalist?'

He waited for any sign of dissent. None was evident.

'Very well,' he announced. 'All those in favour?'

He eyeballed his colleagues as each one in turn raised their hand, their concurrence duly noted by the assistant to the company secretary, his boss still being absent on leave. Armed with that resolution, he turned back to the screens in front of him.

'That gets it sorted, Mary. You're good to go. I'll have the full resolution emailed to you momentarily.'

'We're on the case, Robert,' Mary acknowledged. 'We should get in front of the judge by late afternoon, which means that, assuming that there are no logistical problems, we should certainly be able to serve any order before they begin to produce the early morning editions.'

'Call me, please, Mary, as soon as you have finished in court. We'll be in the office – and probably in this board room – for the next half an hour at least. You've got the numbers. We'll be waiting for your news.'

Mary was about to give her confirmation, but she realised that McBride had already cut the call.

*

Maria was still at her desk later that day as the team of lawyers instructed by the company arranged their papers in Court 37 in readiness for the entrance of the judge. Their application to the High Court had been emailed and faxed to the court earlier that afternoon, and was even at that moment being read by the judge.

The message box on Maria's screen announced that she had received another email from the lads in IT. She opened it to read that Tim was ready to talk her through their interim progress report on the new line of investigation which she had sanctioned. She still harboured doubts as to the extent of her authority in that regard. However, she had already decided that she would cross that bridge once she had learnt what they had found for her so far. The prospect of winning the adulation of her boss and mentor was too great a pull. She therefore wasted no further time, and immediately dialled Tim's extension.

'Hi Tim, it's Maria. Thanks for getting back to me so quickly.'

'No problem. Let me just switch screens so that I can brief you on this.'

There was a short silence as he pulled up the material which he had saved in a separate folder for this purpose.

'OK, here's what we're looking at,' he resumed. 'We've got some good news and some not so good news, although by the time I've explained everything, you might not agree with me which is which, so you'll have to work it out for yourself.'

If Maria had been intrigued before she made the call, she was now desperate to hear what he had to say. She could hardly bear the suspense, and told him so.

'OK, here's the deal,' he continued. 'We've traced a load of emails which we know were sent from this office by Symonds using her Ola web address. Some of these were sent to another email address at Ola with her initials, so we assume it's one of hers, or else it belongs to someone who is assisting her, knowingly or otherwise we cannot yet say. These are the interesting ones because they have got most of the attachments which we think will interest you. Anyway, we reckon that you need to see them.'

'Go on,' she urged.

'We think we've found some stuff that's really useful to you. We've got at least one, no, make that two emails which went from her private address at Ola to the journalist at the paper. And the first of them had attached one of the main documents which were quoted at length by the same journalist in the article. The other one – that's the second email – refers a lot to one of the other documents which she's obviously given to him because they're discussing its contents. But the really good bit is in the second email where she says that she's bringing him copies of other documents which will back up what she's saying in the email. You'll have to judge for yourself, but we reckon we've got her bang to rights on these ones.'

Maria could hardly believe what she was hearing. She had struck gold in less than one day's work, and would now be able to present to her boss more evidence than either of them could ever have imagined possible.

She looked at her watch. It was probably too late to get hold of the lawyers in court, but she would need to ferry this ammunition across to the legal team later that evening, or first thing in the morning at the latest.

'You've done really well, Tim. Do you need me to come over to look at this or can you send them to me in zip format today?'

'We're already putting that together,' he replied. 'It should be ready within the next hour or so. But we've only given you the good news so far. Do you not want to hear the rest? There are some other attachments that you might not be so pleased to see.'

'How bad are they?'

'Depends how you read them, I suppose. They looked pretty bad to me, but you might not think so. Either way, we reckon that you might need to get them checked out by the lawyers before we do anything else with them.'

She considered whether she should tell him to drop the subject, rather than allow him to discuss material which was potentially harmful to the company's case. But he had already told her that they had read the documents, so there was little to be gained there. She therefore decided to let him finish his verbal report. It would be several days later that she realised that, as a result of their conversation, she would be unable to deny any knowledge of the material. As she was quickly to learn to her cost, hindsight is a wonderful thing, but provides little comfort to those who subsequently have time to reflect on their mistakes and repent at leisure.

'Just let me have the basics,' she said, injecting a degree of urgency into her voice.

'OK. Well, you're aware that we're talking about emails that she sent both from and to her address at Ola – they are the ones that I've just been telling you about?'

'Are these different from the ones that went to the journalist with the attachments?'

'Yeah, I'm afraid so. Well, the first two are just copies of the emails to the journalist with the attachments I've told you about. There are a load of others that have got documents attached, but I haven't said anything about those yet.'

'Go one. Let's hear it then.'

'Well, one of these emails attaches a document which looks like a report that's been produced here which is going from her boss – that's the director of CD – to the chief. It seems to be telling him what's been agreed with his opposite numbers within other companies about how to put the knife into the organic lobby who bang on about the links between sugar and the modern epidemic of diabetes. It says stuff like "the time having come when their industry needs to take this seriously", and then there's a page or more saying what they want to do. I haven't read it all but it looks like some kind of action list, including the need for some promotional soundbites.'

She definitely did not like what she was hearing, but thought it prudent to put a brave face on things for the purpose of this phone call.

'Oh, I wouldn't get too worked up about that. Keeping an eye on the opposition is probably an everyday occurrence in this line of business. But are you saying that this has already been sent to the newspaper?'

'No, we're not sure. We just can't tell yet. She seems to have sent herself a copy of the document, but we are still trying to find an email going from her to the journalist which attaches it. But that's not to say that she didn't hand a copy to him personally when they met. And it would seem odd that she's given him the ones which we know about but decided to keep quiet about this little bombshell'

'Can you keep looking for me,' she instructed, 'but include these documents in the zip file that you're sending to me for now so that I can look through them here?'

'Sure, will do. I'm putting together a complete set for you with a report telling you where we found these and when. I'll send this over to you later this evening, or first thing tomorrow, and we'll continue to search for other emails in the meantime.'

'Thanks, guys, I really appreciate this.'

As she hung up the phone, Tim raised his eyebrows at his colleague, Paul, who had been following the conversation.

'Well, she can't say that I didn't offer her the easy way out,' he said with a shake of his head. 'She wants us to zip the whole lot up and send it over to her this evening. And that's not all! She also wants us to carry on looking.'

Paul offered a frown by way of reply, and then added: 'I don't understand why you didn't tell her about the other stuff that we found. That might have made her think twice.'

'Yeah, right, especially as I haven't read any of them yet. You've mentioned a couple, but she's told me to focus on the documents that the paper quoted from. She's hardly likely to thank me for spending all my time reading about the girl's love life.'

'What, when she's clearly been getting knocked off by her boss? That's the sort of info that starts the red lights flashing on the alarm panels. If I was the chief, and I was just about to declare war on one of the major newspapers, that's exactly the kind of info I would want to be told about before I launch a nuclear strike.'

'Our instructions were absolutely clear, Paul. We are to concentrate on finding the paper trail which will show that those documents went from this office to the press. We'll get a right bollocking if we decide not to follow those instructions.'

'And what about all the crap we get given about how we should be using our initiative so that we provide added value to our internal client? Do we just ignore that and just bundle the whole lot over to Maria?'

'That's exactly what we do, Paul. If there's one thing that I've been well taught in this job, seen it with my own eyes too, it's that the messenger is the one who always get shot first. And we are not about to volunteer to be the ones that are first over the top. That means that neither you nor I offer to carry this news to the chief.'

Paul thought about that for a few seconds.

'OK. Maybe you're right there. But I'm really serious about this, Tim. We've got to cover our own arses on this one. That also has to be our priority.'

'And that's precisely what we're going to do. We'll finish preparing the report for Maria to accompany the zip file that we're collating. This will tell her exactly what we've done, and is going to list each of the emails and documents which we've sent her. That way she can't deny having received them. OK?'

'With you so far.'

'So, that's just stage one.'

'OK, I'll buy that. So what's stage two?'

'Did you receive the email about an hour ago from Maria's colleague in the Gestapo asking us whether we would be able to assist him?'

Paul checked his inbox. He told Tim that he hadn't received any new messages from internal affairs.

'Well, as luck would have it, this guy is asking me whether IT might be able to help him shed any light – there's a poncey term for giving him a steer – on what could have been the personal reasons why the Symonds girl left the company.'

'Well, bloody roll on! You're a canny bastard, Tim. How long have you been keeping that one up your sleeve?'

'Just long enough to see how pissed off I could get you!'

'Well you bloody well succeeded, you bastard! So the deal is that we give this guy the full story of what we've uncovered?'

'Remember what I said about messengers? We don't give him any story. We just tell him what we were instructed to do, how we've been carrying out those instructions, and then provide him with the same list that we've given to Maria.'

'But surely we've got to tell him about the important emails? I mean, first there's the one where she's saying that she can't go on seeing him. Then there's this one. Here she is pleading with him to let her go – those are her actual words. Are you telling me that we pretend we didn't find these?'

'Not a bit, mate. He'll get the lot when we're ready.'

'And look at this one. I found it this morning. Here she is saying that she's not going to go on seeing him any more, and that she's not going to listen to his threats any more. I don't know what the fuck that's all about, but if that's not a personal reason for leaving the company, then I don't know what is.'

'Put like that, I couldn't agree more, Paul. But we're not going to be the ones who write that in any report which is going to be seen by the chief. That's the way to be certain that we get lined up against the wall and shot.'

'OK, so what do we say?'

'We'll use words like, "We have listed in the attached schedule a number of emails which appear to us to be personal in nature, but we are unsure of their context, and invite the readers to form their own views on their content." That's the sort of bland crap that we can hide behind if this ever goes pear-shaped.'

'You ought to be in politics, mate. Ever fancied that?'

'Nope. I've just learnt over the years that when the shit starts flying it's always the ones who stick their heads above the parapet who get it in the face.'

'OK. So, do we zip it all into one big folder, or dice it up into a bundle of them? Or have I just answered my own question?'

'That's exactly what you've done, mate.'

'Thought so.'

'And we go further, we scatter the really bad crap throughout the zips so that it will take a day or so for them to reassemble them at the other end.'

'Like burying the bad news?'

'Yep, except with a JCB!'

'Nice one. You've clearly been in the game a while. So what happens when Maria starts to go through the zip files? She's not going to like reading those emails, and I bet the lawyers won't either when they see them.'

'They sure as hell won't.'

'Fuck, Tim. Talk about opening a can of worms, this could all blow up in their faces. What do we do then?'

'You and I, Paul, make very sure that by that time we're going to be fully stretched on other IT business, and we tell her that, regrettably, she will need to look elsewhere for any further help on the IT front.'

'What, just say that we're unavailable?'

'No, we get our boss to say that we're irreplaceable and cannot be removed from another major programme. Which reminds me, I must make sure that both our names are down on the overtime rota. Remember the email that the boss sent round about needing backup for the phased migration of the new software throughout the company over the next couple of months?'

'Yeah. So?'

'Well, think about it for just a second.'

'OK, I've got it. We get ourselves onto the training course later this week, so that by the time this thing blows up, it's too late for them to get hold of us.'

'There you are. You worked it out for yourself.'

'Nice one, Timmo. I can see that I've got a lot to learn.'

'One other thing. Let's make sure that we leave the building as soon as we've sent the report to Maria tomorrow.'

'Good thinking. If I do the list of attachments, can you do the report?'

'That's a deal.'

'What about the report to the lawyer? You know, the one dealing with the crap about personal reasons?'

'We send him the list of the documents that we've sent to Maria, but not the electronic copies. We say that our instructions were that the files were to be shown only to her, and that without further authorisation we're unsure whether the contents are to be shared with others within the company.'

'I know what you're thinking. You're reckoning on fuelling the turf war that's already going on between the Gestapo and legal.'

'Now why would you think I'd be cynical enough to want to do something as aggravating as that?'

'Because you're a cynical bastard at heart.'

'I'm cut to the quick, I am.'

They had a good chuckle at that.

'And remember,' said Tim, 'keep your mobile on airplane mode when you're not using it. They're bound to find the number somehow.'

'Good shout.'

*

Not long afterwards, Mr Alain Gaitsland QC appeared before Mr Justice Hunters in Court 37 at the Royal Courts of Justice. Having introduced himself and his junior counsel, he confirmed that his application was made without notice to any of the intended respondents against whom AlphaOm sought interim injunctions, together with pre-action disclosure and disc-imaging orders.

The format was one with which the court was accustomed to dealing. The judge had read the hastily prepared outline of the case prepared by Gaitsland and his team, known in the trade as a skeleton argument. He had also read the witness statements in support of the application compiled in draft on behalf of Maria and the chief executive, McBride. He duly informed Gaitsland that he had done so. The latter was about to reward this intelligence with his habitual 'I'm obliged, m'lord,' but the judge continued with his initial observations on the evidence.

'I note, Mr Gaitsland,' he began, 'that you are not alleging that any of the respondents acted with the intent of personal gain, although no doubt you will allege that a necessary consequence of publication is that the newspaper will be enriched, and to that end you do not seek any freezing orders against the respondents' assets.'

'That is indeed the case, although to be more precise, my lord, my clients have no direct evidence of any enrichment or intent to enrich.'

'That is very much as I had understood,' continued the judge. 'Which immediately invites the question – assuming of course that your clients can make good their allegations at trial – what was the respondents' motive in acting as they are alleged to have done? Can you help me with that, Mr Gaitsland?'

'My lord, my clients' investigations are at a very early stage, and they are not yet in a position to articulate any allegation on that aspect of the case to which your lordship has just alluded. As present instructed, there appears to be a prima facie intent to harm my clients' business by the publication of incorrect and misleading facts, quoting out of context from confidential property belonging to my clients.'

He paused to give the judge time to make a note on his desktop.

'That said, my lord, it is expected that the disclosure orders, and especially the disc-imaging orders, will provide information that supports my clients' case. What we can tell this court with confidence is that the documents – and more particularly their contents – which the respondents have respectively used or handled, can only have been obtained through unlawful means.'

'Yes, and you have made that point most persuasively in your skeleton,' replied the judge. 'I have no problem at all with that part of your case. The purpose of my enquiry was that, since this is quite a topical issue, to put it no higher, I was inviting you to tell me whether your clients had reason to believe, or anticipated, that the respondents would seek to defend the intended claims on the basis suggested in the article in the newspaper. I refer, of course, to the assertion – and it can be no more than that at present – that the respondents were justified in their actions. The only justification that springs to mind at present would be a desire or intent on their part to expose what they regarded – putting it in its most neutral form – as being conduct unbecoming a conscientious pharmaceutical company. Whether they may have reached such a view on advice or not one cannot tell on the material available.'

'Were that the case, my lord, one would have expected the respondents – or at least one of them – to have confronted my clients with their assertions first before going into print using material which was plainly confidential and plainly the property of my clients. But they have not done so,' answered Gaitsland.

'That was rather my point, Mr Gaitsland,' continued the judge. 'One might have expected such conduct if they had intended to hold your clients to ransom with this material. The fact that they did not suggests that their motive lies elsewhere than in some pecuniary advantage.'

'My lord, with respect,' urged Gaitsland, 'the burden does not fall upon my clients to speculate as to the likely motives of the respondents.'

'I am not suggesting that it does, Mr Gaitsland. What they say is that the documents show three things. First, certain of the properties – the properties known to your clients, that is – of at least one of your client's sugar substitute products have a demonstrable propensity to accelerate both obesity and the early onset of diabetes. Secondly, one of your clients' heavily promoted medicines for controlling diabetes through insulin is specifically designed to render a patient who has succumbed to the disease wholly dependent upon that remedy, quite possibly for the rest of his or her life. And thirdly, that your clients have acted in a manner that is uncompetitive or anti-competitive by arranging with other pharmaceutical entities to disparage articles and entities that accuse your industry of being part of the cause rather than the solution to the current phenomenon of an epidemic of diabetes.'

He paused to allow Gaitsland and his junior to make a note.

'I know that I have taken that at a fair canter, but is that a fair summary?'

'My lord, admirably so.'

'Next, and this is important, your clients' evidence is that there is no truth in any of the allegations, and that is supported by your skeleton, although no libel is alleged.'

'Indeed, my lord.'

'Then your clients go on to complain that the article by *The Daily Chronicle* relies on material that has been unlawfully appropriated by the defendants. They wish the court to restore the status quo to the position that obtained pre-publication by restraining the propagation of the allegations by the newspaper pending further order of the court. Is that about right?'

'That, my lord, is precisely my clients' case. They complain to this court that, unlawfully and with intent to harm them, their documents have been used by each of these proposed defendants, and they wish to restrain such use now and in the future and prevent any repetition of these damaging allegations, which they believe to be entirely unfounded. It is doubly damaging to my clients that the proposed defendants have promoted a story which is not only false, but is one based on documents wrongly obtained and quoted out of context. That is conduct which, in my respectful submission, my clients are entitled to require this court to restrain.'

'Yes, and I am persuaded on the strength of their evidence that your clients are entitled in principle to the orders which they seek,' confirmed the judge. 'I say "in principle" because the court has yet to see any evidence from the defendants, and specifically evidence that would shed light on their actual or likely motive. However, I am satisfied that your clients have presented to me what appear to be serious issues, and that significant damage to their business is likely to continue unless the conduct of the defendants is restrained. I said "defendants", Mr Gaitsland, but have your clients issued their claim form so as to instigate these proceedings yet?'

The silk took instructions.

'I am instructed that the claim form is in the course of being issued, but nonetheless my clients will give the necessary undertaking in that regard.'

'So the order will refer to them as respondents, pro tem?'

'Indeed, my lord.'

'Thank you. Very well, I shall therefore make the orders sought, although I shall need to be addressed on the form of the orders in a moment.'

'I'm obliged, m'lord.'

'One point, Mr Gaitsland. It would make sense for this case to be reserved to me, at least until the return date or dates. I say "dates" because, if my own experience is anything to go by, I sense that there may well be more than one return hearing in a case such as this. I only suggest that because I shall be sitting in London for the next two months, and have read the bulk of the evidence.'

The silk turned around to consult his clients, taking his time.

'Unless,' added the judge, 'your clients might object to this?'

Gaitsland had hoped to get the case before a more lenient, and less diligent tribunal, but had been nimbly outmanoeuvred by this judge.

He gracefully concurred.

'Right then,' said the judge, detecting a distinct note of reluctance in counsel's voice, 'shall we go through the orders?'

Chapter 5

The afternoon sunlight streaked across the bedroom ceiling above the curtain rail, forming patterns against the cornice on the opposite wall. Its reflected rays danced upon the neatly made double bed, and clothes laid out dextrously upon it. The sound of a shower running in the nearby bathroom could be heard above the occasional passing of a car along the road outside.

It was almost 5.30 pm.

Into this tranquil scene intruded the insistent and unwelcome clamour of a bell. This was interspersed with the echoing thud of a door being firmly pummelled by a human fist. The bell, which was an ancient electric contraption, but which had rather appealed to its new owner, was fixed to that very same door. This was the front door of an address in North Clapham, south of the River Thames in London.

That owner, whose form appears female through the steamy glass of the shower door, had now turned off the shower and became aware, through the twin doors of her bathroom and bedroom, of the cacophony that was plainly originating at the front door of her flat. Readers will politely avert their gaze as she quickly reaches for a bathrobe, and twists a hand towel around her hair.

As the banging on the front door becomes louder, she can now distinguish a human voice calling out her name, not once but twice, demanding that she should permit access to the flat.

Her first thought was that it must be her new boyfriend, Tomo. But he would surely never pound her door like that unless it was really urgent. So maybe it was him.

Somewhat confused by the commotion, she found herself preparing to run towards the front door, wholly careless of her state of undress, in order to embrace him.

But then she hesitated. He had not called in advance, and that was not his voice at the door. In fact, not only did she not recognise the voice that was calling out her name, but whoever was addressing her by her surname, demanding entry to her the ground floor flat, sounded distinctly less than friendly.

Very unfriendly, in fact.

She discarded the bathrobe and substituted an oriental dressing gown which she wrapped around herself, poking her feet into frustratingly elusive slippers before warily looking through the spy-hole of her front door, where she was confronted by a 'posse' of people in suits, none of whom she recognised. Two of them at least were thankfully female, which put her slightly more at ease, although not for long.

She opened the door.

A well-dressed man advanced to stand on her threshold.

There he beheld what he considered to be a vision of loveliness, albeit slightly dishevelled, in the form of a stunning brunette. At five foot nine, she was taller than him; taller than many girls that he had known. He tried to avert his gaze away from her legs and bosom, but her face was a vision of beauty, almost intimidating in its perfection, causing him to stammer his opening introduction of his name and role as an independent solicitor acting by an order of the High Court obtained by her former employer.

He cleared his throat.

'Is your name Catriona Symonds?' he demanded, seeking to recover such authority as he could muster by injecting a sufficient menace into his voice to obtain both her attention and respect.

Her brain immediately began to kick into life.

So. It had begun.

Contrary to the confident prediction of those who had assured her that she was not at risk of any vendetta from her previous employers, because the stakes were too high for them, the corpulent face of protectionism had reared its ugly head.

As her brain slowly engaged, she had the presence of mind to demand that her accusers should all identify themselves.

'First things first,' she replied. 'More to the point, please repeat who are you, and what you were doing banging on my door and disturbing the neighbourhood in this way.'

Her adversary had not been prepared for the cultured Virginian accent with which the question had been put to him. He nodded in tacit acknowledgement of this parried thrust, and sought to continue unperturbed.

'As I said, my name is Peter Langer. I am a solicitor. I am independent of those whom you see waiting in the street. They are members of the firm of Pinston Raymond, who are also solicitors. They act for

AlphaOm Pharmaceutical Corporation, whom I believe to be your former employers. I should make it clear that none of them is my colleague,' he said, indicating the besuited posse behind him. 'I am wholly independent of them, and I shall explain my purpose in a moment. But first, now that I have identified myself, I must ask you please to be good enough to do the same. Will you please confirm to me that you are Catriona Symonds.'

Her brain was now functioning, and she weighed up the odds for and against further prevarication. She decided against it, principally because there seemed little point in doing so, since they would be able to identify her – in fact they probably had already done so – from the many photographs held by the company. Her other reason – somewhat bizarrely – was that she had privately anticipated the prospect of such a confrontation.

'Yes I am,' she acknowledged.

The lawyer thrust a menacing document at her, unsure whether to fulfil the traditional task of touching her body with the papers, and reluctant to make contact with her torso in her current state of *dishabille*. Instead, intimidated by her raw beauty, he handed them towards her one by one, as though they were fragile works of art.

'These are two orders which were made yesterday in the High Court against you,' he began, as his carefully prepared words eluded him.

Clearing his throat, the lawyer sought to recall the words which he knew to be necessary in order to announce the purpose of the two documents.

'This first document is a disclosure and search order. This order entitles the solicitors that you see here to search your flat – but in my presence – for any of the documents or classes of documents which are identified in the order. It allows me to take away all copies of these documents and to hold them until further order of the court.'

He passed the order to her. Catriona looked briefly at the document. Her gaze passed over the words 'search order' between the tramlines in the centre of the page and fixed on the words 'penal notice' at the top of first page, which she saw rather than read, and the accompanying threat to imprison her if she chose to disobey the court. She quickly realised the implications of the warning.

Langer was getting into his stride now. He pointed to the second court document which he had just handed her.

'This is a disclosure and disc-imaging order,' he proclaimed, his voice deepening as he found strength in the formality of the words with which he addressed her. 'This order imposes certain obligations on you to permit the independent computer experts identified in the order, one of whom is with me, to provide to me any of the documents or classes of documents which are named in the order.'

She looked at the document, feeling the panic begin to rise inside her. The words 'disclosure and disc-imaging order' meant little to her, but again she focussed on the penal notice in identical form at the top of the page, and the obvious threat to her liberty were she to disobey the court order.

Swallowing hard, the lawyer continued: 'The order allows me as the independent solicitor to remove your personal computer or laptop and to place it into the hands of an IT expert who will cause a copy of its contents to be taken under his supervision in order to preserve these for the purpose of future disclosure in High Court proceedings which the claimant intends to commence against you and others. I must ask you to show me or one of the women here where we can find any personal computer or laptop, and also your mobile phone on these premises.'

She found herself wondering why they couldn't have picked one of the days last week when she wasn't alone. Tomo would have known what to say.

She began to gather her wits as the lawyer droned on in his formal tone, deciding to play her only card.

'The order also …'

The lawyer stopped in mid-flow, his speech arrested by the gentle touch of her fingertips on his wrist. Such a simple, mesmerising act, and yet so utterly disarming.

'Just a moment, and please excuse me for interrupting,' she said, backing into the hallway and inviting him to follow with a gentle squeeze. 'But is it really necessary that I should have to listen to this standing in the doorway like this? And am I allowed to put some clothes on before you proceed any further?'

'Well, you see Miss Symonds …' he began, half paralysed by the contact with her flesh, and forcing his line of sight away from her torso.

'Now here's the thing,' she resumed, playing up her Virginian accent as she turned into the open-plan living room. 'Since y'all are obviously going to gain entry to my flat whether I like it or not, why don't y'all just come in and get on with your business. I'll go and put some clothes on, provided of course that's agreeable to y'all.'

She was going to add that she had no intention of putting the kettle on, but thought better of it, despite the fact that these people were plainly going to be there for some time. But she could not resisting saying, as she removed her hand from his wrist, 'Oh, and I presume that y'all do not need to watch while I get dressed.'

She walked into her bedroom, and was about to close the door.

'Ah yes, and one more thing,' she said casually, 'y'all will find my laptop and my mobile over there on the table.' She pointed towards the extendable table pushed against the wall of the flat.

'Y'all can see that they won't be going anywhere, and I can attend to whatever y'all need me to do in a moment.'

He watched her retreat into the sanctuary of her bedroom.

Realising that the independent solicitor had lost the initiative in this important phase of the campaign, Mary Fellowes (whom Cat had already assumed to be the senior of the two well-dressed women in the visiting team) came to stand beside him.

'Don't fall for that, Peter,' she urged him. 'You've got to finish explaining why we're here and what we intend to do.'

'There's plenty of time for that,' he replied. 'As soon as we resume, we can ensure that the IT bod gets to work on that laptop. That's where you're going to find anything useful. There may well be some useful material on her mobile as well. Meanwhile, you are of course at liberty to look around the flat as well, but my experience in these things tells me that you shouldn't hold your breath on that score.'

'Peter, she's alone in the bedroom,' protested Mary, who had been foiled by such tactics in previous cases.

When he shrugged, she persisted, 'We've no idea what she's up to in there. I'm sorry, but after all the effort we've been through to get the orders ...'

'As I said, Mary,' he replied, without turning to address her, but loud enough so that the younger lawyers could hear, 'the evidence that you need is likely to be on that PC, if it's anywhere.'

'Well, I just hope that we're not going to regret this.'

He was not about to admit that he was mightily relieved that the young woman had gone to put some clothes on.

'As I understand your clients' case,' he continued, still examining the collection of books, 'the mere fact that she had or has certain documents in her possession will not, of itself, prove your clients' allegations. As an employee she could well have worked at home on such documents as part of her job. What you need to find is evidence of communications passing between this defendant and the newspaper, or at least the journalist. And if you can link those communications to the key documents, so much the better. Have I got that about right?'

'Of course you have, Peter. We'll do it your way if that's what you want. But,' she asked him pointedly, 'do you not think it might be easier if I were to continue the discussion with her?'

'Under my supervision, of course,' he rejoined.

She scowled at his back, and went over to talk to the technician who was standing beside the laptop, waiting for further instructions. She noticed that her team had also retrieved some discs from a tray on the floor beside the table.

None of the lawyers had expected Catriona to reappear quite so soon, and certainly not looking quite so refreshed. Less still were they prepared for the casualness with which she addressed them, almost as if she was enjoying the occasion. Instead, contrary to all expectation, once Catriona had emerged from her bedroom, she walked over to Peter Langer in order to resume their discussion.

This time it was her turn to be surprised, as one of the women lawyers intercepted her approach. Catriona never caught her name, but could recall thinking that her eyeliner did not suit her. She wondered how long the woman had been up that morning. Hours? Or perhaps she had never gone to bed?

The woman pulled out two chairs and placed them beside the table. She sat down on one of them, having first invited Catriona to take the other chair, clearly keen to recreate the formality of an office environment in which she would feel more at ease, despite the relative comfort of the flat. Catriona politely declined, saying: 'I'd prefer to stand, if y'all don't mind.' She had elected to re-engage her much-diluted Virginian accent, if only to annoy her opponents. 'And I might just add that it would be courteous if y'all were to introduce yourselves, given that y'all seem to want to make yourself at home in my flat.'

Mary Fellowes had no choice other than to rise and stand beside the younger woman, who was at least three inches taller than her. She sensed a discernible dent in the authority which she had expected to convey.

She gave her name, explaining that she was a partner in the law firm that had the conduct of the case on behalf of AlphaOm, who were the intended claimants.

'Well, y'all must already know that I know plenty about them,' interrupted Cat, searching for any reaction from the other woman, and was rewarded with the briefest of flickers of an eyelid. 'And I guess y'all have read about what they've got themselves involved in? Y'all will have seen that in the newspapers?'

She left the question hanging, inviting an answer.

Mary ducked the challenge, and made to continue her introduction.

'Your names, please, for my record.'

Suitably chastened, she introduced the others.

Cat noted down their names.

A few moments later, Mary went on to explain the effect of the two orders – in terms which Cat found unnecessarily patronising. Mary took care to emphasise that there was little purpose in Cat objecting to the search.

Again Cat interrupted: 'But, I guess what y'all don't know if that every word that they wrote in the paper is true.'

Once more, Mary declined the invitation to respond.

But the ensuing silence hung in the air.

'Like I said,' persisted Catriona, but this time more slowly, 'every word of what they wrote is true.'

Again, Mary ignored her.

Cat turned to look at Langer.

'Now, y'all be sure to make a note of that.'

Mary returned to her task.

'My purpose here is to explain the effect of the order, and to inform you that the only viable remedy open to you and your co-defendants is to complain to the court that the order should not have been made.'

Such formal terms, Cat thought, glancing at the documents she had been handed. Then the woman added for good measure: 'In my opinion and that of a leading queen's counsel, that is to say ...'

'I'll thank y'all, but I know what that means,' interjected Cat.

'As I was saying, it is our view that your prospects of reversing the process which has been instigated by your former employers are negligible.'

'Well, ma'am, that's a mighty big thing for you to be saying, y'all being so new to the story an' all. I'll mind you to remember that when the time comes,' Cat replied, addressing the assembled team.

For some reason she labelled them in her mind as 'the Women in Black Suits'.

Mary did not reply. Instead, she handed Cat a thick lever-arch file of documents. Their weight alone was intended to be threatening.

Cat effected to ignore them, choosing instead to look at Langer, given that he was the one who had originally addressed her.

However, Mary persisted in explaining the purpose of the documents in the file. She used the professional voice that she kept for such occasions. 'These papers contain the evidence which our clients placed before the court. It was on the basis of these documents that the court had made its orders.'

She indicated the text of a letter which accompanied them. For some obscure reason, Cat was later able to recall the heading of the letter, which appeared to record that both *The Chronicle* and its lead writer were also involved in the case.

Since Cat was ignoring her, Peter Langer intervened.

'I think I should explain the purpose of these documents to Miss Symonds,' he told them both, and continued without giving Mary a chance to reply.

'Miss Symonds. The court required the applicant, AlphaOm, to provide you with copies of all the material that had been submitted to the court by them as intended claimants. The court made these orders on the basis of these documents. In addition, there are witness statements by the chief executive, one by an employee of the company, the application itself and counsel's skeleton argument. The latter is in effect a summary of the case being advanced by the claimants.'

'Why, thank y'all, that is mighty helpful. But tell me,' enquired Catriona, moving to address him more closely, 'when do I get my turn to have my say?'

'I'll come to that presently,' he replied, careful to keep himself at an arm's length distance from her, and mightily grateful that she was now suitably clad.

'There are certain steps that you are required by the court order to take immediately in order to comply with its terms. I shall explain them to you. First, you must tell us whether you possess or are aware of the location on these premises of any documents that you obtained from your former employer. Whilst the court is primarily interested in the classes of documents that are clearly listed in the order, we do not have time to go through them individually now. So, let me ask you ...'

He paused for effect.

'Are you willing to tell me whether you have in your control on these premises or elsewhere any documents that you obtained from your former employer? Before you answer, I must advise you that you are not obliged to answer that question before you have obtained your own independent legal advice. However, it may harm your case if you refuse to answer but documents are thereafter found pursuant to this search.'

Cat noticed the woman scowling at the man. She wondered whether it was because he was being overly fair in his treatment of her.

Back to the question, which was an easy one.

Quite truthfully, she told them both that she did not have any such copies in the flat.

'Next,' continued the lawyer, 'I need to ask you whether you have it within your power to obtain any such physical documents. Again, before you answer, I must advise you that you are not obliged to answer that question before you have obtained independent legal advice. However, it may harm your case if you refuse to answer but documents are then found in circumstances where it can be shown that you must have known of their location at the present time and had the means to obtain them.'

That was not such an easy one, so she needed to buy time.

She resorted to the ruse which she had often seen her grandmother use when she was about to outsmart Grandpa.

'Why, I do declare that I cannot rightly recall just now,' she deflected. 'But if it comes to mind that I do, then I'll be sure to tell y'all.'

Mary glared at her, convinced that she was lying, but knew she was unable to prove it.

'Thank you,' he replied. 'Duly noted.'

'Finally, I need to ask you if you have any soft, that is to say electronic, copies of any documents that belong to your former employer, AlphaOm. And I must again remind you of your right to obtain independent legal advice before replying.'

Cat realised that they were going to take her laptop anyway, and would find whatever was stored on its memory, and presumably anything that had been stored but had since been deleted. So, there was little point in evading the answer.

'Well, whatever I may have had from work in the past will be on my laptop. Is that what y'all wanted to know?'

'That is helpful, thank you,' he replied. 'Despite your answers, you will be aware that these lawyers here are now entitled to search your flat. I shall ask these two ladies alone to go through your personal effects. As I have said, if there are any documents on these premises of the type that I have described, it will make things a lot easier if you tell me so now, especially since this could minimise any unnecessary disruption to your flat or its contents.'

That was nicely put, she thought, but did not change her first answer, which just happened to have been true.

She told him so.

He next drew her attention to the paragraph in the order which required her within two working days to swear an affidavit which disclosed to the court the present location of any of the documents or other information which fell within the categories described in the order. This applied to anything in her possession or control.

When she made no response, he told her that her own lawyers would explain this phrase to her, but it covered anything which she possessed or which any other person possessed on her behalf.

That was going to be interesting, was her immediate thought. She considered the messages that had been on her phone. None of them was included in what her former employers were after, but she was quite sure that she did not want them to see them if they found them.

She weighed up her options and decided that it would be best if she were to deal with this now head on.

She looked the man straight in the face.

'Can I talk with you privately for a moment,' she asked demurely, taking his arm and steering him away from the woman.

Such a development was by no means unusual in these cases, and Peter allowed her to exclude the other lawyers. He nodded his head to confirm his assent, assuming that she was about to make a confession of sorts. He swiftly reminded her that he was primarily interested in supervising the carrying out of the search, and not in the underlying dispute which had given rise to it.

She thanked him for that, but explained that what she had to say was connected with the case, but might not be covered by the orders. She would like his guidance on what she was obliged to hand over.

'Do I need to give y'all now ...' she began.

He raised a hand to stop her there.

'No, let me be clear. What you are required to do is to provide material to the court, in respect of which I am the formal conduit as the independent solicitor. So, you are not giving the material to me in person, nor to these people. I shall advise the court what I consider the claimants should see.'

'Why, thank you. So, to be clear, does that include just copies of anything that I sent from the office to my private email address, or do you have to take whatever anybody in the company sent to me?'

He frowned at this. The orders were very widely drafted, and covered communications of any sort between her and any member of her former employers and any of the entities or individuals mentioned in the orders. He explained this to her, and said that she would be able to address the court on the material which she considered did not fall within the scope of the orders.

'But who else will see it in the meantime?' she asked.

That was relatively simple to answer.

'Well, initially it will be seen only by the computer experts, who will report to me. I shall then forward their report to the court and to the parties, describing the results of their interrogation of the memory on your laptop. Your former employers can then apply to see any of this material, and you can have an opportunity to explain why they should not see it. If there is any doubt, the court will normally limit the persons who can see the material to specific individuals initially.'

'And please tell me, who might these individuals be,' she asked.

'They would normally include the lawyers, and perhaps a few key personnel employed by the applicants.'

'So, who would normally get to decide who those key personnel might be? Do I have any say in the matter?'

'Ultimately, it is a decision for the judge who hears the matter when it is returned before the court, but he will almost certainly invite and take into account your views as to which persons you regard as appropriate.'

'And what if some of the material is, like, personal?' she asked.

'Again, that is a matter which will also need to be dealt with before the court,' he replied carefully.

'No, I mean, really personal. Stuff that I can't allow ... I mean, I really don't want anyone else to see.'

'I'm sorry, Miss Symonds, but that is out of my hands. My duty is to present to the court a report of what I have found.'

She persisted, this time more earnestly.

'But if I told you the sort of thing that we're talking about? Would you be able to give it back to me without the others seeing it?'

Oh dear, he thought to himself. One of these fine messes.

'I'm afraid that I would only have limited influence on what your former employers should or should not be permitted to see. I'm just here to ensure that the orders are carried out fairly and properly.'

'But if I showed you some of this on the computer …' she began, reaching out to take his arm again.

He had expected this, and stepped back from her.

'I'm very sorry, but you will have to wait until you see the report from the computer expert once he has interrogated your laptop. That is the way that these orders work, and I cannot change that.'

'But surely …'

'No, I'm sorry Miss Symonds,' he insisted, 'I've already made the position clear to you. I have no discretion in this matter. My duty is to ensure that the orders are executed fairly and properly, and then to report the outcome to the court. There is nothing further that I can do.'

Then he added, so as to head off any further entreaty from Cat: 'Obviously, having heard your concerns that some of the material stored on your laptop is personal in nature, I shall alert the computer expert to your concerns before he begins to interrogate the data.'

'By interrogate, do y'all mean look at everything, even if it's not a document? Surely they can tell the difference?'

'Miss Symonds. I am not an IT expert. What the report will tell me, and thus the court and then the parties, is what is or was at any time contained on your personal computer, laptop or mobile device.'

'Wait,' she asked, a note of real anxiety, panic even, entering her voice. 'Did you say at any time?'

'Yes, that's exactly what I said, Miss Symonds.'

Silence.

Cat absorbed the impact of his words like a punch to her solar plexus. She stepped back, staggered almost, as she began to comprehend the enormity of what the man had told her. She brought her hands slowly up to her face as she retreated, unable to make contact with the man's eyes as she sought the relative sanctuary of the sofa. She slowly collapsed into it, her persona deflating before his very eyes, and almost panting in shock as she hunched into the foetal position.

Langer felt an immediate sense of sympathy, even oddly of guilt, intrusion certainly, as he watched her face slowly descend into her raised hands, her body almost trembling in shock, hair cascading forwards to cover her face.

He turned to Mary Fellows, and whispered *sotto voce*: 'There's something not right here. We shall need to speak once I have received the initial reports from the IT experts.'

Mary did not dissent, but shared the same sense of unease as she observed the younger woman's distress, and her mind immediately recalled the ominous words from the exit interview: 'personal reasons'.

She turned to see one of her two assistants looking first at Cat, then at her, as if to express identical concerns.

Mary had been accompanied by Langer on numerous 'house raids' such as this, and nine times out of ten the dramatics would begin as soon as the orders were served. He had never before encountered a defendant reacting like this to the reality of an electronic search of their private computer.

But what Langer found even more bizarre in this case was that he had overheard this young woman announcing to the claimant's solicitors that the story which the claimants sought to suppress was true. When a defendant reacted with such a 'Bring it on' attitude, it normally meant that he or she had nothing to fear from the claim, and almost welcomed the fact that the claimant was now in possession – or soon would be – of the very material that would destroy its case.

He returned to his checklist.

'One last thing,' he said. 'The order requires you to provide to me the passwords to your laptop and your mobile phone. Both your phone and your laptop will be returned to you as soon as possible, Miss Symonds. I regret that it is unlikely to be over the weekend, but it will certainly be early next week at the latest.'

Cat did not register the instruction. She held her head in her hands, barely conscious of the movements around her or of the words that were spoken.

'Miss Symonds, did you hear me?' he persisted.

Again, no reaction.

'Miss Symonds?'

Still no movement.

This time it was his turn to touch her on the shoulder.

She almost leapt to the other side of the sofa, staring at him with such a wild expression of alarm that he tried to tell himself it was not fear.

'Miss Symonds, I'm sorry, did you hear me?'

'What ...?'

He repeated the instruction, holding out a notepad on which she was invited to write down the details requested.

As if in a trance, she reached up her right hand, and then her left, and took the proffered pen and pad. It took another thirty seconds for her to engage her brain to recall the relevant information. And then, almost like an automaton, she wrote down the series of letters and numbers that he had asked for.

He thanked her, showing them to the forensic expert, and waiting for him to activate both devices. A nod gave him confirmation that everything was in order, and he carefully returned the pad into his case.

The search party concluded their business, and packed their things, having found nothing on the premises by way of hard-copy material.

As he closed the door to the flat, he looked back to see that Catriona had not moved, and that her face had remained buried in her hands.

No, this is definitely not right, he thought to himself.

He caught up with the IT technician, 'A quick word, if I may ...'

*

Afterwards, she reflected that her immediate concern had not been to focus on the effect of the orders or the instigation of this legal process against her. Instead, her mind had conjured up images of public humiliation.

She barely registered the fact that the team of lawyers had concluded their search of her flat and had packed up, nor the somewhat bizarre apology from 'Peter' as the lawyers left her flat as abruptly as they had arrived.

For some reason, Cat also recalled the woman saying that 'the firm' would send her a note of the hearing earlier that day before the judge once this has been typed. It meant nothing to her at the time, other than that she was to expect yet more paper through the post. As if they had not dumped enough of it on her table.

Moments later her radio alarm came on, somewhat incongruously playing the slow movement from Mozart's Clarinet Concerto on Classic FM. It always reminded her of the opening sequence of one of her favourite weepies, with one of the opening lines (spoken with a perfectly delivered Danish accent): 'Once I had a farm in Africa.' She wished she could be somewhere like that now, away from this trauma.

Being recently unemployed, she had worked most of the day on the paper she had begun, and had hoped to put in another half hour before heading off. The unwelcome visit by the black suits had put paid to that idea. And now she did not even have her own laptop to work on. She had not figured on that.

She looked at the time. Almost 6.30.

Damn, she and Ali had talked about meeting at the wine bar in thirty minutes. Ali might be waiting for her.

She reached for her mobile phone, found it absent, and was about to ask herself where she could have put it when she remembered who had possession of it. It was time to start calling for help, but she would need to get a temporary phone whilst the lawyers had custody of her own.

*

Alison Henderson checked her private messages. She was mildly miffed that she had still not heard from Cat in response to her suggestion that they meet up for a drink without the boys. She liked to gossip (although she would never confess to that), but her real interest was to get the latest on Cat's affair. She was highly impressed, perhaps (if she were to admit it) even mildly jealous that Cat had pulled such a hunk.

Ali and Jeremy had been going out now for almost two years, and were generally regarded as 'an item'. She had often chided Cat for being so reserved in her relationships, especially after that dreadful thug that she had met at work. He had given her the creeps, and she had been worried that he had got a hold on Cat which was unhealthy. How right her instincts had proven to be. And when Cat had finally turned to her for help, she found no comfort in the knowledge that her suspicions had been confirmed.

At least that business was well and truly over.

But she had not expected Cat to bring in such a catch, especially in so short a time. Which was why she was eager to press Cat for more details on how it was going.

All right. What she really wanted to do was to find out what he like in bed, but she would have to pick her moment. After that terrible bully, she knew that Cat was likely to be a little sensitive on that score, so she would leave it for a while.

She opened her inbox, but there was still no reply. Surely she couldn't have upset Cat in her last message. That reference to bedtime stories was certainly not close to the bone, especially when compared to some of their recent conversations. They had joked about that phrase when they had last met.

She sent another chaser. Perhaps her own message had not got through. It had been known to happen sometimes.

Or maybe, she thought, Cat had decided to send her a text message instead. But she'd have known that her employers had a 'no mobiles at work' policy, which meant that Ali would not have got it yet.

She prepared to leave and, once satisfied that the coast was clear, guiltily turned on her mobile to check for messages.

She cursed silently as she realised that she had forgotten to charge it this morning. It was out of juice, and she had left her charger behind at home. Worse still, she could wager that the girls on reception who usually lent her one of the firm's chargers had already left for the evening.

She was already running late, and would have to offer her apologies to Cat if and when they met.

She left a trail of expletives as she trudged down the corridor towards the lifts.

*

The sun had begun its descent when Maria opened the first of the emails from the IT operatives. She kidded herself that she had conscripted them into what she believed to be her fighting force. Each email attached what appeared to be a zipped file of electronic documents, the quantities of which appeared to be far larger than she had been expecting.

That was not a good omen.

Parking that for the moment, she opened up the attachments. She immediately saw that some were copies of Word documents, whilst others were in pdf form. Others still were in mixed media – possibly photos or something similar. She would have her work cut out to make any headway with this material before the meeting scheduled for later that evening. She hardly needed reminding that Miss Spooner had convened it in order to monitor the day's progress. If anything, the arrival of these emails was a step backwards.

The documents did not appear to be in date order, which was tiresome, nor were they divided into subjects, which was equally frustrating. That would make her job considerably harder than it already was.

It did not occur to Maria that this had been the precise intention of the authors of the email, nor that the entirety of the zipped attachments had been packaged in as un-user-friendly a form as the two of them could construct in the available time. Nor was there any obvious instruction as to how best to interrogate the attachments.

She had assumed that she could confine her search to any documents that provided an evidential trail whereby the 'confidential' documents used by the newspaper had come into its possession. So, given the very limited number of documents that she expected to be relevant, she had yet to consider the risks inherent in acquiring knowledge which could not later become 'unknown' – absent perjury.

Thus it was that, one by one, Maria began to compile chronological files of both the email traffic between the Symonds girl and her boss in CD, and the confidential documents to which the girl had gained access.

*

The early evening had seemed to drag on for ever. She knew that the phone shop would be shut until tomorrow, so she found a phone box on the high street and had left a message for the new man in her life. Fortunately, she had earlier procured provisions for the weekend from the organic shop, having become accustomed to his appetite. But supplies which might have satisfied an ordinary mortal often left him craving for 'a little something', as Pooh would say. Therefore, substantial quantities of sausages, bacon and eggs, together with her favourite wholemeal bread, had been stockpiled to feed the inner man. She felt it her duty to sustain him physically over the next few days, just as she would look to him to sustain her emotionally.

He is Thomas Butler, or 'Tomo', as his friends call him. She had been instantly attracted to him by his sparkling blue eyes and his engaging smile. These, combined with his wit, could lighten up any room he entered. With his dark brown hair and handsome features, he could have pursued a career on the stage, or perhaps as a professional cricketer. He had fooled many a batsman with his spin, and his broad shoulders and muscular form, all six foot four inches of it, enabled him to despatch opposing fielders to retrieve balls from the boundary with consummate ease.

Instead, Tomo has chosen a career in the law, or more accurately as a barrister. He practices from chambers in London, although to her regret he also appears in courts and tribunals outside London. Still, he has always made time to be with her, and those times are special to her. It has been during her evenings with him that, as she has listened with increasing interest, he has explained to her the chessboard to which he equates the legal process. And she had been really interested to learn about Tomo's work.

Before she had flipped open the files on her table, she had wondered what Tomo would make of this material. She dreaded the possibility that he would be ashamed of her, and that it might bring their budding relationship to a premature conclusion.

And she would have to tell him about the other stuff, and sooner rather than later.

Maybe this was the right time?

Moments later, Cat heard the familiar whistle outside the windows of her flat. Tomo had introduced her to some of Elgar's later works, which she had come to adore – none more so than the *Enigma Variations*. Apparently, so he had told her, it was the same sequence that Elgar used to whistle on his return home. Therefore, when he was struggling to compose a theme for the first Remembrance Day Service in 1919, his wife had suggested that he should use his homecoming whistle. That story had so appealed to Cat that Tomo had taken to replicating the *Enigma* theme whenever he came to her door.

How welcome those opening bars now sounded, and they were all the sweeter for the manner of their delivery.

Cat virtually threw open the front door in order to admit the source of the melody.

She had longed for Tomo's presence ever since the suits had departed; she wanted – no, needed – to talk with him so much. Yet she could find no words as he stood on the threshold. Instead, she urged him into the small hallway of her flat, literally hurling herself into his arms, taking no care to close the door behind them, and embracing both him and the opportunity to release the tension within her.

Tomo knew better than to disturb such therapy. He encouraged the process, holding her firmly in his arms and stroking the back of her head. Not until the initial emotion had dissipated did he steer her gently into the comfortable space that was her living room – the scene of her confrontation earlier in the day – all the while keeping an arm around her. Once in the room, he took her face gently in his hands, using first his thumbs and then his lips to remove the remaining tears, before kissing her tenderly.

'I'm sorry I couldn't get here any sooner,' he said at last. 'My opponent droned on and on for hours. Even the judge couldn't persuade him to give up the points he was trying to make. Talk about flogging a dead horse.'

'That's because he's not as clever as you,' said Cat, realising that she was smiling for the first time that day. 'So you won then?'

'I'm hopeful,' he replied. 'The judge has reserved his until next week. The cogs tend to grind fairly slowly between those ears, and he likes to make his judgements appeal-proof. Tends to work, too, because he seldom gets overturned.'

He looked around the room, surveying the evidence of the intrusion earlier that day, and the sizeable pile of papers which had been deposited on the table.

'I got your message, and I see that our friends have left their visiting cards,' he observed. 'That will make for some fun reading over the weekend. But right now, my mind is on higher things.'

She looked at him quizzically, immediately fearing that he had been instructed on one of his big cases, yet not daring to believe that he could think of deserting her in her hour of need.

'I mean, of course, you,' he continued, and was rewarded by a resumption of her passionate embrace, her face buried deep into the folds of his jacket. There would be ample time for words. Right now, this was the ideal remedy, and his arms and torso confirmed for her the strength of his support, both physical and cerebral. But he guessed that, in the aftermath of the afternoon's trauma, she had forgotten to refuel her body's energy supply.

'I'll wager good money that you've not eaten a thing since breakfast. So, I've taken the liberty of reserving a table at the Italian place that we enjoyed so much the other week. And I suspect that a change of scenery would be no bad thing.'

She smiled in acquiescence, choosing not to reveal the collected ingredients for a Thai meal that she had intended to prepare for him.

'Will you stay tonight?' she asked tentatively.

In other circumstances he might have made light of the invitation by suggesting that he might have to make a few phone calls. But his instinct dictated otherwise.

'As long as you promise not to disturb the neighbours again,' he returned, running the back of his forefinger down the side of her cheek onto her neck, pausing at the top of her blouse. His reply brought back, as it was intended to do, images of the ecstasy they had shared on their last evening together.

'As I recall,' she parried, 'you were the cause of that.'

'That charge is specifically denied, madam,' he declared, using his best professional voice. 'And in order to establish my defence, I shall need to stage a reconstruction of the events to which we refer. I trust that I can rely on your complete co-operation.'

She chuckled against his chest, enjoying the faint trace of the cologne that he had applied in the morning, and of which she had grown so fond.

'That all depends ...' she taunted, relishing the sense of security and comfort that she felt in his presence. 'But in the meantime, since you won't be driving, would you like a glass of wine? I've got some of that Kiwi sauvignon that we both like.'

Tomo accepted with enthusiasm, although he suspected that her need was greater than his. As she disappeared into the kitchen to fetch their nibbles and wine, he opened the first file of papers on the table in front of him. He began to read the principal witness statement (or affidavit) which had been sworn in support of the application for the search order. It told a good story, with plenty of prejudice. It presented a well-slanted version of the events leading up to 'the article', as it so pompously referred to the piece in *The Daily Chronicle* to which the applicants had taken such offence.

He skimmed the bulk of the statement. He noted that the substance of the complaint was that the newspaper had used material which was said to be confidential to the applicants. They had de-emphasised the allegation that the content of the article was false. Interesting, he thought. It was quite a clever tactic. If the material is confidential, and has effectively been lifted, then there's no need to get into a debate about the veracity of the text. You only need to go there if the first line of attack fails. But it did expose them to the risk of a counterattack based on the defences of 'fair comment' and (possibly) public interest whistle-blowing.

He looked up to see Cat watching him from the doorway.

'Tomo, do you think that I have been, how do you put it, a complete knave as well as a damnable fool.'

'Much too early to say, Cat, but whatever you did, knowing you as I do, I am certain that you did it with an intent to do the right thing. That said, to answer your question I'd need time to go through the issues properly.'

'Sorry, of course you're right. It was a silly question.'

'Quite the reverse, Cat. It is an obvious question and one to which you deserve an answer, and which you shall have as soon as I'm in a position to give it.'

She beamed at him in response.

'But,' he added, 'it does give rise to a serious question on my part, Cat. And that is, are you sure that you want me to act for you on this? There may be things in here that you don't want me to know.'

'You're the only person I want on my side, Tomo. I can only get through this if you're with me. If I have to conceal facts about myself in order to preserve our relationship, then it's not a relationship that's ever going to last.'

He took her hand and squeezed it as she said this. He had long surmised that there were matters that she had not wanted him to know, at least until now, and could sense that she had judged this the right time to let him further into her life.

'There speaks the voice of reason.' He stroked her arm tenderly as he spoke. 'We all carry a past, my lovely. The funny thing is that sometimes the facts which we consider to be the object of shame can appear so mundane once they are shared with another, and are looked at in the cool light of day.'

He paused, so as to give her an opportunity to intervene or to steer him away from the subject. Instead, she remained silent, and with her eyes encouraged him to continue in the same vein.

'We had an excellent series of lectures on ethics when I was reading law at Oxford, which embraced the psychology of guilt or shame, both real and imagined. They were delivered by the head of the psychology faculty. She taught us that guilt typically manifests itself in three stages.'

He paused, sensing that he was going too fast.

'Sorry, this is probably not the best time for this.'

'Is there ever a good time, and if there is, is it likely to be any better than the present?' she observed in reply.

'You're probably right. And there's actually no magic to it. It all makes rather good sense when viewed objectively from a distance, which of course is the one thing that the victim finds so difficult to do.'

'Are we talking about guilt or secrets?' she asked.

'Hard to tell them apart, objectively, and it's usually even harder for the one who bears them,' he replied, sympathetically. 'I suppose it embraces any facts that are troubling to the victim that he or she chooses not to reveal to or discuss with another.'

He gave her hand another squeeze.

'Are my feet getting bigger?' he asked.

She shook her head in response.

'So, these aren't her words, but they give you the gist of her wisdom. She preferred not to use the terms "guilt", or "shame" or "secret". Instead, she used neutral terms like "event" or "knowledge". And I could see the reason in that.'

'They're certainly much more sympathetic words.'

'That was exactly her point.'

'So, what are these three stages then? I'm intrigued to learn what stage I have reached.'

'Well, according to the guru, it's all rather straightforward. And what she said made perfect sense. So, stage one arises once the event or knowledge is contained and not shared, at which point it begins to assume both a burden and a malevolence for the victim, which increases the longer they are allowed to remain concealed. After a period of time, the victim enters stage two, whereby the event or knowledge tends only to emerge, clanking in its chains from the dark and lonely recesses of the mind when its gaoler inside the brain has either been allowed to lapse into unconsciousness or no longer has the mental energy to sustain the incarceration.'

She looked at the floor as she heard those words.

'Surely, and I recognise that clanking,' she interrupted. 'You are clever with your words, Tomo.'

'All part of the service, don't you know. Anyway, if left unrectified, stage two in turn leads to stage three. That is when it gets serious. The stress of trying to keep the event or knowledge locked away in the mind consumes an ever-increasing proportion of the body's supply of mental energy, to say nothing of the daily, aggregating side-effects of the consequent anguish. It eventually leads either to a breakdown of the mind, or of the body, and in the worst case, both.'

She nodded in silent assent.

After a long pause, she said, 'You're right, of course. I think I've known that all along.'

Another pause, and then she added, 'That must be why going to confession must be like an act of healing?'

'Well, speaking as a lapsed Catholic, I can't testify to that, but I'm led to believe that it is the received wisdom.'

She began to pour the wine.

'And, as they say,' he continued, 'such inner truths win out. It's just a matter of timing, and of course opportunity. And it's interesting that modern forms of interrogation now seek to use persuasion rather than force. The latter may release admissions from the prisoner, but only bit by bit, and often with key elements withheld right to the end, and sometimes the truth – that is the whole truth – actually never comes out.'

'Yes, I read an article about that,' she replied.

'I can believe it. That's why a counsellor – whether a friend, padre or psychiatrist, it matters not – should always aim to use persuasion to induce the gaoler to hand over the keys to the dungeon voluntarily, and better still get the confessor to open the cell door, rather than try to prise it open through coercion.'

'I've told you before that there's a sage philosopher inside you,' she remarked, soothingly. 'I can see why clients flock to you. They see you as a very good counsellor, as well as counsel.'

'Ha! You flatter me. But enough, there will be time for that in the coming days and weeks. First, we must feed the inner soul.'

He had not eaten anything since that morning – apart from a couple of biscuits which he had liberated from one of the meeting rooms in his solicitors' offices – and the prospect of Sicilian cuisine was already causing him to salivate. And he instinctively knew that, before trespassing onto any delicate terrain that lay ahead, they both needed feeding.

'Just staying with the case for the moment, do we know what the position is with the newspaper?' he asked her. 'Have you heard from them yet?'

'No, but once I've got myself one of those temporary mobiles, I shall speak with the journalist who broke the story,' she confirmed. 'He told me last week that his editor and his board were likely to fight the lawsuit. He also indicated that they would provide funds to enable me to retain my own counsel. I guess that their lawyers are going to write to me formally on Monday once they have cleared things at their end.'

'That makes sense. They will certainly need you onside if they are to have any real prospect of successfully defending the case. I'll explain the issues to you over dinner. No, on second thoughts, let's not mix biz with pleasure.'

As he moved to embrace her again, he realised that she still clasped the two full glasses of wine. For her part, she deftly succeeding in retaining the entire contents of both glasses, thus avoiding any interruption to the intimacy of the moment.

He took his proffered vessel, and tapped its rim against the one in her hand.

'To our success,' he toasted. She joined him, first inhaling the bouquet released from her glass. Taking her first sip, she relished the freshness of the complex flavours on her palate. Wine had become one of her hobbies, and she was especially interested in the emergence of talented growers in South America and New Zealand. They were producing such exciting new wines that they were now challenging the traditional markets to the point of eclipsing them.

He read her thoughts.

'Rather appropriate to the occasion, don't you think,' he mused 'that we should savour one of the products of the New World which now threatens to replace the old?'

'*Exactement*,' she concurred, in her best French accent, so as to emphasise the point, taking another sip.

The first glass was slipping down all too easily, but it was having the desired effect on her. She had realised for some time now that she needed to build up the courage to say what she had to say. Indeed, she knew in her heart that she would have to explain that slice of her past to him eventually if their relationship was ever to develop properly. She dared not think beyond that at the moment. But if they ever did get to the stage where they were gong to take things further, she was not going to 'do a Tess', and like Thomas Hardy's great heroine, slip a hastily scribbled confession under his door on the eve of their union. She could not countenance living her life with him in constant fear that this love affair – the first time that she had experienced being in love – could be brought to an end by a repetition of what had destroyed her last relationship, with all the pain and suffering which that had caused.

She refilled their glasses, fortified herself with another gulp, and then came to stand in front of him.

'Tomo,' she began, hesitantly, still unsure how to begin.

She placed her spare hand against his chest and took one of the buttons of his shirt between her thumb and forefinger.

'I meant what I said ... About us doing this together. If you really are willing to stand by me, that is. But if you are ...'

She hesitated for a moment, then averted her eyes from his. She looked instead at the button with which she had been toying.

'Well, if you are, then there are things that you going to need to know about me. About what happened to me, I mean. Because part of me seems to be saying that this is what this whole business is about.'

'I know that,' he nodded, putting his arm around her again, 'but you can only begin to unburden your mind and hand me the key to that hidden dungeon after you have recharged your batteries – and I mine.'

'What time is the table booked for?'

He looked at his watch. 'In about twenty minutes'.

'I'll just go and make myself presentable,' she announced.

He was about to say, 'But you look lovely as you are,' as he raised his eyebrows inquisitorially, but thought better of it.

She added: 'You know, do my hair and things.'

He released her, and watched her gracefully retire to her bedroom.

He groaned inwardly at this intelligence, resigning himself to the fact that his dinner was likely to suffer an indeterminate adjournment.

Rather like the law, he thought.

He sensed that prudence dictated that he remain mute. As lovely as she looked as she was, in these matters his opinion carried little weight. However, his understanding of the female species was sufficient to make him certain in the knowledge that he could neither divert her from the purpose at hand, nor trespass upon the mystery of the ceremony that was in course of performance.

Dinner would have to wait.

Such was the lot of man, he mused.

*

Meanwhile, Barbara Spooner had convened the team meeting at the appointed hour. She did not need to cite as her authority the chief executive's directive that had been copied to them all. That was implied, and sufficed to impress upon those in attendance the extent of her influence. She tapped her glass bottle of mineral water – which she had not offered to share – at precisely eight o'clock to bring the room to order. Once again, none of the those in attendance had been late.

She smiled icily at the representative of the company's in-house counsel.

'So, brief us on the legal side please, Ted,' she instructed.

Ted Fisher had cursed once he knew that he was to cover this meeting. At thirty-five, and recently engaged, he could have done without this unwelcome burden. The hour was of little consequence to him. He was often at his desk at this time, so he would keep that grievance up his sleeve for another day. No. His complaint was to have to spend any time with the Mamba.

Since becoming involved in this whole business, Ted had acquired considerable respect – if not admiration – for the unfortunate Catherine Symonds, who was now the centre of attention within internal affairs. However, being a sensible fellow, with a well-tuned instinct for self-preservation, he kept this view to himself.

He avoided eye contact as he opened his file, and flicked over the first tab of documents to the note which he had prepared earlier.

'Thank you, Barbara,' he began, with unctuous courtesy. 'Early this morning, the main board of directors, acting with the advice of legal counsel, considered and approved the proposal to instruct one of the magic circle firms that we keep on our books: Piston de Raymond. The name should by now be familiar to most of you. They retained Mr Alain Gaitsland QC as their leading counsel. He is known to us.'

We observed nods of acknowledgement.

'At three-thirty this afternoon, Mr Gaitsland sought and subsequently obtained from Mr Justice Hunters in the High Court in London the following orders on behalf of the company, each on a without notice basis: first, we obtained injunctions against *The Daily Chronicle*, their journalist Ken Baxter and Ms Catherine Symonds preventing any and all further publication of any material which could reasonably be shown to have been derived from confidential information obtained or used either lawfully or unlawfully by Ms Symonds during or as a result of her employment with the company. The order extends to the agents and servants of the aforesaid.

'Secondly, we obtained a disclosure and disc-imaging order against Ms Symonds and the journalist Mr Ken Baxter. The effect of these orders is intended to preserve all relevant and disclosable documents in the possession or control of both defendants. Pistons advise that there is a good prospect that the company will be permitted to have access to those documents prior to service of the company's points of claim in the proceedings, which will be formally commenced next week.'

'Give us a clearer statement by what you mean by the phrase "good prospect", Ted,' interrupted the Mamba.

'I'm quoting directly from the language of the report provided to the company by Pistons, which I understand to convey counsel's opinion. Since it is not my opinion, I ascribe no meaning to the words used. However, I make the observation that, in the vernacular in which law firms habitually seek refuge, the term "good prospect" is generally taken to mean significantly better than fifty-fifty. Is that helpful?' he responded, in suitably diplomatic and evasive terms.

'Please continue,' she parried, giving him another frosty glare.

'Certainly,' he rejoined, again deliberately focusing on his papers.

'Thirdly, we obtained a disclosure and disc-imaging order against *The Daily Chronicle* in similar terms to that obtained against Miss Symonds. It will enable the company to obtain disclosure of documents obtained by the paper prior to commencement of proceedings. This is in addition to the order which was made against the lead journalist with *The Chronicle*.'

He paused to allow the meeting to scribble a note.

'These orders were successfully enforced against each of the respondents earlier today. All further publication of the offending articles has been stopped.'

He enjoyed the collective nods of approval around the table.

'Also, copies of the court orders were served on the editors of all the other newspapers, news channels, online media operating within the jurisdiction and journals which are either published or distributed in the UK. The covering letters included an aggressively worded warning to each of them that they risked placing themselves in contempt of court if they were to repeat the contents of the story which had appeared in *The Daily Chronicle* without the permission of the court. Letters have also been sent to the editors demanding undertakings that they will take no steps which would be inconsistent with or likely to defeat or frustrate the intent and purpose of the orders. We have since obtained letters from law firms acting for most of them giving us the necessary assurances.'

More nods.

'The court will hear us again at what is termed the return date in a week's time in order to decide whether to continue the injunctions. That aspect of the orders may get adjourned if the defendants ask for more time, which is often the case. But the court will also hear our application to have access to all or some of the material which is likely to be secured as a result of the disclosure and disc-imaging orders so that these will inform the content of our points of claim.'

He then added, before he could be interrupted again by the Mamba: 'In answer to Barbara's earlier question, I have relayed the views of counsel on the prospects of such an application.'

With that, he closed his mouth and reached for his glass of water. He had been taught early in his career by a veteran sage never to add 'Are there any further questions?' That was to invite trouble, not least because it implied that his report might be unclear or ambiguous. Confidence was all.

'Thank you, Ted,' said the director. No further praise was necessary. He had merely performed his duty. That was what he was paid to do.

'Is there anything further that you advise that the company should be doing now to improve or protect its position?'

He was too long in the tooth to fall for that ploy.

'We've already advised on that, Barbara,' replied Ted. 'That is primarily your department's turf,' he noted.

Her eyes narrowed, as did her lips, as she said coldly, 'Your point being ...'

The room felt the chill in those words.

'In summary,' replied Ted, conscious of the drop in temperature. 'Pending the return hearing, we need further evidence which will show that Miss Symonds, acting either alone or with others, was responsible for causing the confidential information – over which the company claims ownership – to come into the possession of the paper. That must remain a priority.'

He held up his hand to indicate that he had not finished.

'To date,' he continued, 'we have relied primarily on three sources. First, we have the statements made by the paper itself, which we rely on as an admission. These include quoted extracts from documents which we believe are confidential to the company. We also believe that we can show that they did not come into the possession of the paper by lawful means.

'Secondly, we have the two memoranda which her department sent to the chief executive and others recording their concern that the company needed to take the initiative in countering the assertions that its sweetening products were responsible in part for what was close to becoming an epidemic of obesity and diabetic disorders in the population. She had contributed the section which advocated a shift towards natural as opposed to refined products, and urged the chief to reconsider the company's unwillingness to pursue the marketing initiative which she claims to have conceived. That is circumstantial evidence only, and probably is only relevant on the issue of motive.'

'Third, we rely on the fact that the paper has quoted directly from those memoranda and from the company's confidential documents. However,' he added, 'we need more. Our view, and that of outside counsel, is that without the benefit of the material obtained through the disclosure and disc-imaging orders, the company may be at risk.'

'Let's be clear about one thing,' snapped the director, her forefinger tapping the table as she spoke. 'We have absolutely no doubt that Symonds is the source of the story. I don't want anyone giving her the benefit of any doubt. The board has made it clear that it expects this task force to deliver results, and quickly.'

'We've noted that, and have every faith in your confidence in the case,' said Ted, as politely as he was able through gritted teeth. 'However ...'

'Why do you lawyers always like to plant seeds of doubt ...'

'Because, Barbara, in my profession we can only rely on what we can prove in a court of law. You've asked me to summarise the legal position, and I've done that. You may not like what you hear, but my view –

which, as I say, is shared by external counsel – remains as I've just stated it. We cannot deliver miracles.'

He immediately regretted that phrase, but before he could revise it she had leapt on it like the reptile that she was.

'No one is asking you for miracles, Ted. What you are being asked to do is to produce the right result for the company.'

'I hear you, Barbara. But make no mistake: we are as keen as everyone in this room to deliver the result that we all want. However, what we cannot say right now is that we are sure that we can do so without further evidence. What we are saying is that to be more than sixty percent confident (which is typically the zone where we prefer to operate), we need more evidence.'

Then he added, so as to head off her next assault: 'And I've just told you what the evidence is that would strengthen our case. I'm sure you don't need me to repeat that.'

The director glared at him in the ensuing silence. Then, as if drawing a veil over this last observation, she traversed her torso, like the gun-turret of a tank, so that her piercing gaze fell upon the face of her assistant – she did not care for the term colleague – in her department.

'Maria,' she demanded, 'what leads did you obtain from an examination of Ms Symonds' email accounts with the company?'

Maria cleared her throat, eagerly anticipating the appreciative remarks which she expected would follow her report.

'Thank you, Ms Spooner,' she began, opening her own slim file. 'We discovered that Ms Symonds had been operating two email accounts from her desktop computer located in the Commercial Development Department. We knew about the first account, since it had been provided by the company. Its use was subject to the usual rules about non-company-related communications. We have retrieved a number of email messages from this account, some with attachments, and several in what appear to be some form of code. We are currently working on these.'

'The second account we did not know about. It is an account with a private service provider, possibly using a domain domiciled in Spain, under the name of "ola.com". It can be accessed like most private accounts through the internet, which is the route used by Ms Symonds. However, the IT and telecoms system used by the company requires all outgoing messages to be directed through the company's portal. This portal has a sophisticated retrieval facility. So, with the assistance of our forensics colleagues, we've used this facility to track, retrieve and recreate Ms Symonds' outgoing email messages on her Ola account.

'These messages have been downloaded into a single database which we are preparing in a zip format which will enable our legal team, including external counsel, to analyse their contents for the purposes of this case. Preliminary indications are that these messages are very helpful, and ought to provide the sort of evidence which Ted and his team were hoping to find. In particular, we believe that we have found email messages going from her private Ola account which attach at least one of the documents from which the paper has quoted. We've also found another email in which she discusses another of these documents.'

With that, she sat back in her chair, rather like a contented kitten which has just brought in a young fledgling and laid it on the hearth as proof of its hunting skills.

Barbara nodded her approval, to the glowing pride of her assistant. She turned to Ted for his observation, one of the stencilled eyebrows raised as if to invite his appreciation.

'I assume that you ran this past external counsel first,' he said dryly.

There was an ominous pause. Absent any answer, he continued: 'Speaking for myself, I am not aware that you sought advice from the Legal Department before such a forensic interrogation was instigated, nor have you told us what authority you had to commence one.'

Maria cleared her throat, unsure where Ted was going with this. As far as she was concerned, she had brought in the goods, and she did not wish her moment of glory to be diluted by mere technicalities.

'These emails were sent using the company's emailing facilities and using our internet account, and attaching the company's confidential documents. They are therefore the property of the company,' she asserted, trying not to sound defensive.

'And you felt qualified to reach that view on your own, without consulting either my department or external counsel?' rejoined Ted, trying to look behind the thick lenses of her spectacles.

The Mamba weighed in. She was not about to see her department made to look foolish in front of the whole meeting.

'What's your point, Ted?' she asked dryly.

'My point, Barbara,' he replied carefully, 'is that Maria has just told us that she has caused the company to commit what appears to me – subject to checking with counsel – to be a number of offences, some of them potentially serious, under the Data Protection Act. More importantly, the unlawful acquisition of this material may well mean that this material will be inadmissible as evidence against both the paper and Miss Symonds, since we have effectively taken the law into our own hands.'

He stared across the table at Maria.

'You see,' he continued, 'had you told us about the other email account, we could have applied for an order which required Ms Symonds to give her email password to the two independent officers – that's the solicitor and the computer expert – who would then have had authority to interrogate her private email account. That is how our external lawyers would have approached this, and by now they would most likely have retrieved all the material that you've just described.'

The Mamba intervened once more. 'Well, we probably need to have a long, hard think about all this,' she soothed. 'I'm sure that the position cannot be as bad as all that.'

'No, it's not,' Ted replied. 'It gets worse. Much worse. We shall now have to inform Miss Symonds and her lawyers, once we know who they are, as well as the court, that we have come into possession of this material, and more importantly, how we came by it.'

There was a deafening silence as the implications of his words sunk in.

'And what really gets me, Maria,' he added, just to make the point, 'is that we could have obtained permission from the court today – yes this very day – to access all these messages, if you had only taken the trouble to consult us first. But it's too late now. The damage is done. We shall just have to weather the storm when it hits.'

The silence resumed.

It was broken by the director.

'When do we need to tell the court and the other side?' she asked.

'Either over the weekend, or at the latest on Monday morning.'

Another silence.

Then Ted added, 'And please don't tell me, Maria, that you discovered Miss Symonds' new home address from her private emails.'

When Maria remained silent, Ted groaned.

'Oh, that's great. That's really great.'

'Thank you all for coming,' interrupted the director. 'This meeting is adjourned. Let's meet again tomorrow morning. Eight o'clock please.'

She got up with her papers, adding curtly, 'Maria. A word.'

The icicles hung in the air as she left.

No one looked at Maria, who was studying the front of her file with sudden interest.

*

Further east across the capital, in the hinterland which in former times had contained the docklands of London, the editor of *The Daily Chronicle* drew his meeting to a close. He was an articulate man in his early forties, comparatively young for such a demanding post. But he possessed a fine brain, not inconsiderably improved by a university scholarship which he had gained some twenty years previously. Whilst he was not what one would usually describe as good-looking, not least on account of his pointy chin and prematurely balding pate, his intelligence was readily visible in his eyes and in his spoken words, but more poignantly in his writings. Consequently, his opinions were held in high regard by those with whom he worked.

Before him and his colleagues lay copies of the order which had been served both on him personally and on two of the directors who were in attendance. They had no alternative, at least in the short term, other than to obey the terms of the injunction against them, and he felt sure that proprietors would never be persuaded otherwise. The issue, therefore, was whether they saw enough of a story in this to take on the claimants, and have their day in court.

As was his custom in such cases, he looked to the lead journalist on the story to provide confirmation that his 'source' would hold up:

'So, Ken, your view is that we should trust Cat Symonds to produce the material which she has told you that she can obtain?'

Ken Baxter was a veteran reporter and journalist who had worked with the paper for over twenty years. His opinions were widely respected. And the scandals that he had exposed were seldom found to be wanting in proven source material or (if challenged) subsequent verification. His obligatory leather jacket lay discarded over the back of his chair, and he looked rather becoming in a checked shirt and cravat. His thinning hair, worn rather too long for the editor's taste (but mercifully without any pigtail) spilled over the collar of his shirt.

'Absolutely, Charles,' he replied, with only a hint of a Midlands accent. 'I've no reason to doubt her word, especially since she has come forward with the documents that she told us were already in her possession.'

'Of course,' mentioned the in-house solicitor for the paper, 'you're assuming that her ex-employers have not got there first. I understand that there was a search order against her as well as Ken.'

'Yes, we should not overlook that,' observed the editor.

'Yeah, and a right pain in the arse it was to have had my laptop seized this afternoon,' complained Ken. 'And before you ask, the answer is yes. All my data is backed up both here and at home.'

He received a sympathetic smile from the lawyer, although his boss merely shrugged his shoulders as if to indicate that it was all in a day's work.

'Anyway, they're never going to make sense of the scribbles that I made in my notebook, or the jottings in my directories. Even I can't decipher them sometimes!'

The last remark was intended more for the benefit of the lawyer, who was known to work closely with the IT managers.

The editor moved on, still looking at Baxter: 'Don't take this the wrong way, but are we right to reject the possibility that she may be using us to get one back at her employers, and particularly her former boss? I think I recall you saying that she got close to him at one stage. Maybe even too close? I know we've been over this before, but do we need to reconsider our position?'

'As you say, Charles, we've been here before, and I've seen nothing that makes me think we should change tack now. If you like, I can talk to her again. I could also ask her about the other documents at the same time.'

'I think that would be sensible,' the editor confirmed, 'unless, Simon, you advise that there would be a problem with that?'

This question was directed to the lawyer, who shook his head, adding: 'We need to make contact with her anyway to reassure her that we shall stand by our promise to ensure that she is separately represented.'

'Well, Ken, you can carry those glad tidings to her in person. Simon is following with the formalities. You can then cover those other matters while you're at it.'

'Right, I'll get on it as soon as we're through. But what about dosh?' asked Ken.

'We'll have to pay what it takes, if we're going to fight this, which it seems we are minded to do,' replied the editor. 'Anyway, her lawyers are unlikely to charge anywhere close to what Simon and his gang of blood-sucking vampires will demand.'

'Now there you go with dem negative waves again, boss,' Ken said, stealing one of Hollywood's greatest lines. 'You're forgetting that, when we've won, the grateful board of AlphaOm will be picking up the tab.'

'I wish I shared your confidence.'

'Mine is always half full, you should know that by now.'

This brought a smile from across the table.

'Right, lets' get it done,' concluded the editor. 'Simon, any other points that we need to bear in mind.'

'None that I've got, Charles, although no doubt counsel will produce their own list for us in due course.'

'Well, that's what they're paid to do.'

He got up, saying to Baxter as he packed up his things, 'You know, I've got a good feeling about this story, so keep digging.'

'Sure thing, boss.'

Chapter 6

CT used the interval between the formal end of the conference sessions and the much-awaited reception to scan through his messages and emails. Most of them were from that Ted Fisher guy from legal.

They did not make happy reading. He took in the details of the court orders, the identities of the defendants, and the likely results of the search orders. He clocked the material that Kitty was now accused of having obtained illegally.

As his eye ran down the list, he paused over a number of items.

How the fuck had she get hold of those? They had never been uploaded onto the system as far as he could recall. And they surely hadn't even been shown to the board at any meeting he had attended.

No, that couldn't be right, surely. She could never have got hold of those whilst she was working with him.

Or could she?

A ghastly thought slipped through his mind.

Those times when she'd come over to stay at his place, after their fun and games, she would usually agree to knock up some food for them, and she had been a damned fine chef. Towards the end of their affair she had got into the habit of sending him out to get some ingredients whilst she stayed in the kitchen, or so she had said.

But what if …?

No. How could she have known about them?

And then reality.

'Fuck!!' he said, and immediately realised that he had been overheard by others around him, some of whom would have known who he was.

'A howler from one of my exes,' he lied. 'She was a right bunny-boiler.'

Some knowing smirks from the eavesdroppers confirmed that he had neutralised any potential fallout.

He resumed his thought process.

That scheming little bitch. So that's why she never appeared to have got very far with the cooking whenever he'd returned with the shopping.

It all made sense now. Instead of toiling in the kitchen, she'd had her nose in his office, going through his papers. That would explain that time when he'd found that the power to his scanner had been left on that one morning, when he was always so meticulous about turning it off at both the base and the mains. Is that how she'd done it?

Time for damage limitation, he reckoned. Then he thought about it a bit more.

There were two possible exits from this. First, if the suits had recovered his documents already, the problem might have resolved itself, and he need do nothing.

Alternatively, if the company denied all knowledge of the documents, he could merely hitch his braces onto their carriage, and enjoy the ride.

Either avenue relied on the fact that her lawyers could not get their hands on any electronic or hard copies of the documents, but he was fairly confident that he'd saved them in a place where no one would look.

Either way, Mr Ted Fisher of legal was getting diddly-fuck from him, so that was an end to it as far as he was concerned.

Time to rejoin the party.

*

Ten minutes later, after he had played a few of his favourite tracks from her collection, including a perfect rendition of some of Chopin's Preludes, and after Cat had beautified herself, Tomo and Cat found themselves in Max's Restaurant, already well into their second bottle of the evening. They had jointly demolished the selection of cured meats and salami which their patron had supplied in an attempt to assuage their more immediate appetite. *Prima plati*, in the form of a *Tricolore*, had arrived and were being subjected to a similar fate. Once they had sated their initial need, Cat reached across the table to take Tomo's hand, which he rightly interpreted as a signal that she wished to return their conversation whence they had left it in her flat.

'What I am about to say may sound rather like my confession,' she began, 'but can I ask you to listen to me, just for a bit. Just so that I can say what I know I have to say, not just for your sake but also for mine.'

'Well, let's agree on the tariff first,' he quipped. 'I mean, don't expect that you can get away with a few Hail Mary's in exchange for a bit of carnal sin. I set my standards a great deal higher than that, you know. And, by the way, the tariff doubles for non-Catholics, irrespective of faith or regularity of prayer.'

She chuckled again, as she had been doing for most of the evening, but tried to contort her features into a serious frown.

'Tomo, this is serious. I need you to listen. If you don't want to, that's fine. We can leave it until next week, or whenever.'

'No, from where I'm sitting now seems as propitious a time as any.'

'Okay. So, I want to talk to you about my last boyfriend, and the man I had this thing with at the company.'

'So, he's not the same person?' he interjected.

'No, he's not. And that's part of the problem.' She hesitated. 'Actually, no. It is – or rather was – the problem.'

Then she added: 'And now, what really worries me is that it is about to, or will, become part of this latest new mess that I'm in.'

She waited again, seeking the right words which would convey not only what she wanted to say but also the strength of her emotions.

'It's all a big mess, and ... well, I don't know where to start.'

Tomo came to her rescue. 'Why don't you start with the boyfriend,' he suggested, 'and then graduate to the other man?'

She nodded her acquiescence, moving her cutlery around the edge of her plate before looking at him again.

'His name is James, or rather Jamie, as he prefers to be called. He's related to Ali. You remember my friend Ali?'

'Your best mate that we had dinner with the other night, and her medico man, Jezza, who was interested in your views on nutrition, homeopathy, sugar and all that.'

'Yes, that's her. So, to cut a long story short, after my parents were killed ...'

'You're so brave to speak so lightly of that.'

'But I never really knew them. I was too young. I was a *wee toddler*, as Granny called me. I like to think that I can remember my mother's scent, but Granny told me a few years back that she took to wearing it so as to keep her by her side.'

'What a lovely thing to be able to do.'

Cat smiled at that.

'I guess. But I have so missed having a dad that I can twirl around my fingers like so many other girls do. Anyway, as I've told you, I was brought up by my granny. She told me that my dad, who was old school English apparently, had always wanted me to be educated back in England. So, with the big payout that followed the lawsuit, she booked me into a private girls public school here.'

'What, she sent you here on your lonesome?'

'Oh no. She rented a place nearby. The point is that, almost as soon as I started at the school, Ali sort of adopted me as her surrogate sister, and we became inseparable.'

'That's what best mates usually do.'

'I suspected that it was because she had lost her own mother a few years back, so we shared a common loss. Anyway, Ali would sometimes take me home to stay with her during the holidays, and so the three of us, she, her dad and I, sort of became a family. Then later, her dad met Ali's step-mum, and Jamie was her son. That's how we met. He was about a year or so older than us, and he became her brother, or maybe half-brother. I'm never quite sure how that works. Anyway, before I knew it, she was bossing him about like a younger brother, and has been ever since.'

'No surprise there, she seems to be quite a feisty lady.'

'That she is. So, he used to tease me a lot when I was a teenager, but he graduated to showing me a lot of attention whenever I was down there. It felt a bit awkward at first, you know, almost incestuous because of how close we all were. But later, when I was on a rebound from a failed relationship at uni, he and I started, with a bit of matchmaking by Ali, to get close. And that was before he inherited the family estate in Dorset. He and I went out for almost two years.'

She looked up at him coyly from her doodle with the cutlery. 'We were considered to be "an item", in, what do you call it?' She searched for his term. 'Oh yes, the *modern vernacular*. You know how it goes. Everyone thought that we were perfect for each other, in the sort of Jane Austen fairy tale way that people like to see things. And it's true, Jamie and I were happy enough in our own way. At least, he seemed to be happy, so far as the outside world was concerned. He had his estate in the country, and I would join him most weekends.'

She skewered a piece of mozzarella with her fork, before harpooning a slice of sun-dried tomato with the same instrument.

'I was flattered at first, as he pampered and indulged me with the luxury and privilege of his wealth. But that was as far as it went. I never got that feeling of, you know, being in love, in the way that the girl's father describes it in the book about the soldier with the violin. Or was it a mandolin?'

'It was, and I think you mean *Captain Corelli*,' he prompted, urging her to continue with another squeeze of his hand.

'Go on.'

'Before I met you, I would listen to Ali talking about her passionate bouts with Jeremy, her man. As you said, you've met him.'

'Just so, top man,' said Tomo.

'Anyway, Ali and I used to talk about it; *girlie talk* she called it, especially after a few glasses. I won't betray her confidence, but from the way she described it, I just knew all too well that I had never experienced that sort of ...'

'Ecstasy,' he offered, with another squeeze. 'And I trust that such a sentiment is now in the past tense?'

She blushed in response.

'What I mean is, well ... Jamie and I never really got there.'

She looked down again.

'God, I feel such a traitor saying that, but I can't hide from the truth. What I'm trying to say is that ... is that I just needed to feel like a real woman.'

Another squeeze.

'And so, the relationship had begun to go flat. If, that is, it had ever had any kind of peak. For me, at least. But not as far as Jamie was concerned. He thought everything was great, and he kept on telling me how much he adored me.'

She looked at him again.

'That's the worst bit. I felt so deceitful, so ... so ashamed with myself. Yet, over time I knew that I had become ... well ...'

She paused, trying to find the right word, or rather trying to find a way of not using the word she had been about to speak.

So Tomo said it for her. 'Frustrated?'

She looked up at him again, her eyes supplying the necessary confirmation, grateful for his well-targeted prompt.

'I suppose I thought that the physical side would develop in its own time, and that I was incredibly lucky to be going out with someone like Jamie. He was always so generous, and also so patient, even when I threw the occasional tantrums, which were probably just a way of expressing the feelings which I felt I had to keep suppressed from the beginning of our relationship.'

She took another sip of her wine.

'So, I decided to throw my energies into my job. I had joined AlphaOm a year or so before, and had been recruited into their research department. I was not getting much out of that, so I took the chance to move across into the marketing side, which really interested me. And the work was much more rewarding. Or so I thought at first. But that was where it all began to go wrong.'

'You mean that's where you met this other man?' Tomo interposed.

Cat nodded again.

'CT,' she almost whispered, shaking her head slowly. 'How I came to hate that name. He was – still is apparently – head of the company's Commercial Development Department. It's referred to as CDD or just CD. He was my overall boss.'

'And CT stands for . . .?' enquired Tomo.

'Sorry, it stands for Charlie, or Chuck, Thompson, but he liked everyone to call him CT, especially in the office.'

She paused, wondering if she had the strength to go on telling her story to Tomo. He sensed this, and tapped her free hand holding the fork which still presented the mouthful of her favourite *Tricolore* salad.

'You're not eating enough,' he urged. 'I suspect that this account has some way to go, and you need to fortify yourself.'

She began eating again, noting that he had already demolished his helping. After a pause, Tomo took the lead: 'So, how did he come to be part of your life?'

She thought about that for a moment.

'I suppose that as soon as I moved into his department, he was already in my life, but not part of it, since he was my overall boss. But he had changed that. Looking back, he was like a tiger carefully stalking its prey, preparing his ground for his assault.'

She brought her spare hand to her forehead.

'I was told that I had been co-opted onto one of the top projects on which the department was working at the time. He arranged weekly briefing sessions on the project, which was where I first saw him perform. I must admit, I was hugely impressed. He held the room in his hand.'

'That's hardly surprising,' Tomo interjected. 'He would hardly be able to hold down the job as head of marketing of one of Europe's leading pharmaceutical companies unless he was hugely impressive.'

'I guess so,' she agreed. 'But somehow it's different when you see the guy in action for the first time. Also, he was one of the main board directors, and clearly had influence with the chief executive. The man had a direct link into the ultimate source of all power, and I suppose that this was part of his overall attraction.'

She paused again, almost finishing her caprese, and washing it down with a sip of Tomo's excellent choice of Pinot Grigio, steeling herself for the ordeal.

'God, with hindsight it all seems so ... so tacky. That's Ali's word.'

'But,' said Tomo, 'that is how men like that operate, or used to. They abused their power and their office for personal advantage. Anyway, go on.'

'So, I was part of the team, and after the first few meetings, he invited me to join him for a drink. He made out that he was granting me a special privilege, and, like the blind fool that I was, I was so flattered that I believed him. These drinks graduated into a couple of dinners after work. I think it was during our conversations that he must have skilfully prised out of me, or perhaps detected through his own intuition, my ...'

'Did we say "frustration"?'

She nodded again, looking down at her plate.

'Looking back, I think that I felt that this was my own Achilles heel. I had developed a suit of armour in order to survive at that place, and that was the only part of me that I knew to be vulnerable from the outside. I had persuaded myself that, provided no one knew about it, I would be able to protect myself. And I suppose that I had kidded myself that somehow I would be able to graduate from a naïve debutante into an accomplished lover in my own time.'

She paused again as he encouraged her to take another mouthful, so as to leave the plate empty. As he had predicted, the benefits of food and wine were immediate.

'The next thing I knew,' she continued, 'was that he had asked me to help him with the project launch, which involved the inevitable weekend away at a conference with all the marketing guys. And like a fool, I accepted.'

She shook her head at the memory as she said those words, barely able to credit the folly of her own actions.

'Perhaps I knew what was likely to happen. And perhaps, though I dare not admit it, that's what I actually wanted to happen.'

They suspended their talk briefly as a waitress arrived to remove their empty plates and prepare the table for the next course.

'And so the affair had started?' suggested Tomo, realising that this was the point of no return for Cat, and concerned lest the brief interlude should cause her to lose her flow. But Cat had already decided that it was time to remove the shackles which had kept these secrets hidden.

Again, she nodded, running her hands through her hair as she prepared to continue.

'I can't deny it. The sex was great, right from that first night. Conventional to begin with – no doubt CT had even planned that. But then it became more and more exotic, and all the while it left me with this acute feeling of guilt, that somehow I was being dishonest not just to Jamie, which I know I was, but also with myself.'

Another pause.

'But it also left me with a sense of deep embarrassment at the behaviour of my own body, almost with a sense that it had betrayed me.'

She was looking at the table now, even though Tomo had reached across it to take her hand, which he continued to squeeze in order to encourage what he regarded as perfect therapy, a proper healing process.

'But the worst thing, Tomo,' she went on, 'was that that I couldn't suppress a burning desire for more. And throughout all this time, I was continuing my relationship with Jamie, but always insisting that I go down to his place at weekends. I used to blame my job for the late nights during the week. But I found it increasingly more and more difficult to avoid his invitations to take me out to dinner in London and stay over at the flat. CT had persuaded me to give him a key to the flat. Don't ask me why I had agreed to that, because I should have known – in fact, having thought about it, it was blindingly obvious – that he would take to dropping in without warning. Maybe that's why I did it. No, it is why I did it. But I dared not risk a scene between the two of them.'

'What sort of period of time are we talking about?' asked Tomo.

'A few months really,' she replied after a few moments' reflection. 'Perhaps two or three months, I suppose.'

'And did Jamie not suspect anything at all? What about your friends? Did no one notice a change in you?'

The first tears began to appear on her cheeks as she returned her gaze to the table in order to prepare her answer.

'Just as it had seemed to me that the distance between us was becoming obvious, almost to everyone except Jamie, he had asked me the question that I had been dreading. "Was I seeing someone else in London?" I could have just denied it. Perhaps I should have done, and gone on living the lie until I could bring the affair with CT to an end. Until then I had developed a perfectly plausible story about my work, the project, the prospects for promotion, my career and what I wanted to achieve before I was ready to settle down – as I suppose I intended that to be interpreted as meaning with Jamie. I could have gone on telling and living that lie.'

'But you didn't.'

'No. Instead, I confessed all to him. Or rather, I told him as much of the truth as I could bare him to learn. I said that I had got too close to someone at work, someone that my job required me to spend a lot of time with.'

'And his reaction?'

'Just as I had feared, Jamie was upset, very upset. But he wasn't angry with me, certainly not as furious as Ali was when I told her. What hurt him the most was that I had kept it from him for so long. I tried to explain that I had been hoping that the whole affair would come to an end by itself. There was some truth in that. It was sort of heading that way, because I could see the point coming where I had reached the limit of my need, and the time had come when I wanted to regain control of my own life.'

'And was it just this confession which precipitated the collapse in your relationship with Jamie, or was there more?'

'No, there was more.'

Tomo sensed a hesitation.

'Much more?'

She looked at him desperately, in silent assent.

'And that is partly, no mostly, what makes me feel so awful about it. Jamie was the perfect gentleman. He promised to forgive me so long as I promised to put an end to the affair with CT. And that was the deal. And, true to his word, Jamie honoured it. He bought me flowers; he took me to Paris for a long weekend, and another in Rome, where he bought me some lovely clothes. Then we had a week's skiing together. And throughout, he never once mentioned my affair again.'

'And, for your part, you obviously tried to honour the deal,' he observed. 'So, where did it all go wrong?'

'I told CT one evening that it was best if we were to stop seeing each other. I'll never forget his reaction. He just laughed. I remember it so clearly. He told me that he would be the one to decide whether we should end it and, if so, when. I was furious, perhaps more with myself than with him. To think that I had allowed myself to get into this situation. But I was also shocked by his reaction, and I told him so.'

'When was this?'

'About a week later. This was in the office. I had prepared a paper which I wanted him to approve so that I could submit it to the board. I had been working on it for a long time, and he had helped me with it initially. I saw it as an important new approach for the company. Its theme was that we should start up our own versions of nutritional remedies, using a combination of both Chinese and Western schools, so that we could neutralise what I perceived would become an anti-pharma campaign in the same way that the tobacco companies had been brought to account.'

'Sounds a brilliant idea to me, but you're going to tell me that it got spiked, in the same way as a scoop from a bold young journalist can be consigned to the shredder at the whim of an editor or proprietor.'

'Right first time,' she confirmed. 'But as my consolation, which was the height of irony now I look back, I was told that I would be working more closely with CT. What I didn't know was that I would be working on a smear campaign on behalf of the company – which CT was heading up – intended to put the knife into all forms of nutritional theories and alternative medicines.'

'Didn't you object?' asked Tomo, slightly bemused.

'Funnily enough, I rather liked the idea of being allowed into the lion's den. I played along with the whole idea because I wanted to learn just how far the company was prepared to go. Imagine my surprise when I learnt that CT had agreed to co-ordinate the campaign on behalf of the whole pharma industry.'

'Yes, and I can see where this is going as regards the paper's article, and we shall need to come back to that in due course. But we have digressed. You were going to tell me what had happened to your affair with CT, unless,' he said, with deliberate emphasis, 'you have gone as far as you want to for one night.'

'No, I didn't mean to avoid the ending. It's the crucial part of the whole story, because it gives you the measure of the man, as my granny tends to say. Please don't get angry when I tell you. Promise?'

'Promise.'

'I always knew that he was a classic control freak, but I had no idea how far he could take this. To cut a long story short, he blackmailed me.'

'What!' he exclaimed, volubly.

'You promised,' she chided him.

'I apologise. I shall control myself. So, what did the scoundrel do?'

She paused again, her focus once more on the table in front of her. She steeled herself to continue.

'The blackmail wasn't obvious at first. Initially, what he did was send me – of course I can't prove that it was him – a few photographs of us in bed together, you know, how do you put it?'

'Mid-coitus?' he offered.

She nodded.

'But he was so clever. In each one, his face was obscured, but mine was clearly visible. Each photo was attached to an email sent to my private email address, with an invitation, obviously intended to be an instruction, that I should compile a virtual album. Next came the video clips, each one showing me not just *in flagrante*, but, you know …'

'Surfing through a crescendo of ecstasy,' Tomo supplied, 'for which he could take the credit. Hardly gallant, but it fits with his macho image. And the threat?'

'It was never in writing. Always verbal. And always to me alone. Something like: "Wouldn't it be awful, almost unthinkable, if something deeply personal, which anyone close to you might find embarrassing, were to get into the wrong hands." But I had little doubt as to the meaning. It was all too obvious.'

'So what did you do?' he asked after a while.

'I thought that the best course was to play for time, so I just sort of allowed the affair to continue. Except that it was no longer an affair, and certainly not any sort of love affair. It was entirely one-sided, just as he liked it, because he was able to dominate me, both mentally and physically.'

'The bastard!' muttered Tomo.

'I felt trapped, which I was, until at last I turned in desperation to Ali. I told her everything, by which I mean pretty much all that I've told you this evening.'

'And her advice,' he prompted.

'You probably don't know Ali well enough yet. She's a straight talker, and a hard-headed woman, which is why I went to her for help. Her advice was straight and tough, just as I had anticipated – and needed. She told me to do what I knew I ought to have done months before: leave the job; leave the man; leave the flat. Start over.'

'And did you?'

'To CT's fury, I did precisely that, but not before I had helped myself to enough material that I could use to get me own back on him. Perhaps you don't want to hear about that right now. Anyway, I timed my departures as best I could from all three – man, job, flat – so that these coincided. And I firmly believed that, now that the difficult part was over, I could throw myself back into my relationship with Jamie.'

'I think I can guess the rest,' said Tomo, trying hard to mask the anger which had taken hold inside him, as Cat lowered her head.

'I should have warned Jamie. I should have explained to him what I had done and why. I should have turned to him for help as well. But I didn't. Instead, I ignored CT's repeated demands that I should return to him, hoping and praying that he would not make good the threats which accompanied every conversation I had with him, each one getting more and more menacing. I had been such a fool, and I was even more of a fool to underestimate the extent of the control freak that lurked within CT.'

She took another sip of wine, before turning to her glass of water.

Tomo waited for her to continue, noticing the tears welling in her eyes.

'On one Saturday morning when I was staying at his house in the country, Jamie received the email which I had been dreading, along with a suitably humiliating text. Attached to it were two of the video clips that he had secretly taken of us together.'

'Did he use his own email address?'

'No, he used different email addresses to send daily messages to Jamie, a new one every day, each of them no doubt untraceable, each one attaching either a photo or a video clip. He copied them all to me, with stuff like "remember this".'

'And the texts to Jamie?'

'Each one designed to emasculate Jamie, with obtuse references to his inadequacy with women. Stuff referring to his "shortcomings with girls in every sense of the word" and saying "what a shame you couldn't satisfy Cat". Those were the ones that really hurt him. And they really did hurt him, I know that.'

Tomo watched the tears begin to trickle down her face as she released the pain that she had kept locked up inside. He waited for her to continue, sure in the knowledge that this was the best therapy that any medic could prescribe.

'They kept on coming, these emails. There were plenty which taunted him, saying something like: "Here's how to really satisfy a woman." I remember one in particular that dared him to look at the attachment, saying something like "Have a look at the girl you set your heart on." Another told him to watch me perform like a porno queen while I enjoyed the experience. They were all along the same lines, each one attaching a photo or a video clip.'

'But I don't understand why he opened the emails,' said Tomo. 'Why did he not just accept your word for what had happened?'

'I think it was the headings of the emails more than anything else. They were like a knife between his ribs. And the worst of it was that he knew that the only way that CT could have known about that, you know, the bit about *shortcomings* – God how he loved that phrase – and the other stuff, was through me.'

'Talk about kicking a man when he's down,' said Tomo. 'And he used that phrase because of what you'd told him?'

She nodded. 'I suppose that I must have said something to CT, you know, pillow talk, not meaning it to go any further, although I don't remember it. Or perhaps he eavesdropped on my chats with Ali. I wouldn't put that past him, the bastard. It doesn't matter now, because Jamie believed that I had betrayed him, and whilst he might have been prepared to overlook my *carnal transgressions* – that's Ali's phrase not mine – he could never forgive such a betrayal of trust. He said as much to me at the end. And it was the end for us, we both knew it.'

'But didn't he let you try to explain?'

'It was all too much for Jamie. It was more than he could take. He refused to give me a second chance, despite all my pleas. Even Ali, bless her, tried to explain things to him. But it was no use. It was all too late. He banished me from his life, and evicted me and everything he had allowed me to accumulate at his country house.'

'So, what happened to that?' asked Tomo, his professional interest intervening.

'For weeks I just assumed that he had burnt it all or thrown it into a skip. But later Ali told me that he had consigned it all into one of the outlying barns. I haven't collected them yet, so I assume that they have been gathering dust there, and no doubt much else, for these last few months.'

'And am I right to assume that, if they still exist that is, to the best of your knowledge that is where they still are?' he asked.

'Yes, I suppose so,' she answered, and then added after another pause. 'And I guess that's why you'll want me – no, you'll need me – to ask Ali to help me retrieve them.'

'When the time comes, yes, I think that's probably right,' he replied. 'We shall have to disclose the fact that the documents are or have been in your possession or control, which is the rather wordy way in which us lawyers say that we can get our hands on the relevant documents, or that we could or thought we could at one time in the past. In fact, it may be that we decide that we need them sooner than we think, although that of course depends on what information the documents actually contain. You can tell me about that some other time, but not now. I think we've had enough for one evening.'

He reached across the table to caress the side of her face with the back of his finger.

'I'm so sorry that you have had to carry this burden,' he observed, stroking away her tears. 'Although, I have to say that I think you are being very harsh on yourself, despite all that has occurred.'

Her relief was palpable now, and it manifested itself in a torrent of tears which began to roll freely down her cheeks.

'But Tomo,' she whispered. 'I did a terrible thing. I hurt him so badly.'

She was weeping openly now, trying but failing to restrain herself out of deference to the other customers in the restaurant.

'I never intended to hurt him, and if I hadn't been so selfish it could all have been avoided. I hurt one of the kindest and gentlest men I have ever known, who showed me nothing but love. But I couldn't love him back. I tried. I really did.'

Long sobs escaped her now,

'I really did try, Tomo, especially after I had finished with CT, and before CT began his attack. I sort of felt that I owed him that. But deep down I knew that it was never going to work between us, and there was nothing that I could do to disguise that from myself, and I guess that he must have sensed it.'

She used her napkin to wipe her face.

'Even so, he never deserved the pain that I have caused him. It was all my fault, and I feel so, so horribly guilty, Tomo.'

He took both her hands.

'Cat, hindsight is a wonderful thing. If we could all undo the things that we regret the most in our lives, it would make it all so much easier. But that's not how it works. Put at its highest, you made an error of judgment in an area where you had allowed your personal and your business lives to coincide – or collide even. It happens every day, in every city, in every country. You were not to know the consequences of your actions, any more than you were to know that you had been filmed. I mean, what kind of weirdo does that? No, you were a victim just as much as poor Jamie. And time will heal his wounds, believe me. He will eventually come to understand that. Men have an uncanny ability to survive such things.'

She smiled at him, returning the warmth of his grip. The relief she felt in having told him about CT was immense. But she still harboured two nagging concerns, each of which she needed to alleviate before the moment had passed.

'You don't find me repulsive because of what I've just told you, do you?' she asked, nervously.

'Why on earth should I? At our age, I could hardly expect you to be a prim little virgin from the old colony when we first met – which, by the way, I still remember as if it were yesterday, and shall never forget.'

Her turn to squeeze him back.

'You will have a past,' he continued, 'in just the same way that I have. Anyway, you've yet to ask me what I've been up to since my teenage years, or even how I came to be single when we met. And not even a prod about any of my previous liaisons – there you are, you see, an admission that there has been at least one – nor the ones that got away. But before you do, I should first confess to you that you that you might be a little disappointed that my portfolio won't be quite as colourful as your own.'

He was rewarded by a smile from behind the tears.

'I don't suppose,' he asked, 'that you kept any of the stuff he sent you. I was assuming from what you said that you've already disposed of all the offending material supplied by that brigand.'

'No, I hadn't got around to that. In fact, I was going to try and use them as the basis of a claim against the company. I just hadn't got round to taking advice on that yet, and, to be honest, I didn't have the courage to ask you.' She checked herself. 'I'm sorry, that must seem really offensive to you, but, just as you said, I've kept this all bottled up inside me until now, and it's got all out of proportion.'

'No offence intended, and none taken,' he responded, adopting the well-rehearsed phrase which he delivered with complete sincerity. 'And I mean that. But, staying with that for a moment, if my hunch is right, and if you haven't disposed of them, then you still have them, or at least you had then until today.'

A nod.

'And, staying with my hunch, I'm assuming that those emails and their attachments walked out of your front door this evening in the arms of some IT engineer who is going to download their contents over the weekend onto various sets of disks.'

Another nod, and now her anxiety returned.

'And, knowing the way that these things work, at some point in time, after the engineer has informed the independent solicitor – that would be the guy you would have spoken with at home earlier today – a set of those images will soon be destined to land in the laps of our esteemed opposition. Is that what is concerning you?'

By way of answer, she smiled at him, and transferred both her hands to one of his.

'You know it is, Tomo. I'm surprised you needed to ask.'

'Never take your witness for granted,' he replied. 'It's an easy mistake to make. Believe me, I've done it myself.'

'But this guy, you know, the lawyer who spoke to me this morning, I told him that there was, you know, personal stuff on my laptop. But he just said that the order required that everything on the hard drive in my laptop had to be examined by his IT people. That's what I couldn't bear, Tomo.'

He squeezed her hands to provide assurance.

'Well, now that I know, there are steps that I can take to halt the process, or perhaps even to reverse it as regards this material. But that depends on whether, on reflection, you do – or do not – want the oppo to know about it. Which in turn raises the question of whether you are minded to file a sexual harassment complaint against your former employers.'

She had thought that this was where he was heading.

'Do I have to decide that now?'

'Not at all, I'm just thinking out loud. It seems to me that there may be an opportunity here for you to avoid such a claim altogether.'

She had not expected him to say that.

'How so?' she asked.

'Well, from what you have told me this evening, your case appears to me to be about as strong as any that I have ever come across – albeit, I stress that this is not my turf. But, if we take the strength of your case as a given, which I reckon is reasonable, then early disclosure of the material to the oppo's legal team might actually play right into your hands. I should qualify that by saying that this is just a thought that's occurred to me. I'd want to cogitate on it a bit more.'

When she continued to look puzzled, he added: 'I'll concede straight away that my reasoning is based purely on instinct, which is why I want to think about it more. But it seems to me that, once this stuff has landed in their laps, then their HR teams and their lawyers will never allow such material to see the light of day, and certainly not in any courtroom.'

'But they've got to look at the emails first, haven't they?'

'The lawyers alone will. But that's the beauty of it. We can properly object to your ex-employers having sight of the material, but then theatrically concede that their lawyers will need to be satisfied that our objection is well founded. We go on to insist that they, and they alone, should see the material, and further insist that this must be under supervision by the independent solicitor.'

She thought about that, although the second bottle was proving something of a hindrance in that respect.

'But what if the solicitor decides or recommends that access to this – this stuff – should go no further than the lawyers, but they object?'

'Then we bring the matter before the judge, or at least we threaten to. And again, if my instinct is right, their lawyers will never want to go there.'

Her expression revealed that she was comforted by his logic.

'Does that make you feel any better?'

'Of course it does, Tomo, and I pray you're right. Because what has concerned me since this afternoon is that, now that this business over the paper has all blown up, I'm going to have to go through it all over again.'

She looked at him, searching his face for any sign of doubt. Then she asked:

'You're really telling me that it ain't necessarily so?'

'It's what I'm suggesting, Cat, albeit thinking on my feet, so to speak.'

'But you're also saying that, in the meantime, there will be complete strangers looking at the most degrading stuff about me, and there's nothing that I can do about it. Isn't that the truth of it, Tomo?' she queried.

'Yes and no, is the right answer. I'm going to ask one of my colleagues in chambers who specialises in harassment at work cases to look at all that for me.'

'And he's good? Or she?'

'I'll say. And it's "she". Believe me, they won't know what's hit them.'

She smiled again, the tears abating.

'But,' he added, 'my instinct tells me that the other side may well decide that they cannot risk taking the matter any further. If the emails are as bad as you say they are, that's certainly the advice that I would give them.'

'Aren't you assuming that the emails are seen by the right people on their side, and at the right time?'

'Hey, steady on! You're starting to sound like a lawyer. Any more of that and I'll be out of a job. But yes, you're right. If we are not going to take the initiative, then we have to assume that the bad news does get communicated upstairs as and when it arrives. That is one of the downsides of acting for a big corporation such as our oppo. It's a sad fact of life that messengers with bad news in those organisations tend to get shot first. That's also why no one applies for the job.'

'So, what I think you're saying is that it's up to us to use the emails in support of my case, or in defence of the case against us?'

He reflected on that for a moment.

'I'd need to think about that a lot more,' he said, finally. 'A lot will turn on the strength – as we perceive it – of the case which we intend to advance. Before I'd be willing to express even a tentative view, I would need to have seen much more of the overall evidence. Also, the compromising material which you say is still in your possession may only be useful in support of a separate claim, or perhaps a counterclaim. And it's too early at this stage to say which of these two I could advise you to pursue, if indeed any at all. And, after nearly three bottles of wine between us, I'm in no fit state to offer any opinion, or at least not any opinion of any value, on which course I would want you to take. I shall need to take a completely fresh look at it in the morning, and I may be talking about Sunday or Monday morning, as opposed to tomorrow.'

'But, if we did use the emails, then I'd have to accept that I would be asked about them in court? Isn't that right?'

After a further moment's reflection on the question, he looked her straight in the eyes as he answered. 'I'll obviously think about that, but basically, I think you're right, although I'd exchange *would* for *could*. If it got past the early settlement phase, then you'd need to produce the attachments, and probably the emails themselves, in order to substantiate your claim for sexual harassment or discrimination, in whatever form. But don't get me wrong. Potentially any one of them could be very expensive for the company.'

She paused again, using her napkin to remove her tear stains, and smiled at him, feeling at peace at last.

'So much for my make-up. Do I look a mess?'

A final squeeze.

'Hey babe, you could never look a mess. I love you just the way that you are.'

Cat smiled in reply, knowing that the truth lay mostly on her napkin. She held it up to show him the evidence.

'You're such a bad liar, Tomo. I'll just go and fix this.'

They both smiled at that. It was a mutual recognition that the conversation had gone as far as it needed to for now. Indeed, it had probably reached its natural conclusion as far as confessions go.

She returned just as the waitress arrived with their main courses and – such a nice touch – a clean napkin for Cat.

'Ah, the cavalry,' exclaimed Tomo, as their attention was diverted, but she took him to mean that for the time being any form of dialogue would need to be suspended.

'Thank you, Tomo,' she said, reaching across the table with both hands, 'I feel so much better inside now.'

With that, Cat began to devour her portion of roast sea bass (line-caught, naturally), simultaneously fortifying both herself and her affection for Tomo. The return of her appetite was mirrored by the diminution of the weight on her shoulders following their conversation.

Chapter 7

On the other side of the capital, a solitary and lonely form toiled away at her brightly lit desk in front of a keyboard and screen. A large lever-arch file of documents lay on one side of her, and some unfinished sandwiches on the other.

She had been enjoined by her boss to compile a dossier of every email passing from *'the girl,'* Cat Symonds, and any employee of, or journalist with, *The Daily Chronicle*. In order to do so, she had diligently read through each of the documents contained within the zipped files. She had tried to speak to them with a view to persuading them to change the format of their attachments, but without success. They had apparently left the office for some training seminar and were not due back for another week.

Typical.

Her orders were to find as much dirt on this girl as she could within the material that had been made available to her. The emails were there all right. But that was far from her immediate concern.

What worried her right now was that she was staring at a document which looked horribly like some sort of instruction to professionals loyal to the company. The document was undated, and did not identify – on its face at least – the identity of its author (or authors, if there was more than one). This was one which the girl had emailed to herself, but did not appear to have sent electronically to the paper. That was not to say that she had not physically handed a copy to that journalist.

She read the introduction again, and then moved on to the report summary.

Interview technique when questioned about alternative medicine

> 1. *Do your best to introduce into every sentence the word 'placebo', and wherever possible equate this with a psychological reaction to counselling rather than the effect of physical healing. (One possible comparison would be the effects experienced by the natives who were 'treated' by the druids in pre-Roman Britain, or the witch doctors of ancient Africa.)*

2. *Never allow the conversation to stray into areas such as treatment of animals and young children. (You will be met by the acknowledged fact that the 'placebo' argument obviously cannot carry the same weight in relation to these categories of 'patients', who would be ignorant of the treatment.)*
3. *Always impress on the interviewer the absence of any proven, objective evidence or tests to substantiate the so-called healing properties which are said to be possessed by the remedies supposedly prescribed by those using alternative therapies.*
4. *Always dismiss as being objectively impossible to verify any subjective (i.e. first-hand) evidence from either the patient or the consultant that the patient has been healed or feels better.*

Maria turned away from her screen. She wearily rested her elbows on the desk and sank her head into her hands.

What ghastly can of worms had she opened up? She now realised that she should have been much more circumspect in her interrogation of the girl's private email account. Worse still, she had no valid authority to back up her instruction to the IT technicians.

For the first time in her career she felt completely isolated, alone, and totally exposed to the recriminations of others, including her boss, whom she worshipped – and no doubt the legal team – which would surely follow.

It was the reaction of Barbara that most concerned her. She could not bear to be the harbinger of yet more bad news to her boss. It would devastate what might remain of the confidence that her boss had once held in her over these past few years, and would almost certainly seal her fate within the department.

She dared not imagine the glee with which the news of her own humiliation would be received amongst the other members of the company group. On top of the rebuke at the end of their last meeting, that was too much to contemplate.

She turned the pages to the next document, only to find more incriminating material. She could scarcely bare to read any more.

She closed that file, then opened up the second one.

What struck her immediately was that it appeared that the contents were shown in a new format, distinctly different from the previous files. She wondered whether the original had been encrypted, or protected in a different way.

That should have set alarm bells ringing in her head. Such was her fatigue that her mind failed to register any warning.

She opened first document. It was marked 'strictly confidential' and appeared to be a minute that had been prepared by someone within the Commercial Development Department.

'Oh shit!' she muttered under her breath, despite being the only person in the open-plan office. 'That's where she used to work...'

The document was titled: 'Marketing No-Go Areas for Sweetener Products'.

Her finger hovered over the mouse, querying whether she should open it. But like a glutton for punishment, she could not resist it.

She began to read it.

Strictly Confidential
Summary
The purpose of this note is to record certain matters that have been brought to the attention of the Board of Directors by the Head of the Commercial Development Department, but which the Board requires to be kept strictly confidential.
EFSA Report: In 2013, a report by the European Food Safety Administration gave the green light to the promotion of artificial sweeteners, and confirmed that there is no link between them and cancer. However, the Company (amongst others) provided substantial funds in support of the EFSA's report, and subsidised the costs of producing that report by supplying, via a third party, the 'researchers' who would be primarily responsible for drafting the report. These facts must not be disclosed on any account.
GM Source: The Company's sweeteners are manufactured from genetically modified plants, much of which is grown in the USA. As a result, the Company's sweeteners are several times sweeter than sugar, and at least two of them are over 6,000 times as sweet.
Company Research: The Company commissioned but rejected research that found that its sweeteners would impact on the user's hormonal stimuli, and have three results. First, it caused the body to release more insulin than it required. Secondly, it caused the user's pancreas to believe that the user's appetite and thus need for food had not been sated, thereby causing the user to consume food that the body did not require. Thirdly, the sweeteners were likely to cause the users to seek out increasingly sweeter food products, thereby exacerbating and compounding the effects of the first two causes.

The research concluded that there was a significant risk that the Company's sweeteners were contributing towards, and very possibly causing, both diabetes and obesity.

Publication of the research has been embargoed by the Company, and neither its existence nor its content must ever be disclosed.

<u>Threat:</u> *The Commercial Development Department warned that there was a real risk that over time a link would be found between both the Company's sweeteners and those conditions.*

<u>Action:</u> *A sustained campaign of disinformation was necessary, using whenever possible doctors and professors who received regular funding from the Company.*

Maria stared at the screen for long minutes.

Dear God, what in Heaven's name have I done, she asked herself. How could she have allowed herself to rush so blindly down this alley and get herself well and truly mired in such contamination!

She resolved to sleep on the matter overnight, although she doubted whether she would be able to enjoy any. Meanwhile, she would focus her report on how the documents which had been quoted by the paper had come into its possession via Symonds' emails. She would try to find time tomorrow to think further on what to do about these other documents, although she would have a job explaining how she had discovered them.

What she really needed was to find someone with whom she could discuss this mess within the company. Someone she could trust.

She began to pack up her things and prepared to make the journey back to the tidy and characterless apartment that she called home.

*

CT had 'worked the hall'. As was his custom, he had glad-handed all those with whom he had cultivated his support base across his sphere of the industry. He had ignored the repeated calls and texts from the lawyer, and had taken his new assistant out for a late meal. He was moulding her nicely into a position where he could move in for the feast. He enjoyed this part almost as much as the fornication, which he confidently told himself would be on the cards as the game played out.

All in good time, he said to himself.

As for those documents, they continued to niggle. He cursed first himself for letting his guard down, and then her for her treachery. But something else was bothering him, and it was enough to eclipse his concerns over the paper trail.

Fisher's email had recorded that a court had granted the company an order that would enable the company's lawyers to interrogate Kitty's computer and mobile phone. He was well aware that the IT forensic guys had the tools and the skills necessary to recover any texts, emails and other data that she might have once possessed but had since deleted. But, whilst that might be good news for the company, it was very possibly bad news for him.

He chided himself that he had used the same internet café on Tottenham Court Road to send all his emails to Kitty and her tepid lover. It had been convenient at the time, but he was now aware that the café had been required to maintain digital video recordings of anyone using its facilities. And if the lawyers were ever to pursue that line of interrogation, the trail would lead back to him eventually.

But, he told himself, she would never allow any of that material to get into the public, or even any private domain where it could be viewed by others. The potential for humiliation had deterred the others before her, and he was confident that it would do so again in this case. All the more so if he were to leak some of the other clips to her anonymously, which he was strongly tempted to do.

But he would bide his time, and wait until he was confident that the court had returned her phone and her PC to her.

He would grab a decent night's sleep, then sneak back to London so that he could begin to clear the incriminating material from his house, and use the Sunday morning to do the same in his office when he was reasonably sure that the coast would be clear. He did not want to run into any of the vermin from legal, especially that Fisher fellow.

That guy was becoming a right nuisance.

*

As it happened, a few hours previously, Ted Fisher has circulated a note to his colleagues in legal and internal affairs. He had recorded the current state of play, but had drawn particular attention to the fact that Thompson had not responded to any of his numerous calls, texts or emails. He sought their assistance in procuring a proper response from him, if possible by the next day, and certainly before Monday morning.

He annexed samples of documents that both departments would need to review.

His note recorded that the independent solicitor had in his control Ms Symonds' laptop and mobile, and that both were now being analysed by IT technicians working under his supervision. Thus, it was unlikely that the company would receive any interim report from Mr Langer before Monday at the earliest. More likely on Tuesday.

Meanwhile, Ms Symonds was required to inform the court and the company by Tuesday of the identity and location of any other documents falling within the categories described in the order – assuming that such information was within her knowledge.

Likewise, the paper was enjoined from making any further use of or repeating any of the contents of the company's confidential material. Similar orders had been obtained against Ms Symonds and the journalist.

But the fact remained that the orders against Miss Symonds had been secured on the basis of data that had been unlawfully obtained.

That was the time-bomb.

*

The following morning found Tomo sitting at the table in Cat's living room, reading through the two files of documents that had been left at her flat by AlphaOm's lawyers. She and Cat had literally fallen into bed the previous evening on their return from the restaurant. They were both exhausted: she by her confession and out-pouring of emotion; he following his sleep-deprived preparation for and attendance at a hearing earlier that day.

Consequently, what had been left of the evening had not provided occasion for any display of the 'natural affection and instincts implanted in man' (Tomo envied the Church of England's Prayer Book.) But there was time still to indulge in the liberties usually attendant on a weekend. And the knowledge that a Saturday largely free of commitments lay before them was likely to encourage such intimacy.

And there was always Sunday ...

Instead, as she had lain beside him in bed, he had slowly drawn imaginary patterns across her naked back with his forefinger until her breathing settled into a rhythm. He was content to defer any further contact until her body – and mind – had been fortified by sleep. Not that their relationship had developed any particular pattern by this stage.

Quite the reverse: he was a committed devotee to the maxim of *carpe diem*, and seized every available opportunity to make love with Cat. He did so partly out of necessity, since they were not yet strictly living together, although he sensed that such time was not far off, and partly because as a successful junior barrister he was frequently required to work late into the night in order to prepare his cases. It was a vice – or virtue – he shared with many of his profession which, if 'twere not so, would long ago have become extinct.

Being naturally an early riser, he had let Cat sleep whilst he examined the court papers that had been served on her.

He became aware of her reveille from the sound of running water. This, in his view, augured well. It suggested the performance of a ceremonial ritual, the mysteries of which are known only to the female of the species. Much more to the point, he had learnt during their brief relationship that this often preceded the sort of developments that he had in mind.

So, things were looking up, he thought to himself.

Or perhaps not.

His initial optimism began to falter as he heard the grinding of coffee beans. Whilst laudable in itself so far as Saturday morning activities were concerned, since it heralded the imminent provision of breakfast, it had not been foremost amongst his list of immediate priorities.

Then, for the second time in as many minutes, his spirits were raised again as he sensed rather than heard the swish of silk that advertised her approach across the room towards him.

This was more like it.

The gentle caress of his shoulders announced her arrival beside her Swedish-designed kneeling stool on which he was perched beside the table.

She was clad only in a delicate Thai sarong which was tied around her waist, so that her appearance resembled that of a dusky maiden from a Russell Flint watercolour. However, both her present intent and demeanour held none of the artistic innocence of those fictional beauties.

As she lent forwards, the smooth flesh of her full breasts stroked first his back and then his head, replacing her hands. She kissed the top of his head, her fingers inching inside the bathrobe which he had earlier liberated from her bathroom.

'B'Gad, madam, how's a chap supposed to concentrate on affairs of state with a couple of mammaries flappin' about his ears!' protested Tomo, as he effected to evade the prelude to her seduction.

She ignored the feigned protest, and lowered her hands still further, fingertips fluttering over the hairs on his chest.

'Oh, but sir,' she cooed, in an exaggerated Virginian drawl, 'I was always taught that there is a time and place for everything, and y'all should know that there's a place right close by where you most surely should be spending your time.'

The hands continued their downwards descent, as she added: 'And sir, I'm talkin' about right now.'

He intercepted the next phase of her assault, holding and then raising both her wrists as he revolved a full 180 degrees to engage the assault head on, so to speak.

'Madam, this is intolerable, but you leave me no choice other than to deal directly with the matter in hand.'

He sat facing her, a wrist in each hand as he nuzzled each of her breasts in turn, now releasing her hands so that he could untie the loose knot of the sarong. Before he did so, he paid homage to the two superbly formed mounds before him, each topped by its pert nipple which began to come erect in response to the light touch of his lips, his hands weighing the firmness of each, caressing their undersides. As the silk sarong slowly relinquished its temporary purchase on the gentle curves of her hips, he withdrew briefly and used his fingers to trace circles around each nipple, gradually expanding the radius of each circle so that each orb had eventually been circumnavigated. The fingers now sought new contours, first the taught muscles of her abdomen – honed through yoga, he understood, and occasional exercise at the gym – and onwards towards her lower belly. There they hovered above her mons and inner thigh, indulging in the smoothness of her flesh. She had initially been coyly shy of the depilated skin of her sex.

'And where, madam, might be this place to which you refer?'

'Oh sir, you're so close already ...'

'So, are we getting warm ...?'

'Mmm ... more than warm. Hot.' Her nostrils began to flare, her pulse increasing in tandem with her breath.

'Hotter?' his subtle caress gradually accelerating her arousal. She reciprocated, her hands drawing the gown off his shoulders, head thrown back as her breasts now thrust their sharp cones into his mouth.

He stood up, easily taking her weight as her thighs responded by tightening around his waist, and carried her towards the bedroom.

'Madam, it appears that I have distressed you. Methinks 'twere best if you were to lie you down whilst I investigate the cause of your discomfort.'

'Ooh, yes, please, good sir,' she mewed as they reached the bed, 'search me all over. Don't stop until you're sure that I'm cured.'

*

Afterwards, they lay entwined together for long minutes, their breathing slowly calming, until he gently extracted himself from her embrace. He propped himself on his elbow and began to draw random patterns across her breasts.

'Well, madam, that seems to have resolved the immediate crisis, at least for the moment, wouldn't you agree?'

That provoked a smile, which quickly developed into a chuckle.

She opened her eyes, and detected a schoolboy grin.

'And just what are you looking so pleased about?'

'Me? Pleased? Not in the slightest, I assure you.'

'Now, isn't that just dandy! Why, Mr Butler, I could have sworn that I saw a smile cross that face of yours not just ten seconds passed.'

'You have the word of a gentleman that I was merely observing what appeared to me to be a satisfactory resolution to the matter in hand.'

'Is that so?'

'Indeed it is, madam.'

'Well, if I'm not mistaken, you seem to regard this "matter", as you care to describe it, as having reached a resolution. Well, let me assure you that I have a very different opinion on the subject.'

'Ah ...'

'Ah, exactly.'

'And what, precisely, were you suggesting that I do, given that my current resources appear to be significantly depleted, so to speak?'

She tried to resist a giggle.

'Really?' she replied sitting.

'Yes, really, albeit only temporarily.'

'Is that so? Well, I can soon remedy that.'

'Aha! You mean some of your fresh coffee. Splendid idea.'

'Now don't you be thinking that can quit on me so early.'

'Nothing was further from my mind.'

'Now that is the first word of truth I've heard from you this morning, Mr Butler.'

'Madam, I protest . . .'

'You protest away as much as you fancy, but you should know that a young Virginian girl needs a whole lot more lovin' than just a few kisses and a quick tumble.'

'I am hurt to the quick, madam. But then, post-orgasmic amnesia is by no means uncommon in the female of the species, so I am informed.'

'Is that a fact!'

'Just so, madam.'

'Well then, I'll just have to remind myself what it was that brought about that post-orgy animal, or whatever you're talkin' about.'

With that, she eased him onto his back, and came to kneel astride him. She kissed him gently on the lips, before transferring her attentions down his torso, until her tongue snaked its way downwards. 'Percy', as he affectionately described it, was rapidly acquiring a new lease of life.

Coffee or no coffee, Tomo reckoned this was paradise.

*

Later, once they had finished breakfast, Cat invited Tomo to return to the real business of the day, namely the steps that they would need to take with regard to the court papers that had been served on her the previous morning. She needed him to take her through the logistics of the procedural hoops through which she would be made to dance at the behest of her former employers.

'So Tomo, can you just explain the process to me again. I know that I've heard bits of it from you in the past, but I've never had to play any part in things. What precisely will I be asked to do?'

Tomo came to sit down beside her at the table, taking out his pen and opening his notebook onto a clean page.

'Right. Let's start from the beginning. We'll call your employers "the company" and *The Chronicle* "the paper", just to keep it simple. You are you, the ex-employee. And we'll call the journalist "Ken". Easy enough?'

'All good so far, babe.'

'Good. Now the company reckons that you have leaked its confidential information to the paper, and objects to the paper using it to write an article. It also claims that you can only have leaked its confidential information as a result of a breach of your contract – that is to say your former employment contract – with the company. It says that it was a term of your contract that you would keep confidential any material which they either specified as, or which could objectively be regarded as, confidential information. It also says, in the event that any of that material came into your possession as a result of your employment, then that triggered your obligation to keep it confidential – which in layman's terms means that you cannot disclose its existence or reveal its content to any third party. The contract further says, and the law would imply this anyway, that this obligation will survive the termination of your employment. Still with me?'

'Ahuh.'

'So, once it has prepared sufficient evidence to support these allegations, the company will present that evidence to the court.'

'And this is the High Court, yes?'

'That's right. The company has chosen to go to the High Court in London, which is logical because you and the paper are located here.'

'And where is this again?'

'The High Court has several branches around the country. It calls them "registers", but its principal court is located at the Royal Court of Justice in the Strand, in London. Until now, fortunately, you have avoided the misfortune to having to attend this Victorian edifice. Now, regrettably, you will be required to visit it under compulsion, albeit with your own advisers.'

'Because you'll be there, with me?'

'As you well know,' he quipped with a wry smile, 'I am merely the humble instrument of your desire.'

'Not so humble a little earlier, as I recall.'

He tried to keep a straight face as she said this, but his pretence failed as she gently prodded him in the ribs, before taking his hand again.

'We digress,' he continued. 'Back to matters in hand.'

'Is that an invitation?'

'As I was saying,' he answered, giving her diversion a sensible swerve, 'when a case is commenced in the High Court, it is allocated (either initially or subsequently) by reference to the nature of the dispute. Your dispute is in essence a business dispute, so the claim has been commenced in the business and property section of the High Court where there are specialist judges who will hear and decide the case. You can see that from the heading of the court papers, and it is fairly common in breach of confidence cases, which is essentially what yours is.'

'So how did the company get these orders from the court without me having any chance to say anything in defence?'

'Good question. The way it works is like this. As I've said, the company reckons that it has a strong case against you. So what the company does is to rock up before a High Court judge – either in person or by telephone, depending on the urgency – having given the judge a chance to read its witness evidence in advance. This is usually in the form of one or more sworn documents called affidavits, although these are often provided in draft and then attested or sworn on oath the next day. This exhibits, which means produces, copies of the documents that the company says will make good its case at trial, if there ever is one. The company also produces a written summary of its complaints. We call this a skeleton argument or a case summary.'

'That's the one at the front of the file?'

'That's the badger. It sets out both the factual background to the claims and then gives its legal reasons to say why the court should grant an order in the terms sought. It also needs to explain to the judge why this is a case where, one, not only is the company justified in not giving any of the defendants any notice of its application before the hearing, but also, two, where the court should make the order without giving the other side a chance to present any submissions or evidence in defence. A typical reason would be that the other side would, if given notice, take advantage of the intervening time to hide or destroy the very evidence which the company wants to recover, and which it wants to use in order to make good its case.'

'Which seems to be the reason they have given here?'

'Exactly. So the court – by which I mean a High Court judge – then goes through the process of ticking each of these boxes. He satisfies himself or herself that the company has shown a strong arguable case against each proposed defendant. He then accepts that, on the evidence, the company was entitled to make its application without notifying the proposed defendants. Next, he has to accept that the case is one of sufficient urgency to justify the granting of an order which will preserve the *status quo* pending a further hearing, which this time will be what we call an *inter-partes* hearing, or with both the company and each of the defendants represented, if so advised. We call that the return date. At that hearing the judge will then decide, first whether to continue or vary or dismiss the orders that it had made at the previous *ex parte* hearing (that is to say when he only heard the claimant's side) until a full trial of the issues, and then what to do with any evidence that has been brought to light as a result of those orders.'

'How do we get to see that he's done that?'

'We'll need to wait until we see their note of the hearing before the judge. They have to produce this within the next couple of days.'

'OK. I'll look out for that.'

'So, if each box gets ticked, then the court will make an order or orders along the lines that the company has applied for. In this case, the order against the paper prevents it from using what the company claims to be its confidential information. There is a similar order against you, but in addition it does two things. It permits an independent solicitor to seize and preserve the contents of your laptop and any hard copies of the documents that the company claims are confidential and that you might have in your possession. It further orders you to disclose to the court the current location of any of that material so far as such location lies within your knowledge. There will be a similar order in the case of the journalist. Still with me so far?'

'Yep. There were lawyers here yesterday. One said she was hired by the company. The man said that he was independent of the company, and that he was the one controlling the IT guy who took my phone and my laptop. Which they still have, so far as I know. Would that be normal in this sort of case?'

'Pretty much. They could take a while to interrogate both devices, so I doubt you'll get them back before Monday or Tuesday next week. That would be fairly routine in a case like this. It might even take longer.'

'So, what happens to all my documents and the other, you know, stuff in the meantime? Does the company get to look at them all now before I do?'

'No. That's not how it works. All the court has done is to order that the *status quo* should be preserved until the matter is brought back before it. In the meantime, your material is held by a supervising solicitor, who is called exactly that, the supervising solicitor. He produces a report to the court, with the help of an IT or computer expert, setting out the entire contents of your laptop and your phone so far as these appear to be material to the case. He also identifies each of the hard-copy documents that have been recovered from you or from the search of your flat.'

'So the IT guy is doing that now?'

'Very likely, which means that he will probably produce that report during the early part of next week. If he needs more time, he'll ask for it – usually via the supervising solicitor, who then reports back to the court.'

'And then what happens?'

'You'll see that, on the front of the order, the court has fixed a date for the return date. That's when the court can hear all the parties on the question of whether or not the orders which it made against the defendants should be continued – either as presently worded or in a varied form.'

'And that's, what, a week from yesterday, Friday first, or at least that's what is says in the order against me.'

'Yes, but you or the paper can apply to bring that forward if you can both demonstrate that there are good reasons for that. At present, I reckon we'll have our work cut out just to get your case ready by that date. There's a fair bit to read for starters, and we've not begun to prepare your own witness statement, which is the main vehicle through which we would challenge the company's case against you.'

She nodded in assent.

'So what's the plan?' she asked.

'Well, the first step is to make sure that you comply with the terms of the order. That will involve you telling the court where, so far as you know, you believe any documents that belong to the company are located.'

'Well, for sure most of the documents that I have, or at least I had, were until yesterday either here or on my laptop.'

'You said "most". That implies that there are or were others.'

She hesitated, and his intuition told him that there was something that she was not telling him. He was well used to this.

'Cat, listen,' he began. 'One of the best ways to scupper your chances are to hand the other side an own goal. And the easiest way to do that is to withhold from the court any material which the oppo can later identify was in your possession. You can be sure that they will try to demonstrate that you deliberately tried to conceal it. They would then use that to paint you as an untruthful witness whose testimony cannot be trusted. Which puts you '*Love-Forty*' down in the overall match. Are you hearing me?'

'Loud and clear.'

'So, I need to ask you again, because your lawyers will on Monday morning: do you know the likely whereabouts of other documents that can reasonably be regarded as falling within the category of *confidential material* of the sort described by the company in their evidence to the court?'

She took a deep breath.

'Well,' she almost whispered, 'I know of two places for sure, and I've already told you about one of them. No, that's not quite right. I didn't tell you about my other email address that I used, well to . . .'

He sensed what she intended, and offered, 'To assemble your evidence against the company?'

She nodded.

'Yes. Some of the copies are attached to emails that I sent from my desk at work. They were mostly sent to myself using a special email address that I set up for that purpose. That was Ken's idea.'

'The journalist?'

'Yes. He said that they would probably trace it eventually, but he thought it would be less likely to arouse suspicion in the short term. Anyhow, I suppose that I have to disclose that address to the court and tell them about the emails, won't I?'

'Yes, but only so far as those emails are relevant to this case. Once we've got you a replacement or temporary PC, we can access the account and identify all the relevant messages and attachments.'

'But won't they have already done that?'

'Probably, although I did not see that in the orders. But the court will want to hear it from you. And, thinking about it, that might present us with the opportunity to refer to the content of some of the emails sent to you and to Jamie by that creep.'

'OK, I guess there's no way around that in the end, and Granny always told me that attack was the best form of defence.'

'A veritable sage, I reckon, your granny,' said Tomo affectionately. 'But we digress. Let us keep to the point. That deals with one category. You said there were two. So, do you want to tell me about the other one?'

He didn't push, perhaps because he already suspected what it was that she was finding so difficult to vouchsafe. He squeezed her hand in encouragement. That did the trick. She looked at him, seeking his understanding.

'You remember I told you last night that I would try to spend weekends with Jamie at his place in the country?'

'In Dorset, yes. I remember.'

'Well, I began to leave copies of stuff that I didn't want to leave around the apartment, you know, in case CT found them there, so I took them to Jamie's place. There was a place in his attic where Jamie let me store my stuff.'

'How much are we talking about?'

'Well, from memory, around two or three of those packing boxes that the company used for moving offices.'

Tomo thought about that for a while.

'And did you tell the company's lawyers that yesterday?' he asked her, although he reckoned he already knew the answer.

'No. And to be honest it didn't even occur to me at the time. It was all happening so fast that I guess I wasn't thinking quickly enough.'

'No matter,' he said, 'but did either they or the independent solicitor ask you whether you knew of the location of any other documents?'

She racked her brain, then shook her head.

'I cannot rightly recall, Tomo. I'm sorry. Is it bad for me that I didn't say anything about them?'

He cogitated a moment, before responding.

'Actually, not really, provided we make a clean breast of it now by telling them that we did once have control of the material, but no longer do. That is correct is it, about not having it under your control?'

She checked herself as she assessed her answer.

'To tell you the truth, I cannot say for sure,' she replied, honestly. 'We haven't, you know spoken for months.'

'Yes, I quite understand that. But, do you think that it is at all likely that Jamie will have kept the documents after all this time?'

She shook her head again slowly.

'You know, I really just don't know.'

It was Tomo's turn to nod. As he searched for the right words in which to couch his next question, it was she who spoke first. 'I know what you want to ask me. How can I find out whether or not Jamie still has them – is that right?'

'That's about the gist of it,' he confirmed. Then he added, 'Whilst I am probably not the person best qualified to answer that question, it occurs to me that, if you are reluctant to approach Jamie directly – and I can well understand why not – perhaps the better angle would be via his sister, your friend Ali, unless you feel that this would risk damaging your friendship.'

She had half expected him to make that suggestion.

'She's so protective of him, as I would be if I were Jamie's sister. He owes me no favours and I am so reluctant to ask for one. But ...'

'But, needs must ...?'

She nodded, resignedly.

'Well now,' he said, changing tack, 'for the purpose of your initial evidence to the court, we can only say that you had at one time some documents, the identities of which you cannot be specific, but that these are no longer in your possession or control. However, you are taking steps to ascertain whether they still exist and, if so, whether they can be brought back under your control.'

'Will that not, oh what's your phrase ... oh yes, set hares running?' she asked him, still concerned as to how this would end.

Tomo smiled at her.

'And that is precisely what we want the oppo to do. We want them to come running down the alley that we have prepared for them. Because a nasty claim for sexual harassment awaits them at the end. That's when we'll close the gates behind them!'

'Why, I do declare, Mr Butler, if I did not know you better, I should say that you have the scheming mind of a lawyer.'

'All in a day's work, ma'am. But, compliments aside, let's just close out this issue of the company's documents. We've dealt with the copies on your laptop. We'll deal with the copies that you left at Jamie's place. That leaves the documents attached to any emails that you sent either to yourself or the paper.'

'But I cannot say which they are without access to a computer, and even once I've got hold of one that is going to take a long time.'

'Agreed,' said Tomo, 'which is why we only need to tell them that certain categories exist and that you have not had time to identify them yet.'

She sighed with relief on hearing that.

'And what about the stuff they took from here? I don't suppose the order relates to any of that, and besides, how would I know what they have done with it once it left here yesterday morning?'

'No, you're right. So, what we need to do is to confirm to the court that the independent solicitor took that material, but that you are currently unable to list what it was since it is no longer in your control or possession.'

'And we do all of this by Tuesday,?' she asked. 'I think that is what the order says, but that is a whole bunch of stuff to do.'

'Yep, so we'll need to get a wiggle on.'

She chuckled, edging closer to him.

'I thought that was what we were doing before we had coffee.'

'Now, don't you be getting any ideas,' he chided, although with little enthusiasm. 'We need to focus on this, but in the meantime we need to get you a temporary mobile until you get your own back. And I've got an old laptop that you can use for emails. It will feel like trying to run in waist-deep water, but it will have to do for a couple of days. But if you can't wait that long then we could nip out and buy you a new one.'

He reluctantly removed her hand.

'Either way, some fresh air would be good for you. Come on.'

*

Once safely ensconced in the relative security of his flat. CT set to work on examining the product of the latest witch-hunt by the Mamba. They had been thorough, that much he would grant them. In fact, as he read further into the files, he began to realise that he had seriously underestimated the Mamba's little team of lapdogs. He specifically recalled the one who followed her everywhere.

It soon became apparent to him that either she or someone under her instruction had interrogated the IT system with a passion. As a result, virtually every document that he had created which touched on the twin issues of the properties of the company's sugar substitutes and the repeated warnings from sources within 'traditional medicine' had been faithfully retrieved through the efforts of the Mamba's team. These were now reproduced in the files before him. More significantly, so too had a list of each of the directors and line managers to whom these had been CCd.

As he read through the file, he carefully flagged with a blue Post-it each document that had been copied to the chief. These were his 'Get out of Jail Free' cards. He was not going to be abandoned to the wolves or left to do the decent thing by his boss. They both had too much to lose. He knew plenty of not-so-subtle ways in which to get the message across that he was not about to go down alone if this particular ship hit the rocks.

The next file contained the emails. There could easily be a 'smoking gun' amongst these, and so he took especial care to read them, and those written by him in particular. In one section were grouped those which Kitty – he still smiled at his name for her – had sent from her office PC. Most of them had attachments, and he made a mental note to check each of them on his second read-through.

In the next section there was a reference to her use of a private email address via which she had sent attachments. He had not known about that, and wondered how the company's IT guys had retrieved that information. Either way, he admired their skills, but wondered how they had obtained permission from the court to access that email account and, if granted, then to use the material retrieved. He was well aware of the difficulties that now confronted corporate entities under the revised data protection laws.

He made a note of that address. He was not aware of any emails that had been addressed to him from her using that account. If they existed, these would almost certainly have the potential to compromise him.

But he had enough to contend with the emails that she had sent to him on her own company address. They were not hard to spot. The Mamba's poodle had carefully sorted them into a subsection headed 'HR Issues'. Very discrete, he thought, although he would have expected nothing less from her. Yet it was fucking infuriating nonetheless to learn that at least one other person in the company had now read these. In fact, it was probably more than one.

He had assumed from Cat's silence that he was safe in regarding the whole affair as over. He had resisted the temptation to send her a few more gems from his library. That was one of his more prudent decisions. He still dipped into them from time to time: he could still be turned on by the images of her body. Granted, he had become a bit possessive when she had decided to go back to that toffee-nosed wimp, but that was because he had prized her sensuality and her need. He persuaded himself that, having introduced her to his jaded desires, he had been entitled to resent anyone else enjoying her body. He chose not to admit the possibility that he might harbour spiteful emotions on account of it being her decision to end it.

But this was no time to reminisce, he told himself. In fact, the luxury of time was the one thing he most certainly did not have.

He began at the beginning of the first file again, and started to sort the documents into his own categories. Those with blue flags he put into their own divider. Next, he allocated red flags to those documents which had real potential to harm him, but which he was forced to concede would not qualify for insertion amongst the blue flags. Any which were anodyne in their content, so as not to merit a place in either the blue or red categories, he flagged with yellow Post-its.

He turned to the file of emails. These were more of a problem. Several had attached documents, some of which he could identify within the dividers of the other file. A disturbing number of her private emails now went into the red divider. These would take some explaining, but mendacity came easily to him.

He had gambled at the time that she would not want to retain any of the digital images that he had emailed to her. She had never struck him as having anything of the avenging angel about her. But then again, he had been wrong in failing to predict her willingness to go to the press, so he could just as well be wrong on this score also. In that event he might have to resort to plan B. Although the emails were not traceable to him, he would have to 'lose' his personal laptop for the time being. A temporary inconvenience, he told himself, but necessary nonetheless.

As he re-read the file, he realised that she had referred in her mails to the briefing memos that he had prepared for doctors and other members of the medical profession who had been due to appear on radio or TV interviews. These were the ones that he had emailed to his opposite numbers in other pharmaceutical companies in order to get their 'buy-in' to the script. These were the dangerous ones, because he or his department had drafted almost all of them.

It would be all too easy for some quick-minded lawyer to retrieve the BBC's archives of its flagship *Today* interviews in order to compare the spoken answers given by the 'experts' with his briefing memos. Such an exercise would not make comfortable reading in any courtroom, and certainly not from his perspective.

There was also a fair chance that the memos would be amongst the material that had been seized from Cat's flat. He would learn if that proved to be the case in due course. What was important was that very few of the memos that had the greatest potential to damage him were included within the two files in front of him.

He was puzzled by that.

He made a note to remind himself to ask one of his lawyer mates when the company would get to see these papers. The question of course assumed that Cat still had possession of them before the lawyers swooped on her flat. If they were not there, and if they had not been stored on her laptop, then he should be off the hook. If they were, then he would have to do some serious thinking. They would qualify for bright scarlet flags, and plenty of them!

He realised that, with hindsight, he should have ensured that the chief had been copied in, if only by way of insurance against precisely this eventuality.

He also reminded himself that it was always possible that she had given them to the journalist. But then again, if Baxter had seen them, surely he would have used them in his article? Yet he had not even mentioned them. That was potentially reassuring, at least in a relative sense.

But then, what if they were playing a long game, and were intending to use those documents as part of some defence of justification, or worse still whistle-blowing? That would really get the chief's blood boiling.

Fuck, he really had underestimated her. This was surely hell's fury made incarnate, and they were his bollocks above the raging fires.

Focus, he told himself. Right now, he needed to concentrate on getting hold of these papers, or at least ensure that they did not feature in the lawsuit. Step one was to prevail on the poodle, what was her name, ah yes, Maria, to let him see the disclosure when it arrived. Step two was to ascertain how much of the potentially damaging material could be used in court by the lawyers.

He added this to the list of issues for him to run past his contact.

Step three was to get his hands on her statement. He knew how these orders worked. Cat will have been told by the judge to 'fess up' to the whereabouts of any other document that belonged to the company which she had acquired and retained. Her answer would tell him where to look.

He weighed up the advantages of contacting Cat, if only to shake her confidence. On the one hand, she had come this far, so it was doubtful whether she could be persuaded to bottle now. On the other, there was also the real possibility that she had not expected the reaction from the company to be quite so aggressive or rapid. So, there was perhaps a real chance to rattle her cage.

He would ponder that over a drink later.

In the meantime, he needed to invent a pretext whereby he could gain access to the files. Then he needed to create a reason why he should speak with this Maria girl, then put her at her ease, and inveigle her into his trust.

Time to call in that favour from that lawyer who knew how to sail close to the wind without actually capsizing.

He reached for his mobile.

Chapter 8

The keeper saw Joey coming towards him in his open-backed truck, his mongrel poking its head from behind the rear of the cab, barking at anything it saw that took his fancy. That's rather like his owner, chuckled Charlie to himself. At heart, he was truly fond of the lad, and had helped him develop as a youngster, partly through loyalty to his mother.

He slowed down to pull in at a narrow point in the lane, so that Joey and he would pass close by, making it rude for the lad to drive on without a word.

'Hey, Joey,' he said through the open windows.

'Charlie, how's it going?'

'Oh, the usual aches and pains, but can't complain. I suppose it's a bit early for you to be getting ready for milking time?'

'Yep, just been over to meet with the manager. There's talk of increasing the size of the herd in the autumn.'

'Oh aye?'

'Yep, but I've got my doubts if the farm is to stay organic. These Herefords have got a fair appetite, and them meadows can only hold the stock for a few months a year at best after they've taken off the silage. And it's been a sight less than four months these past few years, what with all this rain.'

'Well,' said Charlie diplomatically, 'Mr Henderson's been trained at agricultural college, and he's been right most other times he's made changes. Might be best to support him on this as well, unless of course you're worried about the extra hours you'll need to spend tending the herd?'

'No, it's not that, Charlie,' protested Joey, rather too quickly. When Charlie gave him a knowing look, he added, 'But why d'you ask that?'

'Oh, nothing special, Joey, it's just that I happened to notice these past weeks that you've been taking the herd in and out at odd times.'

'What! No, regular as clockwork I am. That's what the girls like. But I won't deny that I like to lead what they call a balanced lifestyle.'

'Is that right?' said Charlie, noticing that Joey wouldn't hold his eye.

'It's all part of a structured wellbeing plan. You see ...'

'Now, the reason I ask, Joey,' Charlie interrupted, 'is that we both know that the old barn back up yonder hill is off limits, but I've seen your truck pulled up at the end of the lane sometimes both mornings and evenings. And I can think of only one reason why you'd be parked up there at those times.'

Joey looked across the opposite fields before answering, searching for inspiration. If he'd thought even for a moment, he'd have realised that a straightforward admission would have the sensible course.

'Well, I'm not saying that you're right, Charlie. But let's say you were, with the hours that I work, it's the devil's own job to find some privacy, and ...'

'Joey, I'm not judging you. I'm asking you to think of someone other than yourself. You and I both know the reason why the place is off limits. Have you given any thought to what it'd do to Jamie if he found out that you were using it?'

Joey's feet shuffled on the cab floor. This time he said nothing.

'Joey, his heart is broke bad enough as it is. You know that he'd never do this to you, and it was him that gave you the break to have this job.'

Still silence.

'Joey. I'm asking you nice and proper, like. You know I'm not one to go telling tales behind your back. I'm asking you to show some respect for the man, some decency. And I know you've got that in you.'

Joey nodded, reluctantly.

'Okay, Charlie.'

Not enough, thought Charlie. He held out his hand to the younger man.

'Shake on it?'

With equal reluctance, Joey took the proffered hand and they shook. Both understood the import of that gesture within the unwritten code of the countryside, as the seal was placed on their private pact.

*

Tomo and Cat had just returned from the shops with a pay-as-you-go phone. She had spent time entering from her address book the key numbers that she needed to call over the next few days. These had included those of the admin team on the news Desk at *The Daily Chronicle*. She had asked them to pass on her temporary number to Ken Baxter, and have him call her.

Whilst she was still inputting other details, her phone rang.

It was Ken. She was impressed.

Now she would find out whether she was to be abandoned to the wolves, or whether his employers would be true to their word.

'Hi, Ken. Thanks for calling me back.'

'No sweat, Cat. But I see from the file of papers which the secret police left with me that you have also been dragged into this.'

'Too right. They turned over my place yesterday. And they've got my laptop and mobile as well. Actually, not the company, but the other fella.'

'Ditto, Cat. But look, I thought I should touch base and confirm that the editor will cover your defence costs. You should be getting a letter from our lawyers to that effect. It will probably be hand-delivered later today or tomorrow. They can also help you find a good firm if that helps.'

'Thanks, Ken. That's really appreciated.'

'Whilst we're speaking, I don't suppose you had a chance before the suits turned up to check whether you'd be able to get your hands on those other documents? It's just that my editor would really appreciate knowing one way or the other.'

'Actually, Ken, it's the first thing I'm going to do once we end this call.'

'Okay, then I'll let you get on with it. Good to speak.'

'You too. Bye for now.'

*

Ted Fisher loathed having to work on his weekends. He had little enough time with his fiancée as it was, and he regarded having to work with the Mamba as a major intrusion into his private life; almost a violation. And, as if his cup of joy was not already spilling over, he had received yet another email from her marked 'Urgent!'

As if!

He'd had the good sense to keep his mobile on silent. A glance showed both a missed call and a text from her within the last half hour. He counted the minutes before his inbox announced another chasing email from her team.

Reluctantly, he opened her email:

Ted. Can you please give me a call as soon as is convenient. I wish to discuss the small matter which arose at the end of meeting yesterday.
Your early response <u>today</u> would be appreciated.

Here we go, thought Ted. He could guess what the Mamba wanted him to do, and he was not about to play ball.

He had already called one of his barrister friends who was hot on data protection law. He preferred not to run the point past the company's lawyers, since he was fairly certain that they would advise that the company's position had been compromised.

His friend had duly confirmed his worst fears.

In addition to putting their hand up in front of the court and disclosing the data breach to Symonds' team, the company's compliance officer – namely Ted's head of department – now had an immediate obligation to report to the relevant authorities the unlawful hacking of an ex-employee's email account.

His friend had added that, since these sorts of mistakes occurred all the time, if one made a confession straight away, one was likely to get away with a mild reprimand.

The danger, his friend advised, lay in delay: the greater the lapse of time between the event and its reporting, the more sinister the motives for such delay would appear, and the more severe would be the ultimate sanctions. He strongly advocated that, in this case, the client should take the swift and lawful path.

Bloody great, Ted had thought. No matter how carefully one prepared for these cases, somehow, somewhere, someone within the team would screw up.

Despite the gloom, he could still smile to himself. The fuck-up had occurred on the Mamba's watch. That would be a source of much merriment within his department. Better still, it might even rein her in.

So, time to give the Mamba the good news. He might even enjoy it.

He dialled through to her office. As expected, she did not answer the phone herself, which he found especially offensive for some reason today. Eventually, one of her poodles put her on the line.

The Mamba's cold voice heralded the start of the conversation.

'Ted. Good of you to respond so promptly,' she began with icy sarcasm. 'I'm aware that we did not deal in our meeting with the matter of the girl's personal email account and its various messages.'

'On the contrary, Barbara,' he replied. 'We did deal with it. And I gave you my advice. I told you that, subject to checking with external counsel, we must disclose the full facts to the court and to Miss Symonds' lawyers, once we know who they are. And we must do so by Monday at the latest.'

'Ah yes, now that you mention it, you did say something along those lines, Ted. But we have not minuted it as your advice,' she confirmed coldly.

'That's hardly surprising, Barbara, since you're not a lawyer. Fortunately for the company, we lawyers are required to make full notes of meetings.' Then he added: 'Which, for the record, I did.'

Before she could reply, Ted fired his Exocet.

'And I ought to add, Barbara, that, since speaking with specialist external counsel, there are yet further steps that the company is legally obliged to take in relation to the illegal hacking of that email account.'

There was a discernible pause before Barbara commenced her retort.

'Well, we'll come to that if we have to,' she said curtly. 'But for the time being I want you to consider a different avenue, which I'll run past you if you don't mind. It will only take a minute or two.'

'I'm all ears,' he replied, trying to disguise his insincerity.

'Now. You told us at the meeting that we could have obtained an order from the court giving us access to both email accounts. Correct?'

'It's probable, yes,' he conceded.

'So, I would like you to think about an application for a new disclosure order limited to the girl's personal email account.'

'She is called Catriona Symonds. And she is not a girl.'

'So you say. Now, the order would be against both the girl and her service provider. Our evidence can simply record the fact that we discovered that she used her private email account at the office to send material that is confidential to the company.'

This time she paused, inviting him to respond.

'Well, don't assume that I'm buying into the idea,' he replied. 'In fact, I've got some rather bad news for you. But I'll save that for when you've finished.'

'Also,' she continued, effecting to ignore him, 'I've been re-reading your note on our duty to disclose all relevant facts to the court when we applied for our order against the girl. You also referred to the company's *continuing duty* to disclose new facts as soon as we became aware of them. Have I got that right?'

'That's a fair summary of the position, but only up to a point,' answered Ted, wondering where she was going with this. But before she could continue, he added, 'The key words in your summary are "when we applied for the order". As you will recall, Barbara, my concern is that someone in your department had become aware of the other email account *before* we appeared in front of the judge.'

That was a low blow, but she had never abided by the Queensbury Rules herself, so he saw no reason to conform himself.

She ignored the barb.

'And that duty extends, as I understand it,' she continued, 'to any document in either electronic or hard form to which the girl gained access. Right again?'

'Right enough, as a statement of basic principle,' he acknowledged. 'But don't assume that such a duty confers on the company a free pass to trample on her legal rights.'

He saw where this was going, and he was not going to allow his department to become involved in it. Again, she ignored his unhelpful intervention.

'Just bear with me on this,' she continued. 'So, what I have in mind is this. We make the application as I've suggested, or one which your brief is happy with. We tell the court that we found out about the email account just as we were going to court, but that intelligence never reached the legal team. Meanwhile, we explain that we are disclosing these facts in order to discharge what you say is our continuing duty to the court. The resulting order then allows us to access emails sent from that account, and entitles us to use the evidence which we already know is there. Where is the problem in that?'

She spoke those last words with a note of triumph in her voice.

'Oh, so that's all right then, is it?' he retorted, imitating the director's sarcasm and seeking to control both his rising anger and his desire to ridicule her plan.

'So, your strategy is simple. We commit a flagrant breach of data protection laws. We conceal this fact from the court, from the authorities, and from the girl – as you call her – and her lawyers. We then make your proposed application and, in doing so, again conceal the truth from the court. Have I got that about right?' He let his question hang in the air, and then added, 'And you confidently expect to get away with that? Oh yes, and you're also expecting the Legal Department and the external lawyers to go along with this deceit?'

He laid the emphasis on that last word.

'What I expect, Ted,' she replied icily, 'is full co-operation from your department – and you in particular – so as to achieve what the board is determined will be an important victory for the company – and even for the industry. If you believe that your career here is going to prosper as a result of your obstructive and, I have to say, confrontational attitude, then I invite you to reconsider. And now would be a good time.'

He had wondered how long it would take her pull rank on him. He had over-estimated her. He had assumed that she would put up a more robust defence of her scheme before she pulled that obtuse arrow from her quiver.

But his suit of armour was made of reinforced steel, manufactured in Great Britain under the label *The Rule of Law*.

He replied with his well-rehearsed response. 'You know perfectly well how it works, Barbara. You or the board come up with initiatives, some of which are good, I accept, and some of which on proper analysis might not be so clever. It's up to either the lawyers or the number-crunchers to advise the company which side of the fence any particular idea falls. We all have the same goal, or at least I should hope we do. I certainly do. Do I need to remind you?'

He enjoyed the silence.

'Plainly I do. It is to ensure that the company acts at all times both in accordance with all applicable laws and in the best interests of its share-holders. It follows, Barbara, that if at any time a member of the Legal Department – or for that matter any department – has reason to believe that the interests of the shareholders and the instructions of the directors are in conflict, by which I mean in conflict with any applicable law, then he or she has a duty to record and report that.'

'Spare me the lecture, Ted. I know the rules.'

'I'm very gratified to hear that, Barbara, especially since you were the one who first mentioned career prospects.'

Maybe that was not so wise, he thought, but by God he enjoyed it. Then he continued: 'One of the major differences between our two departments is that I and my colleagues have to live to fight another day,

Barbara. We also have to abide by professional rules and codes of conduct. Those restraints might seem a little quaint and inconvenient to you right now, but that's the deal. And the advice that you are being given by the lawyers, as has been confirmed by external counsel, is that the company needs to come clean right now. That is the position, I'm afraid, and that is the advice which the board will receive from me and from the Legal Department on Monday morning. And that advice will now reference this conference.'

He could feel the venom with which she spat her next words. Until that moment, he had not truly appreciated how much he really detested her. 'Oh, do spare me the sanctimonious sermon, Ted. You really do have a gift for the tedious when you put your mind to it.'

Well, he mused, you didn't get to become head of the Gestapo without punching your way out of a few skirmishes, and he waited while Barbara did just that.

Without hesitation, she continued. 'And it is my department's role, Ted, to ensure that your advice is premised on the right facts. And, as the director charged with getting the right result, it is also my duty to ensure that you properly appreciate how important this whole business is for the company. And just right now, I am not at all convinced that you have got the message.'

'We'll have to agree to disagree on that, Barbara.'

It was almost time to deliver the killer blow, but he bided his time.

'My instructions are clear,' she continued. 'And they come from the top. And to be clear, they are explicitly intended to form the basis of your department's instructions to the external lawyers. And just so that there is no misunderstanding, those instructions are that we are to use whatever tactics it takes to win this fight. Do I make myself clear?'

He declined to answer, sensing a caveat.

Sure enough, it came. 'So,' she continued, 'if that means bending the rules a little in order to win the fight, then so be it. I want you to be in no doubt that I intend to ensure that those instructions are carried out to the letter. The external lawyers have done well so far, but I am not about to risk this entire campaign just because you want to prioritise your professional principles above the interests of the company.'

He checked his phone. Yes, it was still recording.

'With respect, Barbara,' he retorted, meaning that he intended none, 'you are missing the point. It is precisely because I place the interests of the company at the top of my priorities that I have given the advice that I have. If you wish to question that advice, then by all means let us defer to our external counsel in order to seek their opinion on the matter. I can set up a telecom in a matter of minutes.'

The gauntlet was now thrown at her feet, perhaps rather too obviously. Before she elected to retrieve it, he added his bombshell.

'I mentioned at the start of this conversation the requirement to notify not just Ms Symonds and her legal team, but also the proper authorities. The appropriate channel by which that is to be done is through the company's compliance officer. And the advice of external counsel is that if the company were to delay reporting to its officer that a private email account had been hacked by the company's IT personnel on the instructions of someone in your department, the consequences for the company, and those responsible for any subsequent concealment, will be severe.'

Now it was his turn to pause. It reminded him of one of those old *World at War* films of a Lancaster Bomber dropping its ordinance over Nazi Germany, the camera catching the almost balletic descent of the bombs as if in slow motion. He could almost hear that ordinance detonate.

Pure joy.

'Oh, and just so that we are clear, that will include disclosure of the fact that the new home address of Miss Symonds was obtained illegally.' When that met with silence, he continued. 'Which of course would render unlawful our purported service and enforcement – I can explain those terms if you wish – of the court orders that we supposedly obtained against Miss Symonds.'

Silence is golden, he mused.

'So, would you like me to set up that telecon with counsel on Monday morning? He's all lined up. A phone call from me is all it would take.' And then, just for added pleasure: 'Oh, and just one other thing. The report to the compliance officer would of course need to come from you as head of your department, since the breach of data protection occurred on your watch.'

He was already lining up the beers.

However, a seasoned political animal like Barbara Spooner knew when and how to pick her fights. She had already chosen an avenue which she was confident would bear more fruit.

'I don't think that will be necessary, Ted,' she said. 'I had hoped to avoid going over your head, but it seems that I have no alternative. So, thank you for your time. I'll see you at the meeting on Monday morning.'

The line went dead.

So that was her game. But if the Mamba was going pull rank on him, then he would have to prepare a detailed memorandum for his head of department. And that meant that he would have to get his report to him, in hard copy, before Monday morning. He cursed silently as he clocked the fact that he would now have to waste part of his Sunday on this.

Great! He needed a drink.

*

'Ali?'

'Hey, Cat! I get to speak to you at last,' exclaimed Ali.

'I'm sorry if I've been hard to get.'

'No problem, babe. But this isn't the mobile number that I have for you in my contacts. Is this a new phone?'

'No, it's just temporary. One of these pay-as-you-go jobs.'

'Cat, you've not gone and lost your phone again have you?'

'No. It's not that, Ali. I'll explain later, because it's part of what I need to talk to you about. I've just picked this one up.'

'Sounds mysterious, babe.'

'Not really, Ali, but I'll explain later, as I said.'

Ali knew her well enough to leave that that one to soak a while. 'Look,' she said, 'I'm sorry not to have replied to your texts. I did the usual thing of leaving the mobile on all day and all night, and then forgot to recharge it when I got up. Dumb, or what! Anyway, I've just read your message.'

'Thanks for calling back so soon.'

'No worries, babe. But it sounds as though Big Brother has turned nasty. Is this to do with that bastard who took control of your life last year?'

A short pause while Cat thought about the question. The right answer was probably yes, or at least rather more yes than no, if she was being honest with herself. But she wasn't really sure that she wanted to be right now.

'Well,' she began. 'There's a long and a short answer. The short answer is more no than yes, but can we not get into that right now, please, Ali, because there are more important things that I want to talk about with you.'

An audible sigh of disappointment in return.

'OK, agreed, but only for the time being. But you know me. I'm never satisfied until I've had all the juicy details.'

It was Ali's turn to check herself for a moment's reflection. There was no giggle in reply from Cat. And that wasn't the Cat she knew. She sensed, given the tone in Cat's voice, that this was not the time for that. She started again.

'Sorry, Cat. I'm not being very sensitive. I got the vibes from your message that you wanted to talk about this new ... You called it a turn of events. Anyway, whatever it is, your message was fairly oblique.'

'Sorry about that, Ali. I found your number in an old diary, and I needed to be sure that I was messaging the right person. But yes, I do want to talk to you, but only if you don't mind,' replied Cat.

'Of course I don't, babe.'

'You see,' continued Cat, 'you remember that I told you that I had decided to blow the whistle last week on what Tomo would call were some dark deeds by my former employer.'

'Sure, I remember that.'

'Well, I went ahead with it, and it's landed me in some fairly deep, you know ... manure, as Tomo calls it.'

'Holy shit, Cat!'

'Yep, I guess you could call it that.'

'No, sorry, that's not ... Oh, forget it,' she replied, belatedly appreciating Cat's pun. 'Shall we meet up and discuss it, rather than doing it over the phone?'

'Thanks, Ali, I'd like that. But I don't want to bore you with all the detail, but I would really appreciate some time with you.'

'Hey, that's what friends are for, isn't it,' chirped Ali.

'There's a song about that, babe.'

'Now don't start that again ...'

They both managed a giggle as they re-lived their *Jungle Book* memory from school days.

'Seriously, babe, that's what I'm here for. In actual fact, Jez was on the phone just now asking me when we were next due to have dinner with you and your new hunk. I told him that you and I had planned some catch-up time this afternoon, but we could make a date for next Friday. Is that good for you?'

'Uh-huh, that should be fine. Actually, it's the day that I'm due to turn up in court, so I'll probably need a few drinks.'

A stunned silence.

'Court! What's this about going to court?' exclaimed Ali. 'You didn't mention that in your message. Nor in any email. In actual fact, you haven't replied to any of my mails, and I was starting to feel a bit miffed, to tell you the truth.'

'That's because my laptop was seized, you know, confiscated,' replied Cat.

Another silence.

'What did you say, Cat?'

Cat reconsidered for a moment. She hated that word, 'confiscated'. It reminded her of school rules and bossy prefects during her first years at boarding school with Ali.

'Actually, not really confiscated but taken away by what I've called "Women in Black Suits". Well, mostly women. There were a couple of guys too. There's a court order that has allowed them to copy the contents and hand that all over to some independent lawyer. They said that I would get it back in a day or so.'

The penny was dropping fast.

'Fuck, Cat. That sounds like heavy shit, as Jezza would say!' exclaimed Ali. 'I was trying to be flippant when I spoke of Big Brother, but that really is the Thought Police. Shit, you mean they came busting into your home and just took all your personal data, your life, almost? This is scary stuff, Cat.'

'Tell me about it.'

Ali realised just how much data she probably stored on her own laptop, business as well as personal.

'The thing is, Ali, I had them here yesterday going through all my possessions. They took away some stuff, but they were really after my laptop. They say that they're looking for the confidential documents that I helped myself to.'

'Who's they?' asked Ali.

'The black suits acting for my ex-employer.'

'So this is not about the fellow you were seeing – the one that was into all that kinky stuff?' asked Ali, missing the point.

'Oh God, no,' said Cat. 'No. I could deal with him now easily enough. In fact, I'll need to eventually, but that's a different matter. No, this is all to do with the article that came out on Thursday.'

'Of course! Jezza asked me about it earlier today. It's that big story you were going to break about the company and its sweeteners. I missed it, annoyingly, but apparently it was on the news briefly yesterday morning.'

'Uh-huh,' replied Cat, almost with relief that they had got to this point. 'Talk about opening up a hornets' nest. I hadn't expected this sort of reaction from them. And certainly not as fast as this either. Nor was the paper by the sound of it.'

'OK. So they turned over your flat, saying they're looking for stuff which they say is theirs. So what did they take away?'

Cat thought about how to phrase her reply. She was coming to the point on which she really needed Ali's assistance – and quickly.

'Well,' she began, cautiously. 'Apart from the laptop and mobile, and the stuff that's on there – we'll come to that in a moment – they didn't give the impression that they had found any of the important stuff which they'd been looking for. I'll explain more when we meet. I've had to spend most of today wading through their evidence. What they're really after are the documents which they say I must have given to the paper.'

'And did you?' asked Ali, before she could think. 'No, sorry. Don't answer that,' she corrected herself. She knew Cat too well, and this was certainly not the right time for any confessions.

'So where does this go from here?' she asked.

'Well, that's partly what the hearing next Friday is all about. Tomo has been explaining it to me. It gets pretty complicated. I'll tell you in more detail when we meet. Can you still make later today, this evening even?'

'Sure. Your place or mine? I'm easy.'

Cat welcomed the opportunity to get away from all the papers in her flat, and they would only be a distraction.

'I'll come to you, shall I?'

Chapter 9

Chuck Thompson clinked the ice around in the glass of his second large G&T. He had been invited out to a drinks party that evening, but thought it wise to fortify himself first. They would probably serve that awful fizzy wine from Italy, which he couldn't abide. And it was far too pricey for what it was, especially when there were so many cheap offers in town for decent champagne.

He was also revisiting his former idea of a cryptic threat to Kitty. Now suitably emboldened by his beverage, he was crafting something more than just a warning shot. It would need to be seemingly innocent to the outside world, not malicious, yet containing a menace which would register with her.

He was reluctant to send an image of her *in flagrante* from his own email address, despite the temptation. On the other hand, she needed to know that, as far as he was concerned, the gloves were off. And what better way to leave her in no doubt than to send her an image that she alone would recognise.

His logic was that, since he knew how to sell, he would surely be able to sell uncertainty, apprehension even, but best of all self-doubt. And he reckoned that he had come up with the perfect cover. He had selected a gem, which he had discreetly edited.

This one showed auburn hair, perfectly plaited down a naked back, entwined with a thin chord that descended until it connected with two wrists, also tied together, above the unmistakable crevice suggesting the curves of a perfectly round pair of buttocks below. Nothing more; it said everything he wanted to, and spoke louder than any words. Beneath it, an innocent question"

> *Whatever happened to our grand idea of creating an online exhibition? We were going to call it 'Art posing as pornography – or pornography masquerading as art?' I know it's been done before, but I'm game if you are.*

Was it too subliminal? Surely not. Kitty would know they were her buttocks, her wrists, her hair. And there would be plenty of others very similar to that on the internet to confuse an objective reader, in case anyone else saw it.

But the message was clear: '*There's plenty more where these came from, so don't fuck with me.*'

Except you did, he thought, sniggering to himself. And they were good fucks, weren't they? We both know that. No, he really liked it. Sure, there was a risk, but he reckoned that with stakes this high it was about time that he rolled the dice. He took a long swig from his glass.

So, to her mobile … or as an email. No, mobile. More direct, he thought. She won't miss this one, he thought.

He went upstairs to change for the party.

*

A thin length of twine ran down the wall at the rear of the barn. Joey Roberts pulled on it, and the end of a rope emerged from inside the large aperture above him. Attached to the rope was a ladder, which he slowly pulled up, then outwards and then gradually lowered it until it lay propped against the wall.

He dragged a large stone to secure the base, then shimmied up the ladder. Inside, he had piled up old hay bales so as to form steps down to the base of the barn. On the far side lay a thick mat of loose hay, a good three feet thick.

This was his 'den,' his 'lovers' nest' as he liked to call it.

He had brought a large backpack in which he carried the equipment and refreshments that he regarded as essential for the rendezvous that he had planned later that evening with that obliging young girl from the next-door village.

Once he was satisfied that his preparations were complete, and conscious of the hour, he trotted down the lane back to his car, and headed off to the dairy in readiness for that evening's milking.

He was a bit early, but the cows wouldn't mind an early feed.

*

Cat had suggested that they opt for spritzers before they hit anything stronger. She needed a clear head for what she had to say. And she was conscious that she had done fairly well on the booze with Tomo the night before.

Ali had wasted no time in steering their conversation back towards the events of the previous day and their consequences.

'So, the way you said it,' she began, 'or at least the way I understood it, is that these guys, whoever they are, have taken your laptop and mobile away somewhere so that they can access whatever is on there. Is that about it?'

Cat tried to recall accurately what Tomo had explained to her.

'Not exactly. Apparently, the company does not get to see any of the material that's on my devices, as lawyers call them, until the court gives them permission, or we – that's the paper and me – give our consent. That's what's up for grabs at the hearing next week. Tomo said that this could either be a formality, whereby everything gets rolled over to another day, or it could get complicated. I don't really understand the legal side. But right now, and I mean by Monday evening, I have to tell the company, or is it the court, maybe both, not only what documents I've got which belong to them, but more importantly for me at least where they are likely to be right now.'

Cat paused while she searched for the words with which to ask for the favour that she needed.

'And there's something else?' asked Ali, intuitively.

'The thing is, Ali, that Tomo says that either he or my solicitor – I'm meeting with her on Monday – need to see all these documents first before we actually hand them over to the independent lawyer.'

'What, everything?' asked Ali.

'No, I don't think so. Just all the documents that I've got in my possession which could be regarded as the property of the company. It doesn't matter whether they are confidential or not. There's a longer phrase about that, but I won't confuse things any more, even if I could remember it. Tomo wants to see all this stuff so that he can advise me before it gets handed over. Something about the Fifth Amendment.'

'OK. I follow you so far,' said Ali. 'So where's the problem? Don't you just hand over to him all the stuff that you've got —assuming that the suits, as you call them, didn't take them all? It's surely just a question of timing?'

Cat swallowed hard. Come on, she told herself. This is no big deal. You're acting like you're a teenager. Just get on with it.

'Well, you see, Ali. The thing is that I don't actually have the important stuff. I mean, not physically.'

'So. You're off the hook, then, aren't you?' said Ali.

Cat found Ali's announcement irritating, not least because it was spoken with a confidence which was unjustified, or at best premature.

'No. Not really.' She wished that Ali wouldn't be so damned obtuse. 'No,' she continued. 'I meant that I don't have them in my physical possession, but I do know where they are. Or at least, I mean I know where they were. Or at least where I remember seeing them last.'

Go on, just get it out, Cat urged herself. But still Ali seemed to dither, which was so unlike her. She usually prided herself on being quick-witted. She was certainly not a slow thinker.

Cat bit her lip in readiness, and was about to speak.

Instead, she watched Ali as the penny finally dropped.

'Cat, are you telling me that these documents are where I'm thinking they are, or rather where they last were?'

Another pause as Ali realised where this was leading.

'And ... Oh no. Don't tell me. You're not about to ask me to do what I think you're about to ask me, are you?'

Well, Cat thought to herself, a least they had got there. They had taken a roundabout sort of journey along the way, but they were there.

'Ali, you're the only one I can ask. After the way it all ended with Jamie, I just don't feel that I can just call him up, you know, out of the blue. I mean, it's been several months since ... you know.'

Alison had a fiery temper, but she did her best to restrain it now.

'Of course, I bloody well know. Look, Cat, darling. I love you. You know I do. But have you any idea of the damage that you did? The damage that I and Jamie have had to live with every day, every week? You just about broke his heart.'

'Don't you think I know that, Ali?'

'No, come to think of it, you did break his heart. He's not been out with another girl, he's barely spoken to one, since you let that vile marketing spiv emasculate Jamie with his home movies and his venomous emails.'

'Ali, that's unfair. I didn't let him do anything of the sort,' retorted Cat, fighting back her tears. 'And it wasn't just Jamie that got hurt because of all that. You of all people should realise that, Ali.'

'OK, sorry. I know that you were not the cause of that. But you should not underestimate the extent of the injury that Jamie suffered. You have at least been able to move on. You've found a man you can truly fall in love with. But not Jamie. Just the mention of your name re-opens the old wounds.'

Cat had no adequate riposte to that statement, and had no reason to doubt its veracity. That was partly why she had not contacted Jamie since they had split up.

There followed a long silence whilst each of them searched for the right words with which to continue their conversation.

In the end, it was Ali who was the first to speak.

'Jamie's my brother, Cat. And it's my duty to protect him. Right now, the last thing he needs is more grief. Especially coming from you.'

Cat had known that this was going to be hard. She hated conversations like this. She hesitatingly wondered whether in hindsight it would have been better to have continued their telephone conversation instead. She doubted it. She had always preferred face-to-face dialogue. And Tomo had told her this was urgent. She and Ali went back a long way, and were used to discussing things in a mature, restrained manner.

Cat's instinct told her to give it one last go.

'Ali, you know me well enough. Jamie is the last person I would ever have want to hurt. I've apologised to him, and to you, God knows how many times. You know I never meant it to happen that way. No, more than that, I never meant it to happen at all. How I wish that it never had. But I can't turn the clock back, any more than he can. I just ...'

But then she broke. She tried to stop the tears, but they still came as she spluttered an apology, conscious that Tomo had told her to be strong. Yet here she was, not five hours since he had imparted his advice, already dissolving into a weeping schoolgirl.

Ali came to sit beside her, holding out a tissue.

'Hey, Cat, I'm sorry it came out like that. It was unfair.'

Cat shook her head.

'No, Ali. You're right.'

She could feel her shield gradually slipping, exposing her torso to the emotional javelins against which she had resolved to stand firm.

'I shouldn't have said that, Cat. Forgive me?'

Cat nodded, blowing her nose and trying to stifle the tears. She reached for the words that Tomo had used. She knew he was right when he had advised that her best approach was to appeal to Ali's good sense.

'Ali, I just think that Jamie would take it better if the approach came from you, rather than from the lawyers, or worse still from me. No, let me finish. I need to give you the full picture, because I don't want you to think that I've held stuff back.'

She looked at Ali.

'Okay? Will you hear me out?'

Ali nodded quickly.

'Well. There are two parts to this. On the downside, I have to comply with this court order that's been served on me. You'll have heard it called an injunction, right?'

Ali nodded again.

'Okay, so it orders me to tell the court what documents I know exist and where they are. Tomo tells me that I've got no choice in this, and that if I get caught lying then I risk going to jail. I know where I left them, Ali. What I don't know is whether they are still there, and the last thing I want is to have the company's lawyers crawling all over Jamie's house and bringing his name into this. Tomo says that's what will happen if I just say where I think the documents are. But that won't happen if I've already given the documents to my lawyers. So that's the first reason for asking you.'

She took a breath.

'The next bit . . .'

'You mean the upside?' asked Ali.

'Well, it's only an upside in that it is something that I need. It's not about the order. It's about the case, but not the order itself. And I'll be utterly straight with you. The reason that I need those documents, if Jamie still has them, is that I don't believe that I can prove my case, you know, as to why I blew the whistle in the first place, without them. I need them to defend myself and to prove what they did.'

'And what you're asking,' said Ali, 'is that you want me to act as your go-between in order to obtain them?'

'I am, yes, Ali. Tomo says that there is another way. He says that my lawyers could ask Jamie for them, but I really don't want to go down that route. I think that would be just as bad for Jamie. So all in, I'm asking you to believe me Ali, that I'm honestly trying to do what I truly, truly believe will be best for Jamie.'

Alison seemed to appreciate the sense in this. She tried to detect the fault in the logic of Cat's argument, and in her request, but reluctantly acknowledged to herself that there was none to be found.

But she still had one major concern.

'And just so that we're clear, Cat, we are just talking about documents. You're not going to ask me as well to get Jamie to hand over any of those dreadful emails which that vile creep sent to him.'

She said it as a statement. It was not a question.

Either way, it hit Cat between the eyes. She stared at Ali for an eternity, since the thought had never even occurred.

She shook her head firmly.

'Ali, I told Tomo about him last night. About it all. Everything. And I mean everything, and that includes those fucking emails.'

'In every sense,' said Ali.

They both laughed at that, and it was enough to stifle Cat's tears.

'Ali, I was so scared that he would find me, you know, repulsive once I'd told him, and that I would lose him as well.'

This time she fought off the tears, or thought she had.

Ali gave her a hug.

'How did he take it?' she asked as only a caring friend could.

Cat smiled, as Ali wiped away the remains of a tear with her thumb.

'He was what you would call a brick.'

'That understanding, huh?'

'Better. He said that I was just as much a victim as Jamie was. And, to answer your question, he explained to me that we could use the ones he sent me, you know, of him fucking me, to bring the creep down. A sexual harassment claim. But to be honest, Ali, I'm not sure that I'm ready for that yet.'

'Well, there'll be time enough for that, I dare say, Cat.'

'Maybe, Ali. But I told him what you said.'

'Remind me.'

'You know, that if I didn't bring a complaint, then he'd only do it to the next girl that he grooms in that awful place.'

'Well, it's true, isn't it? These sorts of guys are serial offenders.'

'I know, Ali. But yesterday ...'

'When you told Tomo?'

Cat shook her head.

'No, I asked the lawyer supervising the search what was going to happen to the personal stuff that they would find on my laptop.'

'What did he say?'

Cat took a moment to think about it.

'Oh God, Ali. I cannot describe to you how I felt when the guy told me what they would do with my laptop and mobile.'

'Your mobile? Is that why I couldn't get hold of you? And why you didn't show up yesterday evening or call to apologise?'

'Yep. And they've still got it. They'll keep it until they're ready to return it.'

'So what did the guy say to you?'

'He told me that his IT technicians were going to provide him with copies of everything that is on my laptop and my mobile.'

'Everything?'

'That's what he said. I went into meltdown. I couldn't speak. It was as if he was telling me that I was going to have to go through it all over again, but this time with a bunch of lawyers gaping at the photos and videos of me.'

'Hold on,' interrupted Ali, 'surely Tomo can stop that?'

'He reckons he can stop it being used in this case, but not before all the IT guys and the lawyers have had a good look at them first.'

'And afterwards?'

'Tomo says that the harassment side of it is not what he calls his turf. He's going to ask one of the specialist lawyers in his chambers to deal with that.'

'But Cat, I'm no lawyer, but that company is not going to want those emails coming out in court, surely. They'll keep well away if they've got any sense.

'Maybe, but Tomo thinks that it will help me if the company get to know about the emails, even if they didn't come from any address at the office. But I've still got to prove that they were sent by that bastard.'

'Come on, Cat, who else would have sent them? More to the point, who else had the motive to send them to Jamie. That was more than malicious. That was pure evil.'

'*The devil incarnate* – isn't that the term?'

'And how.'

They fell silent, neither wanting to be the one to steer the conversation back towards Ali's earlier question. In the end, it was Ali who spoke.

'I think I know the answer, but is Tomo saying that he'll need Jamie to testify to bring that loathsome creep down.'

Cat thought about that.

'Actually, we didn't discuss that, because he said it wasn't his turf. But I would not ask Jamie unless he wanted to help. And it's not about the money, Ali, believe me. It's much more than that.'

'Hey babe, I know you better than that. But if you don't bring him down, he'll just keep on doing it to other girls.'

Cat nodded.

After a bit she said, 'You know, Ali, it's almost easier now that other people have seen them, or at least will have seen them.'

'I was thinking the same thing. In a funny sort of way, it could stop being a weakness, and would become a strength.'

'Except that I don't have all of the emails, Ali.'

'How many do you need? Surely one's enough?'

'I don't know, Ali. And I don't suppose I will until I've spoken to the specialist barrister.'

'Sure. But for now, we need to focus on those documents. Now that I understand the whole picture, I can see that they're the priority.'

Cat nodded, reaching out for Ali's hand.

'So, will you help me? Please?'

Ali did not need long to answer, and gave Cat a reassuring hug. 'You know I will, babe. I'll call Jamie tomorrow.'

Chapter 10

'Good morning, twenty-one Gray's Inn Fields,' answered the confident voice on the telephone. Mary-Anne had been the loyal and devoted servant of this set of barristers' chambers for many years. She had followed their migration from their cramped rooms in the Temple to these newly refurbished buildings in Gray's Inn overlooking the gardens, which were known as 'the Fields'. Hence the chambers' address.

'Morning, Mary-Anne,' replied the caller. 'This is Tom Butler. I trust that you are keeping well and healthy, as always?'

'Hello, Mr Butler,' answered Mary-Anne in her customarily convivial tone. 'I'm very well, thank you. And how about yourself?'

'Overworked and under-paid – that is, when I do eventually get paid. But that is not your concern.'

'Alas not. I'd soon sort that, mind you, if you were in these chambers. But for now, what can I do for you?'

'I was wondering whether Andrew Sutherland might be free to speak with me.'

'Just hold the line, Mr Butler. I know he's in chambers, but I'm not sure if

he has finished his telephone conference. Just bear with me a moment.'

Tom was on the point of returning these pleasantries, but the phone began playing the slow movement of one of Mozart's piano concertos, No. 19 if he was not mistaken, and mercifully performed at the right speed. He elected instead to indulge himself with this mellifluous melody for almost a minute. The recital was interrupted by an irritatingly high-pitched note, disturbing the tranquillity, as Mary-Anne abruptly announced that he was about to be 'put through'.

He was returned briefly to the concerto, before this was again interrupted by that confounded beep, and then: 'Hi Tom, what a pleasant surprise.'

Andrew Sutherland had this uncanny ability to be able to make each person with whom he spoke, either in person or electronically, to think that he or she was the most important individual to him at that time. He did not do this consciously. One had only to meet him – and indeed his parents – to learn that this was not some art which he had acquired through careful schooling. His entire family, who hailed from fine Yorkshire stock, were known and reputed to be one of the warmest and kindest people in the county. At the same time, like their ancestors, they embraced the Gospel with a passion and devotion that was an example to all who had the good fortune to share their company. Andrew's obvious intellect, and his polite and persuasive manner, had secured his appointment as one the youngest queen's counsel (as they were before the queen's death). He was of course now king's counsel.

'Andrew. Hi. Sorry to disturb you,' said Tom. 'I'm calling in connection with the injunction served on *The Daily Chronicle* and Miss Catriona Symonds last week by AlphaOm. I shall be acting for Catriona, and I understand that you have been instructed – or are about to be – by the newspaper. Is that about right?'

'Yes. That's right,' said Andrew. 'In fact, I've just come off the phone to them now. Looks as though it could be quite a spat.'

'My view precisely,' said Tom. 'Now, are you aware that your clients have agreed to underwrite Catriona's legal fees?'

'Yes, I've just been told that. Apparently, a letter has already gone out to that effect. And I suppose you'd like to know whether I am at liberty to not only discuss the case with you but also to work with you in formulating the defence?'

'Hah, no flies on you, Andrew! That was the principal purpose of my call, but there is another.'

'Well, let's deal with that point first. In short, I am at liberty to work with you and to discuss the case with you, and should be delighted to do so, if that is what your client on advice would wish me to do.'

'Indeed she does, Andrew. Thank you.'

'Not at all. So, before we go on, you said that you had another point.'

'Indeed I did. We'll come on to it in due course, I'm sure, but it concerns the scope of the material that, as part of the *quid pro quo*, Cat is obliged to make available to your clients.'

'Right, got that. I've made a note of that, and suggest that we deal with it in stages. So, the first is whether your client will confirm the statements that she made to my clients that led to the article.'

Tomo was expecting that.

'That's an easy one, Andrew. She will stand behind her statements and do whatever she can to help with the defence.'

'Excellent,' said Andrew. 'So, next, is your client willing to support a defence based on justification and public interest.'

That was also easy.

'In principle, absolutely,' said Tomo. 'It's early days, of course. But my instructions are that the piece which occupied the front page in your people's paper can be supported, if not by direct testimony then by documents which, all being well, we hope to be able to show are or were created by AlphaOm and are in their possession.'

'I'm relieved to hear that,' noted the older of the two. 'But I'm not reassured by your use of the past tense there, nor your use of the word "hope". Forensic technology is a thing of great wonder, but there are ways and means of bleaching out the past. By the time that we obtain a disclosure order against the claimants, the documentary trail – assuming it ever existed, even in electronic form – could have become squeaky clean.'

'Granted,' noted Tomo. 'Which is why I think we need to focus on what our clients say was – indeed, still is – the threat which AlphaOm were so anxious to neutralise. We start by showing that they have a vested interest in propagating the myth that the consumption of their artificial or refined sugars is not causative of the early onset of obesity or diabetes. We produce the claimants' marketing material that supports this, along with their material that suggests that their products might even help to combat those diseases. We produce their sales figures for all related products in that category. Then we refer to all the evidence to the contrary that proves the link between their products (amongst others) and the diseases. So far, nothing special, one might say, because that is all out in the public domain, agreed.'

'I'm following you so far, Tom.'

'Right, then we produce the text published by your clients, meanwhile seeking disclosure of that and other documents, referring to the claimants' unpublished research data that contradicts all their own published material. We know it exists, because Cat has a copy on her laptop ...'

'Sorry, Cat I presume is short for Catriona?'

'Apologies, that's right,' said Tomo. 'And I need to come back to that in a moment, but I just want to finish my line of thought.'

'Forgive me. Go on, I'm listening.'

'Okay. So, we then follow the research data evidence with the document, also quoted by your clients. That records the concerns internally expressed within the claimants that there exists a proven link between certain sweeteners and the tweaked insulin produced by them. It also records that the claimants categorised as "high" the risk that this market sensitive information could fall into the public domain.'

'Which is the thrust of the main lead in the article, no?'

'Precisely. So, then we produce the memo that goes from the head of marketing to the chief executive drawing attention to that intelligence, information, call it what you will. In short, that this goes right to the top.'

'Which is also the gist of the article – at least that is how I read it. But is this enough to get us home so far as our defence goes?'

'Well, I fully agree that that material would probably not be enough to establish a claim for personal injury against the claimants, but in my view it would help to get the court onside as regards justification.'

'Let me think about that,' said Andrew. 'On one view it is circumstantial evidence only, since we have no evidence that the chief executive replied to or reacted to the document – if, of course it is genuine. And before you answer that, I am going to assume that our common instructions will be that they are all genuine.'

'Those are indeed my instructions.'

'Excellent. But one of the things that concerned me about the article is that it suggested that there was a link between diabetes, on the one hand, and not just all sweeteners, but also one in particular ...'

'The claimants' best-seller?'

'Indeed, and it suggests that the link between that product and the claimants' own insulin-based products, or at least one of them, is deliberate. So my concern is, do we have any material with which to substantiate that assertion so far as it appears in the article?'

Tomo had expected this.

'Cat is adamant that there are documents that either exist or did at some point exist that will point strongly to that link, and even establish it outright. She is fairly sure that she had them in her possession at one time, and thinks she knows where they were, but cannot be sure that they still exist. The story is complicated, and I'm in the process of finalising her affidavit now. We are due to serve it this afternoon.'

'I see. And I don't suppose that you can give me any indication as to whether or not we are likely to be able to see these before Friday.'

'To use that time-honoured phrase, *as present advised*, I regret not, but Cat is working on it as we speak.'

'And what about this other suggestion, actually it is stronger than that, this assertion in the article, the one alleging some form of cartel?'

'Oh yes, what Cat dubbed "the diss campaign" – I rather like that – about trashing any form of dissent as regards pure health links.'

'The *diss* campaign. Yes, that's good,' said Andrew. 'What the article appears to have said is that the claimants acted in league with other pharmaceutical companies with a common purpose, and took active steps towards achieving it, of taking every opportunity to discredit any medical opinion that sought to demonstrate a direct link between refined sugar and both obesity and diabetes. So, my question is: do we have the material to support that assertion?'

'I fear the position as regards the existence and location of any relevant documents is very much the same.'

'Ah. As I feared.'

'Still early days, Andrew. Give Cat a chance.'

'Well, at least it's not in hell,' Andrew quipped, amused at his own droll wit.

'Actually,' replied Tomo, 'You are not far off the mark. That is one of the points that I wanted to mention.'

'That sounds ominous, Tom.'

'That rather depends how we play it, Andrew. I appreciate that what I am about to tell you relates primarily to Cat, but it does raise issues of motive. And I have Cat's authority to disclose this to you in confidence.'

'Now I'm really intrigued, Tom. And it goes without saying that I shall not pass this on to those instructing me without your client's permission.'

'No, I took that for granted, Andrew. So, there are two aspects to this; three to be more accurate. The first is that Cat had what began as an affair with her boss at the claimants, but what soon became something more disagreeable. I shall call it sexual bullying so as to avoid the more obvious labels. This went on for a period of several months, and ended more or less at the same time that she quit her job. And yes, it would not take a genius to realise that the two are not unconnected.'

'I see,' noted Andrew. 'But you say there's more?'

'I'm afraid so. Meanwhile, by which I mean before, during and after the duration of the affair with her boss, Cat was actually in a steady relationship with a young man who owns an estate in the country. Dorset actually. The boss had been aware of this throughout. However, as soon as the affair ended, and Cat had gone back to her young man, her boss began to send a series of emails to the young man attaching images of Cat, to quote Saint John's Gospel, "in the very act itself". The emails were malicious, and his intent was to destroy Cat's prospects with the young man. In which regard, I should add, his campaign was singularly successful.'

Andrew cogitated as he digested this. 'One hears about this sort of thing,' he said, as calmly as he could, 'but it is very different when one has to confront the reality of it.'

'Just so. I learnt about it over the weekend.'

'You said there were three things, as I recall. The third being?'

'Ah yes. That's to do with how I came into possession of this intelligence.'

'I suspected as much.'

'Still no flies there, Andrew. So, as you can imagine, Cat's relationship with her boyfriend did not survive the deployment of these foul communications. Several months later she bumped into me. After a time, we became what I believe is colloquially termed "an item". And, before you ask, yes, I have counselled in favour of someone wholly independent, but she will not hear of it.'

'There's nothing in the bar standard's rules that prevents you acting for her, Tom, as long as she knows the score. Your solicitors will see to that, no doubt.'

'In fact, it was I who put her in touch with them. We've got a right Rottweiler acting for her there, and I've recommended someone else in chambers to deal with the harassment and other employment issues.'

'Very wise, Tom.'

'So, my dilemma is, what if any use do I advise Cat to make of what I shall call the malevolent communications in these, as opposed to other, proceedings? On the one hand, it exposes her to the charge of revenge, thus potentially both distorting the strength of her evidence, and simultaneously weakening your clients' case. On the other, in order to explain and prove how she knew the documents to be genuine, she has to tell the court how she first got to know about them and then how she got hold of them. And the answer to that is partly pillow talk, and partly post-coital sleuthing by her at his house.'

'Yes, I see,' said Andrew. 'My instinctive view, but I'd want to think about it, is that if she is to establish the provenance of these documents, then she has little choice but to disclose the affair, and in the event that the claimants seek to deny it then she will need to produce these ... these, shall we say unchivalrous, emails.'

'That was rather my thinking, Andrew. Thank you. And thank you also for what I might call that inspirational description. I shall use that.'

Andrew pondered for a moment. 'Are your solicitors aware of this aspect of the case, Tom?'

'They are aware of the outline facts, but no more, following my telecon with them this morning.'

'But they will need to see the offensive material in order to advise your client properly, won't they?'

'For sure, Andrew, but Cat cannot supply that until she gets her laptop back, which could be either today or tomorrow.'

'Of course. Sorry, senior moment!'

'Not at all, and she's still not got her mobile.'

'So be it. So, thinking out loud, am I right to suppose that your solicitors have asked you how you think they should use the material?'

'Indeed they have.'

'And either you or they suggested that, in order to answer that question, a second opinion would be very useful?'

'Pretty much spot on, Andrew.'

'And are you fortified by my instinctive view that in the end your client may have no option if she is to establish provenance?'

'Very much so, Andrew. Thank you.'

Andrew thought it wise to change subject at this point. 'Can we return to the central issue, Tom, for a moment? I just want to be clear how it is that on your scenario we make good our defence on what I am calling the conspiracy allegation. What Cat calls the diss campaign.'

'Sure.'

'Well, it seems to me that it is not sufficient to show that the claimants possessed both the means and the intent to achieve their goal. We have to go further than that, and prove that they went so far as to achieve it. This will fall into that grey area where, although the claimants have the burden of proving their claim, we shall need to embrace the burden of proving what they achieved if we are to get our clients home.'

'I agree, Andrew. But my instructions are that we can show that the board at AlphaOm were briefed on the campaign, which went as far as the chief executive. We have the evidence, admittedly verbal at present but hopefully soon to be supported by documents, to show that the company was using the relevant information as recently as last year, and even this year. And we have evidence of material being published with the sole intent of rubbishing opinions from respectable sources. What we are missing is evidence as to how the campaign was orchestrated. But we hope to be able to prove that when we can find the documents, assuming that these do indeed materialise.'

Tom waited while this new intelligence was being considered at the other end of the telephone.

'Well,' said Andrew, after a long pause, 'it may be all we've got. But I'd be very reluctant to go into bat with just our verbal evidence. Surely, we do not want to have to rely on their disclosure to get us home?'

'Agreed,' said Tom. 'But we think that there's a reasonable chance that we know where to find the smoking guns. You'll have to bear with me on that.'

'Tantalising,' noted Andrew. 'Please don't keep me in suspense for too long. It's not good for my health.'

'Watch this space, as they say. Meanwhile, can I run past you some of the points which I should want to pursue at the *inter-partes* hearing? I want to make sure that none of these will queer your pitch, so to speak.'

'Delighted for you to do that, Tom. But first, tell me about the other theme which ran through the article. As I understand it, we have made the allegation that AlphaOm have deliberately suppressed the results of certain tests. We said, apparently, that these had been carried out on drugs which were in the course of being developed but at a stage before these drugs became refined into their eventual ... constituencies, if that is the right word. Does that just about sum it up?' asked Andrew.

'Pretty much,' agreed Tom. 'I query whether AlphaOm are going to want to make much of that issue. My understanding is that, until recently, it has been common practice for the big pharmaceuticals only to publish the tests results of their choosing. That practice may either now be about to change, or has been forced to change.'

'Ah, how so?'

'Apparently, as a result of pressure from an unlikely source, namely independent medical journals. The editors apparently spoke with one voice and laid down an ultimatum that they will not publish the results of any tests unless the company promoting the results has itself subscribed to and complied with a new code of practice. Under this code, the company is obliged to inform the journals when it is about to start each test, and will also provide the results of each test, irrespective of whether the results are good or bad for the relevant product.'

'So, where's the scoop then?' asked Andrew.

'Well, there might not be one,' replied Tom. 'If these are results of tests which were carried out before the code came into effect, then there's nothing to the story. On the other hand, if AlphaOm signed up to the code, but then said nothing about these tests, then we definitely have a story. Your clients were careful not to say which side of the fence they were dropping the dirt. So we shall have to wait and see on that one.'

'Got it, thanks,' said Andrew. 'Now, let's go back to the points which you wanted to run past me. Fire away.'

Chapter 11

The director of the Office of Internal Affairs was used to getting her own way. She had the measure of most men in the company. This included the short and balding director of the Legal Department, who doubled as the company secretary. It irritated her that this title gave Laurence James a seat at most board meetings.

She had done her best over the years to try to limit his authority, but even she could not control the legislation and other regulations that were binding on the company. That said, she had to respect the fact that he made a point of ensuring that his team kept on top of the law so far as it concerned the business of the company. Also, she was seldom less than impressed by his regular briefings, both verbal and written, to the board.

Lawrence was regarded as a man for detail, which she noted with regret did not extend to his wardrobe, nor his appearance generally. She loathed his practice of growing the few greying hairs he had left on one side of his head and, using some vile sort of lubricant that some men of his age thought attractive, spooning these across his scalp like a layer of mouldy treacle.

And his aftershave was vile.

Her revulsion notwithstanding, she resolved to be civil to him when they met this morning. She knew only too well that she needed his support.

The previous evening, she has taken the precaution of calling Laurence, or 'Larry' as she made a point of calling him, whilst denying him any reciprocal cordiality. She had known that he and his tedious spouse would have just returned from vacation that very afternoon. That did not deter her one bit. Quite the reverse: she intended to intrude upon his privacy, exploiting the fact that she would catch him 'off-guard'.

Her scheme had produced fruit in the form of his reluctant consent to a meeting 'first thing' in the morning. The ease with which she had procured it confirmed her poor opinion of him as a man.

She suspected that he would seek to evade her in the morning, and was reasonably confident, to the point of near certainty, of two things. First, that he would be ignorant of her ability to be alerted to the precise second that he logged on to his desktop PC in the office. And, secondly that, no sooner had he done so, she would be able to impose her presence upon him.

She liked to start the week like this.

Failure was not a phenomenon with which she had made any acquaintance during her career. However, she was very much alive to the significance of the violation, or rather the alleged trespass as she preferred to call it, which her assistant had committed in respect of the 'rights' of that treacherous little upstart in Thompson's department. She looked again at her profile.

Damn her for good looks, she thought, conscious of her own flat chest. And why does she have to smile at the camera like a model?

'Focus!' she told herself. She was not about to have her own department blamed if the company failed to nail that scheming bitch.

A bleep on her computer alerted her to the fact that Larry had logged on to the office network, so she swiftly made her way to the lifts.

What she had not reckoned with was the fact that that she would find Larry's door locked. A frosted glass door it might be, but it was nonetheless locked.

Locked! And despite their arrangement the previous evening. Intolerable! She had to stoop down to peer through the clear portals in the wall to survey proceedings within. She! Stoop! This would not do.

And on the other side of the door was not just that useless fool of a company secretary, but also his erstwhile poodle, whom she regarded as nothing but a thorn in her side, and right now a rather barbed hawthorn.

She glared at the back of Ted Fisher's head. That little toad had slipped in before her in order to poison her target before she could get to him, and was proving to be very much less than helpful.

Although she cursed silently beneath her breath, she had to admire her adversary's guile. There was more to him that she had given him credit for.

She must be getting slow! This was her trade, damn it. Yet, despite this being the appointed hour on this Monday morning, that little shit had stolen a march on her. Bastard!

And it might even be a good deal more than a march if they

continued to obstruct her! Did they have any idea what was in those emails? Of course they didn't. They were far more interested in their wretched principles.

She was about to turn away when first the company secretary and then Ted turned to see her. Larry beckoned her in to join them.

She could hardly retreat now, and certainly not once Fisher had seen her and had got up almost languidly to unlock the door.

'Ted,' she acknowledged, giving him an icy stare by way of salutation, and contrived her best smile towards Larry as she graciously accepted the chair beside Fisher.

Larry James began by thanking her for joining them, then before she could reply moved swiftly to the business at hand.

'Barbara, I think you know Ted,' he began, once she was settled.

She gave the faintest of nods.

'He has just been briefing me on developments on the Symonds business,' he continued. 'It seems to me that you are both to be congratulated on your achievements so far. We appear to be in a reasonably strong position, save for this one aspect that Ted and I have just been covering. But I think that we can treat this as a piece of normal housekeeping. It happens all the time, I'm sure, in other companies, and we should be able to ride any storm that comes our way. Of course, I'll need a full statement from you, and the relevant member of your staff, so that I can submit a full DPA report. But that will probably get filed away by the bureaucrats somewhere.'

Barbara made as if to speak, but Larry raised his hand.

'That deals with the internal procedural stuff. Which leaves only the matter of what we say first to the court and then to Miss Symonds.' He raised his hand a second time. 'Ted is due to speak again with our external counsel today. So, it's just a question of how soon you can let me have the statement covering the detail.'

She took her time before responding, her eyes fixed menacingly on Larry, whom she knew to have a reputation for compromise. He was usually susceptible to the views of the last person to speak to him, which she intended to ensure was herself. To that end, she needed to get Fisher out of the room, and fast.

'I'm grateful, of course,' she oozed, 'that Ted has taken the trouble to brief you so fully. However, Larry, this is really a matter which needs to be discussed at board level, and is not something that can be delegated to Ted. There are important issues at stake here, Larry. The chief has made this a priority for the company, although I know that you were not at last week's board meeting, and might not have picked that up given your annual leave. And even if you did, I doubt that you have had a proper chance to read all the papers and emails sent to board members from the chief.'

She glared at him knowingly, nodding towards Ted, and indicating that it would not be appropriate to discuss board matters in front of him. She enjoyed making the most of her advantage over him.

Larry took the hint.

'Ted, would you excuse us for just for a while. Don't go too far. I'll need to speak to you again in a few minutes.'

'Certainly, Larry,' replied Ted graciously, fully conscious that Larry was being played by the Mamba. 'I'll be in my room.'

He turned to Barbara, smiled politely and bade her good morning.

'I'll await your call, Larry.'

*

Monday morning's post had brought a series of letters from AlphaOm's lawyers, each addressing her as 'Ms'. Her immediate reaction was to take offence at that. She had been one of many within the company who had elected to be being addressed in the traditional form of 'Miss'. They had joked that the term 'Ms' suggested that they had been neutered, like stray cats. She was also thoroughly irritated that the company's solicitors should presume that she preferred that prefix. However, on reflection, it suggested to her that they had not consulted with the Human Resources Department, because they had a policy of adhering to the prefixes selected by former employees. It would also suggest that they had not yet discovered her reasons for leaving the company. She would make sure to mention that to Tomo and her lawyers.

The letters were numbered 'first letter', 'second letter' and so on consecutively. Tomo had told her to expect that. It was a blunt but typical tactic of some of the big firms, and in his experience usually counter-productive. Cat barely skimmed over the first paragraphs of each, and decided that she could not bring herself to read any of them.

She was due to meet that afternoon with the firm of lawyers that

Tomo had said she should instruct to act for her. She and Tomo had held a conference call with the partner there. She was called Rosalyn. (Cat liked that name, and instinctively her.) Somehow, after her 'confession' to Tomo over the weekend, it had seemed rather 'matter of fact' to discuss what Rosalyn had tastefully described as the 'less agreeable aspects' of her case with a complete stranger. It was even more bizarre that it had taken place remotely over the phone as well.

She put the letters back into their envelopes. She would give them to Rosalyn later, and maybe ask Tomo to tell her what they meant when he came round to his flat that evening, or *vice versa*. She didn't want to spend the night alone in her place.

She had walked absently towards the table where she normally kept her laptop in order to check her emails. The empty desk had shocked her at first, and it took a while for her brain to register why her laptop was not there. She would probably not see it again until the following morning.

However, this was a timely reminder that she needed to make proper provision for backing up all her documents and addresses in case – which was becoming increasingly common, and not just in London – either her laptop or her mobile phone was hacked or her flat was burgled. And there was every incentive now for the company to set their spooks on her, especially after this whole business.

She checked her temporary mobile, wondering whether Alison had replied to her text message. Oddly, her inbox was empty. Perhaps Ali had enjoyed another of her 'naughty nights', as she liked to refer to them, with Jeremy. She would probably text or call either over lunch or this evening after work.

Cat had been due to call Ken Baxter, the journalist at *The Daily Chronicle*. However, Tomo had cautioned against this, sensibly warning her that the newspaper would be taking stock of the situation with their lawyers. They would almost certainly have told their staff not to speak with anyone on the subject until they had decided on which course of action they intended to take. So, she had put that idea on hold for the time being.

Instead, she would have to do what Tomo had advised, namely, read through the affidavit evidence which had been served on her by the company, and make careful notes of the points which she wanted to contradict.

Tedious, but necessary, he had said.

You sure are right there, Tomo, she thought.

The principal affidavit had been sworn by someone from the Department of Internal Affairs at the company. The name Maria Lutherson meant nothing to her. She was vaguely aware of the existence of the department, but only by reputation and specifically that of the Black Mamba, whom she had never encountered.

She felt particularly uncomfortable that she had been targeted by the department. The affidavit portrayed her as a disloyal and self-interested schemer, motivated by greed and publicity. She was both surprised and impressed by the language employed in the affidavit. Oddly, if she didn't know the full story, she would have been convinced by the tale which had been spun.

Clearly, the judge had been persuaded by it.

However, what struck her most was the outright denial on behalf of the company that the board had been put on notice of the risk of any proven link between their bloody pills and the two 'conditions'. They had even denied the existence of the document from CD that she had helped to compose.

As bold as a thieving racoon, her granny would have called it.

Well, they were in for a surprise when they saw what she'd taken from CT's desk and his briefcase over the last weeks of their affair.

More intriguing still was the denial by the company that the board had ever condoned the 'diss' campaign which she and the newspaper had since exposed. Why would they do that, when there were plenty of other members of the department who had played a part in that campaign? Some of them were probably still there.

But what it did mean was that she really would need those documents that she'd left at Jamie's. Sure, it was a while ago, but she was certain that these included the ones that showed that her department had been an active participant in the formulation and the subsequent orchestration of the campaign.

Did that mean that the company was going to say that they had never seen any of the key documents? Surely the board was not going to pretend that it had given CT a free hand with regard to the campaign?

How did Tomo put it? Ah yes, 'without even a nod and a wink'.

She resolved to speak with Ali to see whether she had made progress in getting hold of Jamie, and whether he still had those boxes. And more to the point, whether he would release them. She knew that he would listen to Ali.

Tomo had said that the court would insist on her providing a full account of the documents in her control, and that she had to promise to preserve all such documents. Maybe, once Ali had explained that to Jamie, he would see that there was no alternative, really, other than to let her have them.

Back to the main affidavit. More references to her memoranda and other confidential documents. Those would be the ones that, as Tomo put it, she had 'liberated' from the company. Then long quotes from the article in the newspaper. Cross-references from the piece back to the memos and other documents, and then conclusions drawn – or inviting the court to draw – from the assorted evidence. Then lots of legal guff about breach of confidence, urgency, damage, the *status quo* and something called the 'balance of convenience'. Tomo had tried to explain that to her over the weekend.

She flicked through the rest of the file. More affidavits. One from a computer nerd about how to retrieve and recreate electronic documents. Another confirming that the company had lined up an independent solicitor to supervise the implementation of the court's various orders – she presumed that in her case they were referring to the guy who had explained the orders to her. But what struck her as really odd was that there was no statement from Chuck, nor for that matter from anyone else in commercial development.

Perhaps they had not spoken with them yet. That was certainly possible, if not likely. Knowing CT as she did, he would have found a way to keep his head down as soon as the story came out.

She could just see him, probably sneaking into the office by the rear door, so that he could start to prepare the 'spin' which the company's lawyers could be persuaded to swallow to cover his own role in all this. And then there'd be more spin which the company would use to brief the media, as and when considered appropriate.

But if they had asked him for a statement, he had obviously not obliged. Or perhaps, once he had put on his 'let me be utterly candid with you' frown as he prepared to tell a whole bunch of lies with a straight face, what he had told them had been considered less than useful by the lawyers.

Neither would surprise her. And maybe he even expected to get away with this by saying nothing? Well, she would see about that.

Chapter 12

Peter Langer prepared his notes for his telecon with the claimants' solicitors. He had just come off the phone to the principal technician at ITerrogate, the firm designated by the court, at the suit of the claimants, to conduct a forensic analysis of the mobile phone and laptop of two of the defendants, Symonds and Baxter.

The technician had told him that their analyses had been completed that morning, and that they would be sending over details of their findings shortly. They had also told him that they had sought to separate the various files into populations comprising what they called business, private, cross-related and unclassified. They had told him there was a quite separate population of emails, and also texts, which they regarded as 'sensitive'. When pressed, they had explained that these were of a nature that the technician recommended that the existence thereof should be made known to the parties, but that their contents should not be disclosed without further order of the court or with the owner's consent.

The 'owner', he had told him, was the third defendant, Miss Symonds.

From the young woman's reaction in the flat, and from what she had said to him, Peter had suspected as much.

But it was what the technician had said next that concerned him more. There were text messages and emails that appeared to be malicious in nature, and had been sent both to Miss Symonds and to a third party. It was unclear from the email address and content who the sender was.

And then the bombshell.

There had been a flurry of these emails and texts about five months ago, but then they had had dried up.

Until this weekend.

'Are you sure about that?' Peter had asked. He had kicked himself afterwards because the technicians were precisely the people who would know.

They were. And they did.

And the coincidence really bothered him.

*

Mary Fellowes pressed the 'phone down' button on the speakerphone console. She looked across at her team of assistants, whose expressions of anxiety confirmed that they had not only overheard the conversation, and especially the closing exchanges, but had also appreciated the import of what had been said.

She turned to her senior associate, whose razor-sharp mind and mental agility ensured that it was not long before he was on the firm's notepaper. He had been responsible for supervising the drafting of the witness evidence and liaising with the clients' Legal Department.

'Tim. Formalities first. Our engagement letter went out on Thursday. Has it been returned signed by the clients yet?'

'I've chased this morning, Mary. Ted Fisher is my point of contact at the clients. He tells me he's on the case and is getting it signed today. The head of legal was due to return from annual leave this morning.'

'Okay. Keep the pressure on. Any news on the affidavits that the defendants are due to file at court?'

'Nothing in yet from any of the parties. But we've got a notice from JWT Legal that they are acting for *The Chronicle* and Baxter. We've acknowledged.'

'And Miss Symonds?'

'No, we've had nothing in from her, nor any news of who her lawyers are, nor her counsel for that matter.'

'Well, there's time enough. Let's move on to inspection. We'll need to seek consent from the defendants to inspect the business and cross-related files once these have become available. Who's on that?'

A hand was raised by the smartly dressed assistant whom she had hired that year from a rival firm.

'Thank you, Jane.'

Good, that was in safe hands.

'Private emails. We'll follow the usual practice of seeking permission to inspect at the premises of their solicitors but not take copies without consent.'

Jane raised her hand.

'On it already.'

'Excellent. Which leaves this last category, the one that's been described as "sensitive". I think we can all guess what that means.' She said that with a straight face.

And there were no smiles in response.

The tone of Peter Langer's voice had sufficed to warn them that there could be more to this than at first met the eye. And she was not at all sure that she wanted to set eyes on any of this material. But her duty to her clients came first.

'I think that I should deal with this. And I should add that Jane and I had a distinctly bad feeling that something was amiss when we served the orders on Friday. Miss Symonds had appeared to be up for the fight until she understood that other people would be looking at this . . . what I now presume to be this sensitive material.'

Jane nodded.

'Which reminds me, Tim, did Ted Fisher ever get back to you with regard to Miss Symonds' exit interview?'

'No, he hasn't. And it's on my list of things to speak to him about this morning. I think he is trying to obtain instructions from within the company. But there is one thing that I should mention, if you'll allow.'

'By all means . . .'

'Roger tells me that he has been able to delve into this a little. He's spoken with some of the people who worked with Miss Symonds in CD, and also with one of the managers in the company's HR department. The overall picture is one of a near perfect employee in virtually every aspect.'

'I sense a "but" coming,' said Mary.

'There is. Miss Symonds began to raise what she – and I understand that she was not alone in this – what she believed were legitimate concerns regarding the company's ethics and business model. Those concerns were initially verbal, but were eventually condensed into a series of papers submitted to her boss, and in one case eventually sent to the main board itself. But apart from that, there is nothing to suggest that she had any motive to damage the company.'

'So, where's the but?'

'That's the point,' said Jane. 'If our instructions are correct and there is no truth behind any of the allegations made by the paper, then what game was Miss Symonds playing at by going to the paper with this story?'

Mary had enough experience of this sort of thing than to speculate on motive. The answer invariably lay in the evidence, of which they had so far seen little.

'That, I fear, is what we are about to find out,' Mary replied. 'But let's keep chasing, and above all make sure that we stay on the front foot. I think we all feel strongly that this is certainly one of those cases where we most surely do not want to be ambushed or taken by surprise by the other side.'

'And especially not by JWT,' chirped another assistant.

'Exactly, although I suspect that it is not them we shall have to worry about on this score. The trouble will come from whoever acts for Miss Symonds.' Then she added more out of instinct than necessity: 'And remember. Detailed file notes on all calls with the clients, please. I want a full audit trail on this one in case there is a post-mortem.'

The team was all too aware what she meant by that.

Tim raised his hand.

'Have you read my note of the hearing? If so, I was wondering whether you're content for it to go across to Alain Gaitsland or his junior for approval.'

'Yes, thanks. Friday seems such a long time ago now. But yes, do please get it off to counsel as soon as we're done here.'

She consulted her list.

'Costs schedule for Friday – have we got estimates from counsel's clerks? And what about the techies? Have we had a bill off them yet?'

A hand was raised across the room, confirming that the team was on it.

'Finally, Tim, where are we on collating all the disclosure from the clients? I appreciate that they've only had a day or two.'

'It's on my list for my telecon with Ted later this morning.'

'Fine. Will you ensure that he understands that we shall need to get as much material as we can to counsel so that they can begin to draft the particulars of claim. We've got less than two weeks.'

'On it,' confirmed Tim.

'Excellent. Thank you all. Shall we reconvene at two-thirty?'

*

'As I was saying, Larry,' cooed Barbara Spooner, 'this is essentially a board matter, and one on which the chief is going to look to us for a decision. If he detects that we are not of one mind on this, he will insist that we defer to our external counsel. And we both know that they will take the safe course in order to protect their heavily overpaid posteriors. Which is why I'm looking to you to be strong here.'

The appeal to his manhood was well aimed. It was common gossip within the company that Larry's wife, who worked up in the City as a PA to the CEO of a freight company, took her pleasures other than in her home port. Barbara's suggestion that Larry, as the company secretary, had the ability to assert his own views in preference to those of his deputy was carefully designed by her to provoke him into adopting the stratagem which she had already proposed to Fisher.

'What I proposed to Ted – and I have to say that his response was somewhat pedantic – was that we should apply for an order from the court which would give us access to the girl's email account. I'm not talking just about the emails which were sent from this office. There must be plenty more which she sent from her home. We might not find all of these on her PC, but we might obtain copies through her service provider. I want us to apply for a new disc-imaging order against both the girl and the ISP which is limited to the girl's personal email account. In our evidence, we can tell the court that we've discovered that she used her private email account at the office. I can't see the problem with this, can you? We can present this as part of the discharge of our continuing duty to the court. Also, if we make the application in the way which I've suggested, we don't have to tell the court how we found out about the email account.'

She stared at him with her penetrating eyes.

He shuffled his feet with indecision.

'Well, you see ...'

'It's remarkably simple and completely effective, wouldn't you agree, Larry? And it means that the lawyers don't compromise our case.'

She was deliberately including him in the term 'lawyers'.

Laurence James was rubbing his chin, which he usually did whenever he was confronted with a decision which he was required to take himself rather than delegate. There was certainly attraction in the idea, as Barbara had said. What concerned him was that it would be his department that would be compromised, and thus his own reputation might be at stake. He knew that Ted Fisher had already refused to go along with the plan, and would do so again, which meant that he – James – would have to give the instructions to the lawyers. This offended one of his basic rules of survival, namely, that there was to be no trail, no smoking gun, that could lead directly to him.

'Let me think about this a bit more, Barbara,' he proposed, purposefully avoiding her eye. 'This is not something that we should rush into. Also, I'm not sure that I agree with Ted's assessment of the urgency of the matter. Let's discuss this again in the morning, once we've all had time to reflect on it.'

The director beamed her oiliest smile at him, sensing victory.

'Take as much time as you need, Larry. Like you, I think that this is not a matter which demands an immediate decision. Tomorrow may be a little hectic, what with the hearing on Friday morning. So shall we arrange to meet up after the hearing, say around four pm on Friday. Or next Monday might suit you better?'

'OK,' nodded James, delighted to be released from her presence. 'I'll have my PA schedule a meeting.'

'Oh, and Larry,' she added, on her way to the door. 'I suggest that we don't involve Ted any further on this particular point. I'm sure that the chief would want us to deal with it ourselves, and at our level within the company. Don't you agree?'

'As I said, Barbara,' he replied evasively, 'let's discuss this again when we meet.'

*

'I'm sorry, Mr Fisher,' said the voice on the telephone, without even a hint of an apology. 'Mr Thompson is still on his conference call, and he has people in reception waiting for him. He's already overdue for that meeting. I've put a note in front of him to tell him that you've called before, and I'll make a point of reminding him that he needs to call you as soon as his meeting is over.'

Ted ground his teeth as he forced himself to remain polite on the phone. It had been a long night.

'We were due to speak at eight this morning. That's over three hours ago. I realise that you're not his PA, but can you please try to make sure that he calls me before he goes into his next meeting. I really do need to speak to him, urgently.'

'I'll be sure to try, Mr Fisher,' replied the cheerful voice down the line to him, 'just as soon as he's free. But he's already got clients waiting for his meeting that was scheduled some time ago. So, I can't promise anything.'

'Do you have access to his email account?' he asked hopefully, realising the futility of his question.

'I'm afraid not, Mr Fisher,' came the inevitable reply. 'You'll have to ask his PA, but she's on the call with him now and is also due to attend the meeting. Then, she has a doctor's appointment this afternoon. But I will be sure to give him your message.'

Ted thanked her for her time, and replaced his handset. There was nothing to be gained from taking out his frustration on her. What really concerned him was the total absence of co-operation from Thompson, who was likely to prove a key witness. The reluctance of the head of Symonds' department to become involved was understandable in some ways, but he had an uncanny sense that there was more to this whole business than he had been told so far.

And he disliked uncertainty.

Also, there remained the unresolved issue of the data protection breaches by the director's office. His boss had ducked the point during the meeting with the Mamba that morning. Consequently, his instincts told him arms were being twisted – and he had a pretty shrewd idea as to who would win that particular contest.

It was going to be a long week!

Chapter 13

Rosalyn Hills concluded the formalities of her engagement as Cat signed the letters confirming her firm's appointment. Cat was even more impressed with her in person than she had been on the call earlier. She was well dressed, articulate, businesslike, but above all personable, and had immediately gained Cat's trust.

She also liked her colleague, Alex, whom Rosalyn had introduced as an 'associate' of the firm. She was told that he would be working with her.

Rosalyn had explained to Cat that she had spoken to the independent solicitor to inform him that her firm would be acting, and had filed the necessary notice at court and sent copies to the other parties' lawyers. She had received confirmation from JWT Legal, who acted for *The Daily Chronicle*, that her firm's fees and those of Tomo would be covered by the newspaper in return for Cat's full co-operation. She had explained the terms offered, and had recommended that Cat accept, which Tomo had approved.

They worked their way through the orders. Rosalyn had prepared an agenda for that purpose, and they had reached the point about the content of her affidavit, which was due to be served the following afternoon.

'I've read the draft that you and Tom prepared over the weekend. I am more than happy with this as it stands, but can you update me on any developments with regard to the documents that you say that you once had. You're saying that you left them somewhere last year and are not sure whether they still exist and, if so, what or where is their current status and location. Is that still the position?'

'Why yes,' replied Cat. 'I've left messages with my friend, Ali, to call me, but I've not heard from her yet today. I met with her over the weekend, and she told me that she would call her brother. That's Jamie, he's my... um ... my ex.'

She glanced at Tomo, who gave her a reassuring smile.

'I can't say for sure,' she added, 'but if they still exist, he'll be able to tell her. And he'll know where they are.'

'Well, if that remains the position as at …' Rosalyn looked at her watch, 'As at 1.45 pm, then my advice is that you simply say three things. First, that as late as last year you did have certain documents that belonged to the claimants. Secondly, that some of these would in all likelihood fall under the description of confidential. And thirdly, that you are currently unsure whether they exist and, even if they do, what their location is. Would you agree with that, Tom?'

'That was indeed my verbal advice to Cat, save that I would probably go one stage further. Given the absence of further intelligence on their whereabouts, I would have Cat say that she has taken and will continue to take reasonable steps to ascertain whether the documents still exist and, if so, whether and when they can be retrieved, either by herself or more likely with the aid of others.'

Roslyn looked quizzically at him. 'Are you sure about that? I mean, is that not rather a hostage to fortune? If she never finds them, won't she lay herself open to the charge by the claimants that she contrived their disappearance?'

'Yes and no,' said Tomo. 'But we have to face facts. Cat has been ordered to tell the court what she knows. That means that she has to tell the court the fact that certain documents may either be in the hands of a third party, or that this third party may know whether and where they can be found. The fact that such knowledge lies in the hands of another goes only to matters of timing and logistics. It does not affect Cat's obligation to return them if they belong to the claimants.'

Rosalyn thought about that for a moment.

'No, you're right. We don't really have a choice here, do we? If she can, then Cat must take steps to return them.'

'Exactly,' confirmed Tomo. 'And, to a large extent, I think that she would do far greater damage to her case if she does not offer that commitment – we might row back from an undertaking – especially if the court is compelled to force it out of her. She needs to be telling the court that she has nothing to hide.'

'Yes, I see that. That is a sensible approach,' agreed Rosalyn.

She turned to address Cat.

'Well, you've heard Tom's advice. So, the question I have to ask you is whether you are willing to give that commitment to the court?'

'Sure, but aren't we missing something? Surely I need these documents myself anyway to help prove my defence.'

Tomo answered her. 'The two points are connected, but different, Cat. We're talking here about what you're prepared to promise the court that you will do to try to find and return these documents – which are not lawfully your property. That is wholly separate from whether we actually want to make use of them ourselves. Does that make sense?'

'I guess.'

'The thing is that, as your lawyers, what we're concerned with right now is whether or not it is in your best interests to be making promises to the court which it may be difficult to show that you have kept. In some respects, it is or may be cosmetic, in that we are trying to present the court with the best impression of you.'

'Okay,' Cat replied reservedly. 'I guess I follow that.'

Rosalyn amended the draft as she followed the discussion.

'Right, that's gone off for printing. I'll get hard copies brought in for you both to check.'

She picked up some further documents.

'So, that brings me conveniently to the next item on my agenda.'

She passed them each a hard copy of an email.

'Whilst I amend our covering letter to the court and the claimants, have a quick look at this email from the supervising solicitor.'

'What is this?' asked Cat.

'This came in just before you arrived. It's from the solicitor who supervised the search orders at your flat. He's called Langer. I've dealt with him on other cases, and he's always been entirely reliable and, importantly, straight. He's sent over a list of the data that his IT technicians have retrieved from your two devices.'

Cat immediately noticed that the solicitor had confirmed that the 'forensic analysis' of her devices had been completed.

As Tomo continued to read his copy, she asked Rosalyn, 'So what happens to my laptop and my mobile?'

'I've asked for them to be couriered over here,' replied Rosalyn. 'I am hoping that they will arrive before we've finished.'

'Well, I can survive on my temporary mobile for now, but it's a drag trying to find addresses and numbers, and such.'

'My PA will alert us as soon as they arrive.'

'That's kind. Thanks.'

'In the meantime, between us we need to decide, and sooner rather than later, which of the emails and documents we – i.e. you – will object to the other parties, principally the claimants, not just seeing but also copying.'

'There's a difference?'

'Indeed there is. Let me explain. We can consent to their lawyers looking at – we call it inspecting – certain documents but only for two purposes. First, they may say that they need to see them to establish the relevance of the documents to the case. Secondly, they may want to assert their right to take copies of the originals.'

'So, what if we say no?'

'Well, what usually happens is that we come to an arrangement whereby we either allow one of their counsel to see these, or we jointly appoint someone to decide or advise on whether they should see the documents. Or sometimes we ask the judge to look at them and decide the issue.'

'Okay, that makes sense I guess. So can you just talk me through the process from our perspective, and explain what I have to do?'

'Right. Well, the majority of requests will come from the claimants, and we'll need to decide how to respond. Now, we may decide that there is no point in disputing that some of the documents and emails are their property. In those cases, we make no claim to retain them, and offer to return the documents. We would, however, assert a right to use them in the proceedings, on the basis that the claimants would have to disclose these anyway. That may cover most or all of the items in what has been termed the "business" category. So, we may find those the easiest to deal with.'

'And I guess I'd recognise some of them, at least.'

'Exactly. So, the tricky category is going to be the one containing material that has been labelled by the IT firm cross-related. Now, I take that to mean that whoever was charged with sorting the data was unsure whether these were private and personal to you, or whether they were likely to be the property of the claimants. They've offered no view, and seem to suggest that could fall into either category.'

'And you need me to go through them all, is that it?'

'I do, yes. You can either do that here or at home, but I'd suggest that it would be easier here because Alex can be on hand to assist you. It's very likely that you will have some queries or need things printed.'

'And,' Cat added, 'you think there will be less distractions here.'

Rosalyn smiled.

'Well, I didn't mean that, but I won't deny that I was thinking it.'

It was Cat's turn to smile, but not for long.

'Say, what if we consider that there's stuff there that's private, even though it came from within the company?'

'That's the hard bit,' replied Rosalyn. 'And it's why we need you to examine each email and attachment, and explain why you think the claimants should not be allowed to see it, let alone take copies.'

'And the same would go for, you know ... what the guy emailed to Jamie and me. That IT firm has called it the sensitive stuff?'

Rosalyn glanced at Tom to confirm that she should be the one to answer that, from which Cat deduced that they had already discussed this.

'It's OK,' she said softly, 'Tomo knows what's in them, and who sent them. But we've agreed that, you know, it'd be best if he didn't see the images, but that you should tell him what the messages said.'

Tomo nodded his concurrence.

'In due course, Cat, we can discuss whether or not you want to make these the basis of a claim, and whether you would be well advised to do so. But there will be time enough for that after we've weathered the initial storm. And Tom has recommended a barrister in his chambers who can advise on that aspect — in fact, another partner in this firm has used her in the past, and speaks very highly of her.'

Cat looked at her hands for a few seconds, then at Rosalyn.

'There's a book I sometimes read about politics and morals. There's a chapter in it about how tyranny comes about, and how it becomes self-perpetuating. It will be the same with all these celebrities who turn out to have done awful things. The reason is almost always because the victims either say nothing, or if they do they are not believed by the people who are meant to protect them – at least not at first.'

Neither Tomo nor Rosalyn spoke.

'But now,' said Cat, almost to herself in a whisper, 'I know why people do say nothing, and what it does to them by doing nothing.'

Rosalyn offered a sympathetic smile. 'That's all it takes, Cat.'

'Was it Burke or Cooke?'

'Sir Edmund Burke, I think you're referring to,' said Tomo.

'I've never forgotten what he said about evil, and what happens if you do nothing. It's what Ali said. If I do nothing, then that man will just hurt another girl, someone just like me; maybe more than one. And I'd have to live with that.'

Rosalyn gave her a long look.

'I realise that, Cat. Believe me, I'm not making light of what you've told me, and I don't even need to see the material to understand the damage that they did. But right now, I need you to focus on these other documents, because we've a deadline to meet. There'll be time enough once we've met that.'

Cat could recognise sound counsel when she heard it. And she was hearing this advice loud and clear.

'Okay. Okay, so should I go someplace else to start?'

'In a moment,' said Rosalyn. 'Let's get your statement signed and filed first, then you and I can move on to the documents. I know that Tom has got another conference back in chambers later this afternoon. This is enough for now.'

*

It had been a long morning's work under the sun, and the keeper was grateful that the meeting with his employer had been brought forward to the early afternoon. He had used the appointment as a convenient reason to excuse himself from any further exertions under these sweltering conditions. He left his underkeepers to finish the reinforcing of the fences around the new pen, instructing them to take regular breaks using the refuge provided by the woods from the heat of the sun.

He set off on the short journey to 'the big house', as the manor was generally known on the estate. It was a lonely place now, what with both the man's mother stopping up in London and Jamie rattling around inside it like a solitary pea in a pod. Charlie could still remember when the sounds of children playing in the gardens used to drift up into the woods in front of the house. And his sister, Alison, used to keep a horse there. Happier times were those.

The keeper needed little reminding of the length of time that had elapsed since he had last been invited to follow the (once familiar) routine of visiting Jamie in the big house. He was able to observe that little had been done to alter the layout of the flowerbeds in the garden behind the house. Those had been replanted under the direction of the 'southern belle' and would soon be in bloom again.

'My,' thought Charlie, 'but she had been a catch for Jamie.' And Charlie remembered her fondly. She had always found time to chat with him.

She might be long gone, but the flowers were still allowed to blossom. He asked himself whether to interpret this as a positive or a negative indication. He wasn't sure. Time alone would tell.

The thick tyres of his Landy crunched up the gravelled driveway to the house, and he was greeted by a reassuring bark from Jamie's Labrador, Biscuit. Reassuring because the bark signified recognition rather than alarm, and was intended as much as an enthusiastic greeting as an alert to the owner of the house. It conveyed a special warmth to the keeper, since he had helped to train the dog, and had worked him during the last season when Jamie was conspicuous by his absence.

Charlie returned the greeting with a friendly command, whereupon the barking ceased abruptly from within the house.

He parked beside the car belonging to Sandy McQueen, who doubled as both the manager of the estate and as the shoot captain. He suppressed a sense of guilt that he was relieved to learn that Sandy had arrived before him, and that he would be spared the embarrassment of engaging in small talk with Jamie pending his arrival.

Charlie had never discussed with Jamie the reasons why he had sold all the days last season which were reserved for the family. Whilst he knew better than to raise the issue himself, he dreaded the prospect of being alone with the man whom he had schooled as a young boy in the art and etiquette of the field, only to watch him break his heart over a woman. The subject was best left well alone for the time being, at least until they had got the new season underway, especially if they got Jamie to come out with his guns again and, more importantly, with his family and friends.

He let himself in through the 'kitchen door' at the back of the house, raising his hand as a command for Biscuit to sit. He would let him taste the back of his hand in a moment. He had long ago instilled in Jamie the importance of ensuring that a dog should always be the last to be greeted and the last to be allowed to greet, such was the significance of hierarchy to the canine brain. He called out his greeting to his host, who appeared from the next room.

Charlie completed the ritual salutations with his fellow delegates to this overdue conference. Only then did he turn his attention to the dog, earning an appreciative smile from Jamie and a nod of recognition from the shoot captain in the process.

'Sandy and I have already started on the beers, Charlie,' began Jamie.

'Would you care to join us, or are you going to shame us by making us watch you drink tea?'

'I'll thank you, Jamie, for a long glass of water if I may, followed by a beer. It's thirsty work under the sun today. We've been putting the final touches to that new pen in front of the woods besides the river. That will make for some truly sporting birds. They'll test the best of 'em, of that I'm in no doubt.'

'Ah yes, I recall you saying something about that a few months back,' replied Jamie, doing his best to disguise from Charlie his obvious lack of enthusiasm for the subject. 'I'll be interested to see how that goes.'

Unenthusiastic, perhaps, thought the keeper, but at least this was a start.

No, he corrected himself, it's more than that. This meeting was a huge step forward, as was any contribution from his employer. In recent weeks, Jamie had eschewed any form of social intercourse and had confined his communications to those he deemed essential for the efficient management of the estate.

A short silence ensued. It was slowly filled, in the same awkward pace as were the various glasses around the table, whilst the host opened a large diary in front of him. He placed Sandy's list of proposed dates beside it.

As the ritual of glass-filling was being completed, Charlie was able to observe the changes which a broken heart had wrought on the features of the person whom he had known man and boy these past thirty-odd years.

The mass of thick, slightly unruly hair had not diminished in quantity, but what struck him immediately were the sallow features of Jamie's face, especially in his cheeks and around his eyes. Gone were the warm smile and friendly, if at times awkward, manner, to be replaced by a sullenness to which this man had been a stranger not twelve moons previously. And there was no sparkle of amusement around those large blue eyes, which he had inherited from his father, God rest his soul.

And Jamie's eyes too would normally reveal a keen interest in all they observed around them. Yet now they seemed only to advertise that his mind derived no pleasure from any of the surroundings.

'Lord love us,' thought the keeper to himself, 'but he's still hurt bad.' What a difference from the boy that he had groomed in the field as if he were his own son. Now there was no emotion visible upon the man's face.

If there was ever a sight to pity, it was of this poor soul. What that man needs, thought Charlie, more than all the gold in all the world, is for another woman to put his arms around him and give him the kiss of life.

His philosophical musings were brought to an end as a long glass of fresh water, straight from the spring beside the house, was passed across to him, alongside a tankard of ale. He made short work of the water, and quickly refilled his glass before upgrading to anything stronger. He needed a straight head for the time being, especially if they were to be discussing figures.

The list of dates before the assembled team had been prepared and circulated by Sandy earlier that month to Jamie and the keeper. Some days were firm bookings, with deposits already paid. Other dates were not yet fixed in stone, but were a tentative attempt by the shoot captain and the keeper to engage – or rather regain – Jamie's interest in what had once been one of his favourite activities. The dates now needed to be firmed up, and this required Jamie's agreement, or at least his blessing, to allow the others to fix them without reference to him, as had been the case last season.

Hence this meeting.

'First, thank you both for coming today,' began Jamie, 'and for switching the venue at short notice. It's quite a help for me.'

'Delighted, Jamie,' responded Sandy, a definite Scottish lilt to his tongue. 'The quality of your beer is far superior to mine, and if we'd stayed with plan A I'd have got landed with the washing-up, or some other chore that I shall be accused of neglecting by the domestic management.'

Fred shot him a sideways look by way of reprimand. Big feet had the captain, and he'd missed the grimace that had flickered briefly on Jamie's face at those words, although he had let the comment pass. The last thing that Jamie needed reminding of right now was the absence of domestic bliss in this house. But the captain could stand alongside a herd of rhino when it came to comparing thickness of skins.

'And thank you also, Sandy, for providing us with this list. I've only got a couple of suggestions. And as for the draft account that you've produced – for which again many thanks – I need to go through this. But the figures look about right. And I can see now why you want to lose some of the profit by carrying out the schedule of works on the estate that you and your team have produced.'

'There ought to be enough fat in the budget to spend on other maintenance,' observed Sandy. 'The shoot bus being one of them.'

And so the meeting progressed through its informal agenda. Midway through, Jamie's telephone rang – quite a rare event, thought the keeper. Which was probably why Jamie had never got round to replacing the old message recorder attached to the phone, a relic of the previous century, no doubt. He let it go through to the answerphone which he had kept permanently switched on this past year, forgetting that his device proclaimed the content of the incoming message, rendering it audible to all those present.

Jamie was about to continue with the meeting when he heard – as did the others – the voice of his sister, Ali. None of them missed the sense of urgency which her message conveyed.

'Hi Jamie. It's Ali. I sent you a text, but I realise that I sent it to the new number. Sorry. Could you give me a call as soon as you get this. I need to speak with you. Something's come up which only you can help with, and it's got to be dealt with as soon as poss. Can you call me back when you get this message. I'm leaving work now, but I'm on my mobile, and I'll be at home this evening. I'll call your new mobile with the same message just to be sure. That's all for now. Love you.'

A look of combined irritation and resignation passed across Jamie's face. He looked across at the other two men, who both knew that Jamie's sister ranked above all else in his list of priorities.

Accepting that the scheduled discussions would have to be curtailed, Charlie greeted this intelligence with mixed emotions. He was partly relieved that there would be no time for small talk once the main purpose of their meeting had been achieved. He was also partly frustrated that the intervention would give Jamie an excuse to avoid some of the difficult decisions which had been held over from last year.

But, he thought to himself, at least they had got this far. They could always reconvene on another occasion, and he might even suggest that. But he'd achieved his first task, which had been to regain Jamie's interest in what he and Sandy were planning. All he had to do now was to keep the man interested.

Less than half an hour later, after they had made further progress down their agenda, the phone rang again. The same voice, distorted by its electronic transmission through the recorder, played into the room. Once again, the flow of their conversation was temporarily halted by the interruption.

> *'Jamie, it's Ali again. I'm not sure if you picked up my earlier message, but I do need to speak to you quite urgently. Jamie, it's ... it's actually about Cat. She's in trouble, and I mean real trouble. She really needs your help urgently this week. I'll explain when we talk. Love you.'*

This time the metallic recording left an awkward silence hanging in the air between them, and even the thick-skinned captain knew better than to catch Jamie's eye.

If they had been alone, Charlie might have seized the opportunity to speak. Instead, both he and Sandy elected to examine the papers in front of them. It was as though Jamie had walked into the room with his pecker hanging out, but neither had wanted to be the one who mentioned it to him.

Jamie sensed that neither of his guests wanted to be the first to speak. After a brief pause, he said: 'That's all right. I'll call her after we've finished.'

Charlie nudged Sandy under the table.

'No, Jamie, we'll reconvene later in the week. You have other pressing business to attend to, and we should be on our way.'

Chapter 14

'Hi Ali,' said Jamie. 'Sorry to be so long getting back to you. I had a meeting with the estate team that had been fixed for weeks.'

'Oh, Jamie. Thank you for calling. I didn't mean to interrupt you, but I don't think that this can really wait. As I said, this is about Cat.'

A cold pause at the other end of the line left Ali in no doubt that this was going to be as difficult as she had predicted.

'I know. You said,' he eventually replied.

'Well, you know me, Jamie. I like to get straight to the point.'

'I was expecting nothing less, sis.'

'So, do you still get *The Daily Chronicle*?'

'As a matter of fact, I do.'

'And did you by chance read the headline article in *The Chronicle* last week about Cat's former employer, you know, AlphaOm?'

'I did, actually. And yes, I did recognise the name.'

'Well, Jamie, Cat's the mole.'

'What!'

'That's right. She's the one who has blown the whistle on them.'

He had certainly not anticipated this intelligence.

'Well, how about that! Hats off to her!'

'But that's not the whole story, Jamie.'

'No, I don't suppose it is.'

'As you can imagine, the company have not taken this lying down. They've come after her and the paper with a vengeance.'

'As the old saying goes, money means power.'

'You'd better believe it. They've put their lawyers onto her. And I mean for real. She's due in court at the end of this week.'

'What! On a criminal charge?'

'No. At least I don't think so. Not yet, anyway. No, these are civil proceedings in the High Court, in London.'

'I'm lost. Can you explain?'

'OK. This is what I learnt from Cat so far. The lawyers have obtained some kind of injunction against Cat and the newspaper. Cat has been ordered to produce to the judge all the documents in her possession that she took from the company, and any others that were given to her when she was employed by them.'

'So?'

'Apparently that includes any documents that were in her possession but which are now held by someone else on her behalf.'

As she expected, there was silence from the other end of the line.

'I see,' he said, eventually.

She let him digest that statement for a while, although she suspected that its significance was not lost on him.

'The thing is, Jamie,' she continued, 'Cat is pretty sure that some of the papers that she's going to have to hand over to the judge are amongst the stuff that she never collected from the house.' Then she added: 'You know, when you two split up.'

She had tried to introduce that painful issue as softly as she could, but she could almost sense the old wound reopening.

'You don't mince your words when you get to the point, do you, sis!'

'Look, Jamie, this is not easy for either of us. God knows how much I wanted it to work out between you two. But I can't undo the past.'

Silence.

'Jamie, the only person who regrets more than we do what happened between you two is Cat herself. She's still eaten up with remorse about what she got herself into, and how it all ended.'

'Well, she didn't look too remorseful on camera.'

'Jamie! That's horrible!'

'OK. OK. Sorry, sis, that was out of order.'

'Look, Jamie, all she's asking you is whether you kept any of her stuff. It's because if you did, she's going to have to tell that to the judge.'

'Is that all, seriously?'

'For now, yes. But if you have got the papers, then the court has told her that she's has to ask you to let her have them back.'

'And what happens then?'

'Then, she has to hand them over to the court.'

He thought about that for a moment.

'So, will I have to give them to her in person?'

'Not necessarily. You could give it to her lawyers directly. Or they can arrange a courier to collect them from you. Unless you want me to come down and collect the stuff.' Then she added, as if mirroring his thoughts, 'If you feel that it might be better?'

He realised that he was being childish.

'No, that's a real chore for you,' he said. 'A courier is the answer, surely.'

It was time for her to pop the question.

'So, do you still have any of her stuff?'

There was another long silence, as he looked through the kitchen windows towards the valleys of the estate.

'Jamie?'

'Sorry. What?'

'Have you kept any of her stuff?'

He gave a slightly croaky response, then added: 'Not in the house, but yes, I think I can get it.'

'And did it include any papers?'

A lump had developed in his throat.

'I think so, yes. I can't really remember. No, I do. I remember her saying that there were some files of papers that she wanted me to hold onto down here, because she didn't think they would be safe in her flat. Half a dozen files; perhaps more. She had put them in some cardboard boxes. I don't recall how many.'

'And you've still got them?'

'I reckon so, to quote the great Clint. She said that she wanted to leave them with me for safekeeping at the time as a precaution. She didn't elucidate, but I suspect that she did not want, you know, *him* to know that she had them.'

The word 'him' was said with a bitterness that was foreign to him. Ali was astute enough to realise that it reminded Jamie that the only reason that 'he' might find the papers would be if he went round to her flat.

'So, what do you want me to say to Cat?' she asked delicately.

'Why don't we just say that I've still got some of her stuff, and that it probably includes the papers that she left here.'

'And can she also say that, once you've found them, her lawyers can arrange for a courier to come down to collect what you have?'

'Yes, let's leave it like that. Just as long as she's able to comply with whatever the judge has ordered her to do.'

'And is there any chance that you might be able to tell the lawyers tomorrow morning, one way or the other, whether or not you have definitely got the papers? I can give you all the details.'

Another silence, as he contemplated the prospect of opening up that barn. He could still remember the scent of her perfume on her clothes. Just the thought of smelling it again was painful.

'Jamie?'

'I'll need to find the keys or get one of the lads to help me open some locks and doors, so it could take a couple of days.'

She decided not to push him further.

'OK. I'll tell her that, but it's Monday today, and she's due in court on Friday. So that doesn't give her or her lawyers much time to consider them. I don't suppose you could make it a priority?'

A heavy sigh, then: 'Okay, sis. I'll start to make some calls.'

'Thanks, Jamie.'

Next, she summoned the will to trespass onto even more sensitive terrain. It was a subject that had been off limits between them for so long.

'Oh, and Jamie?'

'Yep.'

'There's just one more thing, and it's better that you hear this from me rather than via any third party.'

That sounded truly ominous to Jamie. 'Come on, sis, it's not as if she haven't asked enough of a favour.'

'No, Jamie, this is different.'

'Oh yeah?'

'Yes, Jamie. The thing is that Cat wants to file a claim herself against the company. She's been advised that she's got quite a strong one.'

'So?'

'Well, you see, her claim would be for constructive dismissal, but also with the additional grounds of sexual harassment.'

A longer silence this time.

'I think you can guess what that means, Jamie. And before you say anything, AlphaOm got a search order against Cat's laptop and mobile, which the court has seized. Cat's been advised that this means that her former employer will soon know about all those vile emails and photos that she was sent by that creep, and that their lawyers will soon get to see them too.'

This was met by stony silence.

'Cat says that her barrister will try to prevent the photos from going any further than the company's lawyers, but not before her solicitor has told the other side what the emails and text messages contain.'

The import of what she had said dominated the short silence in the conversation, until Jamie eventually said in a strained voice, 'I see.'

'But Jamie, Cat wants your consent before she tells her lawyers that she is definitely going to use the emails and texts to support her claim.'

Again, the silence hung in the air.

'You don't have to decide right now, Jamie. Cat wants you to think about it first. She does not have to say anything just yet. It can wait.' She waited for him to say something. When she realised that he was not going to speak, she continued, 'Jamie, she's not going to take this any further until you've had a chance to think about. She won't do anything without your permission.'

Silence again.

'Jamie?'

'You're saying that she's going to need to use those fucking emails, isn't she!' he finally exclaimed. 'The ones that ... that cunt sent to me and copied to her. She'll need to use them to prove her claim, won't she?'

'It's possible, Jamie, even likely, yes. But it's primarily the actual videos and the photos that she needs to use, rather than the emails themselves. But, yes, there's a risk. And that's why she's asking you for your permission first.'

More silence.

'Jamie, it's going to take a lot of guts for her to make the claim. I haven't seen the photos or the videos, but she's described what they involve. I would never allow photos of myself like that to be shown to anyone else, let alone seen in open court. Imagine what she's got to put herself through!'

'Frankly, Ali, she didn't have to "put herself through it" in the first place. Why did she ever have to get involved with that pervert?'

'Jamie, darling, if she'd known the answer to that question at the time, we probably would not be having this conversation.'

She was right. Jamie could see that. But by God it still hurt. But then again, he knew that he couldn't go on hiding from the past forever. In a way, perhaps he had been waiting for something like this to happen.

'Maybe you're right, Ali. Perhaps it is time for me to face up to what happened between us. I know I can't just go on like this. It's just that ...'

She sensed his voice about to crack.

'Jamie, we'll have plenty of time to talk things over when we meet up. I could come down this weekend, if that would help.'

'That would be really nice, sis.'

'Okay, but let's not rush things until you're ready, yeah?'

'Okay.'

'I'll call you again tomorrow, okay?'

'Yeah. Thanks, sis. You're a real brick. You know that, don't you?'

'I'm always here for you, Jamie. Love you.'

'Yeah. Same here. Bye, sis.'

Chapter 15

Tuesday morning found CT still evading his pursuers within the Legal Department. He knew that he would need to speak to them at some point. Yet the delay was important. It had provided him with valuable time in which to cover his tracks. He had spent the weekend 'cleaning' both his personal and business computers. He was now reasonably confident that there was nothing that a cursory forensic trawl would uncover which could either compromise his department or embarrass him personally.

He had sorted his files into an order of his own choosing, and had removed beyond trace – except perhaps to the most able and experienced IT expert – any material which an impartial tribunal might regard as potentially incriminating to him, at least as far as any alleged affair with Miss Symonds was concerned.

In the business of public relations, CT lived by a simple maxim: knowledge is power. Adherence to this rule required CT to acquire not only knowledge of what his opponents or competitors had done, or were doing or intended to do, it also required him to obtain, by whatever means, knowledge appertaining to the conduct of his own side.

Such a fixation with the control of information is a common feature in many despots, and CT was no exception. It was why he had proved himself so useful to his chief, whose posterior he had made it his business to guard so efficiently over the years. Thus, it was entirely consistent with his need for control that he was determined to limit the extent of the knowledge which the lawyers on both sides would obtain about his world, either professional or private.

Yet now, to his intense frustration, he lacked such crucial knowledge. Specifically, he now needed to know in detail what material the company was using or was about to acquire in its ill-advised campaign against both the paper and Kitty. That included what they knew, and what they had said.

The obvious route to such knowledge lay with the very person whose calls he had evaded for the past few days. But CT did not do obvious. He was nothing if not versatile. And if there was one thing on which he prided himself, it was his ability to wriggle out of a sticky corner or, more to the point, how to needle his way into a seemingly impregnable fortress.

As to the latter, long years in his trade has taught him – and he had schooled himself in military history – that ever since the Middle Ages many a citadel had capitulated not as a result of a superior force of arms from without, but more often from an inherent weakness betrayed from within. Sometimes such infidelity was innocent, but more often it was executed for personal gain.

'Follow the money' was the mantra applied by many an inquisitor, and CT was adept at scenting out the weakest link in a seemingly secure chain. What little knowledge he possessed of classical literature included the value of discovering the Homeric equivalent of a vulnerable heel. Such knowledge in the hands of an adversary was a dangerous thing. It had brought about Achilles' downfall.

Right now, he needed to get hold of the information which currently resided or was shortly to reside within the team of which he was not a member. His absence abroad during the past few days had proved a short-term blessing, in that it had enabled him to cover his tracks. But it had also removed him from the immediate axis of influence.

He needed to rectify this, and soon.

To his credit, CT had already discovered the identities of the constituent members of the committee formed and empowered by the chief executive to prosecute his campaign. That committee reported directly to the CEO. And, as CT had expected, the conduit to the CEO, and thus the chair of the committee, was none other than the Mamba, as opposed to the head of legal.

No surprise there, he thought to himself. The guy's a fucking wimp.

He realised that he could expect no joy from the 'Mamba' in terms of relevant information, and assumed that she had contrived his exclusion from the committee, no doubt on grounds of 'conflict'.

Fucking bitch.

However, standing back, he was able to appreciate the dual advantages – and the irony – of being excluded from the centre of operations. If there was to be a PR disaster as a result of this fiasco, he could avoid any subsequent recriminations. He was already spinning his line about how the result would have been so very different if only the committee had consulted his expertise. His conceit excluded the possibility that anyone had a higher opinion of his expertise than he did himself.

To business. His attention focussed on the Mamba's lapdog. He was unsure how she would react to his charm offensive, not least because he harboured a strong suspicion that the girl was gay, or just not interested in men. But that did not deter him, for he had scored notable successes in the past with girls whose confidence in their own sexual orientation had been less than certain.

This girl was not a beauty, that much was clear. Yet from her photograph she seemed to have made no attempt to mitigate the rough hand she had been dealt through her genes. Instead, it almost seemed that she had merely adopted the Mamba's appearance in all matters cosmetic and stylistic, such that the end product was hardly designed to accelerate the flow of any red corpuscles – and that went for either sex.

He reprimanded himself. If he was to have any chance of exploiting any weakness in her persona, and specifically her persuasions, he would have to overcome his prejudices and feign an ardour worthy of Don Giovanni.

No time like the present, he thought, and opened up his laptop again. He saw and ignored a score of emails in his inbox as he pulled up the company's intranet and searched for her details on the system.

Maria. That was her name. Maria Lutherson.

He moved the cursor across his screen to highlight her name, and pulled up her details. There she was, part of the Black Mamba's team in internal affairs.

He read the internal CV which the girl had posted onto the company's intranet. He always liked to start with 'interests and hobbies' when preparing for these sorts of campaigns. If a touch of reconnaissance worked for generals and lawyers, then it was certainly good enough for him. And, he thought to himself, there was surely nothing to be lost by throwing in a little advance planning, especially if he stood to gain a modest advantage in the subsequent engagement.

As a seasoned gigolo, CT was a stranger to any codes of honour. He was no team player, and the concept of chivalry wasn't on the substitutes' bench, and had never even made it into the squad.

He scanned down her CV until he came to the section on 'personal interests'. A rare smile crossed his lips as he read on.

'Secretary of the company's wine-tasting club; member of the company's bridge club; enjoys music and reading.'

Well, that was a start, he thought. He could at least work with the first two. He ignored the others. He always reckoned that 'reading' was a bit of a cop-out. One might as well say 'breathing'. Reading what? English literature? Classical literature? Not much of a clue there. The same went for music. It covered anything from Mozart to rap.

His department was charged with promoting attendance and participation in the clubs which were sponsored by the company. This gave him ready access to the activities of these internal societies. These were meant to promote and facilitate team-building and cross-fraternisation within the company. But he had always regarded these as being rather incestuous, with the usual suspects pitching up. He suspected that the wine-tasting club was no exception.

Still, access had its advantages, and he was able to realise one of them at the click of a mouse as he pulled up the membership of the wine-tasting club on his screen. As head of his department, he was a nominal member, although he seldom put in an appearance. He flicked through the minutes of their last meeting, wherein Maria had dutifully recorded in fastidious detail the attendance and proceedings, and gave notice of the date, venue and purpose of their next meeting.

In faithful dedication to her duties, Maria had annexed to the minutes the agenda for the forthcoming meeting, the principal item of which was a 'Focus on the red wines of the Rhone,' both northern and southern.

A doddle, he thought. He could score some easy points. In fact, he could almost run the meeting single-handed, noting that it was scheduled for the following week. The test for him was how to ingratiate himself with this girl enough for her to take him into her confidence – or her bed. It mattered little to him which of them occurred first. Either would yield him the results he desired.

Well, that wasn't quite true, he admitted to himself. Whilst the latter would present the greater challenge, it also brought with it the added potential of an opportunity to indulge his private vice.

*

'If I might say so, Tom,' said Rosalyn, bringing matters to a conclusion, 'that is a first rate letter. One of your best, I'd say.'

'All part of the service,' he replied. 'But thank you.'

'The thanks are on Cat and me, Tom. I really like the strategy on all fronts as regards our so-called admissions regarding the material that was thrown up by the search of Cat's laptop. They won't be expecting this, especially so early in the case, and it really does not leave them much room for manoeuvre.'

She turned to Cat.

'And thank you, Cat, for putting in the hours to go through all this material, and including what Tom describes as the unchivalrous items.'

'Actually,' corrected Tom, 'that is not my phrase. It was the term that the silk who is acting for the paper used when I explained the, um, background. I sought a second opinion from him on how we should use it.'

'And free advice from such an eminent source is not to be dismissed lightly. We've used him in the past, and he's first rate.'

Cat had been listening to the exchange between her lawyers, and was comforted by their demeanour and the confidence in their advice. She half expected what Rosalyn was about to say next.

'So, the key question for you, Cat,' Rosalyn began, 'is whether you are ready – and I mean mentally prepared – for us to disclose the provenance of the offending material at this stage. As you know, my initial view had been to hold this back for the time being, but I have been persuaded by Tom – and especially following his discussion with the paper's silk – that we should hit the other side with it now. They have already asked about it, so there is little to be gained by delay. Add to that the fact that we do intend ultimately to reveal its existence and provenance, but specifically not its content, which is to be viewed by only one or two lawyers by the other side. Also, there is a powerful case for confronting the other side with it now.'

'I should add,' Tom interjected, 'that I have run this point past my colleague in chambers. She's the one that I recommended for your harassment claim. She agrees that there is little to lose by this strategy, and quite a big potential upside.'

But still Cat hesitated.

'Cat?' Rosalind prompted.

Her thoughts were about Jamie, with whom she had still not spoken about this. And Ali had told her that she had left matters on the basis that she, Cat, would not take any action regarding the emails and photos without his consent. She feared that the strategy that was being advocated by her lawyers would compromise that position, and leave

Jamie feeling that she had forced his hand. She had said as much to Rosalyn.

'You see, I hurt him so badly last time. I feel terrible about it. I cannot bear to think that I would be putting him through this all over again, and especially when Ali – she's his sister – has told him that I would wait for his consent. Won't he think that I have betrayed him all over again?'

Tom looked across to Rosalyn as if to consult on who should be the one to answer Cat's perfectly fair question. Rosalind took the lead.

'I think it is important if I explain the distinction here between making use of this material for the purpose of a claim, and conceding its relevance to the issues in dispute. The letter as drafted by Tom does three things. It explains the provenance of the material, and that is important in order to establish, or at least corroborate, the provenance of some of the other key documents that we intend to use. Secondly, it asserts your right to privacy in respect of content, as opposed to provenance, which as I said we want to concede is relevant to the case. And thirdly, it does no more than reserve all your rights in respect of both the provenance and content of the material. It specifically does not advance a claim based on the material, which I think is the point that concerns you.'

Cat thought about that for a moment.

'Does that help, Cat?'

She could see the force of what Rosalyn was saying. 'So, what y'all are saying is that we – by which I suppose I mean "I" – don't really have much of an alternative?'

Both Rosalyn and Tom nodded.

'Not really, Cat,' Rosalyn confirmed. 'We could delay this, but on balance we think that will do more harm than good, especially since the other side have asked us to consent to inspection. In each of the three respects that I explained, the letter is doing no more than is necessary to protect your position, bearing in mind that you are subject to a court order that obliges you to disclose anything of relevance.'

'Yes, I keep forgetting about that.'

'That's perfectly normal, Cat. I'd be surprised if you were not urging me to take the fight to the other side.'

Cat looked across at Tomo. 'And I guess, Tomo, that I don't need to ask you if you agree, since you were the one who drafted the letter?'

'You're doing the right thing, Cat,' he reassured her. 'Trust us.'

'Okay. But I've got to speak to Ali first. Can it wait another day or so? I just want to get her take on how Jamie will react.'

'Actually,' suggested Tomo, 'why don't I just revise the letter to record that we are in the process of obtaining the consent of the owner of the premises to release his personal data to the claimants' lawyers? That would buy us the time we need.'

'Fine. Let's go with that for the time being,' said Rosalyn.

*

CT prepared himself to make his call to the Mamba's lapdog. He had studied what passed for her profile long enough.

He dialled her internal extension.

'Maria Lutherson,' announced the crisp, slightly nasal voice.

'Hi Maria. This is CT,' he oozed. 'Clive Thompson, from commercial development, but everyone likes to call me CT.'

That was a lie, and he knew it. He avidly promoted that abbreviation. And he could think of quite a few people in the company, her boss for one, who would like to call him something else to his face

'Oh, hi,' she replied cautiously.

'I know that we've certainly met before. I think it was at the wine club a year or so back. And I've just been reading your extremely informative minutes of the last meeting of the club. An excellent analysis of the Loire wines, if I might say so. I especially liked your description of the 2022 Saumur Champigny which you all seemed to enjoy. Don't tell me, but I'm guessing that you had a hand in its selection?'

'Well, I . . .'

'I only had to read your piece and I was ready to buy a case. Right on the button, if I might say so. I sure could use someone with those skills in my department, but I suppose you're going to tell me that Barbara would never let someone with your talents make such a move? Sorry, don't answer that. It was unfair of me to go there. But your article was still excellent stuff.'

'Well, thank you, Mr Thompson . . .'

'CT, please Maria,' he interrupted, oozing charm, instantly recognising the discernible change in her tone. Flattery was such a useful tool,

'Of course, CT. Sorry. Yes, it was a good meeting last month, and everyone enjoyed the reds as much as the whites. Actually, CT, it's funny you should call, because I was just about to drop you an email.'

Well, there's a surprise, he thought, immediately on his guard. Had she been put into bat by Ted Fisher, he wondered. But this was an odd route for Fisher to take. He was usually one for the direct approach.

Still, CT told himself to tread carefully, and blandly responded, 'If it's about next week's meeting of the wine-tasting club, that really would be a real coincidence, because that's one of the reasons why I was calling you.'

'Actually, CT, I'm sorry to say that the reason why I wanted to speak with you was business rather than pleasure. I'm afraid it's to do with those articles in *The Daily Chronicle* last week.'

'Stranger still, Maria,' he lied. He had to hand it to Fisher. He certainly had not seen this one coming. He had already had to dodge several calls from the lawyers over the last few days, and thought it best to maintain the pretence.

'Actually,' he continued, 'that was the second reason for my call. We hardly know each other and you're reading me like a book. Forget telepathy, this is primeval!'

'Yeah, well, coincidences do happen,' she replied, chiding herself at once for such a sissy response. The truth was that she had been unprepared when the call came through, and now she was struggling for some words that would enable her to move the conversation onto her agenda. What she had yet to appreciate was that one had to be fleet of foot if one wanted to stay ahead of CT in a one-to-one, and Maria's skills lay in pedantic foot-slogging through mountains of paper.

Quick-witted she was not. Thus, he was first off the mark.

'I tell you what,' he declared, more as a decision than a proposal. 'We'll take it in turns. Since I called you, I'll go first with my ideas for next week's wine club meeting. That will not take up too much of our time. And then you go second with *The Daily Chronicle* number. How does that sound?'

His enthusiasm was infectious, as he had intended. And, if she was honest with herself, such was her degree of stress that she almost found it easier to let their discussion run the course which suited CT. And there was the small matter of him being a director.

'Sure,' she acquiesced. 'But only because you started the call. And then we'll move on to the important stuff, yeah.'

'Sure thing, Maria. That's a deal.'

She was unaware of the python's tail. Surreptitious, oily and sly, it began to curl around her ankle. Meanwhile, on the other end of the line, CT's tongue began to dart in and of the side of his mouth in that dreadful habit.

He had not acquired the label of 'Mr Twenty Percent' during his university days by concealing what he regarded as his radiant light behind a bushel. With practised ease, he began to steer his charm offensive towards its well-rehearsed pattern. The telephone was not his preferred medium, and if he were to be honest with himself (which he seldom was), he would have to concede that his strike rate was perhaps not as benign as he had been able to boast in his younger days. Still, he was by no means displeased with the initial exchange, and even allowed himself to contemplate the earnest expectation that his target would prove to be another of his victims.

'Right then,' he began. 'Rhone reds. That's an ambitious programme for one meeting; but I'm sure you already know that. It's really a question of emphasis, or to use your word, *focus*, which, if I might say so, is exactly right. If the meeting is going to cover both north and south, which I assume it will, one must first decide what wines should be highlighted. Now, I'm not sure if you have already chosen the wines which you wish to include for tasting, because, if you have, then my proposal may not be as helpful as I intend it to be. Am I too late to be making suggestions?'

'Actually, no, we – that is the committee – have not finalised the list yet. We're still – or rather I'm still – chasing up members who have not yet booked to say that they will be attending, and more importantly, paid their subscriptions. That's all part of my job as secretary, I'm sorry to say,' she added, with a note of bitterness.

'Oh, I've been there, I can tell you,' he lied smoothly. 'It's the old story. Until you know how many will attend, you can't fix the budget. And without a budget, your committee can't decide which of the wines you have shortlisted you can actually afford. Is that about right?'

'Yup, that's where I'm at,' she agreed, subconsciously imitating his language. 'That's the bit that I don't like. I get really narked having to chase the club members every month. It takes all the fun out of organising the meetings.'

'Tell me about it,' he empathised. 'I used to run a similar club at my last place, and I know only too well what a thankless task it is.' Mendacity came so easily to him that he was often able to convince himself as to the veracity of his own words. 'I really admire you for taking on the role here, especially since the potential numbers are so much higher than I had to deal with. Running a department is a push-over by comparison, which is why I think you're doing such a great job.'

'Well, someone's got to do it, and I do really enjoy learning so much about a subject which I'm fairly new to.'

'Sorry, I'm not buying that, Maria. Anyone who can write about wine the way you do is way beyond the beginners' class. There's no way I'm going to let you sell yourself short by describing yourself as a novice. And you wouldn't have become elected as club secretary if you were.'

'All right, CT, since you insist, I do know a bit more than I did a few years back when I started with the club. But I'm grateful for your confidence.'

'Nothing more than you deserve, I'm sure.' He gloated to himself as he said this. He was so slick it was almost too easy. It was almost like stealing candies from a kid. Just a touch more of the smoochy stuff and he should be right on track. 'And I bet we could compare notes all day on the agonies of trying to run a club. Herding cats would be easier, wouldn't it?'

'Absolutely right,' she agreed, slowly falling for the charm.

'But let's stay with the Rhone reds for the moment,' he insisted, diverting their conversation onto his carefully prepared ground. 'I'll tell you why. It just so happens that the Rhone is one of the valleys – quite a big valley, I agree – that I have got to know rather well. In fact, I spent some of my annual leave there again last year, testing out some of my favourite vineyards.'

'Dream on,' she applauded.

'And, as part of the spoils of my visit, I brought back a shedload of wine which will keep me going for at least a decade. In fact, I've got so much left that I was proposing to offer you a couple of cases for your meeting next week. Unless, of course, you'd prefer to do the choosing with your committee, as you said.'

'Wow, CT. That's really generous. It's a bit like Christmas coming early for us. But you'll understand that it's not just my decision. I can't speak for the whole committee, but I'm sure that they would be really grateful once I tell them. And I'd need to know what we were talking about. No, that sounds all wrong, and I don't want to be rude. What I mean is, so that I can persuade the committee to accept, can you tell me what would be in this case?'

'Most certainly. And I apologise if I gave the impression that I expected your committee to accept the offer in complete ignorance of what was being proposed. That would have been totally out of order.'

'Oh no, CT, you didn't give that impression at all. It was just me being a bit slow; stepping in it as usual.'

'Now there you go again, Maria, putting yourself down. I won't have it. You'll be telling me next that you don't think you're attractive, and if I'm allowed a say in the matter, I would be at the front of a long queue looking to tell you you're dead wrong.'

The embarrassed silence at the other end of the phone was a joy to his ears.

'And to prove my point, at the end of this conversation I'm going to try to fix a date in your diary when we can meet up for a drink after work. But, staying with the issue in hand, to the best of my recollection the wines that I have got left include a few of the big names and one or two which some of the club members will not have heard of before. I'm assuming that you normally get through two bottles of each wine, yes?'

'Normally, yes, but that doesn't mean that you have to … you know, provide that many for the meeting.'

'Of course, but on the other hand I wouldn't want to change the usual agenda. Now, let's see what I've got on my list. First, there's a rather unusual Fleurie to get them started, followed by an especially good vintage of Chateauneuf du Pape – 2007 I think, or possibly 2009. Then there's some 2010 Crozes Hermitage and Saint Joseph which are both starting to drink really well. Next, I've got a wine which you might not have heard of; it's from a small estate called Rasteau which is just starting to sell under its own label rather than to the big houses. And, of course, the evening would not be complete without a couple of bottles of Cote Rotie, and a 2007 at that. Does that sound like the sort of list which you and your colleagues might have put together, or would you want to put something rather more exotic on the table?'

'Wow, CT, that's going a bit up-market for us. It's going to be quite an act for us to follow in future meetings.'

'Oh, yes, I hadn't thought of that,' he lied, 'and I promise you that I hadn't intended to upstage the committee in any way. I shall quite understand, Maria, if you would prefer to choose your own list.'

'Oh, no, CT, that's not what I meant ...'

'You see, it's just that I've got so much of the stuff and these vintages are drinking really well now. I know that I wouldn't be able to get through all these Rhone's before they begin to go off.'

'Well ...'

'It really would be a crime to let those wines go to waste.'

'Well, that's really generous, CT, and if you're sure ...'

'Absolutely positive, Maria, I swear. And it would give me a real pleasure to know that I'd be introducing some of my favourite wines to the club, especially since I'd be helping you in the process.'

'That's very kind of you, CT.'

'Not at all, Maria,' he replied, and then added as if reading her mind, 'and I would prefer if this stayed just between you and me, provided of course that you wouldn't mind taking the credit for choosing the wines.'

There was a pause as Maria reflected on the kudos which would attach to her as a result of procuring these vintage wines for the meeting.

'I can live with that, but only, CT, as long as you're really sure that you want to keep your name out of it.'

'I'm sure, believe me.'

'OK, then I'll just say that the wines have been supplied to us by an anonymous donor, because otherwise I'll be asked questions about how we were able to afford to buy in those wines.'

'Fine with me, Maria.' Time to change tack here, he thought, whilst he still held the initiative. 'Now can I ask you about the other matter which we both wanted to discuss. That is the articles in *The Daily Chronicle*. I've been abroad for most of the week, and all weekend, but I understand that the company has decided to involve the lawyers on this and to go on the offensive?'

'Actually CT,' she replied candidly, 'our lawyers have gone a lot further than that. They've have obtained an injunction against the newspaper, and ...'

'What! Maria, you have got to be kidding me! That is a fucking – sorry, forgive my language – that is a PR car crash waiting to happen. Surely the board can see that the story will just die a death if we ignore it.'

'You see ...'

'And why wasn't I consulted?'

'I suppose it's because the lawyers also obtained an injunction against a former member of your department.'

'What?'

'Well, they, and we, have good reason to believe that this person was responsible for leaking our own confidential material to the paper. She's Catriona Symonds. I'm not sure how well you knew her.'

'They've done what!' exclaimed CT, avoiding the question and injecting a little of his amateur theatrics. 'I really hope that they know what they're doing, and the potential downside. Russian roulette is child's play compared to this.' Then he added, 'I assume that the other reason why I wasn't consulted was because this came from the top. Am I right on that, Maria?'

'That's my understanding, CT, although you need to understand that I don't have any first-hand knowledge of how this all started. I didn't become involved until the decision had already been taken to bring in the lawyers. But I am now.'

'Really? How so?'

'Yes. You see, I now sit on the committee set up by the chief which is chaired by my boss and which is co-coordinating the company's strategy. And I was put up as a lead witness for the company.'

'What? You mean that Barbara has let you show the way into the lion's den, instead of leading from the front?' Before she could answer, he pretended to check himself: 'Sorry, Maria. That was out of order. I shouldn't have brought Barbara's name into this. I'm sure there was a good reason.'

She had not expected such an outburst from him, especially one that brought into doubt her loyalty to her boss and mentor. Yet, despite her distance from the original decision-making process, she needed someone to speak to, and he could be just the right person.

But she could not find the words.

CT had half expected her to resort to the well-tried Nuremberg defence of obeying orders. So, perplexed by her silence, he continued: 'I'm not blaming you, Maria. Of course I'm not. But has anyone given any thought to the possibility that this could all backfire on us? Even if we're in the right, which the lawyers must obviously think we are, we're never going to win the PR battle on this. Companies like us never do.'

'Well, you see ...'

'I have to be honest,' he lied, 'it really worries me that this could all turn out very badly for the company.'

'Well, the advice we're getting is that the paper had no right to use our own confidential documents, especially if these have been unlawfully obtained, and we say that they have been, and by Ms Symonds when ...'

'Even so, Maria, we're taking a hell of a risk.'

'Well, the lawyers say that we're entitled to prevent the paper from publishing our own confidential material. It should be an open and shut case.'

'Not that old label again, Maria. If you only knew how many times I've heard of that advice being given, and the number of companies who have regretted taking it. These things have a habit of going badly wrong.'

There was silence from the end of the line. That made CT's ears prick up. He decided to push a bit further.

'The real trouble is, Maria, that there's a big difference between what the law says about the rights and wrongs of the case and what the buying public thinks when the whole business gets opened up in court. They really are two very different things, which is why I should have been consulted.'

No reply. He cast his baited line further across the flowing waters.

'All you need is for our team to foul up on some technical point and the whole house of cards comes crashing down.'

Still silence. Hey up, we could be on to something here, he thought.

'I've seen it all before, believe me.'

The stillness on the other end of the line was tangible.

'Maria, are you still there?'

'What? Oh ... yes, I'm here.'

Well bugger me sideways, thought CT. There has been a foul up, and she bloody knows about it. Talk about a stroke of fortune.

'Obviously I don't want to pry, Maria, but are you aware of any areas where you think we could be, you know, exposed?'

Another silence. This was too good for a mid-week call. What her silence was telling him was that the *suits* in the Legal Department – he'd even got Kitty to call them that – had already dropped the ball, and the match had barely even begun. This was fucking magic!

'Don't go there if it's difficult, Maria. I don't need to know right now.

We can always come back to that when we've covered the other stuff, yes?'

'Yeah, fine,' came the choked response.

All in good time, he thought. There was no need to rub salt into this particular wound right now. He would pick his moment. In the meantime, he would retain the initiative in this conversation.

'As you probably know, I'm going to have to speak to the chief and the rest of the board on the PR issues arising out of this.'

That was another lie, of course, but he decided to maintain the façade, and he doubted whether the girl would see through this. Then again, she would have known that he hadn't been consulted by her department before the decision was taken to go to law. And he'd told her that none of the other board members had spoken to him first, least of all the chief. So, it was probably logical for her to assume that he would need to offer them his advice.

On the other hand, he had a strong hunch that the Mamba had ensured that he had been excluded from the committee charged with overseeing the legal proceedings, no doubt citing a fundamental conflict of interest on his part. The Legal Department would have bought into that, and he would bet good money that the Mamba had not made Maria privy to her scheming design. Even so, it was odd that she should be willing to confide in him of all people when her boss had no intention of doing so.

'The chief will obviously have his eye mainly on the share price and the reactions of the big fund managers and brokers. I guess that's the message that you're getting from the top, isn't it, Maria?'

'Pretty much,' she agreed.

'But my job is to focus on our market profile and the public image associated with our range of products, as I'm sure you will appreciate.'

'Yes, of course.'

He was over-egging it a bit, but so what, he thought. He seldom missed an opportunity to share with each new acquaintance his exaggerated views on his own self-importance. He wasn't going to make this an exception.

'Right then,' he continued, 'in order to put me in the picture, you'd better tell me where we've got to in the case. And I suppose that we can start with the sort of evidence that is going to come out in court.'

'What exactly do you need to know?'

Gotcha, thought CT to himself, as he slowly began to wind in his line in readiness for the moment – fast approaching – that he got this fish to take the bait. She would soon be well and truly hooked. CT was in his element now. This was going better than he could ever have predicted, and they were still at first base.

'Well,' he said, in answer to Maria's delightful invitation to him to reveal the material he was looking for, 'first, what's the evidence that we're using at the moment; next, what evidence are we looking to use; then, what evidence are we expecting the other side to use; and finally, what are we intending to get out of this?'

'Wow, that quite a list, CT.'

'That's just for starters, believe me! The reason that I'm asking you is that I have to know this if I'm going to have any kind of sensible conversation with the chief. I don't mean to sound pushy or anything.' Then he added for good measure: 'We can leave to one side any own-goals that we might be about to score, or that are already in the back of the net.'

He was biding his time on that score, but he wasn't going to let her off the hook any time soon on that hot potato. He didn't get to become head of the Commercial Development Department of one the world's largest pharmaceutical companies without acquiring a sixth sense for that vulnerable heel.

'OK,' she began, after clearing her throat again, 'our lawyers went to court last week – Friday afternoon, actually – and obtained an injunction against *The Daily Chronicle* and the girl, Catriona Symonds, and also against the journalist who wrote the main article. As I said, the principal affidavit has been sworn by me.'

'And now I come to think about it, I'm glad that the company has recognised your worth,' he lied. 'Seems only right and proper.'

How typical of the Mamba, he thought, to get one of her lapdogs to put their head on the block in such a high-profile case, rather than step into the breach herself. There were almost fewer flies on her than there were on him. But this did conveniently play into his hands.

'And in a nutshell, what does it say?'

'Actually, my affidavit is quite a long document,' she continued. 'It runs to over fifty pages. It has a file of exhibits which attach all the documents that we can also show have been either quoted or used by the newspaper in the article, and which we can prove are confidential to the company.'

'OK. That tells me what's in it, but not what it says. And just to be clear, I'm not asking you to tell me over the phone in detail what you've written in a fifty-page document. I'm just after the main line of attack in it.'

'No, I fully appreciate why you need this. But you need to know that my statement was drafted all through the night at the lawyers' offices, along with some other affidavits and statements which we've produced.'

'So, you're saying there's a fair bit to read?'

'Exactly, and it's probably best that you do.'

Time to back off, he thought, and to change the angle.

'Hey! You're right. I didn't mean to impose. I can hardly expect you to be word perfect on a document that's been written for you, especially one that long. But I guess you've had to live and breathe this for a day or so?'

'Yeah, pretty much, although it wasn't exactly all my own work, if you get my meaning. The lawyers had a big hand in it.'

'So what's new! I wouldn't have expected anything different. Which was why I was going to suggest that you let me read through the evidence bundle. That would save you a lot of time. And it would also let me see where there might be holes in our case which I would be able to fill.'

There was a time in such a conversation when he instinctively judged it right to prepare his net to land whatever had taken his fly. And if the fish was a person looking for an easy way out of a corner into which they had painted themselves, even if the reality might be objectively different, so much the better. His instinct and experience told him that he had reached such a moment.

So, in his best bedside voice, he said, 'I was going to suggest that we meet up. That way, if there happened to be any areas where you considered the company to be weak or in any way exposed, you could then tell me about them.'

She didn't answer, so he added: 'In strict confidence, of course. Just between you and me.'

The ensuing silence was exactly as he had predicted. The longer she hesitated, the more likely she was to consent. He could almost hear her weighing up the benefits of securing the sympathetic ear as opposed to trying to carry the load by herself, asking herself how badly she needed to obtain advice from an informed colleague. At the same time, she had to assess the gravity of the risk that she would expose herself to by disclosing sensitive information outside the claim committee, and to someone who had deliberately been excluded from it by her boss.

He decided to obey the first rule of a salesman which he religiously taught: when you're looking to close a deal, and you've asked a closing question: *Shut The Fuck Up*.

His patience was rewarded.

'OK,' she said at last, 'but on the strict understanding that you can't show the file to anyone else. You must promise me that.'

'Promise, and cross my heart and hope to die,' he said with a wry smile.

That was one of the very few promises that he was more than ready to keep.

'And you won't make any copies of anything.'

'Of course not.' And the cheque's in the post, he said to himself.

'Tell you what,' he suggested enthusiastically, 'why don't you let me have a copy of your court files to read overnight, then I could return them to you in the morning, and at the same time I could bring the wine in to the office so that it would be here for your meeting next week. Does that sound like a fair deal to you?'

'If you're sure that's not too much trouble, it would be great to get the wines in now. I would then have time to prepare the notes for the tasting forms.'

'It's no trouble at all,' he lied.

He would have to drive to his friendly wine merchants to buy the cases, but he could get the company to pick up the tab for that.

'Also,' she added, 'it would mean that the evidence files would only be out of the office for one night, which would be good.'

'So, would you like me to come down before my next meeting starts and collect the files directly from you? Otherwise, if you prefer to meet up in the car park, we could do that. Which would be more convenient to you?'

'Actually, coming down here might be a bit obvious. Let's meet up in the car park. Where are you parked?'

He sensed opportunity here.

'Mine's the silver Merc parked along with the other directors. It's the sports coupe. I think it's still got the sunroof down.'

'Cool car, CT.'

'Proper wheels, that's what they are. Not like the souped-up sewing machines they're making now. Tell you what, can I give you a lift somewhere after work. Or better still, what about going for a drink first?'

Hesitation. That was good.

'The trouble is, CT, I can't really leave before seven. My boss has given me so much to do, and not just on this case, that, you know ...'

'Including helping to sort out the stuff which you might want to discuss with me? I mean, the stuff where you think the company might be at risk?'

A longer pause this time, indicating that he'd scored a bullseye. He couldn't even have written the script for this.

'Yeah, that as well,' she confessed in a quieter voice.

'Well, it's up to you, of course,' he soothed, reverting to his bedside manner again, 'but if you'd like a sympathetic ear or a shoulder to lean on, then I'm your man.'

Another pause.

'What sort of time were you thinking of?' she asked at last.

Fuck, but I'm good, he told himself. 'I'll fit in with you, Maria. You just tell me what would suit you best, and I'll figure out how best to use the time.'

'Well, would, say, seven-thirty be too late?' she asked tentatively. 'I reckon I could finish up here by then.'

'Seven-thirty in the car park it is then,' he announced. 'I'll look forward to it.'

'OK. See you then.'

Chapter 16

Dusk was already falling as the gamekeeper completed his inspection of the last pens on the south side of the estate which he had volunteered to cover. He had wanted to give the lads an evening off, and was ensuring that all the water troughs had been filled and that each fence was firmly secured against any vermin or predators that might trespass onto his 'turf' from neighbouring farms. He glanced at his watch and cursed. He would need to hurry if he was to be back in time for his meeting with the estate manager which had been adjourned as a result of those calls from Jamie's sister. The captain wanted to go through the diary to re-schedule all the dates for the forthcoming season, including those which would be taken by 'the family'. This was the euphemism which the captain employed on these occasions when he was seeking to avoid direct reference to Jamie in this or any other context.

The keeper had only just been informed that the venue for the meeting had been switched to the 'big house' at the express request of Jamie. This appeared to the keeper to be something of a landmark – twice in one week; one day even. Could this really herald the re-kindling of Jamie's interest in the shoot? It was certainly the first occasion since the beginning of the last season, so far as he was aware, that Jamie had exhibited any interest in it. Perhaps this really could mark the turning point as regards Jamie's life. It was too soon to think in terms of his love life.

The keeper pondered that possibility for a moment before entertaining a less charitable but probably more realistic interpretation. In his present humour, Jamie seemed almost to go out of his way to avoid the company of women. Also, the original venue would very likely have involved an encounter with the shoot captain's buxom and voluble wife. And it would involve accepting her hospitality at their house on the far end of the estate down the lane from the Puddletown Road.

The keeper reckoned that Jamie was not ready for that yet. Whilst the possibility of his renewed interest in the sport was not to be dismissed, of the two alternative reasons, the keeper regarded the latter as more likely.

Either way, it would be the second time in almost as many days that he would get to enjoy the rare privilege of an audience with Jamie. Consequently, he was anxious not to be late for such an occasion.

Having made a mental note to remind one of the underkeepers to check the vermin traps in the woods at the rear of the pen, he hauled himself behind the wheel of his Landy and began the short journey towards the drive to the manor house. His route took him across the valley and into the lane which then followed the meandering course of the River Piddle. He knew it so well he could almost drive it blindfold.

The lane was lined with hedgerows, which themselves marked the boundaries of the lush green water meadows, each beginning to bloom with wildflowers. He glanced across at the padlocked gates at the bottom of the track which ascended from the lane and up the slope to the deserted barn halfway up the opposite valley. He was about to check the thick metal chains advertising the forbidden territory when his eye caught sight of fresh tyre tacks by the gate.

They had not been there when he had last looked.

Don't tell me that Joey has broken his word already, the keeper asked himself, and so soon after giving his bond.

He could not be certain, but someone had. And for sure, Joey had plenty of form in that department.

He would tackle him on the matter when they next spoke.

*

Mary Fellowes re-read the emailed letter from the firm acting for Catriona Symonds for the third time. She was struck by its frank and co-operative tone, which seemed to mirror the impression given by Ms Symonds' affidavit that had arrived the previous day. What had impressed her on her first perusal, and did so again now, was the unequivocal admission that many of the documents that had been identified on Ms Symonds' laptop were in all probability the property of the company. This admission covered almost all of what had been termed the 'business' category, and also a large proportion of those listed under the 'cross-related' file.

But what the letter did not concede was that any of the documents in either category were 'confidential' to her clients.

So, whilst on its face that did indeed concede the first limb of her client's claim, namely the issue of property in the documents, it also provided a very convenient platform for the defendants to launch a defence based on justification, as well as non-disclosure, or even worse deliberate concealment by the company.

Her instinct smelled danger here.

What the defendants were saying was that the documents cited by the paper were genuine, along with a host of other material which none of her team had yet seen. She read on, and digested again the further admission that many of the documents in the second category were copies of emails passing between the director of the Commercial Development Department and other board members.

She did not like the sound of that one bit.

But what she disliked more was the admission – more of an allegation in reality – that the material identified in the 'sensitive' category had been sent to Ms Symonds by a senior employee of her clients. The letter conceded that the material was relevant to the issues in dispute, but only as regards the provenance of the sensitive material, and not the material itself.

Her firm was invited to nominate a senior representative or counsel, in either case preferably female, to whom the material could be shown. The letter contained an explicit invitation to her firm to concede the issues of provenance and relevance without the need for inspection of the material.

Now that, she had to admit to herself, was very cunning. The author would have known that her firm could not seriously countenance making any admission as to provenance without having first inspected the sensitive material. And the author would also have known that, once her firm had inspected the material, then her firm – and by association her clients – would become privy to knowledge of the content of the material. So, she would be damned either way.

She read on. The letter asserted a right to retain copies of the material in the first two categories for the purposes of the proceedings, subject to an undertaking to hand over such copies at the conclusion of all proceedings – which, she noted, Miss Symonds intended to contest vigorously.

She would have to advise her clients to concede that right, and to accept an undertaking along those lines, which was of course worthless. Her clients would almost certainly ask why. There was, as in all such cases, a simple answer. It was because she knew that, if the proceedings were contested in open court, then every man and his dog would get to read the contents of the material, which would do the usual rounds through social and other media.

The final paragraphs proposed arrangements regarding the logistics of inspection of the material in each category, and went on to request disclosure of a not insubstantial number of documents that were said to be in the possession of her clients during the time that Ms Symonds had been employed by her clients.

This was very clever. Someone had been burning the midnight oil on the other side, and she had that all too familiar uneasy feeling that the initiative in the case was about to be wrestled from her. And Mary Fellowes did not like that. Not one bit.

She convened a meeting of her team.

*

Jamie brought the meeting to an end, having offered beers all round.

'Just one other matter, please before we pack up for the evening. There are some bits and pieces that I need to retrieve from that disused barn just up from the valley road. I thought that I had the keys to the various locks there, but I must have mislaid them. I don't suppose either of you kept the spare set?'

Charlie swallowed a mouthful of beer, before responding. 'Well, if they're not in the Landy, then they'll be in the game room down besides the farmyard. If you give me a minute, I'll just take a look.'

'I'd appreciate that, thank you.'

'Oh, and of course Joey has a key to the gate so that he can let the herd in and out of the fields there when he's using them.'

'Of course. Why didn't I think of that?'

'I'll just be a second.'

Shortly afterwards, Charlie returned with what appeared to be a set of padlock keys on a ring with a blank tab on it.

'I reckon these must be the keys to the barn. I've called Joey, and he could meet us there in ten minutes if that would help.'

'Actually, that would be really helpful.'

'Right, I'll call him back right away.'

Joey was duly summoned, and Jamie announced that they should set off once they had finished their beers. Charlie's offer to accompany him was politely declined, and Charlie had the good sense not to ask a second time.

They indulged in small talk for a few minutes until Charlie deemed it expedient for him and the captain to leave, allowing Jamie to lock up and make the short journey down the road to the gate, where he found Joey waiting.

'I very much appreciate this, Joey, especially since you'll have had an early start.'

'No bother at all, sir. Happy to be of help.'

Joey could have won an Oscar with his over-dramatic heaving and grunting as he feigned his epic battle with the gate's padlock at the foot of the pot-holed lane. This was by no means the first time that he had unlocked these restraints of an evening, both for work but usually later for pleasure so as to provide access to his 'love chamber'. Indeed, he had performed the very same act just twenty-four hours previously, and had done his best to disguise his tracks in an attempt to avoid detection, not least by the ever-vigilant head-keeper.

He effected to sound a note of triumph as the chains clanked noisily down the rusty metal bars of the old gates. He looked for a sign of approbation from Jamie, for whose benefit his theatrics had been performed.

Alas, he was not even rewarded with a smile. Jamie was barely conscious of the stage-managed uncoupling of the links around the padlock, nor indeed of much else. His gaze was elsewhere.

Joey followed Jamie's gaze up the lane, and realised that his eyes were firmly fixed on the old barn way up the slope. He suddenly felt an unfamiliar sense of guilt, as if he had trespassed on another's soul. He knew when to keep his mouth shut.

He now felt ashamed that his primary concern, when Jamie had first asked for his help, had been that Jamie might suspect that the barn had been put to irregular use, despite the very clear instruction to stay away. He was equally ashamed that he had sneaked into the barn the previous evening via his usual entrance, and had done his best to dismantle any evidence of his amorous pursuits inside.

He pulled open the gates, and jumped into his pick-up, expecting Jamie to follow suit, and privately dreading the prospect of small talk. Instead, Jamie began walking slowly up the lane, almost trance-like, seemingly in no great hurry, his eyes still firmly fixed on the doors to the barn.

Once he had reached the barns, Joey pulled over. His rear-view mirror told him that that Jamie had brought some form of wrench, which he gripped tightly. Even at that distance, Joey could make out Jamie's knuckles, which were prominently clenched around the solid weight of the tool.

That puzzled Joey, because Jamie had given him what he thought were the keys to the padlocked door, and he could see that the lock was barely a year old. Which made it all the more curious that Jamie had asked him to bring plenty of de-ruster as a precaution. Perhaps Jamie was expecting the lock to be less than obliging, or maybe he had no keys to gain access to the barns.

He stepped out of his pick-up as Jamie approached. He held up the key, waiting for Jamie to give him the green light to set to work. Instead, Jamie dropped the wrench by the wall, and came to stand in front of the double doors. Then, very slowly, he placed his hands against the seasoned wood. Joey could have sworn that Jamie was speaking to it, his head almost touching the course surface, and his body perfectly still. After what seemed an eternity to Joey, but was probably less than a minute, Jamie stood upright, and turned to Joey.

'Joey, would you oblige me and open these doors.'

Somehow conscious that he was about to perform some act of spiritual significance to Jamie, Joey moved slowly, almost solemnly, towards the doors. He sprayed some of the penetrating lubricant into the keyhole and around the links before inserting the key and turning it.

The lock sprang open, and the chain rattled through the rusty door handles so that Joey could form them into a pile. He heaved open the first door, thereby releasing the sweet, musty smell of last year's hay. It seemed to welcome the fading evening sunlight, which caught the particles of dust that the movement of the doors had disturbed. That dust now seemed to dance in the reflected rays of light as these moved to the rhythm of the gentle breeze which swirled in and around the barn. It found an exit through the window at its far end that had become so familiar to Joey.

The sunlight seemed to point accusingly at the aperture, as if to announce that the special tranquillity of this shrine had been disturbed, and that the perpetrator stood before it, 'convicted by his own conscience,' to quote the book.

Joey avoided Jamie's eye, and took hold of the second door, which he tried to heave open, this time with genuine effort. For some reason, the door was reluctant to surrender the secrets within, almost as if it knew that by exposing them to daylight, it would somehow facilitate or conspire in the revelation.

Joey instinctively held back, sensing that this was a private moment for Jamie, wondering whether he should withdraw. The silence hung between them.

It was broken by Jamie. 'Could you give me a couple of minutes, Joey.'

'Sure thing, sir,' said Joey, almost too enthusiastically. 'I'll just wait in the truck. Just shout if you need me to help with anything.'

Jamie nodded and waited for Joey to disappear.

He tried to cast his mind back to that awful day. He had stripped everything of hers out of the wardrobe in the spare room. Her perfume had wafted out from behind the oak doors, which had squeaked in protest at their sanctuary being violated. The scent had still been breathable on some of the clothes that she had kept at the house. But right then, it had represented the scent of failure. Of inadequacy. And ultimately, of rejection.

He looked at the old trunks, relics from happier times around school holidays. Here they acted as a dungeon, their feeble locks standing guard over the past. His past, which had accumulated dust and bat droppings, much like his own life over the same period. And he'd not even told Ali about this.

He shook his head. What sort of pathetic gesture was this! What purpose had he served; what good had he hoped to achieve by hiding from the reality of the pain, other than to exacerbate and prolong it?

These were her clothes, for fuck's sake. What the fuck is all this about?!

'You're a fool, Jamie,' he told himself, 'if you think that feeling sorry for yourself and hiding from the past, from her, is going to make things better. You're not helping anyone, least of all yourself.'

Certainly nor her, he thought. Ali was right. It was time that he stopped just thinking about himself, and thought about what it had done to her, what it was doing to her, and for all he knew would do to her if she pressed ahead with a claim. She needs you, you fucking idiot! She needs you to help her, and you're stood here moping like a teenager.

'Idiot,' he said out loud, not caring whether or not he was overheard, and dragged his gaze away from the trunks.

There, stacked against the hay, was a brown packing box, and he could see another one poking its nose out from under the hay. Those were what he had come to collect, and they were the priority.

But why stop with these? Why not offer to give everything back to her. They're not going to walk out by themselves.

He suddenly felt galvanised.

He walked across to the boxes, and opened the first one. Just as he remembered, it was filled with light-blue lever-arch files. The other one, so far as he recalled, would contain more of the same. He carried the first one out of the barn.

Joey looked up from his mobile, and instantly stepped out of his truck to offer assistance, opening the rear door.

'Thanks, Joey,' said Jamie. 'Could you grab the other one in there? I've got to get these back fairly pronto. There's a courier coming from London to collect them in the morning. I'm told they contain enough explosive to bring down an empire.'

He immediately regretted saying that. This was 'need to know' stuff, and Joey most certainly did not need to know.

'Oh, aye,' Joey replied. 'I've heard it said that the pen is mightier than the sword, so I can well believe it.'

'But keep it between us, eh Joey?'

'Mum's the word, sir.'

'That's the stuff.'

He placed the boxes on the back seat, and Joey noticed that Jamie was not going back to collect the heavy trunk that had been visible beside the boxes, but thought it best to say nothing on the subject.

Joey had counted only two boxes going into Jamie's truck. He was sure that there was a third stuck under the hay. He'd seen it only last night. He hesitated. How could he say anything without giving himself away? He could not risk losing the confidence of his boss, and potentially much worse besides. He'd only known him a year, but he admired him as a manager.

And then inspiration beckoned.

'Just a thought, sir. That's a tidy amount of dry hay in those bales. Would you object if I used it as fodder in the shed, or even as matting?'

Jamie needed little time to respond. The barn had served its purpose, and it was time to move on.

'It seems a shame to let it go to waste, Joey. I can't vouch for its vintage, but you're the right person to say whether it's still edible.'

'You'd be surprised, sir. If the animal is hungry enough, it'll eat it whatever the condition. We just need to check it for thistle and other stuff.'

'Right. Do you mind giving me a hand with this into the back of my car down there? It shouldn't take too long.'

'It'd be a pleasure, sir. Shall I hang on to the keys once I've locked up so that I can come by and collect the hay tomorrow or the day after?'

'For sure,' said Jamie, realising that he almost felt relieved that he would no longer be in control of them. Then he added. 'Let's leave this be for a week or so. Hang on to the keys for now.'

So, Joey swung the heavy doors shut, and jammed a large stone under the outer door to prevent any wind damage, and relocked the padlocks.

They drove back down the track from the barn, and turned onto the lane towards the big house, and paused at the gate. Once they had pulled up alongside Jamie's car that he'd parked at their rendezvous, Jamie hauled the first of the boxes into his car.

As Joey heaved the second trunk into Jamie's car, he said casually, 'I'll make a start on shifting that hay, once I've repaired the tyres on the trailer. There's a fair quantity by the looks of it.'

'Thanks, Joey.'

'And thinking about it, sir, they'd likely be grateful for some of it down at the paddocks. I hear there's a new foal due next month.'

'Good idea, Joey. Can I leave you to organise any extra muscle that you might need? There's not a lot that the promise of a few pints won't sort.'

'Too right there, sir. I'll get on it first thing.'

Jamie turned his back on the barn. And drove towards what he hoped was, for him at last, a new future.

*

At around the same time, the internal affairs meeting room found Barbara Spooner in a frostier than usual mood in her office, frostier still after she had cut the call to Ted Fisher. A stony silence fell upon the room as she and her team digested the latest intelligence from the lawyers. Their email and subsequent telephone call to Ted had briefed the team on the outcome of the preliminary forensic trawl of the girl's computer and mobile phone by the IT specialist.

None of the team was prepared to be the first to speak, especially given the scowl across the Mamba's brow. They had seldom, if ever, witnessed such fury.

'They have retrieved over 450 documents, they told us. 450! How in God's name did she manage to obtain that amount of material?'

None of the team caught her eye. Each of them, heads lowered, sought the answer amongst the papers in their files.

'And we're also told that there are potentially more that could become available via the girl's solicitors, coming from an as yet undisclosed destination.'

Again, silence.

'Maria,' Barbara resumed, seeking to prompt her assistant into speaking, 'you've looked at her email accounts. Would you say that there were as many as 450 documents attached to those communications?'

Maria had expected such an interrogation. 'Whilst I can't be specific, I would have to say that I would not find that figure surprising. The reason I say so is that, whilst there are not that many attached to the emails she sent, from what I've seen there are references to at least that number, if not significantly more than that, in her mails.'

Barbara absorbed that information, and then slowly began to shake her head, almost as if in disbelief. 450! The enormity of what she was hearing began to sink in. There was no need for her to articulate what the room was thinking. There had been a serious security failure here. And on her watch. She cursed silently.

'And we can expect them later today?' she said.

She made it sound like a question even though she was repeating what they had just been told by the lawyers.

Nods all around.

'And the further material that we know will be incoming?'

The question was again addressed to Maria.

'They did not tell us when we could expect those, but as Ted said just then, they have to go to the supervising solicitor first. So, at a guess I'd say that it will be tomorrow afternoon at the earliest that we get to see those. More likely the day after.'

'Right. Terry, Maria, I want you to prioritise the analysis of all this new material in the morning. I want it in date order, oldest at the front, and fully indexed.'

They both acknowledged, only too glad of the opportunity to absent themselves from her presence, at least for the time being. And in Maria's case, to be relieved of her other duties.

'One other thing. If you have time, I'd like a separate categorisation index alongside the chronological index.'

'We can cross-refer the two indices as well,' said Terry.

'Good. Do it.' Before he could reply, she said to Terry, 'Can you get Ted in legal to instruct the lawyers to do whatever is necessary to identify the email address or mobile from which that so-called sensitive material was sent. I know we can't see the content, but we need to know where it came from.'

'On it,' he said.

A final glare around the table from the Mamba. Then a curt 'That will be all.'

*

Tomo re-read the document again. It appeared to have been prepared by some of the junior researchers at AlphaOm using data compiled over the past decade or so, but it bore a date from early last year. It relied heavily on similar research that had been carried out at two leading universities in the States, inevitably trashed by the spokespersons acting as the mouthpiece for the pharmaceutical industry, as a result of which they had not received any significant dissemination internationally. The British media had been particularly reticent about running the story.

Until now, thought Tomo.

The paper's central theme was that almost all the data that the company had used to substantiate its claims relating to the links between sugar consumption and obesity had relied primarily or sometimes exclusively on self-reported dietary analysis. Virtually none of the data used by the company had been objectively obtained or peer-reviewed, and certainly not outside the industry.

The American study went on to record that self-reported analysis was statistically much more likely to underestimate the consumption of sugar substitutes. The authors had run control samples using several thousand participants, and the results were consistent in virtually every participating nation.

But there was a much more interesting feature to the document that Tomo was holding. This was that the very same researchers who had prepared the report had warned that, by adopting and utilising data based almost entirely on self-reported analysis, the company had exposed itself to some very serious risks.

The first was that there was an increasingly high risk that the company's justification of the 'recommended' daily consumption of sugar or sugar substitutes would be shown to be flawed. That was bad enough. But there was worse.

The paper continued by warning that it followed that, if the company's 'recommended' daily consumption, which it effectively advocated in its literature, could not be relied upon, then nor could the guidance that accompanied all of its products, which, by extension, its consumers would have relied upon.

And, so the paper reasoned, that meant that the company had been wrongly advocating as 'safe' a level of sugar consumption that was not just unsafe, but was potentially life-threatening.

The paper then referred to a separate study by the company of the links between obesity and cancer. This was potentially even more serious. The consequences of that were blindingly obvious. In short, the company had exposed itself to the risk of a huge class-action suit that would make the fight over smoking look like a walk in the park.

But there was yet more. The really bad news was that the document concluded that the policy of only selecting data based on self-reporting had been deliberate. Why? Because, the researchers revealed that a decision had been taken at board level within the company not to publish the results of its own research that had been based on objectively recorded sugar consumption data obtained through urine and blood testing of participants over sustained periods. Those results were embargoed, because they went to the heart of the company's profits.

The paper concluded by urging a change of course before the new European Union rules, which were already drafted and could soon come into force in the UK, obliged the company to publish all its research data, however unfavourable.

And then the bombshell. This report had been annexed a note, apparently sent from the office of the director of the company's

Commercial Development Department, to all board members advocating urgent action. That had been some eighteen months ago. And the point to which Cat had drawn attention before she left the company was that nothing had been done to change the company's policy. And that was one of the three main threads in the article by *The Chronicle*.

So what we have here, if I am not very much mistaken, thought Tomo to himself, is a proper smoking gun, and a sack of warm cartridge casings.

He picked up the phone to call Andrew Sutherland.

Chapter 17

Rosalyn terminated the call from the courier firm. The agent had confirmed that their driver had collected two boxes from the address in Dorset, and that these would be delivered shortly after lunch-time, traffic permitting.

She dialled Cat's mobile.

'Cat? It's Rosalyn.'

'Oh hi. Any news?'

'So far, so good. There are two boxes on their way to my offices as we speak, so I'll need to make use of your time again.'

Cat frowned at the other end of the line.

'Only two, did you say? I'm sure that I left at least three at Jamie's place. I've not spoken with Ali, so I've no idea where they were found.'

Rosalyn thought about suggesting that Cat could go straight to the horse's mouth, but thought better of it.

'Leaving aside logistics for the moment,' she said, 'I shall need to inform the supervising solicitor and the claimant's lawyers of the discovery. I shall also need to provide the court with an undertaking, on your behalf, to hand over the documents to the independent solicitor once we have received them. As I explained previously, I have no choice in the matter, since my primary duty is to the court.'

'Yes. That's fine, Rosalyn,' Cat confirmed. 'But I thought that is was in our interests to rub the company's nose in this stuff as soon as we can.'

'Once we've reviewed the material ourselves,' cautioned Rosalyn.

'Oh sure. Yes, sorry, I keep forgetting.'

'No matter. So, we shall get the documents copied as soon as they arrive, and then I'll get them over to the independent solicitor first thing in the morning.'

'Sure. Do you need me to come over in the morning?'

'That would be very useful, thank you.'

After a pause, she continued, 'Cat, you said you thought there were three boxes?'

'Yes, I'm sure that I left three down there. Whether one of them got thrown out or lost, I've no idea. But I'll keep asking.'

'Yes, please do,' said Rosalyn.

Then she added, 'One last thing, Cat. Regarding what's been termed as the sensitive material, the partner acting for the claimant has nominated herself as the person who will review it on behalf of the company. She will do so in the presence of the barrister recommended by Tom to act for you in connection with the images.'

Cat was grateful, and relieved, to hear that. It meant that there would be just two women who would see her like that. And there would be less scope for voyeurism.

'Did you get that, Cat?'

'Oh, yes. Thanks for arranging that.'

But there was something else that Cat had omitted to tell Rosalyn. It was important, but acutely embarrassing. *Now or never*, she told herself.

'Rosalyn. About the ... you know, the images. I said that you can't see the guy's face in them. What I didn't tell you is that you can see his back. And I mean clearly see it. And the reason why that's important is because he's got two large moles just below his right shoulder. Can you ask our barrister to look out for them, and when she sees them, can she point them out to this partner person?'

'Of course, Cat.'

Rosalyn instinctively knew when a client was holding something back.

'And should I tell them anything else?' she asked.

Cat hesitated, then relented.

'On the video, and in the photos, my ... he'd tied my hands behind my back with a cord, and he's ... you know ...'

'Enough said,' Rosalyn interrupted. 'I'll pass that on.'

'It's the one that hurt the most,' said Cat softly, almost to herself. 'It was the one that he sent to Jamie at the end.'

'I understand, Cat.'

'It killed off what was left of our relationship.'

Rosalyn waited for her to say something else. When Cat remained silent, she said, 'Shall I see you in the morning, Cat? Let's say the usual time?'

Still silence, requiring a prompt from Rosalyn.

'Sorry, what was the question?' asked Cat.

'More of a request, actually, Cat.'

Rosalyn repeated it, and having obtained the required confirmation, put the phone down. She proceeded to prepare a letter to the supervising solicitor. She told him about the discovery of the boxes, and that her team would check the contents. If, as she expected, they contained copies of material that belonged to the claimants, she would cause them to be handed over, and would invite him to suggest a time that would be convenient the next day to receive them.

She prepared a draft of a further letter to the claimants, taking care to be as vague as she dared about where the material had been discovered.

*

CT looked at his watch. It was approaching 7.00. He packed up his laptop and notes, and made his way towards the lift. He was waiting by the car when Maria emerged, and immediately switched into his pre-prepared greeting.

'Hey, Maria.'

'Sorry if I'm a bit late. I had to wait until the others had left so that I could assemble all the files that I think you might need.'

'No, we're cool, and anyway, I'd only just arrived,' he lied.

'Also, our lawyers just sent through an email from the girl's lawyers telling us that they'd found some more documents.'

'More documents? That doesn't sound good. But let's come back to that, because I'm concerned that you said "files that I might need". Didn't you mean to say the files that "we" might need?'

Maria had not been sure what to say, so she replied with a rather feeble, 'Well, I didn't want to presume anything.'

CT was on that like a panther. 'Presume away, Maria. We're going to have to act as a team if we're to have any chance of sorting this.'

He was rewarded with a smile.

Maintaining his silky tone, he took the box of files from her, and opened the passenger door to his car, motioning for her to get in. They drove to a hotel that the company used for some of its corporate events, and where he knew he'd be given a meeting room for a few hours. CT waited until a friendly waiter with a foreign accent had brought in complementary refreshments and biscuits before he began to interrogate Maria.

'So,' he began, removing his jacket and placing it around the back of a chair, 'do we know where these new documents have appeared from?'

'Well, we're told by the IT person who had possession of Symonds' laptop and mobile that this first lot have been discovered on those.'

'You say "first lot". Does that mean that there's more?'

'Well, according to the girl's lawyers, there are some more documents that Symonds left with a friend at an unspecified address.'

CT pretended to look confused. 'So, what's with the secrecy?' he asked.

'We're told that the details have been withheld to protect the owner's identity. We've also been advised that we're unlikely to get those details.'

Don't break a leg trying, though CT to himself. I know exactly where that is, and he had some unfinished business on that score.

'If it was my call, I'd tell our lawyers to keep chasing for the details, because I wouldn't put it past the press to create plenty of fake documents. They're good at fake news, so why not fake photocopies?'

Maria was puzzled. 'Sorry,' she queried, 'I don't follow.'

'It's simple,' he replied. 'We're going to need to challenge the authenticity of this material. And in my book, the best way to do that is to get the paper to tell us precisely how they got hold of it so quickly.' As an afterthought, he added: 'And it also means that they need to tell us where it's been stored.'

She gave that some thought.

'Okay, I get that, but you need to know that the documents have been disclosed by the girl's lawyers, and not the paper.'

'Not a big difference, really,' he replied. 'The same point applies to her as it does to the paper. You need to get your boss to tell the lawyers to chase that. We have to make them prove authenticity.'

'Okay, thanks. I'll make sure to do that.'

*

'Hi, babe!'

'Hey, Ali! Thanks for calling back. And thank you so much for talking to Jamie. I've been on the phone to the lawyers. Two boxes of papers have just arrived at their offices which they've collected from Jamie's place earlier today. I'm going over to their offices tomorrow morning to sort through them.'

'You know what, babe? I think it's been the best thing for Jamie. He sounds like the bro I used to know. Apparently, he'd been keeping them in one of the olds barns on the estate, which he'd kept locked up. He sounded almost poetic when he described releasing the chains and opening up not just the old doors, but the future. Early days, I know, but this could be a new start.'

This was indeed music to Cat's ears.

'I cannot tell you how good it is to hear you say that, you know. If good can come out of bad amidst all this- this vileness, then at least we may have achieved something, if only for Jamie's wellbeing.'

'Here's hoping, babe.'

'I know that my lawyer has dropped a line to Jamie to thank him for getting us the papers so quickly, but I just wondered if you were aiming to speak to him again; like either later today or early tomorrow.'

'Sure, babe, I can do. I wasn't planning to speak to him until tomorrow evening, but it sounds as though you want me to ask him something.'

'You know me too well.'

'Well enough. So, shoot ...'

A voice inside her head told Cat that, if Jamie had summoned the courage to confront the past, then so should she.

'Do you think it is too soon for me to meet with Jamie, so that I can thank him, and also perhaps ask him if we can still be friends?'

Ali had already given it some thought. 'Not having had a great deal of experience in repairing broken hearts, I'm probably the least qualified to advise on how long wounds need to heal. But, just going with my instinct, I'd be inclined to say, following my conversation with Jamie earlier, that the iron was hot, so it's not a bad time to strike.'

'So, are you suggesting that I should call him?'

'I think not, Cat. What I was going to suggest was that I ask him whether he feels it is too soon for the two of you to meet.'

'Thanks, Ali. I'd like that.'

'Cool. I'll try to drop it into our next conversation.'

Cat had one more favour to ask, but was now fearful that she really was pushing her luck with Ali's patience. But it needed to be said, and best coming from her.

'Ali, when you're speaking with Jamie, I know I'm pushing it, but would it be too much to ask that you just run something by him?'

'When you push, babe, you sure do put your shoulder into it!'

'Well, I just think it might be better coming from you, rather than the lawyers. It may be nothing, or it may be important. But when you do speak with him, can you just tell him that I definitely remember leaving three boxes at the house, not two. If he still has another one, it could contain something that's really important. Could you ask him if it's possible that one of the boxes might have been overlooked?'

Ali was not expecting that.

'Oh, so you think it could be there still?'

'I really don't know, Ali. But I told my lawyers there were three, and they will just pester him if we don't give them an answer.'

'And your concern is, applying Murphy's law, that it will turn out to be the one that has all the crucial documents?'

'It's certainly possible, Ali.'

'OK. I'll get on it.'

'You're a brick, Ali.'

'Just always there for you, babe.'

*

CT had ordered a bottle of wine for them, and they paused their conversation while the waiter did the honours.

Once he had left, Maria remembered something. 'Oh! Symonds' lawyers have told our people that they intend to pass two boxes of papers to the independent solicitor some time tomorrow.'

CT's ears pricked up. 'And we've been given no clue as to where this this undisclosed address might be?'

Maria shrugged her shoulders. 'CT. The thing is, that ... well, I think they will be able to prove that the girl emailed a lot of these documents to herself.'

He stared at her now, eyes alert.

'How do you know this?' He corrected himself immediately. 'I mean, how do we know this?'

He saw her feet shuffle beneath the glass table top. She hesitated. He let the silence hang between them until she answered.

'We ... no, I mean, I, or rather our own IT people found her private email account. She was emailing stuff to herself from the office using that address.'

Right under my very nose, thought CT. But he had to credit her –

she'd played the dumb brunette to perfection. He'd not seen that coming.

'And can we do that – legally?'

She looked away from him. 'That's what I wanted to talk to you about, CT.'

His mind raced. 'And this forensic examination of her laptop. The one ordered by the court. Has that not confirmed that she received the documents?'

She nodded. 'That's what the lawyers told us today,' she said. 'They said that, so far, the IT report had identified about 450 documents that she had obtained that way.'

Fuck! 450! And counting! That's a fucking security car crash. Trouble was that the motor came from his lock-up!

He effected to maintain his calm exterior. 'So, whether or not we acted legally, we've got hold of the information by the front door anyway. So what difference does it make?'

Maria wanted to agree, but she'd heard the legal advice.

'It's something to do with data protection, and the consequences of concealing a breach once it's been discovered.'

CT shook his head. 'No. It's just a matter of how you sell it, and – just as important – when you sell it. So, if you're selling bad news, you choose a time and a way to sell it so that it gets swallowed up with lots of other crap.'

She liked the sound of that. The simplest solutions were so very often the right answer to a tricky problem.

'You mean, we just say that we've been trawling through our internal disclosure, and we've came across all her mails which we are now volunteering to disclose to the defence now. You know, as opposed to later in the case?'

He beamed at her.

'There you go,' he crooned. 'You're a natural. You just need to pick a good day and a good way to bury the bad news.'

For the first time in days, she felt something like her old self. 'Thanks, CT.'

'Hey! That's what I'm paid to do.' Time to change the subject. 'Now about these documents: can you talk me through what I need to read in order to brief the chief.'

Chapter 18

The following morning, Mary Fellowes waited for her team to arrange the lever-arch files into numerical order before she addressed them. She could sense that they were all conscious of a subtle shift in her body language, unspoken yet seemingly tangible. Even the two junior members had experienced a moment like this: the dawning realisation that the client had failed to vouchsafe the whole truth.

They had been told some of the truth, yes. Perhaps some of it, but not the whole truth, and certainly some way short of 'nothing but the truth'.

It had begun, innocently enough, as a niggle. A niggle in each of their own minds, barely recognisable at first, but gradually evolving into a whispered seed of doubt, onto which was sprinkled droplets of new evidence.

That whisper acquired a voice as each new document was revealed. It germinated into a suspicion that would heed no dismissal. It nagged at them incessantly, Iago-like, urging them to ask themselves the questions that every lawyer hates to ask, especially as they approached the eve of a hearing: 'Look into the mirror and ask yourself, *Can I trust what I have been told by those who have been instructing me?*'

And then: '*Can I trust what those instructing me will say in answer to the questions that I am about to ask them?*'

And finally: '*How are we going to explain these documents to the court?*'

This was such a moment.

Mary looked up at her team. As professionals, they all knew what had to be done, and now was the time to act professionally.

'Who is taking the detailed note?'

A hand went up from her bright new recruit. She nodded in acknowledgement.

'Tim, have they all had the agenda that you prepared for the telecon, together with the list of document references?'

He held up a hard copy of an email. 'They went by email first thing.'

'Good. Thank you.'

She looked around at them. 'Any points before we call the dial-in?'

Heads were shaken in response.

Mary nodded to Tim, who connected them to the telecon, and introduced the firm via the automated voice.

There was a delay of a few minutes as they waited first for Ted Fisher and then Barbara Spooner and her assembled team to join them.

'Good morning,' Mary began. 'Are we missing anyone?'

'We're all here,' came Barbara's stern reply.

Mary noted that she was taking the lead on behalf of the client. She had rather suspected that would be the case.

'Good. First, can I thank you for the excellent arrangement of the provision of the first tranche of the defendants' disclosure. That has saved us significant time. I'd like to focus on this if I may to begin with.' There being no dissent, she continued. 'Could you please go to the document at bundle two, page forty-seven in your indexed bundles. The versions sent over last night.'

She gave them a few seconds to find this.

'Do we all have it?' Assent followed. 'Good. This appears to be a research paper created within the company. I'd like to know what steps have been taken to establish its provenance, leaving aside the email that Ms Symonds used to send it to herself.'

Barbara seized on that before Ted could intervene. 'We've run some checks here. We can confirm that the email appears to have been sent from the company's offices, along with a number of others. We are aware that we shall need to include all such emailed material in our own disclosure, and are taking steps to download all that we've found on our cloud.'

'I see,' Mary said cautiously. 'You are referring to her emails from her company account, as opposed to her personal account?'

'I understand it to be the latter.'

'I see,' said Mary cautiously.

'And before you ask,' Barbara continued, 'our internal IT support team accessed the girl's email account on the mistaken assumption that the company was obliged to do so as a term of the court's order. However, I note that the relevant emails have been obtained from the girl's laptop anyway.'

Mary looked at her team, whose expressions spelt distrust.

'So,' continued Barbara, 'you and we now have an original set.'

Ted Fisher was fuming, silently. Barbara knew full well that such a false approach had specifically not been authorised by his boss, whom she knew to be the company's compliance officer. However, he was instructed to defer to the Mamba on all matters that concerned the proceedings.

He made a note to call Tim after the telecon.

'We may need to come back to that point later,' said Mary. 'But for now, can we please concentrate on the documents?'

'Certainly,' replied Barbara curtly.

'Good. So, staying with the research paper, is the company in a position to confirm or deny its authenticity?'

Barbara's response was instant. 'We are currently looking into that. However, as for the supposed covering email, we have reason to doubt its authenticity, but again we are looking into it. For present purposes, we cannot confirm that either document is genuine.'

Mary looked across at her team. Each of their faces displayed the same sentiments that were going through her own mind.

'And what are the chances that you will have some clearer instructions for us prior to the hearing in what is less than two days' time?'

This time there was a slight silence.

'As I say,' replied Barbara, eventually, 'we are looking into it.'

Mary decided to move on.

'Can we go please to bundle one, page 125.'

She waited until the sound emanating from the other end of the line had abated.

'This is a summary of the academics and other institutions who were engaged, to use a neutral term, by the company, amongst other entities, to carry out or contribute to certain research material. One of the papers, you will notice on page 186, is the report from the European Commission's Research and Innovation Unit into the links between sugar consumption and diabetes or obesity.'

When neither Barbara nor Ted spoke, Mary asked, 'The report de-emphasised the risk of sugar consumption. Yet the point made by *The Chronicle* last week was that the company, amongst others, had deliberately skewed that report in its favour by crossing the palms of those academics and universities with large doses of silver.'

'You can take it that we've all read the article several times.'

'As have we,' replied Mary. 'But it will not surprise you to learn that we were concerned by the contents of the documents that have been obtained from Ms Symonds laptop in response to the order made at the company's instigation.'

Barbara did not respond to this, which Mary thought rather odd.

'Is the company not equally concerned, Barbara?'

Again, there was silence.

'You see,' Mary continued, 'the document suggests, in fact I would go further and say that it suggests strongly, that there was indeed such engagement.'

Again, Barbara remained silent.

'In short, what I need to know is whether the company is yet in a position to confirm or deny the authenticity of the summary.' She added, before she could be interrupted, 'Indeed, I ask the same question regarding the various supporting papers that identify the recipients of certain of the payments.'

'Mary,' said Barbara coldly, 'I think that I can save us a lot of time. We are looking into the provenance of all these documents.'

Mary shook her head in frustration. 'So, are you able to instruct us that any of the documents within the disclosed bundles are ones that we can confirm to the defendants are genuine, or are otherwise regarded by the company as fake.'

Barbara effected a weary sigh. 'We received these documents yesterday, Mary. As the saying goes, we're quite good at miracles, but the impossible takes a little longer.'

Mary winced at the titter she could overhear down the line.

'So be it,' she said.

Tim passed her a note. It read 'counsel'.

'So, I take it that you are not confident that I shall have anything of substance to convey to counsel this afternoon?'

'We'll certainly do what we can with the resources that we have,' replied Barbara coldly, and with little conviction.

'But what you're telling me, if I've heard you correctly, is that with regard to key documents such as the ones that we've been discussing, it is likely that by close of business today I shall have to instruct our counsel that we cannot assist the court at this early stage with matters of provenance.'

'That would be a sensible precaution,' agreed Barbara

'Very well. But I should warn you that, when he hears this, counsel may well advise that, once he has spoken to the defendants' counsel, we may have to propose that the hearing should be adjourned.'

She expected vociferous protests from her clients. None were forthcoming.

'Look,' she continued, 'it is vital in cases such as this that the claimant is seen, both by the court and by the defendants, to be maintaining a sense of urgency with regard to the proceedings.'

'But how, tell me,' replied Barbara, 'were we to know, let alone expect, that the search of the girl's computer and other so-called records would produce quite such a volume of material?'

Mary's team looked alternatively at her and the speakerphone in astonished silence, scarcely believing what they had just heard.

'Because, Barbara, as we specifically advised you and Ted at the time, that is the very purpose of a search order. It is why we sought such an order on your instructions. We wished to recover the company's confidential documents, and your witnesses told the court that it was their firm belief that Ms Symonds had that very same material in her possession. That was the basis for the order.'

'Indeed.'

'But now I am being told that we are not at all sure that any of the material that has been seized was the property of the company. Have you given a moment's thought to the legal implications of such a position?'

'Please enlighten me.'

Mary almost snapped the pen she was holding. 'Gladly,' she began, through gritted teeth. 'Because it begs the question, which you can be sure the defendants will ask, as will the court, as to whether the company was in fact justified in seeking the orders that it did.'

'You're the lawyer, Mary, but the answer to that question is surely that we are entitled to be satisfied that the defendants have not slipped into their disclosure some documents that are not genuine?'

'I beg to differ, Barbara. The defendants will make the point, if the judge does not do it for them, that it should only take the click of a mouse for the company to verify whether a document is genuine.'

Ted Fisher kept quiet. He was relishing the demolition of the Mamba in front of her own team. He was recording it for posterity.

'Mary, there are almost 500 documents that those of us on this committee have never seen before. Some of them are extensive, and you tell us that there are yet more to come. Verification will come from a number of sources. There is a limit, surely, to what the court can expect.'

'Up to a point, Barbara, I'd agree. The key point is that the company has asked the court to use its most potent weapon in the limited arsenal that it uses to right a wrong. We cannot sensibly tell the court that we suspect that the majority of the documents that have been retrieved have been fabricated.'

'But we are not doing that, Mary. We are just asking for more time. Surely that is not so unreasonable?'

'Barbara! My point is that we are doing what no claimant should do. We are allowing the defendants to take the initiative.'

'We are permitting no such thing.'

'Delay will allow the proceedings to drift. It will have the same effect. I must urge you in the strongest possible terms to revise your instructions.'

'Mary, we are here to be advised.'

And to obstruct me, Mary said to herself. 'That is not an instruction, Barbara, and you know it. I have to be in a position by close today where I can instruct counsel either to press ahead, or to stall. I have warned you of the consequences of the latter.'

The taciturn tension was tangible, visceral. After several seconds silence, Mary said, 'So, Barbara, best case scenario: when do you expect that my firm will be in a position to confirm provenance?'

Barbara was long enough in the tooth to see that one coming. She had never fenced, but she understood the purpose of a parry. 'I've always preferred to work on the basis of reasonable case, Mary. So much more realistic and manageable, don't you think?'

'As you say, Barbara, I am here to advise. The court will demand best case performance from the claimant in these circumstances, especially at the return hearing of a search order. However, it is only obliged to accept reasonable case from a defendant. You might not know it, but you are making my point for me.'

'Forgive me, Mary, which is?'

'Which is, Barbara, that my advice is that the company should strive to achieve best case performance as regards our interrogation of the disclosure, so that we are in a position to provide as much assistance to the court as we are able. It is also my advice that the court will expect such assistance from us. And I should add that I expect counsel to concur with that view when we speak later.'

'We are discussing semantics, Mary, as you should know. We shall do what we can in the time that we have available.'

'Which only leaves today, Barbara, or what's left of it, and part of tomorrow!'

The gauntlet was well and truly down. But Mary had yet to wrestle with this particular reptile, adept as it was at slithering out of danger and baring her fangs when the need arose.

'I've given you my answer, and my instructions, Mary.'

'And they are duly noted, Barbara.'

And that, all things being equal, would have brought the conference, if such it could be called, to an end. But things were not equal. The Mamba had yet to sink her fangs. She had been attacked, and in front of her own team, and before witnesses. The eyes narrowed in readiness.

'Before we sign off, Mary,' said Barbara, deliberately changing the subject, 'I have a question for you.'

'By all means.'

'It concerns the latest batch of material supposedly and very conveniently discovered by the girl somewhere in the country.'

'Fire away.'

'Why did we, by which I mean you, not obtain a court order requiring that material be immediately surrendered to the independent IT people, instead of her lawyers first before being allowed to copy it and then pass it over?'

She had intended it as a low blow, and to a less seasoned warrior than Mary Fellowes it would have drawn blood. But, for once, the Mamba had not read her brief. The answer lay on the table in front of her, and in front of Ted in his own office, who sat back and beamed.

'There are three reasons for that, Barbara, which I believe we set out in our email to you yesterday afternoon.'

Barbara would have looked at Ted for an answer, but he was not in the room. Instead, she was obliged to defer to Ted over the phone. She hated that. 'Ted?' she prompted.

This was a joy for him.

'The email is addressed to you, Barbara, and copied to me. But it might speed things up if Mary were to repeat the gist of her advice for your benefit.'

Fuck, but he enjoyed that, and even more so because the Mamba was unable to retaliate with any poisonous looks or words.

'Certainly, Ted,' said Mary sensing the power game at play between them. 'I'd be more than happy to do so.'

Tim passed her a copy of the email, on which he had highlighted the relevant advice from Mary's firm in yellow. 'The first and obvious reason, Barbara, is that Ms Symonds' solicitors had volunteered an undertaking on her behalf to hand the material over to the supervising solicitor upon receipt, unless he was content for them to photocopy it first. Such an undertaking would, by itself, have been sufficient to satisfy the court, and would have removed any sound basis for any further order.'

He allowed Barbara and her team a moment to absorb that.

'Secondly, given such an undertaking, and given that their request for permission to copy the material was eminently reasonable and practical, we could not sensibly object.'

Silence. He loved that.

'Thirdly, we had even less reason to seek a restraining order with regard to the material once the supervising solicitor had confirmed to all parties, as he did in the email annexed to my advice, that he was content with the undertaking.'

'But they could have tampered with it first,' objected the Mamba.

'So, do you have any evidence to support that very serious allegation against my fellow professionals, and a member of the bar by extension, Barbara, given that they could just as easily have destroyed the documents wherever they had been held? Because they have had the opportunity.'

Of course you don't, thought Mary. So please do not waste my time with idle speculation about what might or might not happen.

When Barbara remained silent, Mary said, 'And we need to bear in mind that Ms Symonds appears to have retained a great many of the company's documents, which her solicitors have conceded are the property of the company. That constitutes strong evidence of her preservation of material, rather than its destruction. In those circumstances, our case would have been hopeless. And it is my job to advise the company to take on fights that it has a reasonable chance of winning, rather than enter into battles that invite defeat.'

She regretted that last sentence. It implied that she believed that there was a reasonable prospect that she could still win the overall case. That was looking less likely by the hour. By the minute even.

'I should add, Barbara, that I understand that that we are likely to be given copies of the new material either some time later today or more likely tomorrow, which – needs must, and all that – I am conscious will add to your already significant burden.' She told herself to disguise her pleasure in making that point. She failed. Instead, she continued. 'Forgive me, Barbara, but I only say that because I shall need to ask you and your team to carry out the same authenticity verification of each of the new documents that are contained in this latest population of disclosure.'

'As I understand it,' said Barbara, 'there are already two whole boxes. If so, that suggests that there are almost double or three times the quantity of documents that we're already reviewing.'

'So I believe, Barbara, but we're the claimants, so we have to be the party forcing the pace in the proceedings.'

'As I've said, Mary, we shall do whatever it takes in the time that we have to review this material,' said Barbara, tersely.

Mary felt like saying, 'In your own time, but today would be nice.' Instead, she took a deep breath and said as politely as she could, 'Thank you, Barbara, I appreciate that, but ...'

Barbara cut off her response. 'Mary, I want your firm to put the girl to proof as to how she got hold of the documents, and more importantly, where she claims to have kept them since she left the company.'

'That is already in hand, Barbara,' said Mary, looking at Tim, who gave her the 'thumbs up' sign in reply. His colleague produced a copy of the firm's letter to Rosalind asking that very question.

'Tim will send over a copy of our letter after this call.'

'Noted. Please understand that this is important to us, not least because I am now told that the girl left us under something of a cloud.'

Ted almost leapt out of his chair.

What the fuck, he thought. *Where has that come from? From which hat has the Mamba mysteriously produced that rabbit?* Mary looked at her team. She could sense that they were fast becoming wholly distrustful of their principal client contact.

'This could be significant, Barbara. When are you proposing to share the details with us as regards the relevant circumstances?'

'You will receive the detail just as soon as we receive it, Mary.'

'Thank you, Barbara.'

The frost between them had well and truly settled. She looked at the agenda and hesitated, unsure whether or not to raise the last item on it. It was headed 'sensitive material'. Reluctantly, she felt that she had no option.

'One last thing, Barbara, more for your information at the moment, I think right now, but it could become important.'

'How so?' asked Barbra.

'Well, I am scheduled to meet at the offices of the supervising solicitor tomorrow morning to review the contents of the data file whose contents were labelled by the IT specialist as being sensitive.'

'I see.'

'The point is that Ms Symonds' lawyers have conceded, strangely I think, that this material is disclosable but not relevant. Ordinarily, I would regard that as a contradiction in terms, but given the surprises that we have already encountered in this case, I'm not at all sure that such a label is not intended to be deliberately provocative. So, I am assuming that there is nothing that you or your colleagues can think of that might link this material to the issues in our case.'

Barbara looked around at her team, whose negative expressions left her in no doubt that their cupboard was currently dry. 'Nothing, as yet, Mary,' came the reply.

'Very well. I shall report back to you in due course.'

'Noted.'

'Right, then, subject to the point that we touched on a little earlier, that's just about it for now, Barbara, unless you or Ted – or indeed anyone else – have any further questions for myself or my team here?'

'Nothing further from me,' said Barbara curtly.

'Thank you, Mary,' responded Ted, 'likewise nothing from me. This telecon has been most helpful.'

The truth was he had plenty to ask them, but not with Barbara on the call. Mary paused as Tim passed her the note they had prepared earlier.

'So, Barbara, I'd like to come back to the matter of Miss Symonds' private email address to which we've now been told that the company had gained access.'

To her surprise, there was silence from the other end of the call.

'So, can you tell me when this account was accessed?'

'Apparently some time on Friday evening, I am told, Mary.'

'And can you tell me who within the company became aware of that fact, and equally importantly when?'

Time for payback, thought Ted, so he responded. 'I can answer that, Mary. I became aware at a meeting with Barbara's team shortly after seven pm on Friday evening that a member of Barbara's team had given an instruction to some of the company's IT staff to access the account, assuming that it formed part of the orders that the company had obtained. I can let you have a copy of my advice to Barbara on the Saturday morning in light of that intelligence if that would help.'

'It would be. Thank you, Ted.'

'I should add that my advice is no longer being sought on the matter. However, you need to be aware that Miss Symonds' new home address was obtained as a result of that "search", if I might so dignify it.'

He could hear the javelins hurtling through the airwaves towards him from Barbara, but he knew he needed to be bomb-proof on this.

'I see,' replied Mary, joining the dots for herself. 'So, can we be told who is dealing with this particular issue within the company?'

Ted said nothing.

After a pause, Barbara spoke, 'The matter is currently with our head of legal. He and I intend to provide you with our board's instructions very shortly.'

Mary looked at Tim, who raised two fingers to his head as if shooting himself.

'And by very shortly, Barbara, I take it you mean later today?'

A further pause.

'I'm not sure. He has got a lot on his plate right now, having just returned from a long holiday, so it could well be tomorrow.'

Tim shook his head at Mary.

'I'm not sure that you appreciate quite how serious this could become, Barbara. This is not a matter on which any further delay can be justified.'

'Very well, Mary. I shall convey that advice to him directly after this call.'

'Thank you. That would be very wise. Tim will be on hand here to handle matters whilst I am inspecting this other material tomorrow morning. So, Ted, please copy him in with your note.'

'Will do.'

'Thank you for your time, all of you.'

After some tart replies, Mary indicated to Tim to cut the call. She shook her head slowly at her assembled team.

'Shall we reconvene tomorrow at eight? Right now I think we could all do with a drink!'

Chapter 19

Cat had spent most of the day going through the boxes that had arrived from Dorset. She was on the second box when she came across the document that she had most wanted to find amongst the papers. She almost ran across the office to Rosalyn's room, pausing just in time to check that she was not engaged. She knocked, even though the door was open, and Rosalyn invited her in with a smile.

Cat sat down on the small table opposite Rosalyn's desk. On it she placed a set of the documents that she wanted to show her.

'I knew I'd copied these. They're the instructions to two of the universities regarding the "findings" that the company wanted researched and proven for submission to the reporting committee. When the report came out a few years back it caused a real controversy, even in the medical profession.'

'Yes, I think I recall reading something about that. I think one of the big medical journals got in on it.'

'And there's a separate note setting out the scale of payments that the company was prepared to make. As I read it, they are saying that they are willing to pay generously for the right results.' She pointed to the entries. 'There's a record here also of payments made to them before and after the publication of the report.'

Cat pointed to the entries in the account, and then to the note. She asked Rosalyn whether she would like her to send this sort of document over to Tomo, or whether she would be stepping on Rosalyn's toes. It was a tricky one for Rosalyn, accustomed as she was to this sort of balancing act. On the one hand, she did not want to cause her clients to feel that they were being excluded from the legal process; quite the reverse, in fact. But, on the other hand, she needed to keep a tight rein on the administration of that process. And one of the most important aspects of that, especially in a case such as this, was the flow of material that she provided to counsel.

So, Rosalyn wisely suggested that Cat should certainly keep bringing these documents to her attention, and should also feel free to mention them to Tom when they next spoke. Meanwhile, Rosalyn said that she would continue to compile the indexed bundles that she was preparing for counsel, which she intended to share with the legal team acting for the paper. She would include anything that she considered to be important at this stage of the process.

'Whilst you're here Cat, can you take a seat for a moment? There are a couple of matters that I should like to discuss with you.'

This sounds ominous, thought Cat. She could see that there were several letters from the claimant's lawyers on Rosalyn's desk.

'The two matters are actually related. The first concerns a letter that came in last night from the other side with regard to the documents that you retrieved from Dorset. Whilst they have not yet expressly disputed the provenance of the documents, they are putting us to proof both as to provenance and storage. In plain English, they are requiring us to provide evidence of the circumstances in which you obtained the documents, specifically where and how. They also want us to confirm where they had been stored from the time of their acquisition up to the time of their discovery, and lastly how they were obtained. Which, to put it mildly, raises a number of delicate points.'

It certainly does, thought Cat.

'Tomo said that they might try that, but would probably back away from it once they knew about the ... you know, the other stuff.'

'I would have been inclined to agree with that view, certainly as regards the means of acquisition, but for the content of the documents. I've read most of them. Speaking for myself, and without having discussed it with either counsel, my initial view is that some of these have the potential to be really damaging to the company, and that's not including the ones that you've just shown me. So, I'm starting to wonder whether the company intends to argue that the documents have been fabricated.'

'What?' asked Cat in surprise. That idea had not even crossed her mind. 'But that's crazy. I've held a bunch of the originals, and I copied or photographed many of them myself at CT's London flat. And there were a bunch of others that I sent to my own email account from the office, so the company surely can't argue about those. Anyways, some of them went to the board, so they should already know about them. And most of the others will have been attached to emails sent internally. Others they will have already retrieved from my laptop. I mean, surely ...'

Rosalyn held up her hand to acknowledge the point.

'I cannot disagree with that, Cat. But I'm sure that their tactic is to create doubt in the mind of the judge who hears this. Which means that we are going to have to deal with that issue in your witness statement, or tell the court that we shall provide the detail to the court in a separate statement.'

'Okay, I get that,' said Cat.

'But it leaves open the question of where the documents have been stored since you originally acquired them.' They both knew what that entailed. 'What did you tell Jamie about how we are going to explain that? I told Ali that you would try to keep his name out of it.'

'Precisely that,' replied Rosalyn, 'but with the clear caveat that we had limited control in that department if the question were to be asked.'

'Which it now has been.'

'Exactly. Hence the necessity to review our strategy, which, as you have surmised, means that we need to involve Jamie.'

Cat's silence spoke volumes. Despite the obvious logic in Rosalyn's advice, Cat had been privately dreading this moment, which she had half expected would come at some point, but not this soon.

'It's probably best if I write to him in the first instance,' Rosalyn continued, 'because I suspect he will find it easier to hear it from me, especially if I explain the circumstances. You and his sister can of course blame me if that helps, but I don't believe we really have a choice.'

Cat had come to the same conclusion.

'Should I speak with Ali to tell her about it as well?' she asked.

'Well, the thought had occurred to me, Cat, but on reflection I think it would be better if you didn't explain our thinking behind this – the fewer people who know about our strategy, the better. But I'll copy you in on the letter that I send him.'

Cat nodded. After a while she asked, 'And the other thing?'

Rosalyn pushed the letters to one side of her desk, and came to sit in the chair at the table beside Cat.

'Well, as it happens, I have been rethinking our overall strategy on the harassment issue. My initial thinking, as you know, was that we should hold fire on any claim until we have resolved the initial issues arising out of the injunction and the urgent disclosure obligations. Fortunately, as it so happens, that has proved much more straightforward than any of us had been anticipating.'

For you, perhaps, thought Cat.

'So, the upside of that is that I've been able to give this quite a lot of thought overnight. I also took the liberty of running the options past Tom yesterday, as much for a reality check as anything else, but also so that he could run it past the QC acting for the paper. I think he may have told you last time that he knows him well from a previous case. They were both going to chew the cud on it, so to speak, and let me know their combined wisdom in due course.'

'Yes, he said something about the two of you having a rethink on strategy, and that he wanted to bounce some ideas off someone whose views he respected. I took that to mean he was getting a second opinion.'

'And I believe that is precisely what he did, such that I have now indeed received such wisdom. In a nutshell, but very much subject to your prior endorsement before they reach a final view, their advice is that they are attracted by my revised strategy.'

'Which is . . .?'

'So, here's the thing. I learnt yesterday that the partner who is running the case for the claimants' solicitors is due to inspect the sensitive material today at the offices of the supervising solicitor. The timing of her visit, if you can call it that, is – as it turns out – highly convenient to us. In fact, she should be there early tomorrow morning, along with Diana Thomas, who is the specialist counsel whom Tom recommended should act for you on that side of things. I've briefed her to draw attention to the "detail" that you mentioned to me, along with the other matters that we have discussed.'

'I see . . .'

'So, whilst she is being distracted by that, I propose to send a letter to her firm which I'll pretend to be in response to her firm's enquiry about provenance. If you agree, the letter will identify Mr Thompson as the generous provider, albeit unwittingly, of the collection of documents that you acquired. My letter will state – again, only if you agree – that my firm is instructed to write to the claimants separately in connection with the circumstances surrounding both the relationship (if it can be termed as such) between the two of you, and more particularly its termination. It will also highlight the reasons for the termination of your employment. Needless to say, the letter will also set out the basis of your claim against the company for sexual and malicious harassment. I think the activity is known in modern-day parlance as sexting, and will probably also entail criminal liability. We'll need to await Diana's advice on that aspect.'

'Wow,' Cat exclaimed. 'That should make them sit up. I think Tomo would call it setting the cat amongst the pigeons.'

'That is certainly the intent. I should add that this strategy has been endorsed by Diana, who also helped to draft the letter.' She gave Cat some time to digest this.

'I guess it would at least explain why I felt that I couldn't go to Jamie before now and ask for the stuff back,' she offered.

'Indeed it would.'

Yet Cat felt uneasy about this change of tactic. Events had moved so fast since that early evening raid on her home that she had not prepared herself mentally for the prospect of going on the offensive. Rosalyn sensed this.

'You're looking concerned,' she prompted.

'It's just that, when we discussed it together, you were worried that the judge would think that my motive in all this, you know, all this exposure, was revenge, when it's not. It's about letting the world know that these people cannot be trusted, that their motive is nothing but greed. No, it's more than that. It's greed, yes, corporate greed, but it's also reckless and dishonest, and it is causing harm every day.'

'And that comes across strongly in your witness statement. That said, I cannot deny that there is a risk that a judge could be persuaded to think that your motive is revenge, and that is very likely how the claimants will push it. But there is another important factor that we need to bring into the equation. It is one that, whilst I have not ignored until now, has been in the back of my mind for a while.'

'Go on, you're making this sound like a suspense thriller!'

'Apologies. My concern is that the claimants might do what I would be tempted to do if I were in their position, namely to be the first to expose the relationship, asserting that it had been you who had seduced Mr Thompson. They will say that you took advantage of his infatuation with you, and that you did so you with the specific intent of gaining access to his private papers, and then inserting into his files what would become a Trojan horse, or in fact a whole squadron of them, which you would then use to your advantage. To that end, you provided certain documents to the paper so that they would run the story, and you kept some back so that these could conveniently be discovered in response to a disclosure order. And all this had been part of a carefully orchestrated campaign.'

Cat looked at her in disbelief. 'But what about his emails to me, and the ones to Jamie? They won't know about those until he confesses to be the guy who sent them, and that he's the guy in the photos and stuff, and he's never going to do that.'

'Believe me, Cat, these huge companies will go to any lengths to survive. And if it means that they have to hang out a director or two for the vultures, that is precisely what they will do. And they will keep a perfectly clear conscience whilst doing so. You have to trust me on this, Cat, because I've seen it played out all too often.'

Cat still wanted further reassurance.

'But couldn't they still say all that, even if we decide to go first and expose what he did to me, and to Jamie above all?'

'True,' rejoined Rosalyn, 'they could, but they'd have to explain why their evidence to the court had failed to disclose the relationship when they first applied for the injunction. In my line of work, that is a big black mark. Moreover, once we expose the relationship and its termination, their task of explaining their non-disclosure becomes a whole lot harder, and the court will give them very little wriggle-room.'

'But surely the board knew nothing about it?'

'At least one of their directors knew all about it, and as far as the law is concerned, that equates to the knowledge of the company.'

Cat had not allowed for that. 'Oh, I see. I thought it had to be reported to the board or something?'

Rosalyn pressed home. 'Not for the purposes of UK law. So, this new strategy is designed to leave the claimants with no room for manoeuvre, and it also hands us the initiative, which in this game is crucial.'

'How so?'

'Here's why. We can now seek an order from the court that requires a director of the claimants – preferably the head of their Legal Department – to disclose the originals of each of the documents that you have exposed. If they refuse, we shall seek a disclosure order against them.'

Cat's face lit up. 'You mean you can turn the tables on them?'

'Yes. That is precisely what I intend to do.'

Cat was impressed. The strategy now made obvious sense.

'Tomo said you were good, Rosalyn, but that is really smart.'

'Thank you. As Tom is inclined to reply, "We aim to please."'

They both chuckled at that.

'So when do you hope to get this order?'

'As I said, we must first ask them to provide the documents voluntarily. They will almost certainly prevaricate and try to fudge it. We shall persevere, probably with one or two chasing letters, until finally we seek an order from the court, saying that we were left with no alternative. In fact, for starters, Tom might even decide to table our application at the return date hearing – assuming that it goes ahead.'

Cat was surprised to hear Rosalyn say that. 'You sound doubtful? Why is that?'

'There's another letter in from the claimants' lawyers suggesting that counsel discuss the merits of adjourning the return date, saying that they need more time to consider the large volume of disclosure. They even have the temerity to presume that we would be in favour of an adjournment, which we might have been in other circumstances.'

'Why's that?'

'Sorry, I should have explained. Normally the defence would grab the chance to postpone such a hearing. I say normally because this is far from being a normal case because we now actually welcome the opportunity to get before the judge. Having said that, I can see the benefit of a few more days to prepare for it.'

'Will it affect your strategy?'

'Not at all,' replied Rosalyn. 'The timing of the letters is very much under our control, as is their content.'

Cat sensed the nuanced pause. 'The content?'

'Yes. It's a convenient way for me to introduce the letter of claim that I had asked Diana to approve. We aim to ruin my opponent's morning tomorrow, but only if you are content to give me the green light to the revised strategy. I shall need to go through some of the details of this with you first.'

'Can we first speak to Tomo together?'

'Surely. I'll set it up now.'

Chapter 20

Diana Richards, or 'Di' to her friends and colleagues, was an experienced employment law specialist in Tomo's chambers, with a side line in harassment and abuse claims, having appeared in a number of high-profile cases. Her slight build and greying hair might at first suggest that she was past her prime, until one met her eyes. They were bright blue, alert and razor sharp, advertising one of the brightest minds in her discipline. She had elected not to take silk, and so continued to practice as a junior, but only the foolish or reckless underestimated her as an opponent.

She was at the top of her game.

She had bided her time as she watched Mary Fellowes go through the attachments to the emails and texts in the file listed by the IT specialist as 'sensitive'. She sensed that Mary was not herself used to seeing such images in her line of work, or indeed privately, and was finding the exercise distinctly awkward. She waited until the image appeared with the clues to the identity of the second of the two participants in the *flagrant delict* – if, that is, the scene could be elevated to such a genteel phrase.

She asked the IT manager to hold the image.

'I am instructed to draw your attention to the detail of the skin on the back of the second person visible on the screen. You will notice two distinct moles just beneath the right shoulder blade. In due course, I understand that your clients, the *intended* claimants in the principal proceedings, will be invited to confirm that the person that we can see here was none other one of their main board directors to whom my client reported. Indeed, we believe that he remains so to this day.'

'Thank you. Duly noted,' said Mary, although she was silently cursing her clients. She would demand to know why had she been exposed to this ambush.

'The provenance of the emails, and the device from which they were sent, is a matter that is likely to form part of a disclosure request that will be sent to your firm later this morning by those instructing me, in addition to the invitation to the claimants to which I have just referred.'

'Again, duly noted,' replied Mary, biting her lip.

'There is then the question of the identity of the second on the two recipients to whom some of these images and videos were sent. I am instructed that those instructing me will address that matter in due course in a separate communication to your firm. That assumes, of course, that the director concerned has not already confessed to being both the second participant and the sender of the emails. Were he to do so, he would no doubt at the same time also vouchsafe to your firm of his own volition the identity of the second recipient of his emails.'

Di left that dainty morsel hanging in the air for a few moments, and then added, 'How likely that is, I can only speculate.'

'Thank you. Again, duly noted,' was Mary's terse reply.

She had the uncomfortable sensation that her firm was now in the process of being outmanoeuvred by her opponents on not one, but two flanks. She now understood Miss Symonds' horror when she realised that others would see these images.

Di thought that this was the perfect time to end the meeting.

'Is there anything else that you specifically wish to see in this file, or that I can help you with now in order to save time later?'

Mary detected an element of mischief in the question, but decided that now was not the right time to make an issue of it. 'No thank you,' she replied. 'I think that I have seen enough for the moment, so we need not trouble this gentleman here any more.'

'Very well,' said Di. 'That then just leaves outstanding the twin questions of the relevance and the desirability of admission of this material in the principal proceedings.'

'In principle, I agree.'

'Good. So, dealing with the first point, as I intimated, later this morning those instructing me will be writing to your firm. As regards the second point, I am instructed that having spoken with Rosalyn, whom I believe you know, the supervising solicitor will expect us to agree that, now that this material has been inspected, it should not be inspected by or disclosed to any other person or entity without either Miss Symonds' express written consent or by further express order of the court on notice to all parties. I suggest that we save time and consent to that mutually.'

'So, what about the claimants' counsel?'

'I am instructed that Miss Symonds insists that the material should only be inspected by you and me. Neither her own counsel nor Rosalyn are being permitted to inspect it, and she wishes the position to remain that way.'

Mary could see the plain sense in that arrangement, and had little hope of persuading the court to overrule the supervising solicitor. She thought about trying to buy time. However, before she could do so, Di continued.

'As I understand the compromise proposed by Peter, the embargo would only apply to the images and the videos. The emails themselves would of course become available for disclosure and inspection in the proceedings, unless the parties otherwise agree or the court orders to the contrary.'

'Thank you. Once I receive the letter form the supervising solicitor in those terms, I shall of course seek instructions.'

'I expected nothing less. And off the record?'

'Speaking off the record, and without instructions, I can see the sense in the proposal, especially at this stage of the proceedings.'

'Duly noted. I shall report back on that basis.'

Mary nodded.

'It goes without saying,' Di added, 'that it will be our suggestion in the current proceedings that counsel should agree how best to inform the judge, should he enquire, as to the contents of the attachments in the event that the issue becomes material.'

'Duly noted. And I thank you for your time, both of you.'

*

Ted Fisher rose from his laptop, or rather stumbled sideways, numbed with shock and seemingly unable to grasp the enormity of what he had now read. His arms, at first limp, slowly rose from his torso, initially without purpose, and then directed his hands towards the crown of his head. There they rested, purposeless, inert, as he turned towards the window as if in search of salvation.

'Oh fuck! Oh my holiest and saintly, what have I just seen!'

It was not a question, for he already knew the answer. His was a statement of despair, as the realisation dawned on him that no one in the company was going to come out of this well, least of all his department.

He had belatedly got around to disassembling the plethora of electronic material that had been sent to him by an operative within the company's IT resource commissioned by the Black Mamba, or her poodle.

What a fuck-up!

True, it had not been her, but one of her personal terriers who had gone chasing off on a limb of her own – and crucially without authority or legal mandate. She had tried to steal a march by accessing electronic communications sent by the former employee whom the company had been advised to sue. But what was worse, what was much worse, was that some of these were plainly Symonds' personal data, much of it highly personal.

This was a textbook example of the consequences of acting in haste. The trouble was, much as they would like to repent at leisure, the one thing they did not have right now was the luxury of time. The company was due back in court on Friday morning, unless it could secure an adjournment of the hearing.

The trouble was: that would signal retreat, if not imminent defeat.

He had wasted the best part of today going through all the material that had been recovered by the IT guys and subsequently downloaded into zipped files. None of the files had been properly divided into any form of order or subjects, which was a damned nuisance: hardly surprising since his department had no idea which 'haystacks' to look for, let alone which needles.

He had initially attributed such an oversight to an absence of clear instructions from internal affairs. However, on reflection, given that these were IT guys, that excuse would not wash. They could have easily performed an initial classification of the material so as to make it more accessible to him and to others.

No, on reflection, this must have been deliberate. Those guys knew exactly what they had done. They had created a series of haystacks with the clear intention of rendering any subsequent analysis by his and other teams substantially more complex. They must have appreciated that the explosive properties of the data that they had intentionally scattered amongst those hybrid pyramids were no ordinary needles. They were bloody great pitchforks. And he could guess why.

This stuff was the legal equivalent to a kilogramme of Semtex being smuggled into his office under cover of an internal disclosure request. It had been copied by the IT guys deliberately – no doubt in the certain knowledge that this would protect their sphincters once the post-mortem was commissioned. As it surely would be, in no short order, he expected.

What infuriated him – and he could imagine them sniggering to each other on their way down to the pub after they had pressed the send key – was that by dutifully arranging the material into subgroups, he himself had now helpfully supplied the detonator, expertly primed and connected to its electronic circuit. And now, by reading this material, and thereby acquiring knowledge of its contents, he had pressed the firing pin.

Fuck, he thought to himself. 'Oh Fuck! Fuck! Fuck!' he whispered at the window.

If these documents were all genuine, they proved that the company had as good as bribed the academics to falsify their papers, in the clear and certain knowledge that they were concealing the truth, or at least not telling the whole truth. This was even worse than the newspaper had claimed. This was corporate deceit.

Unless, of course, the documents were fake. That might be the company's best response to all this material. But could all of this really have been faked?

He'd already checked the provenance tables twice, and had seen the recorded sources of this material checked by the IT operatives. With a few irrelevant exceptions, they all appeared to have been generated on the company's own server. The IT guys had made that point loud and clear in their covering emails.

As a result, it seemed likely that the one avenue of hope that he had floated would in reality be blocked off. At any rate, on the basis of the material that he had seen, he had no reason – or at least none that was likely to satisfy the court – to doubt that these papers were otherwise than genuine.

They confirmed the newspaper's primary accusation, and revealed a combination of the suppression of some key test results and the deliberate skewing of others in order to deceive the company's primary market. And it had taken place under the very eyes of the profession that they were supposed to be helping, and also under the noses of its regulators. Yet only last week the company's lawyers had told the court that there was absolutely no substance to the allegations in the newspaper.

How in the name of all that was sacred was the company going to explain this material to a judge? Come to think of it, he thought, how did they expect to do so when the paper had already boasted in its article that there was more to come. More to the point, how should he break the news to his boss? The Mamba he could manage without difficulty, but Larry was going to take this very badly. No, worse than badly! He might even have to consider resigning.

No, hold on. How could he have known that all this was going on? None of this material had been copied to him, and Ted had yet to see any email that suggested that Larry had been privy to any part of the deception. No, Larry was as much in the clear as he was.

Yet still the question haunted him: how the hell did no one in the company raise the alarm! Surely someone, one of the chemists even, who had procured the so-called research papers, would have queried the ethics of all this if they had got wind of it?

No, this conspiracy could not have been widespread. It must have been limited to a handful of people in the company with the deliberate intent of concealing this from the entire industry.

And, he realised, from the Mamba.

Even so, the question still bugged him: why did no one raise the alarm? He checked himself.

No, someone clearly had. And that someone had to be the person who had blown the whistle last week.

And now the truth was about to come out. He went to make himself another strong coffee in order to fortify himself for the brief that he needed to send to his boss and to the Mamba.

Chapter 21

Back at her offices, Mary Fellowes prepared for the team meeting that she had convened earlier that morning. They were due to speak again to the clients later, but she wished to obtain the team's feedback on their various tasks, including their review of the disclosure material from Miss Symonds' solicitors.

But first, she needed to ensure that she was up to speed on all recent developments, which included new correspondence from Miss Symonds lawyers. The first had arrived yesterday evening, the second this morning.

Tim had circulated, and they had all read, the first letter received yesterday evening from Miss Symonds' solicitors dealing with matters of disclosure. It was both reactive and proactive in content, the latter being the more concerning. Tim's note had helpfully summarised the letter, and she had identified the two key elements that they needed to address.

First, the letter had identified the provenance of the two boxes of material. According to her opposite number, these had been retrieved two days ago from an estate in the south of England. The precise details of the 'custodian' were going to be vouchsafed later that morning once certain legal formalities had been observed, which included obtaining the necessary data protection clearance from the relevant 'data subject'.

Secondly, the letter dealt with the twin issues of the provenance and relevance of the material produced following the interrogation of the laptop and mobile phone that had been obtained from Miss Symonds' flat last week.

The forthright admissions in the letter were not only unusual, indeed unwelcome, but were also concerning. They were unusual because a defendant would normally be a great deal more reticent on the question of provenance, not least for reasons of self-incrimination. They were unwelcome because it rendered the prospect of being able to challenge the authenticity of the material commensurably much more difficult for the clients. They were concerning because they heralded a counter-offensive by her opponents, but in circumstances where her own clients were being less than forthcoming. And that was a bloody big concern, in fact.

But that was the least of her clients' problems — and therefore that of her firm. Something else also concerned her. It concerned her very much. She would need to address it during their internal meeting.

She returned to Tim's note. He had recorded that Miss Symonds' solicitors had now requested that her clients should provide voluntary disclosure of the originals of each of the copy documents that had been retrieved either from the mysterious estate in the south or from Miss Symonds' laptop and mobile phone. And their letter had made the point that the disclosure had been the product of the search and disk-imaging orders that her firm had obtained on behalf of her own clients.

Now, that was clever. That was very, very clever.

Finally, the letter had recorded that Miss Symonds' solicitors were not currently minded consent on behalf of their client to an adjournment of Friday's hearing. However, they might do so in return for certain undertakings and/or assurances, which included the disclosure by her clients of the originals, as requested.

'Talk about a gun to the head,' she said to herself.

And then the bombshell.

Her firm had received, as a matter of courtesy, a draft of a letter that would, in the absence of certain undertakings, be sent to the chief executive at AlphaOm. Its contents had come as a surprise to her team, but not to her, given that she had been forewarned earlier this morning during her 'inspection' session at the offices of the supervising solicitor, which Mary had found acutely uncomfortable.

As threatened by Miss Symonds' counsel, the draft pre-action protocol letter would be sent to AlphaOm by Miss Symonds' solicitors unless AlphaOm admitted liability and gave the requested undertakings, which were wide-ranging but at first glance not wholly unreasonable.

The letter was laden with menace. It set out claims for sexual harassment, constructive dismissal and malicious transmission of indecent images. It further named her client's commercial development director specifically as the person primarily responsible for, or personally involved in, each category of claim. It concluded with a demand for damages and compensation in excess of three million pounds.

'Cheap at the price' was Mary's immediate reaction.

The undertakings which were sought in the letter concerned, amongst other matters, the return of the originals and all copies, electronic or otherwise, of any images or recordings of a sexual content involving Miss Symonds. They also concerned the confidentiality of all such material. Again, Mary's instinctive view was that no sensible commercial entity worthy of the name, properly advised, would readily resist giving such undertakings if one of its directors had got himself mixed up in all this.

She had to hand it to Rosalyn: she had played a blinder here. She would have to think how best to advise her clients to respond to this development, unwelcome as it was. No, she told herself. This was not her firm's field. She was professionally obligated to tell her clients to instruct a specialist firm.

Time enough for that, she thought.

So, as was her custom, she had already circulated copies of both letters amongst her team, but this time with the proviso that the second letter was to be treated as highly confidential for the time being. She would need to involve the HR specialists elsewhere within her firm so that that could advise how best the clients should deal with the substantive allegations in that letter. But that, of course, assumed that the clients would accept her advice that they should instruct another firm to deal with this new matter, given that it was not her firm's speciality.

And the more she had thought about that, her best course was to rely upon a likely, if not probable conflict of interests.

For present purposes, the relevance of her opponents' letter to the current proceedings was limited to the provenance of the material now disclosed by Miss Symonds pursuant to the court's orders.

Time for her to join the meeting.

She walked down the corridor and offered her apologies to her team for her slightly tardy arrival. She was handed the agenda for their internal meeting, and cast her eyes down the list of items. This could take a while, she thought. A separate agenda had been emailed to the clients, identifying the issues on which her firm required urgent instructions.

Don't hold your breath, she thought to herself.

'Good morning everyone,' she began. 'Before we start, can one of you remind me, are we still due to speak to the clients at eleven, or has this been pushed back again at the clients' request?'

Her junior assistant, Emma, raised her hand. 'An email has just come in from Ted Fisher in legal,' she said. 'He's asked us to move the call back to eleven-thirty.'

'That sounds ominous, but we may not have the luxury of that amount of time. Did he give a reason?'

'He mentions internal discussions at the clients.'

Mary shook her head, almost in disbelief. The team as one picked up the sentiment, but it was Tim who spoke out loud what they were all thinking. 'Look at it this way, Mary. We've had some difficult clients as claimants in the past, but this one surely takes the biscuit. You'd be forgiven for thinking that they'd forgotten about the hearing. What the devil are they playing at?'

'Well,' said Mary, well versed in these scenarios, 'we are where we are, so we shall just have to do what we can. Let's start with counsel's brief fees. Have the funds come in from the clients to cover these?'

Emma raised her hand again.

'Yes, these came in late yesterday.'

Mary ticked that off on her agenda.

'On that note,' Tim interjected, 'I've had counsel and their clerks on to me again. Between them they had two points. First, they told me that both counsel are booked out on another matter for most of next week, with Friday looking the only free slot at the moment. So, logistically that makes an adjournment distinctly less than attractive from our side.'

Great, thought Mary.

'Secondly, counsel chased me again for instructions as a matter of urgency. They will need to inform the court this morning if we are likely to adjourn, or else risk a big black mark with the judge. As claimants, that is the last thing we need. They also reminded me that they are required to file their written submissions with the court by three pm today, with particular emphasis on the material disclosed by Miss Symonds, and our reasons for continuing the restraining injunctions. Further delay risks censure from the judge and, as you might expect, they are anxious to avoid that.'

'What have you told them on that score?' asked Mary.

'I've held the line that they will need to form an orderly queue behind us, but that went down like a lead balloon.'

She turned to Emma. 'I think you need to go back to Ted and tell him that we really cannot wait until eleven-thirty. Ask him if possible to keep our telecon at eleven. You can pass on counsel's concern that they have to file their submissions this afternoon.' Then she reconsidered. 'Actually, now that it's come to it, tell them that we need to instruct counsel by noon today at the latest. And we can't do that without first having taken instructions from the clients. In short, we do not have the luxury of time.'

Then she added: 'Oh yes, and remind him to tell his team that they are the claimants, and that the court will be expecting them to force the pace.'

In other circumstances, that remark might have generated comments around the table, but today was not such an occasion.

'On it,' said Emma, and began to type her email.

She returned to Tim. 'I've seen nothing in from the clients in connection with the disclosure from either of the defendants, but especially from Miss Symonds' team. I've seen the communications going to and from the universities regarding the research, for want of a better word. It does not exactly make for pleasant reading.'

Tim flicked on the PowerPoint, and pulled up a list of key documents, each numbered and in date sequence.

'Our team of paralegals have been through most of the disclosure. What I've highlighted here are what I regard, from an initial trawl, as the really dangerous ones from the clients' perspective. I consider that, if they cannot explain these, the clients are going to find it very hard to resist an application by the defendants to set aside the restraining orders, in part if not as a whole.'

The team digested that intelligence in stony silence.

'Have counsel seen these?' asked Mary.

'Indeed, and they share my view entirely. Hence, they were chasing me all day yesterday and again this morning for instructions. They have pretty much told me that, absent clear instructions from the clients this morning, they will inform the court – subject to any application that the defendants are minded to make – they will be seeking to adjourn the return hearing in order to give our clients more time in which to interrogate the large volume of disclosure from the defendants.'

'So, absent clear instructions from the clients, counsel will have to do what all claimants should never do, namely, to ask for time?'

Nods around the table.

She turned to Tim. 'Are there other documents which you would place in the same category as the ones that you circulated yesterday?'

Tim tapped his laptop and brought up two further electronic copies.

'Several more, but let me show you two of the worst. The first document is the initial draft of the report from the researchers. Its conclusion is far more equivocal than the revised version, which I've put alongside it. You will not be surprised to learn that the first version never saw the light of day. But what is damaging – if the emails are genuine – is that the revisions pretty much track the heavily telegraphed suggestions from the clients to the researchers, and in at least one case almost verbatim. As I say, if the clients confirm that these are genuine, then we have a very serious problem.'

'You mean *the clients* have a problem,' corrected Mary, 'which will likely become our job to help them to resolve.'

'That's about the sum of it.'

'So, the key question, as before, is whether these are the real thing, or whether a degree of creative artistic licence has been deployed.'

'Oh, I like that,' chirped Emma. 'That is so much more preferable to "fake news". Oh, and before you ask, nothing back yet from Ted.'

'Right. So, in short,' said Mary, 'without clear instructions from the clients, we cannot take that further for the time being.'

The team agreed. Mary scanned down the agenda.

'Let's deal with the disclosure request from Miss Symonds' solicitors. Any immediate thoughts on this?'

Her other junior assistant, Ben, raised his hand. 'My immediate thought was that they are turning the tables on us, but on reflection I query whether they are not being too clever for their own good. In the short term, won't the clients be able to say that they need much more time, since this would be equivalent to a standard disclosure exercise, which normally takes up to three or even six months. So, the oppo are really playing into our hands.'

Tim was nodding. 'I'm with Benjy on this. I think that this buys the clients valuable time, but only as regards the new stuff.'

'Go on,' encouraged Mary.

'Well, they have had over a week to search out the originals of the documents that were cited by *The Chronicle*, and they've gone on oath to tell the court that they had reason to believe that those documents were confidential. Are they seriously going to suggest that they should instruct us to turn around now and say to the court, "Oops, frightfully sorry and all that, but it looks as though these documents were faked by the defendants." Leaving aside just how awful it will look, they would be trying to shift their claim from one based on breach of confidence into one alleging libel.'

'And we all know where that can lead,' Mary observed.

'Yep,' said Tim, 'but the difference is that we'd be dealing with something rather more important than the contents of a hamburger.'

They were all fully aware of the implications of that statement.

Mary took up the reins again.

'So, we've gone full circle, and we're back to getting instructions from the clients as to the authenticity and provenance of the disclosed material.'

She looked across at Emma.

'Sorry, still no reply,' reported her assistant.

'As I expected, but can you please chase again.'

Emma signalled her assent, and began to type another email.

After a brief silence, it was Tim who spoke next. 'Given that we have an elephant in the room, should we all take it that your inspection of the sensitive material and the draft protocol letter from Miss Symonds' lawyers are, with no pun intended, connected?'

Mary nodded gravely.

'Alas, I fear very much so. And I don't mind admitting to you all that, as I left the meeting yesterday, I had the acute sensation that we were being outmanoeuvred on virtually every front, including this new one.'

The team digested that for a moment.

'Well,' said Tim, 'we've been in the manure before, and we've lived to fight another day. There are some wars that with hindsight one was never going to win, and we always knew that this could be one of those. And, if I read it correctly, your file note of your initial instructions from the client, on that fateful evening, raised the very point that the clients might be better served if they just issued a denial and let the story die its own death, as so many of these headline grabbers so often do.'

'More than that,' Ben interjected, 'you repeated the point in your letter of advice to the clients when we issued the engagement letter.'

'Indeed I did. I don't know why, but I had an uneasy feeling about this case from the very start. A genuine whistleblower either goes straight to the authorities or to the press. A fake will try to extort a ransom. This one had all the hallmarks of being the genuine article right from the word go.'

'But I'll wager that you didn't see this one coming,' observed Tim.

It was Emma, with her acute female intuition, who was the one who replied first. 'Actually, once Miss Symonds had been identified as the likely culprit, and we'd all seen her photograph, I suspect that we all instinctively feared that there might be a darker side to the whole story.'

The team's silence provided the tacit confirmation.

After a few moments, Tim, who like all the other members of the team had read the draft protocol letter setting out the claim, asked the question that was on all of their minds, including her own: 'So, do I take it that we going to find a way to decline the instruction on the harassment brief? No, let me rephrase that. Do you reckon that our existing duties to the clients would oblige us not to take the brief, but to declare a conflict?'

'I'm not sure,' replied Mary. 'I'll need to run the point past our compliance team here first, but my instinct tells me that they will want to divert the instructions to another firm with the right expertise in order to avoid any conflict down the line.'

There was an audible sigh of relief round the table.

'Shall we give Ted Fisher a call?' she suggested.

Chapter 22

Cat had spent most of the previous day going through the remainder of the documents that had been retrieved from Dorset. She now had divided the material into discrete subjects as best she could for the convenience of both her own lawyers and for those advising *The Chronicle*. She had given priority to the full chain of communications, both internal ones at AlphaOm and the external ones to and from the universities, recording the arrangements with those responsible at the universities for the research that had exonerated, amongst others, AlphaOm's sugar substitute products.

She had to keep reminding herself that she was no lawyer. But despite that limitation, she wanted so much to believe that this material ought to be enough to convince the court that her employers had set out to deceive not only the politicians in Europe but also the public at large, and no doubt some of the medical profession.

But there was important material missing. She was certain that she had taken copies of the emails between CT and the chief, along with the communications with some of the other 'pharma' companies.

And she was sure that those were the real dynamite.

She checked the time. Rosalyn had scheduled a telecon with Tomo later that morning, after they had spoken with the legal advisers to *The Chronicle*. There had already been a discussion earlier in the week about a common strategy. The outcome of the previous discussions had been that it was agreed that neither she nor *The Chronicle* was yet in a position to apply to set aside the injunctions. She doubted that the position would be any different today. But she had got the distinct impression from her conversation with Tomo when they had spoken earlier that such a time was not far off.

Her 'inbox' told her that she'd just received an email from Rosalyn's PA. It provided the dial-in details for their telecon. She followed the robotic instructions, and was connected to the call. It was Rosalind who welcomed her, in what seemed to Cat to be a surprisingly cheerful voice, which was a very pleasant change from previous days.

'Thanks for joining us, Cat. We've just put the phone down on a very useful conference call with *The Chronicle*'s legal team. You won't be surprised to learn that they need more time in which to launch an all-out attack on the injunction. However, they like the idea of pressing for a disclosure order against the company, and have agreed to take the lead on that front, which is a relief. Their concern, however, is the same as ours. They think that all that the company will say is that, at this early stage, they have reason to believe that some or all of the documents have been fabricated. On that basis, they will ask the court to give them more time in which to verify that.'

From their earlier meetings, Rosalyn had prepared Cat for such a scenario, such that this did not come as any great shock to Cat. In fact, she almost felt a sense of relief that the tension that would otherwise have accompanied the scheduled hearing would be significantly abated.

'So, just that I'm clear,' she began, 'does that mean that there's no hearing in court this week?'

It was Tomo who answered. 'Actually, Cat, we consider that if, which we think is likely, the company does not agree to provide voluntary disclosure of the originals, nor for that matter all other relevant material in its control, we should get the court to focus on this. It's too good an opportunity for us to waste. Also, the fact that the company has invited us to adjourn makes it even more desirable for us to keep the pressure on them. After all, it was only last week that they told the court that you had taken their confidential information and were using it to cause them harm. So, I'm working on my submission to the court as we speak. It will need to go to the judge mid-afternoon.'

It was that aspect that Cat found difficult to comprehend.

'Well, I'm no way as clever as y'all, but I just don't get how the court will allow them to say that I've stolen their documents when it suits them, but turn around and say the opposite once the tables are turned.'

'Believe me, Cat,' replied Tomo, 'that point will not be lost on the court, and we shall be making it in spades. Does that help?'

'I guess,' she replied, slightly hesitantly.

'Just to be clear,' intervened Rosalyn, '*The Chronicle*'s lawyers will be asking the court either to make an order for disclosure or to give the company a deadline in which to confirm whether or not they consent to such an order, failing which the court will be asked to make the order itself.'

'But what if they deny that the documents are real?' asked Cat.

'In that event,' replied Rosalyn, 'as we discussed in these offices, our co-defendants are agreed that we should apply for a disc-imaging order against the company. And we think that we've a fair chance of getting such an order.'

'So, is that all that the hearing will be about?' asked Cat.

'Not quite,' replied Rosalyn. 'First, there will be the formality of adjourning the main issue for another return date, which is whether the restraining injunction should be continued. We have advised you that we should agree to adjourn on the strict understanding that your rights – and those of *The Chronicle* – are fully preserved as regards setting aside the orders. The court will very likely agree to that. Then we'll need to agree a revised date for the hearing with the company and the court.'

'And I guessing from what you've already said,' Cat remarked, 'that, since we're not ready yet, this suits us just as well?'

'Indeed it does,' Rosalind confirmed. 'Tom and I are in agreement on that. Do you want to add anything, Tom?'

'No thanks. That just about covers it.'

'You said "first" …' prompted Cat.

'I did, yes. I forgot that not much slips by you.'

'Well, it is *kinda* my problem.'

'Quite so, Cat. So, the court will then hear us on the terms of certain undertakings that we've asked the company to give. Those concern two matters which we consider to be important. First, we want the court to approve the *status quo* with regard to the content of the sensitive material found on your devices. Given that this arrangement was proposed by the supervising solicitor, and our opponents have not challenged it, the court is very likely to rubber-stamp it.'

'That's good to hear.'

'The second aspect concerns the location where the recent disclosure had been stored. As regards that, we've told our opponents that, since at least one of the directors of the company has form in harassing people close to you, we – by which I mean you – will only consent to the information regarding the details of the location being seen by their lead solicitor and their lead counsel.'

'And what have they said so far?'

'We wrote to the company's lawyers twice yesterday, but have yet to hear back from them.'

'So why are they holding out on you?' asked Cat.

'We've chased again, but I think it is quite likely that this is not high on their agenda right at this moment. As we have discussed before, Tom and I reckon that they will want to keep as far away from the unpleasant stuff as they can. And as regards the recent documents, the location of their storage only becomes an issue if the company decides to challenge the authenticity of the material. If they do, they will almost certainly want to know where those documents have been stored on your behalf over these past few months.'

'I guess that's an answer of sorts,' said Cat, 'but do we actually have to deal with that in court? Why can't you guys just agree it?'

'That's exactly what we're trying to do, Cat, but we can only do that if and when they condescend to engage with us.'

Cat thought about that for a moment.

'Fair point, I guess,' she acknowledged. 'So, if we're not dealing with the main issue, do I have to come over to your offices again today?'

'No, not at the moment. But I'd like us to catch up again this afternoon so that we can deal with any late developments before the hearing. Shall we say three-thirty? We can use the same dial-in details.'

'You got it.'

*

CT had been up all night reading through the volumes of paper that Maria had copied onto a CD and sent over to him. He had to hand it to Cat; she really had been thorough. He had known that she was good at her job – amongst other attributes – but this had been a class act. And all the more impressive on account of the fact that she had stolen this material from right under his nose.

But where were the emails between him and the other pharmas? More to the point, where were the memos that he'd sent to McBride to get his …? His what, exactly? He'd been canny enough to avoid actually approving the operation overtly. CT had to give him the credit for that.

But he'd fucking well known about it. CT had made damn sure of that. To a court of law, his tacit approval was enough to condemn him, since he'd done bugger all to call a halt to the scheme.

I mean, fuck! Their whole business depended on these sales. Sure, he'd seen plenty of articles from the 'organic' lobby and the self-styled

'Earth mothers' condemning their sweetener products. The most recent was entitled: 'The poison that lurks in your cereal'.

There were piles of such hysteria every month. Every other year it might grab a headline or two in the national press, usually in the silly season when those jokers had nothing much else to write about.

But, the public's appetite for sweetness just kept on growing. They liked it in their 'low fat' foods, in their confectionary and in their mechanically processed meals whose natural nutrients were neutered and replaced by manufactured substitutes that AlphaOm peddled so effectively.

In his mind, he reckoned that he and the chief were no different from every drug peddler on the street corner. They dutifully and consistently fulfilled a public need, which had virtually become a worldwide addiction. I mean, fuck, just look at the obesity rates in the USA and elsewhere! And the diabetes epidemic. Oh baby, just keep it rolling!

He turned back to his screen. He wondered whether Maria might have omitted a whole tranche of documents, perhaps deliberately. It was possible, he told himself, but not altogether likely, because it had been her idea to involve him, and he doubted whether she would have been able to recognise some of the potentially damaging documents without his background knowledge.

So, if they weren't here, then the most likely explanation was that neither Cat nor the newspaper had those incriminating documents. And, if that was right, and it was certainly beginning to look that way, there was a fighting chance that he and the chief might come out of this in one piece. Sure, they would have to lie through their pants, but they were well schooled in that game. Hell, it almost came as part of his job-description.

But how had she missed them? CT was as certain as he could be that he'd filed them on the same server as all these other documents. If she had got access to the server through his laptop – and the more he thought about that, it must have been how she had done it – then she would have seen the links. So, where were they?

It was time to contact Maria again.

Chapter 23

Joey and his mates had loaded the last of the hay bales onto the trailer in readiness for the short journey over to the stable. He'd let the girls decide whether it was still fit for the horses to eat, or whether it was bedding material.

He had carefully placed the two trunks and the remaining box in the corner of the barn. They seemed so insignificant now that the building was empty, like some abandoned hovel for refugees seeking shelter from the storm. He tarried a while, conscious of the fact that he was now able to admire the structure of the barn, which was remarkably intact after all these years. The beams could maybe do with some help, but so far as he could see from inside, most of the stone tiles were still in decent shape, despite the decades of neglect.

It was a lovely building. He wouldn't be at all surprised if Jamie decided that it was time to give the old girl a new lease of life.

He was proposing to drop by the house later to ask Jamie what he should do with the stuff in the barn. However, thinking about it, he was pretty sure that he knew the answer, and certainly so far as the box was concerned. But he'd need to play the part, lest his conduct cause Jamie to become suspicious. Or Charlie, for that matter. He had eyes in the back of his head, for sure!

He reminded himself that there was just one more thing he needed to attend to before he went over to Jamie's. He would nip into Dorchester to get copies of the keys cut in order to facilitate his nocturnal pursuits. And he wanted to get one of those blow-up camping beds that he could use to good effect over the summer evenings. The girls did so like their comforts.

*

Their attempts to contact Ted Fisher had eventually elicited a begrudging consent to speak at 11.00 with the 'cabinet' chaired by Barbara Spooner. However, it was with a heavy heart that Tim made the connection to the telecon at the appointed hour.

The minutes ticked by. The Mamba was taking her time to dial in when eventually Ted was able to join them.

'Good morning again, Ted. Mary is here, and will lead from our end. Any news on when your team will join us?'

'Hi, Tim. Hi, Mary. I had understood that she would be with us. Just give me a second and I'll mail her again. I'll copy in her assistant, just to be on the safe side. I'm pretty sure one of them will pick it up.'

After a pause he signalled his readiness to proceed.

'Thanks,' said Mary, taking over the reins. 'As I think Tim has already flagged, we are going to have to tell the court whether tomorrow's hearing will be effective or not. In order to do that, we need your instructions, Ted. So, if, as I suspect is the case, you or Barbara are going to tell us that the company needs more time, then the sooner we say that to the court the better it will look.'

'Sure, and I have passed on that message loud and clear,' said Ted. 'We also have some other issues internally that we are looking to resolve that may or may not have an impact on the case generally. However, I am not yet in a position to brief you on these, so I must ask you to bear with us for a while. And that includes the issue of the apparent discovery of Ms Symonds' new home address.'

'Well, please don't keep us in suspense for too long, Ted. We have enough on our plate as it is without any more excitement.'

'If only that were in my gift, Mary. I seem to spend my time playing catch-up on this case, and I hear that there has been a development which relates to the case, but I'm not privy to the details. Apparently, it's already gone upstairs.'

'That is what I understand, Ted,' replied Mary, being careful to avoid giving the impression she was herself very much privy to the details.

The robotic voice announced Barbara's entry to the call.

'Are we all here?' demanded Barbara brusquely, and without even a hint of an apology for her delayed arrival.

'We are, Barbara,' said Ted tersely, 'and have been since eleven.'

She affected to ignore the jibe. 'So, I understand that counsel have unilaterally imposed a deadline on us,' she began, 'and that is high noon today.'

Mary saw her team wince and shake their heads.

'No, Barbara, that is not the case. On your instructions, we sought and obtained a date and time for the return hearing. That date and time has been in your diary for a week. It is tomorrow, at ten-thirty, in Court 37. If the company, for whatever reason, is unlikely to be in a position to proceed tomorrow, then counsel have a duty to inform the court promptly. Counsel advise that two pm today is the latest that they can properly leave it before they inform the court of the company's intentions.'

'Well, no one consulted me about that,' said the Mamba. Tim suppressed a guffaw at Barbara's tart reply, but still she persisted: 'As I think I have made clear before, Mary, I dislike having deadlines imposed on me by those whom I employ.'

'Barbara, the company, at your cabinet's behest, imposed the deadline on itself when it applied for the orders last week.'

This had got off to a bad start, and she could sense that the longer it progressed, the more unpleasant it was likely to become. However, it was Ted who rode to the rescue.

'Barbara,' he said, as calmly as he could, 'can I suggest that we stop pointing fingers at each other, and instead concentrate on the key issue. And, as Mary has made clear again in her emailed advice overnight, that is whether or not the company is or is not in a position to proceed with the hearing or whether it needs more time. From our discussions internally, it seems to me that it is now highly unlikely that we shall be able to proceed with the return date issues tomorrow. But I need to hear that from you, as does Mary, since you are the lead client contact. So, to put it simply, is the answer to that very simple question a yes or no, Barbara.'

There was a stunned silence from the other end of the phone, but Mary's team were variously giving 'thumbs up' signs or silently applauding. Over the course of the week, they had come to share Ted's dislike of their primary client contact. They also assumed, correctly as it happened, that she had never been spoken to before like that, and certainly not in the audible presence of others. But more than anything, they admired Ted for his courage.

The silence was eventually broken by Barbara. 'I'll not stand for any more insolence from you, Ted. I'd be grateful if you would leave this conference call now.'

Ouch, thought Mary. That was not going to help anyone, least of all her and her team if she lost the one person at the client who was making any sense.

'No can do, Barbara, as you well know,' replied Ted. 'I am here in Larry's stead, and for the purpose of this call I hold the same status as you. And can I suggest that it will hardly be an edifying sight for Mary and her esteemed team to witness a turf war between our two departments. So, can we please just get on with this.'

It was time for Mary to intervene. 'When we spoke yesterday, Barbara, we left matters on the basis that you would let me know this morning whether or not the company was in a position to confirm whether or not the documents disclosed by Miss Symonds are genuine. As I have advised, whilst it would be preferable if we *were* in a position to proceed, the court will probably understand if we tell them why we need more time.'

That seemed to calm the waters, so she continued.

'Meanwhile, we have heard from the solicitors acting for Miss Symonds. They intend to agree to an adjournment of the hearing so far as concerns the restraining orders, in the event that the company does request that, but on terms. They intend to support the solicitors for *The Chronicle*, who wish to be heard tomorrow on their application for an order for specific disclosure against the company. You will both have received my email yesterday afternoon dealing with that and other issues. Can I take it that you have both had time to read and digest its contents?'

'I have Mary,' said Ted, 'and I can give instructions in a moment as regards the requested undertakings, which Larry and I have discussed. As regards the defendants' disclosure request, Larry and I would prefer you to resist this on the basis that all of the disclosure will be made available in the ordinary course of the proceedings following the court's usual case management directions. That is the only persuasive basis that we can think of at the moment for resisting the application. That said, the other possible basis is that the request presumes that the original documents exist and that we have them under our control, which is, of course, an entirely different matter. That is what Barbara and her team are working on as we speak.'

'Thank you, Tim, and that is duly noted,' said Mary. 'We'll give some thought to that and consult with counsel later today. We'll come back to the undertakings in a moment. Meanwhile, Barbara, are you and Ted in accord on this?'

'I shall deal with that directly,' said the Mamba, ice now blatantly evident in her voice. 'First let me confirm the position with regard to our analysis of the disclosed material. In that regard I can confirm that it is correct that we are still interrogating our system to ascertain whether these documents are genuine.'

'Thank you, Barbara, that is noted.'

'I have not finished yet,' continued the ice-cold voice. 'For the record, I would be grateful if you would henceforth only take your instructions from me.'

Here we go again, thought Mary.

'Sorry to be a pedant, Barbara,' Ted retorted as calmly as his gritted teeth would permit, 'but under our articles, as revised, all undertakings which are to be given on behalf of the company must be approved by the Legal Department and then cleared with the board. So please, can we just get on with this.'

'Now listen, Ted,' Barbara spat in her authoritarian tone ...

'No, I'm sorry, Barbara,' he replied, 'this has to stop. We have not got time for games like this. The limits to your department's authority are crystal clear, so there is nothing for us to discuss. But I have to insist on an answer regarding tomorrow. Between us, we have to give instructions to Mary. Until now, I have been hampered by the fact that you had still not told me – nor Mary, for that matter – what is the status with regard to Miss Symonds' disclosure. It has become increasingly obvious to me that you are not in a position to confirm to Mary and her team that you have finished your interrogation of that material. If that is the case, can you not now at least have the good grace to confirm that. Because, if that is the case, then it must follow that we are to instruct Mary to instruct our counsel to apply to adjourn the hearing tomorrow as regards the restraining orders. Is that now our agreed position?'

The question was met with silence. It hung within the cables between them, poignant amidst the urgency of the hour. Five, ten seconds passed. But no response. Mary found this excruciating. In any other circumstances, she would have made her excuses and terminated the call. But these circumstances demanded that she persevere, despite the difficulty.

'Barbara?' she prompted.

After a further interval, a response was at last forthcoming.

'I consulted my board this morning. The company's instructions are that, for a number of reasons, which I must stress have to include the incomplete state of our interrogation of the disclosed material, we must reluctantly seek an adjournment of the hearing tomorrow. However, our instructions go further than that. The board has resolved that provided it does not prejudice the company's position, we should aim to avoid any form of attendance in court tomorrow.'

It was the turn of Mary and her team to sit back in stunned silence, and even Tim was for once speechless, although he shook his head firmly at Mary.

Mary took the hint. Thus, it was she who spoke first. 'Barbara, I hear what you say. However, the only way that the company can avoid its attendance at this hearing is by conceding the defendants' disclosure request. Were it to do that, the company risks causing significant harm to its position in these proceedings, and perhaps even more widely. Conversely, if we attend the hearing, we at least have the opportunity to limit the scope of the order sought, if not to resist it altogether.'

She allowed the silence to hang for a few minutes.

That advice met with a stony silence from the Mamba, but Ted had found his 'mojo' again and came back into the fray.

'I'd have to add, Barbara, that I have just come from a meeting with Larry, and he made no mention of any such resolution by the board.' And then a sudden thought occurred to him. 'Just a minute, Barbara. Are you saying that there was an *actual* board resolution, or was this just a decision made at the very top?'

Mary could sense their turf war breaking out again, and was quick to intervene before the Mamba could reply.

'Actually, Ted, that may be academic, given that I have now explained to you both that there is an inherent contradiction in the decision or resolution, it matters not which. I take it, therefore, now that you have both had the benefit of my firm's advice, and that of counsel, that between you, by which I mean you, Barbara, and you, Ted, will now cause the company's instructions to be revised on this issue?'

Ted was first to respond. 'That's a yes from me.'

After a pause, Mary prompted: 'Barbara?'

'I shall convey your advice to the board,' said the Mamba frostily, 'and in due course inform you of our position.'

Tim wagged his finger hastily and pointed to his watch. Mary and he were in accord.

'Just to be clear, Barbara, it is now gone 11.30. In half an hour's time,

I need to be in a position where I am able to provide counsel with clear instructions as to what is to happen regarding tomorrow's hearing. That has two aspects.'

Tim put three fingers of his hand up, pointing to his highlighted note.

'Make that three, actually. First, what is to happen with regard to the restraining orders. Secondly, what should the company do and say with regard to the disclosure application by the defendants. And thirdly, what is the company's position with regard to the recent request for undertakings by Miss Symonds' solicitors. Are we agreed?'

Like a sulking child, Barbara elected not to speak, so Ted replied for them both: 'Let's take that as a yes and move on.'

'Very well. So, as regards the restraining orders, counsel are to request that this aspect of the hearing be adjourned. Yes?'

'As Barbara has said, we have no real choice,' agreed Ted.

'Thank you, Ted,' replied Mary with evident relief. 'Could one of you please drop me a line to confirm that?'

'Consider it done, Mary,' said Ted quickly.

'Thank you. As regards the disclosure application, both or one of you is going to revert to me before noon. Agreed?'

'It will certainly be one of us,' replied Ted, consciously assuming command in the absence of any coherent strategy from the Mamba.

'Thank you. So that leaves the undertakings, of which two have been sought on behalf of Miss Symonds. From what you said earlier, Ted, I understand that there has already been some consultation within the company on these, which is helpful. I should like to deal firstly with what has been termed by the supervising solicitor as the sensitive material. Is that agreeable to you both?'

'Sure,' Ted cut in first.

Furious, frozen silence oozed from the Mamba.

'So, the undertaking that Ms Symonds lawyers are seeking, which was in fact suggested by the supervising solicitor, is that inspection of any of that material should be restricted to myself alone. There are two points to note here. The first is that the court is very likely to adopt the suggestion from the supervising solicitor in the absence of compelling reasons to do otherwise, and none has been put forward. Secondly, I have already inspected the material. Dealing first with the email traffic, which is entirely one way, I can confirm that this is of limited relevance to the case. As regards the content and attachments, these are of no relevance. Therefore, my firm's advice is that the company should not hesitate in giving the undertakings. Would either of you like to comment on that?'

'Mary, I can confirm that a recommendation in those terms has already been given by the Legal Department to the board, citing the reasons which you set out in your email yesterday. I expect it to be ratified shortly.'

Mary waited for assent from Barbara. She was tiring of this infantile display by a woman who appeared significantly older than her.

'Very well. I shall convey that message to counsel, but should like to have that instruction in writing please, Ted.'

'Of course. I shall ask Larry to send it after this call.'

'Thank you. Can we therefore then turn to the undertaking relating to the location of the material disclosed by Miss Symonds, and the identity of its custodian. You will have seen my firm's advice yesterday. We consider that the company will need to produce a strong and compelling reason to persuade a court to do otherwise than order that knowledge of such location and identity should be restricted to counsel and myself. So, is either of you in a position to give me such a reason?'

Again, Ted took the initiative. 'Just so that we are all clear, Mary, would the undertaking be couched in such terms as would enable us, if new facts came to light, to ask the court to either vary the undertaking or release us from it altogether?'

'That does not strike me as being altogether unreasonable in principle, Ted, and we can certainly offer a revised undertaking in those terms, although I cannot promise that a court would accept it. The purpose of such orders or undertakings is to protect an individual in circumstances where the court considers on the evidence that he or she may otherwise be at risk.'

'Just hold on a moment,' came the voice from the iceberg.

The Mamba had not spoken for so long that Mary had assumed that she wished to take no further part in the conference.

'Sorry. Yes, Barbara?'

'First, what is this so-called evidence? And secondly, how are we supposed to investigate the authenticity of these documents if we don't even know who stored the material, where they stored it, and for how long? Are you seriously suggesting that the company should tie its hands like that?'

God give me patience! thought Mary. In any other circumstance that might have been a fair question. But the evidence strongly suggested that Cat's former boss had form on the harassment front, and the last thing they could risk was this evidence being shown to the court, especially at this delicate stage of the proceedings.

'I understand your concern, Barbara, but I must ask you to trust me on this one. You have not had the misfortune – as I have – to have inspected the sensitive material obtained from the laptop and mobile phone of Miss Symonds. You have to take my word that it does not make for pleasant reading, nor viewing for that matter, and I've already said too much. It is my very strong advice that the court should not become aware of the content of that material. And, I'm afraid to say, that this is not all.'

She let those last words have the desired effect for a moment.

'There is also a further document that has just surfaced, but I am not sure that now is the right time to discuss it, if indeed you and Ted have seen it.'

'Sorry, Mary, what document is this?' asked Ted before Barbara could shut him off. 'Does it relate to this case?'

Mary was unsure how to respond. She had assumed that the draft letter of claim, which had been addressed to the 'Head of Legal' at the company, had by now been seen by Ted and his colleagues. However, Ted's question suggested that this was not the case. But now was certainly not a good moment to be discussing its content.

'So, Ted, judging by your answer, it would appear that neither of you have seen this letter, which explains your question. Very well. When you do get around to reading it, you need to be aware that it is my very strong advice that we and the company should do everything lawfully in your power to prevent it from being displayed in open court. As regards its content, all I shall say for now, and I say that advisedly, is that the document is a draft of a letter which is intended to be sent to the head of legal at the company by the solicitors acting for Miss Symonds.'

If there was one thing that Barbara hated, it was being told that she was not allowed to become privy to a secret known to others. As head of internal affairs, secrets were her trade, her currency, her life blood.

No, this would not do.

'I'm sorry, Mary,' she began, an air of authority returning to her voice. 'It is entirely unsatisfactory that you should dangle something like that in front of me and then keep me hanging in suspense. At least tell me what this letter says.'

Mary noticed the 'me' rather than the 'us' but elected to ignore it.

'Very well. So far as relevant to this discussion, the draft letter alleges that Miss Symonds and a third party were subjected to a campaign of highly unpleasant harassment by a director of AlphaOm, which continued for a sustained period. I have good reason to believe that, unless the undertaking is given by consent, the allegations in the draft letter will be repeated in these proceedings by way of justification for the terms of the two undertakings that are currently being sought on behalf of Miss Symonds. As I have said, it would be very unfortunate and damaging for the company if that were to happen. For that reason, it is my strong recommendation, and I mean *strong*, that my firm should now be instructed by the company to give those undertakings to the court.'

Before Barbara could respond, Ted intervened, 'Can I suggest, Mary, that you send a copy of the letter over to Larry. I shall alert him to expect it. He can then decide what course of action should be taken in relation to its contents. Meanwhile, in view of what you have told us, Mary, I shall recommend to him now that the board should resolve to give the undertakings sought, subject to Barbara's caveat that we discussed a moment ago.'

'Thank you, Ted, duly noted.'

'Perhaps I could add, Mary,' he added, 'that it would assist me greatly if you or Tim could drop me a short line to summarise the advice that you have just given us, which I can then attach to my draft recommendation.'

'Certainly, Ted.' Then she added quickly, 'I am going to assume, unless you or Barbara tell me otherwise, that Larry will decide whether the draft letter should be copied to any of his other directors, including the chief executive and Barbara.'

She was rather pleased with the way in which she had implicitly elevated Barbara's status by mentioning her alongside McBride.

'Also,' she continued quickly, 'I am going to assume that he will decide which firm should be instructed to act in respect of it, since he will not want my firm to act on this for fear that it will give rise to a conflict of interests.'

'Noted, Mary.'

'Once again, Ted,' she concluded, 'can I ask you to put your instruction in writing, along with a copy of the resolution once it is formalised.'

'Of course.'

'Thank you. So, we shall leave matters on the basis that one of you will confirm to me in, what, the next twenty minutes, what are the company's instructions regarding the disclosure application by the defendants. Agreed?'

'Yep,' said Ted, 'and I reckon that just about wraps it up for now.' Then he added, without giving Barbara the opportunity to intervene, 'One of us will be in touch with you or Tim very shortly.'

'Thank you. Speak later.'

Mary directed Tim to cut the call, anxious to avoid the inevitable tantrum that would very soon erupt within the head offices of her client.

Chapter 24

As Robert McBride habitually reminded himself, indeed prided himself, his meteoric rise to the top of AlphaOm was due mostly to his addiction to control. Actually, that was not quite accurate. It was entirely due to it. He was the ultimate control freak, and as such had trained himself to make do with little more than three hours sleep each night. He reckoned that it gave him an extra five hours of working time.

He employed two personal assistants, and each was supported by a small team. Like so many tyrants, he had come to regard the company as his own personal fiefdom, a private empire that existed to advance his international renown – and pocket.

Thus, early that morning before his team had begun to arrive for work, the last thing that he had expected was a call to his mobile from his oily spin doctor over in commercial development, and he had been caught completely off-guard. No, more than that: he was so stunned that he had to steady himself on a desk.

He had almost whispered a question to himself, despite being alone in his suite of offices: 'How the fuck was that girl allowed to gain access to those documents?'

But he already suspected that he knew the answer.

When he had put that question to CT, the latter had reasoned that, if he knew the answer, he'd have put a stop to this before it had all started. He had then had the cheek to tell him that the question was irrelevant, since the 'girl' and the paper had got hold of them. How they did would have to wait. But right now, they – and yes, he had meant the two of them – needed to decide what to do next.

McBride had not taken kindly to being chastised by that greasy weasel for causing the company to reach for the holster without consulting him, especially when he must have known that his own name was written all over those papers, and even some of those emails. As a result, CT had warned him that Spooner was quite capable of shooting off every toe on their corporate foot.

So McBride had been persuaded that they needed to buy time, and that involved slowing down the legal process, and preferably halting it altogether. That was why he had issued his instruction to Spooner to do her best to vacate the court hearing the next day.

He had also been persuaded that CT should be consulted by the cabinet currently being chaired by Spooner, particularly as regards any press statements that were considered necessary. He had hesitated, because he had not got a straight answer when he had asked Thompson whether he had got himself involved with the girl. The guy had been evasive, but had eventually fessed up. However, ever the salesman, CT had argued that it gave him a useful edge, since he now knew things about her that would make her vulnerable, and provide him with the opportunity to exploit her weakness.

In other circumstances, McBride would have let the guy fall on his sword. The trouble was, he and CT had worked on that project together, and that slimy snake was more than capable of using that sword to stab him in the back first. CT's reference to McBride's name being 'all over the emails' had clearly been intended as a firm warning that, if CT went down, he would take McBride with him.

Meanwhile, CT had told him that there was potentially some good news, if it could be called that. From what he knew about the case, the girl had not got hold of the crucial emails relating to the research papers. He wasn't sure how she had missed them, but they were not included in any of the stuff that had been retrieved from her devices as a result of the court orders.

So, if the defendants didn't have the emails, then it looked as though the two of them were in the clear.

'Just make sure it stays that way,' McBride had told CT.

He was fairly sure that he had deleted most, if not all, of those communications from his own private devices, but he had little control over where his PAs had backed up his mail. Also, he was fully aware that, in the world of IT, nothing stayed hidden forever.

'I don't want any more of these unpleasant surprises, Okay,' he pretended to command, already regretting his decision to instigate the court process.

'On it, boss,' CT had replied in his best oleaginous tone, and then had hung up. Loathsome toad!

Chapter 25

Rosalyn thanked Jamie for his call, and for his intelligence that another box had been discovered on the estate. She began to make arrangements for the extra box to be collected from his estate in the morning. She had taken the opportunity to confirm to him that her firm had received the requested undertakings from the company's solicitors that any knowledge of his identity and address would be restricted to their counsel and Mary. Jamie had been both relieved and grateful to hear that. Armed with the assurance from a fellow professional, she had emailed to Mary Fellowes the 'password' to a letter which would contain the relevant details regarding the who, what, when and where in respect of the storage of the new material.

Rosalyn had then added that her client would require the undertaking to be read into the transcript of the proceedings in court tomorrow and, alongside the separate undertaking dealing with inspection of the sensitive material, expressly set out in a formal order by the court.

Next, she had copied and pasted into a separate letter the terms of the qualified assent on behalf of her client that Tom had drafted in response to the claimants' request for an adjournment of any substantive discussion of the restraining orders at the hearing tomorrow. However, she had also informed her opposite number that her client would seek to be heard through counsel at tomorrow's hearing on the matter of the disclosure request, the reach of which her client was willing to reduce, as appeared from the revised request which she enclosed.

Finally, she had sent another short letter to confirm which documents her client (in short, a euphemism for Tom and her firm) wished to see included in the bundle that was about to be sent to the judge for the hearing. As expected, she had heard nothing back from Mary regarding the draft letter in respect of Cat's harassment claim. Her instinct told her that Mary's firm would be very reluctant to accept instructions from the company on that claim, and would get it farmed out to a firm of specialist employment lawyers.

But the damage would have been done, and the nexus between the sexual harassment, the electronic images and the acquisition of the crucial evidence by her client had been as good as established. To her mind, at the very least those factors would make it difficult for the company to argue to the contrary.

Tom had been very reassuring in that regard. His view, which she had come to share, was that the longer the company sought time in which to establish the provenance and authenticity of the evidence, the worse it would look in court. Also, as Tom had reminded her, the company had broken the first rule in litigation: as the claimants, you never give the defendants time.

And time, to quote the Stones' 60s hit, was definitely on her client's side.

The Chronicle's lawyers had set up a conference for the following week at which it was intended to review their analysis of the evidence now available, and to prepare the ground for their application to have the restraining orders set aside. They had previously sent her a copy of a recent report prepared by some respected academics. This had revealed the fact that the vast majority of research papers in the field of medicine – and they were talking in the high eighties in percentage terms – were funded by the corporate entities who later relied on them.

Well, there's a surprise, she had said to herself.

The clear inference in the report was that it resonated with the old saying that 'he who pays the piper calls the song'. The report was helpful, she agreed, but only up to a point. Very few universities were sufficiently endowed to finance research on a scale which had been undertaken over the past few decades, and therefore their academics would be reliant on external funding. So, the fact that money changed hands was not of itself sinister. The opposite was more likely.

But this case was different. The material that Cat had unearthed revealed that AlphaOm, by causing the researchers to rely solely on a specific and limited source of data, had deliberately biased the outcome of their resulting report. It was wholly misleading, in that it had intentionally only included some of the truth, and had omitted – *The Chronicle* had suggested deliberately – substantial and crucial evidence. And that, in Tom's view, amounted in law to deceit. He had shown her an extract from a recent High Court judgment in which the court had cited and relied on the words of a judgment given over 200 years previously in 1803 dealing with deceit by omission:

If a man professing to answer a question, selects those facts only which are likely to give credit to the person of whom he speaks, and keeps back the rest, he is a more artful knave than he who tells a direct falsehood.

That was spot on, thought Rosalyn.

*

Across town, Mary Fellowes opened the emails, and out of habit printed them out. She was not especially interested in the identity of the custodian of the material retrieved from the country, but nonetheless felt obliged to address the point. She immediately recognised the name of Jamie Henderson as the unfortunate recipient of those disagreeable emails which she had been obliged to 'inspect'.

Of course, why hadn't she made the connection before? He must have been Miss Symonds' previous boyfriend to whom reference was made in the letter of claim. His house in the country would have been one of the last places that her employers, and in particular her line manager, would have imagined that she would be stockpiling confidential material. But it would have been a convenient and relatively secure location for her to choose.

She put that letter to one side, and then read the next one. It informed her that another box of material had been discovered, having previously been concealed from the view of the proprietor of the property where they had been stored, but that arrangements would be put in hand for that material to be collected in the morning.

The letter conceded that Miss Symonds was working on the presumption, which might on analysis be rebutted, that the contents were relevant to the proceedings, albeit that they were at present unknown. However, once they had been screened for relevance and ownership following the procedure previously approved by the supervising solicitor, the originals of any relevant material would be provided to Mr Langer. Copies thereof would be retained by Miss Symonds' solicitors on the same undertaking as before. A further set would be supplied to Mary's firm.

Mary knew that her client would object to that procedure, but given past precedent she had little doubt that Peter Langar would side with Miss Symonds. Still, she would have to ask one of her assistants to explain that again to the clients. Finally, she read the revised request for disclosure from the defendants' solicitors. It informed her in no uncertain terms that an application would be made to the court on behalf of the defendants at the hearing.

Her instinct told her that this was likely to be much more difficult to resist. A glance ar her screen showed that it was almost 3.00. Time was against her, and she needed to consult with counsel urgently.

In haste, she scooped up the letters and asked her temporary PA to copy the letters to her team and to get copies of them off to counsel. It was an innocent enough instruction, one that she had given on countless occasions. This one was no different, save for one critically important factor. The bundle included the letter that she had undertaken would only be seen by herself and counsel.

The young PA was covering for Mary's experienced PA, who had been struck down with food poisoning the evening before. She was new to the role, but was keen, efficient and eager to please, having been told that if she performed well in her current role there was every prospect that she could be offered permanent employment at the firm.

She made pdf copies of the letters, and sent copies to each member of Mary's team. She then pulled up on her screen the last email that she had used to distribute material prior to the last telephone conference. It was addressed to Alain Gaitsland QC and his junior, and copied to Mary and her colleagues, and marked 'Very Urgent'.

She attached the pdf copies to the draft email, and pressed the return key, before moving on to her next assignment, satisfied that she had done precisely what was required of her.

Which she had – save for one crucial thing. The PA had failed to notice one of the 'cc' addressees.

It stated 'mlutherson@alphaom.com'.

Chapter 26

Cat and Tomo had been the first to dial in to their telecon. Whilst they waited for Rosalyn to join them, she had used her feminine charms to get him to commit to coming round that evening, quite reasonably arguing that it would be unkind of him to let her spend the night alone on the eve of the hearing. He had pleaded, entirely fairly, that her interests were best served if he prepared for the application which he was due to make in conjunction with *The Chronicle*'s lawyers. They hadn't quite had a tiff, but he could sense a major sulk unless he relented.

They had compromised on a late supper at her place, but on two conditions begrudgingly conceded. First, that she had to let him finish off any late adjustments to his submissions after supper, and secondly that she would not instigate what he termed any 'hanky-panky' either later or in the morning. A sixth sense told him that several of her fingers were crossed when he had eventually secured her reluctant agreement. But, as professional conflicts went, he told himself, that was quite a nice one to have.

Rosalyn announced herself into the conference.

'Apologies, both,' she said as she joined them. 'It's been pretty manic here, but we've managed to prevent the other side from making any substantial last-minute additions to the agreed bundle, Tom. As you've advised, the judge won't allow it for a start, and in my view most of what they wanted to insert was irrelevant. I've agreed that they can re-insert documents to which, ironically, they had initially objected, and you've seen all of them anyway. Your clerks now have this in pdf form, and they're printing it out for you as we speak. Leaving aside the company's undertakings, we've got our revised application and draft order, my supporting witness statement which you drafted, together with the one from the partner acting for *The Chronicle*, which you have already seen. There is nothing in yet from the claimants in response to my statement. We'd all assumed that we could expect something earlier today, but that has proved not to be. So, given the hour, I don't expect that we shall see it until later this evening.'

'For Cat's benefit,' Tomo interjected, 'that sort of delay by the claimants is hardly going to endear them to the judge, who I'm told will be "Spitty" Hunters again, since he has already assigned the case to himself. And if he is true to form, my oppo had better put some blotting paper in his pants, because he can expect a pretty severe thrashing.'

'Rather him than me, I agree,' Rosalyn replied.

'Turning to your recent discussions with *The Chronicle*'s counsel, Tom,' she continued, 'are you still all on the same page? You seemed to be making good progress when we last spoke this morning.'

'Yep, all going to plan,' said Tom reassuringly. 'Cat knows that we're taking a bit of a flyer, but we're all agreed that this is too good an opportunity to pass up, and right now the claimants don't seem to know where they're going.'

Cat chimed in at that point.

'I know that I've asked you this before, but is the judge really going to believe them when they tell him that they need more time to review all the documents that they have obtained through the court orders?'

'Shall I answer that?' asked Tom.

'Please do,' agreed Rosalyn.

'As I think I explained this morning when we spoke, the substantive issues relating to the restraining orders are going to be adjourned to another day. That means that the question of the authenticity of the disclosure obtained pursuant to the orders is not strictly on the agenda for tomorrow.'

'I know that, Tomo, but ...'

'Just let me finish. So, that said, whether it's on the agenda or not, both Andrew – that's the silk for *The Chronicle* – and I intend to take every opportunity to remind the judge that one of the primary grounds on which the company applied for the restraining orders was that you and *The Chronicle* were in possession of confidential and commercially sensitive material that belonged to the company. Yet here they are saying that they are now not sure of the provenance and authenticity of the material. So, they face a dilemma. Do they claim that none of the material is genuine, and thus change their case to one based on an alleged libel, or do they abandon the case altogether, and let the media have a field day? And if they do the former, how do they square their amended case with the evidence that they submitted in support of the orders? Whichever way you look at it, their case seems to be in a real mess.'

He paused to let the other two both absorb that advice. It allowed Rosalyn to add her own input.

'Let me just add, Cat, that it's often very difficult, not only for the clients but also the lawyers, to comprehend the tactics that the other side have chosen to deploy in the course of litigation. This case is no exception, save for one significant feature. Neither Tom nor I are confident that our opponents have actually come up with any coherent strategy other than to buy time. As I see it, that is not even the beginning of a strategy, and it's probably doing their prospects significant harm.'

'That is indeed how I see it,' Tom confirmed.

'So, they can't say tomorrow that this is all fake?'

'Let me answer your question,' he continued. 'We consider that it is too early to predict what the judge will or will not believe. What I can tell you is that he is unlikely to be impressed by the company's conduct to date. Quite the reverse, in fact.'

'Okay, I sort of understand, I guess, and it's kind of reassuring to hear you guys say that you reckon that the company has got itself into a mess. But tell me, do you still need me to be there tomorrow?'

'We both think it would be a very good thing, Cat,' said Rosalyn. 'And I'm told that either the editor or the deputy editor of *The Chronicle* will be there as well, as will the journalist. Moreover, the court will be hearing your application for disclosure. I should add that you will not need to say anything, but it always looks good for the court to see that a defendant is taking an active interest in the case.'

'I would agree, Cat,' said Tomo. 'Shall we meet at my chambers just before ten? We can remain in email and mobile contact until then.'

'That sounds like a plan,' confirmed Rosalyn.

'Oh, and in case my clerks forget to tell you, the hearing has been moved to Court 37, in the Thomas More Wing at the RCJ. It's a pain, but there we are.'

'Thanks Tom, I had not picked that up. Can I take it that you will be giving Cat the directions and address?'

'All in hand, although I do not expect there to be any last-minute initiatives or surprises from the other side. But we'll be in contact in the interim if there are.'

Except that I have a rather different kind of contact in mind, thought Cat to herself, but had the good sense not to give voice to such a sentiment.

*

An hour or so later found Alain Gaitsland QC in his room in chambers with his junior, Richard. He held up the index to the application that had been filed on behalf of the defendants, and pointed it at the younger man.

'If I am not very much mistaken, Richard, I'd say that a fair few hours have gone into the preparation of this application. I reckon that Andrew and his team had been keeping this up their sleeves, and were waiting for the right moment to strike. And what better time for that moment to arrive than when they realised that we were left with no alternative other than to play for time on account of what I think can best be described as recent unexpected developments. Would you agree?'

There were alone, and had convened in order to settle their submissions for the hearing the next day.

'That is precisely how I see it, Alain. They clearly smell blood, and they believe that they are on the scent of a wounded prey.'

Alain laid the paper neatly down before him, ensuring its edges were perpendicular to the sides of the polished desk.

'Tab fifteen caught my eye. It is the note made by Mary Fellowes of the execution of the search order at Ms Symonds' flat.'

'Yes, I read that too.'

'So, at para eleven, she records that, once she had got over the initial shock of the raid, which I'd say is par for the course, Ms Symonds looked her in the eye and told her: "You know, it's all true, and your clients should have told you that." Now that is a very unusual thing for a defendant to say in those circumstances. True, she had not received any independent advice, so there might have to be an argument as to whether any judge should admit the statement. But that has not happened. Instead, not only did Ms Symonds' team not object to its inclusion in the bundle, but they have actually exhibited the record to their own application.'

'It certainly adds a nice ring of consistency to the application,' ventured Richard, and then immediately regretted saying it on seeing the older lawyer raise an eyebrow. However, Alain let the comment pass.

'Tell me, what do you make of Symonds' reasons for the late disclosure of the documents from the country?'

This time Richard had already thought about the point.

'What do I think? Well, her compromised relationship with her boyfriend, Henderson I think he's called, would ordinarily be nothing out of the ordinary, but what is in my view are the circumstances in which her relationship was destroyed. Mary tells us that the sensitive material recovered from the laptop would have been deeply embarrassing to Ms Symonds, and its transmission to Henderson would be more than enough to undermine any relationship, however strong. That, in my book, is more than sufficient motive to wish the material to be concealed. It also explains why she had assumed that Henderson had disposed of not only all of her clothes but also all the other material that she had left on the estate once the relationship had terminated. And you're going to ask me, will the judge buy it. In my view, now that she has given him the full story, and I mean the *full* story in what I foresee as the precursor to a harassment claim, then in a word, yes.'

Alain realigned the index on his table, as was his habit when thinking.

'Yes, I rather feared you'd say that. It is the view that I have reached too, which leaves us with fairly limited options as to how to tackle the issue of provenance, despite the last-minute adjournment.'

'As to that,' Richard intervened, 'without having seen any of the first tranche of documents that have been released by Ms Symonds, or rather her legal team, it's hard to tell whether we live or limp to fight another day.'

'Perhaps both,' Alain suggested. 'Either way, our clients have broken one of the first rules of the game. They have given the defendants time. I've been doing this for thirty years or more, and in my experience a claimant seldom recovers its dominant position once it has ceded the initiative to the other side.'

Richard gave a brief nod in concurrence.

'And we surely do not want to allege malice, because of the can of worms argument on which our instructions are concise.'

'Quite so. But we are where we are,' Alain continued, 'as the saying goes, and right now we need to find some more persuasive arguments as to why our clients should not be ordered to provide copies of all their internal communications relating to the subject-matter of the claim. Beyond the usual unfair advantage point, which frankly is always rather thin when our clients have themselves obtained disclosure orders against the defendants, I confess I am rather struggling.'

'I agree.'

'Then we've got the standard argument that all of the clients' disclosure should *in due course* – which in reality means months away – be made available following the usual case management directions. That in my view is just a refinement of the unfair advantage point. Would you agree with that?'

'With you so far.'

'We've then got the argument that the clients have promoted, namely that the request for disclosure presumes that the original documents exist and that they remain under our own clients' control, which is, of course, an entirely different matter. On that point the clients' evidence is that they need more time, but that does not address the principle, and the draft witness statement in response is silent on the point.'

'I agree with that, and I think the "time" point is weakest with regard to the research that we have to concede was commissioned by the company, either on its own or in conjunction with others, into their sweetener products.'

'Precisely,' agreed Alain. 'As to that point, our instructions are that the clients want us to argue that the defendants are on a fishing expedition, based on the "when did you stop beating your mother" argument.'

'The trouble with that,' said Richard, 'is that the defendants have already anticipated that point, and have included in their application evidence of our clients' own announcements regarding their appointment of the research teams, including the apparent tender process and the conclusions in the research papers.'

'Exactly,' agreed Alain, 'which is why I do not understand why it is not a relatively simple task for our clients to identify and locate the relevant material.'

'I agree.'

'So what's left?' Alain asked himself. 'We cannot seriously argue that the documents are not relevant, nor can we say that they are inadmissible. So, I think we are back where we started with the unfair advantage point, but also coupled with what we've been told is a substantial logistical challenge, assuming that the judge buys that.'

'That's just about where I had got to,' agreed Richard, as he turned to one of the pages in the bundle that he had flagged. 'And we face the added argument that this is precisely the sort of litigation risk that a man in a glass house takes when he starts to throw stones. But if the logistics argument is all we've really got, let's see if we can't gather enough material to be able to run with it.'

'Well, I've helped with disclosure when I did a couple of short stints with a firm of solicitors in my long vacs, and I can confirm that the sort of exercise that Mary has described in her instructions can take a very long time to undertake. And that is all the more so in a case of this complexity.'

'Just so,' observed Alain. 'And that, of course, is why as a rule the courts do not order disclosure until the parties have formally articulated their cases on paper.'

'Exactly. And, as you say, it may be our best point.'

Once again, the papers were rearranged neatly in front of him before Gaitsland looked across the table.

'So, now seems as good a time as any to get on the phone to Mary and run our thinking past her and her team. Agreed?'

'I'll get her on the line.'

Chapter 27

CT opened the text from Maria. It told him that there had been some developments, on which he would very likely want her to bring him up to date.

'That girl is proving to be a very necessary, as well as useful, asset,' he observed, making a mental note to call her as soon as he could conclude the tedious marketing meeting that he was supposed to be chairing. He was doing his best to chivvy this crowd along, but McBride had stressed that it was essential that his department appeared really interested in the product these guys were peddling. Fair enough, but it meant that he had to allow them to run through their whole sales pitch.

He knew he liked the sound of his own voice, but these people were in a league of their own. They all seemed to have been born with identical twin defects: they lacked any 'off' button to close their mouths, and possessed no discernible circuits running between tongue and brain.

He checked his mobile beneath the table again. He was being perpetually harassed first by Ted Fisher and then by Larry, and would have to remain agile if he was to successfully dodge the numerous calls, texts and emails that he had received from them that afternoon.

Fisher had stated at least twice that serious allegations that had been levelled against the company, all of which pointed to CT as the guilty party.

Yes, but who was making those serious allegations? That's what he needed to find out from Maria before he spoke with Larry or Fisher.

At last, the lead presenter asked them if they had any questions. Before any of his own team could think of anything to say, he replied in the negative and thanked them profusely for such an interesting demonstration, and gave them his earnest assurance that they would be hearing from the company very shortly.

He made his way back to his office, pleading another urgent 'virtual' meeting as an excuse to avoid the tedious debrief. Once there, he texted Maria and asked him to call him as soon as was convenient. Which broadly meant 'now!'

Within five minutes Maria called him. CT immediately detected a note of caution in her voice, and she seemed to be speaking in little more than a whisper.

'Maria, sorry, but I can hardly hear you.'

'That's because it's very difficult for me to speak right now, and especially about the case. There are just too many people near me, and ... you know ... this whole thing has become quite ... topical, and I'm really not enjoying it.'

His first thought was that the Mamba was onto her, and that she was trying to tell him that her days as his mole were over. He tried his innocent voice.

'Have I got you into trouble, Maria?' he asked.

'No, it's not that. I can explain. Where can we meet, and when?'

CT looked at his watch. It was gone 5.30, which meant that the car park would start to get busy any time soon.

'Do you still have work to do?' he asked.

'Not a lot today, in view of what's happened. I should be able to get away just after six. How about you?'

'That should be fine. Let's avoid the car park, it'll be too busy. Why don't I pick you up outside the Italian place; you know, the one that's about three blocks down past the station on the left. Say at six-fifteen?'

'Okay. I'll call if I can't find it.'

Each one of the next forty-five minutes seemed like an eternity to CT, all the more so on account of the 'missed' calls from Fisher that he contrived not to answer. They exacerbated the stress that he was experiencing through his ignorance of the 'important developments' to which Maria had referred.

This state of ignorance was a wholly new experience for him.

Knowledge provided him with intelligence, and that in turn gave him control. Control gave his own sense of power. It was his life blood.

But without knowledge and thus control, he could not 'spin' to weave into yet another of his many tangled webs. Truly, the Artful Dodger could learn a few tricks from him.

Consequently, he felt unarmed and unarmoured, completely vulnerable to the slings and arrows of the many enemies that he had acquired during his career, the success of which had its very foundations in deceit. So, here we was, deprived of knowledge, for the first time that he could remember, and certainly in his role as a director.

His entire body felt stiff with fear – a fear that he was rapidly losing control of events. He was like a junky without a fix; a gambler without his dice who could not rely on that one final roll to reverse his losses.

Unconsciously, his reptilian tongue was working overtime, sliding sideways in and out of his mouth. As the seconds ticked by, he imagined others using the very knowledge of which he had been deprived to gain a tactical advantage over him, manoeuvring the forces at their disposal to outflank and out-think him.

He had to stop himself leaving the office early, because it would only mean that he would have to drive around in endless circles until Maria arrived at their rendezvous. As a result, he was like a restless, fidgeting child, knots slowly forming in his stomach as his fear grew that events were moving beyond his control.

He dared not open up his office email account, because the Mamba or one of her thugs would be alerted through IT that he was contactable via that medium. Instead, he had switched to his alternative mobile phone, and was using his private email account to which his office emails were automatically forwarded. In this way, he hoped to evade pursuit for the rest of the day.

Eventually 6.00 came and went. He grabbed his laptop bag, and took the back stairs down to the car park, forcing himself not to run.

Five minutes later, having checked that there were no other executives or senior managers in the vicinity, he eased his 'pimp-mobile' out of the basement car park and turned left, nervously watching his rear-view mirror every other second to satisfy himself that there was no need to evade any pursuit.

He spotted Maria standing by the doorway of the 'taverna', holding the straps of what appeared to be a small shoulder bag. She furtively began to move towards his car, but he had the sense to turn into the side street before coming to a halt and reaching across to open the passenger door for her.

As soon as she was on board, he headed towards a nearby multi-storey car park, thinking that if anyone noticed their brief visit, they would be taken for an adulterous couple out for a quick snog.

'Thanks again for this, Maria,' he said to her, giving her his earnest 'you need to trust me on this' look that he saved for those moments when he was looking to close a deal. 'You know, I reckon that I owe you and the wine club at least another case or two of those Rhone reds. Maybe more.'

She was flattered by the compliment, and also delighted to have pleased him. She gave him a brief, if nervous, smile, along with a shrug as if to indicate that her help was a small token of thanks for his advice and support.

'No, seriously, you've been a real help to me, and for that matter to the chief as well, because both he and I have been getting the distinct impression that we are being left in the dark on all this.'

He maintained his earnest frown.

'Neither of us are pointing fingers,' he added quickly, lest she should think that he was suggesting that her boss was the culprit, 'but it's very difficult for me to advise the chief if we only know half the facts, and then only a day – a week even – after everyone else. So, your help is really appreciated, Maria. And let me add that you only have to say the word and I shall make it my number one priority when this is all over to make sure that the chief thanks you personally.'

Now she was really listening, purring like a kitten as it watched the jug of cream being removed from the fridge and heading in the direction of a saucer.

'It's nothing, CT, really,' she assured him, 'I'm just glad that I'm in a position to help. And you've been just as much help to me, don't forget. But I don't mind admitting that I am really nervous about this coming back on me.'

'I have given you my word, Maria. The only two people who know that we are talking are you and me, and it's going to stay that way unless – or perhaps I should say until – you tell me that you'd like the chief to know about your help.'

She looked for and found the reassurance in his eyes. After a brief hesitation, she elected to continue with their interview; or was it a conspiracy? She was not so sure now. He sensed this, and quickly moved to the purpose of their meeting.

'So, I'm all ears, Maria, and I can't wait. Please tell me what you've got.'

It was difficult for her to shuffle her feet in the confined space afforded by the passenger seat, but she shifted her body weight awkwardly in response to his prompt, which she had known was coming.

'Well, there's quite a lot, actually,' she replied, 'and it's hard for me to know where to start with it all.'

'Well, why not follow the chronology since we last met? I often find that it's the simplest way to do it.'

That made sense to her, yet she clutched the shoulder bag nervously, acutely conscious of the gravity of what she was about to do.

He sensed her hesitation.

'You have my word, Maria, that this stays between us.'

She smiled at him, relaxing her grip on the bag.

'Okay,' she began, taking the plunge. 'You remember I told you that there is a hearing in court tomorrow?'

He nodded.

'Well, it's been agreed with the defendants that there will not be any discussion in court about the actual injunction, which is a relief for us. I can explain in a moment. But there is going to be a fight about whether the defendants are entitled to require us to hand over copies of all our documents and emails that are said to be relevant to the reasons why the injunction was granted.'

'What, so the paper has asked for these?'

'Exactly, and our lawyers are saying that we should oppose their application at this stage, because it will give the defendants an unfair advantage.'

'Which is no doubt why the other side are pushing it,' he volunteered. Then he added, 'You know, this would never have happened if I had been consulted before this all started, but that bridge is well and truly burned.'

He chose that moment to throw in some of his 'drama queen' theatrics.

'As a PR disaster, this has the potential to make the hamburger fiasco look like a walk in the park. But – and we can be thankful for small mercies – at least it will give us a chance to regroup and have a rethink.'

Maria had already come to that conclusion. She held secret doubts as to whether the company could deny that the documents recovered from the Symonds girl were genuine. But of far greater concern to her was the prospect of her illegal hacking of the girl's private email address, and its subsequent concealment, becoming disclosed not just to the girl's solicitors but also to the authorities.

She had told herself that, if there was any way that she could turn the clock back, she would grab it with both hands. Her only hope was that CT could persuade the chief to walk away from all this.

'Yes, but that's not all, CT,' she said.

He let the silence build, again giving his earnest 'trust me' look.

After further hesitation she added: 'This is highly confidential, CT.'

God, how he hated 'one more thing' moments.

'I overheard a discussion today. I probably shouldn't have been there. I was outside Barbara Spooner's office. She was talking with the head of legal about, you know, not just the case but ... well everything.'

She paused.

'And?' he prompted.

'Well,' she continued uncertainly, 'according to the company's lawyers, the Symonds girl is making some allegations ... new allegations in fact ... and, the lawyers say that she is threatening to make a claim against the company.'

She left the sentence hanging, hardly daring to whisper the charge.

'And?'

She looked at him earnestly, seeking reassurance, and believing, convincing herself that she had found it, ploughed on.

'I'm sorry, CT, but there're actually quite unpleasant ones, about ... well ... about you and her actually.'

In order to stay in character, he should have done his best 'Well, fuck me, here we go with another "MeToo" bunch of fucking lies.' But, instead, CT felt an icy hand squeeze his heart and his stomach simultaneously. He tried and failed to restrain his tight-knuckled grip on the gearstick. Mercifully, she failed to notice the tension in his arm as, with a practised art, his face remained a cold mask of deceit. In that moment, he made the gear stick his rock.

Hold on, he told himself. She needs to believe in me. Hold on.

His first reaction was disbelief that she had been prepared to go public, coupled with fear of the short-term consequences. He knew the form only too well. Immediate suspension; an internal enquiry; surrender of his company laptop and mobile; email quarantine; loss of all perks. The first accusation swiftly followed by others. And on it would go.

That was just for starters.

For the first time for as long as he could remember he felt lost for words, silenced by the enormity of what he had just heard. Inspiration eluded him, so he reverted to what he knew best and what came naturally to him: an initial shake of the head, then a dismissive wave of the hand, accompanied by a derisory snort.

'You have to be kidding me, Maria!' It was more of a statement than a question. 'Has the girl totally lost her mind? And why wait until now to raise it? I mean, does she really think that this is going to help her win the bigger battle?'

Maria had no idea how to answer that, any more than she had understood her own reaction when she received the intelligence regarding such a liaison. She adamantly refused to entertain the possibility that she might be jealous of Symonds. She was only too well aware that she lacked the girl's attractive features, and had found the reports of the girl's popularity unsettling. Moreover, the whole situation was so unfamiliar to her. She might at one stage have entertained the hope that something more might come of her own 'relationship' – if it could be called that – with CT. However, in light of this latest development she had already reconciled herself to the probability that her own dealings with CT were unlikely to progress beyond symbiotic.

Yet here she was, sat in the guy's sports-car, trading secrets with him in return for his influence and assistance. But was there more to it than that?

Sure, he was nice to her, and occupied a position of power and influence which, if she was honest, was probably what had attracted her to him in the first place, but there was no way that they were anywhere close to being an item. But, on the other hand, she had to admit to herself that, were the opportunity to arise ...

No, she needed to stay focussed.

'There's more CT, I'm afraid,' she continued, but in a soft, almost apologetic voice. He gave his best 'why does that surprise me' look, but his insides were turning to ice.

'It's to do with the disclosure order that was made against the Symonds girl, and the boxes that she had been storing.'

What now, he thought, as if this could get any worse.

'And?' he asked, immediately fearing that they had discovered the email chain that he had persuaded himself had been buried.

'Well, her solicitors told us initially that Symonds had taken two boxes of documents from the company. These were the ones that were handed over to the lawyer who is supposed to be supervising how the court order is carried out.'

'And these are the ones that we suspect she has faked, right?'

'Yes, but that's not what I was going to tell you.'

Oh fuck, please not more of this, he found himself praying.

'No, the thing is,' she said cautiously, conscious of the enormity of her disloyalty to her boss, 'the thing is that her lawyers have emailed today to say that a third box has been discovered.'

Hold on, boy, hold on, he kept telling himself.

'Well, isn't that convenient,' he managed to whisper between gritted teeth.

She pressed on. 'I learnt earlier that a courier has been hired to collect the box from the place where her lawyers say it has been found, and then bring it to the independent lawyer, where they can be inspected by him and her lawyers after the hearing tomorrow. Her lawyers will take copies of whatever there is, and then leave the box and its contents with the independent lawyer. Apparently, he then decides whether and when we get to see the documents, or at least which ones we get to see.'

He continued to shake his head in his best 'oh, the poor, demented creature' impression that he hoped would command both respect and sympathy. But then a germ of a plan began to emerge in his mind. Not a seed yet, just an embryo of an idea ...

'So, this new box of tricks, these "ha, got you now", documents, where exactly are we supposed to believe that these have been so mysteriously discovered at this convenient moment in time?'

This was the steer that she had wanted.

'Well, CT, that's just it. Our lawyers have been told ... in fact I'm pretty sure I was not meant to see it – they've been told that the stuff has been sitting in some derelict barn on a country estate in ...'

Don't say it, CT almost begged.

'I think it's Devon,' she said uncertainly.

'Really?' Almost daring not to believe it.

'You're sure it was Devon?' he asked, perhaps too urgently.

'Well, I'm not ... no wait. It's down in the south, either Devon or Dorset. Yes, maybe it's Dorset. Any way, it's down south somewhere. Apparently, there's a connection there with someone that Miss Symonds had known in the past ...'

That was enough for CT.

He wanted to leap out of the car, kick the wall, shout every expletive he knew at the top of his voice into the void beyond the car park, then grab an iron bar and smash his car into a pulp.

Instead, holding on to the gear stick as though his life depended on it, he brought what little remained of his self control to bear on to what he had just heard. This, for him, was now about nothing less than self-survival.

'And this convenient material, where exactly are we supposed to believe that it currently resides – or has Miss Symonds' lawyer declined to say?'

Maria was eagerly nodding and shaking her head at the same time, not quite sure which was the correct gesture to use in response.

'We've been told where the box is being collected in the morning, but apparently that is not where the box is now. They've not told us that.'

CT read her anxious face, looking for signs of duplicity, but saw none. Instead, he detected in her a new, urgent tension that had hitherto been absent. He did his best to feign casual interest in the detail.

'So, this pick-up rendezvous, do you actually have the address?' he asked her, looking in the read-view mirror out of habit.

A host of emotions raced through her mind. This was, she knew, the point of no return for her. If she told him the truth, there was little doubt that he would not stop until he had the details that had been unwittingly provided to her. But, if she disclosed this secret, she also knew that she would have no control over the consequences.

He sensed her hesitation.

'You know, Maria, if we can show that whatever the other side now magic out of, this … what was it … this barn is no different from the other manure that has been kept there …if we can show that, the chief's gratitude will know no ends.'

He let the carrot dangle for a moment. Then the stick …

'On the other hand, if he finds out that we had the opportunity to expose the lies that are being thrown at the company, but failed to help him, then you don't need me to explain what his reaction is likely to be.'

As he said that, he turned to look at her, holding her nervous eyes until she looked down at the file on her lap. Still she hesitated. He let the silence burn for a few more seconds before he spoke again.

'Well, do we, Maria?'

Stabs of guilt jabbed at her. But, alongside that was her realisation that CT was probably right in forecasting the likely reaction of her employers if they were to learn – as they surely would in time – of her failure to act on her knowledge. She pulled out the copy of the email that she had received, conscious that what she was now doing could bring either reward or censure from those who employed her. The choice was not in her gift.

He observed the hesitant decision, followed by the production of what he presumed was the document that contained the intelligence he required. As if performing some ancient ritual, she placed one hand over the central paragraph of the email, whilst holding the communication in the other.

'CT, if I show you this ...' she began.

'Which I really hope you intend to do,' he suggested as a way of finishing her sentence.

She persisted. 'If I do show it to you, what will you do with it?'

He had not expected that, and the question threw him for a moment. She had surely not come this far only to get cold feet?

He opted for what seemed to him a plausible lie: 'I'll do what I presume you would want me to do. I shall tell the chief, so that he can decide what to do with it.'

She looked for and thought she saw sincerity in his eyes. A final hesitation, and then, 'Okay CT. As long as you are sure it's the right thing?'

He gave her his best reassuring 'rest assured – this is the right remedy for you' smile.

'Of course I'm sure, Maria. The chief has been kept in the dark for too long, and it's our job to help him now.'

He held out his hand.

'Now tell me, how can I be of help to you?'

Chapter 28

For the second time that evening, McBride was taken completely off-guard by another call from Thompson bearing yet more shattering news.

'What did you say? Just say that again,' he hissed into his mobile, 'but this time say it nice and slowly.'

'As I said, I don't know who's advising her but, whoever they are, they have just informed our lawyers that the girl, or whoever she's working with, has found another load of our documents. They're in the country, some place in Dorset, and they are being collected by courier tomorrow morning.'

McBride absorbed that news like punch in the nuts. The odds were narrow that these ones would be the research material and the communications relating to them which until now had not seen the light of day.

'The thing is, boss,' CT added, pausing for effect, 'the thing is that I've got hold of the address where the handover is due to take place, and the details of the courier firm that the girl's lawyers intend to use.'

Once again McBride was stunned.

'What, you mean ...'

'Yeah, that's precisely what I mean,' interrupted CT. 'Don't ask me how, we can discuss that once the dust has settled. The point is that, with your help, boss, we could intercept the delivery.'

He had laid the emphasis on 'your help' so as to exclude any possibility that McBride might not understand that this crisis involved both of them. That was not lost on McBride.

'Yes, but I told you to handle it,' he hissed into his phone.

CT had anticipated that.

'I am, boss, and have been, but this has gone way out of my league. And you're the only one who's got the contacts with the heavy mob that we've used in the past to sort out this kind of problem.'

Now that really is cute, thought McBride to himself, not least because CT had a habit of trying to slither his way out of tricky holes. But he also had to acknowledge that this boil had to be lanced.

'So, you're passing the buck now that there's brown stuff is incoming? Is that it?'

'Hardly, boss. This ranks as an emergency, and I don't have the muscle for what's called for right now. And besides,' he added with a deliberate pause, 'there's something that has come up today that will probably take me out of the picture.'

'Explain,' demanded McBride, his executive voice returning, but privately suspecting that this particular rat was about to desert his ship.

'Well,' began CT, 'the Symonds girl has chosen this particular moment to bring a claim for sexual harassment against the company. She has identified me as the principal offender, although she claims that there was a culture within senior management that protected the kind of behaviour that she's alleging.'

He let McBride digest that last point for a moment, then continued, 'The guys from legal, including Larry and the HR lot, have been trying to get hold of me all day. I've eluded them up until now, but it's just a matter of time before they catch up with me. And we both know what will happen then.'

Again, that statement required no further explanation, but McBride was not going to let CT off the hook any time soon.

'Look,' he replied, almost with a snarl in his voice, 'you let me worry about the likes of Larry and the guys in HR. Right now I need you to help me sort this, because you are the only person who can identify the really damaging stuff – assuming, that is, that this is not just one big bluff by the girl's team.'

McBride thought about that for a few seconds.

'Come to think of it,' he continued, his suspicions deepening, 'Are you sure that we are not being set up by the girl and the paper? We're told the details of the pick-up point, along with an address where the stuff is mysteriously said to have been all this time. This could have been leaked to you as a bait, you know, as a lure. What I mean is, our guys could be walking into some sort of trap.'

'No boss, I'm sure this is for real. The detail was in an email that came straight from the lawyers acting for the girl, and was intended as an eyes-only message to the company's head lawyer across town. You and I were never meant to see it.'

McBride considered, and then accepted the reassurance.

'I'm going to give you the pick-up details over the phone now so that we don't leave any electronic trace. And believe me, boss,' he added conspiratorially, 'you don't want to know how I got hold of it.'

That remark was rewarded with a derisory snort

'Okay,' said McBride, as he made up his mind. 'I'll make some phone calls, and get back to you. Can those guys get you on this number?'

Answering that question had not been part of CT's game plan. He was looking to put as much distance between the company and the case as he could, starting that very same evening. He already had his bags packed.

'Wait a minute, boss,' he tried, 'the guy down there knows what I look like. If he sees me, he's going to put two and two together. It's too much of a risk.'

Another snort from McBride.

'Nice try, but you don't get to weasel your way out of this just when the going gets tough. We're both in this mess together. You try to keep out of sight when anything is handed over, but be the first to get a look at whatever it is that they produce. Got it? I need you there. Then you phone me.'

'Okay, boss.'

*

Ali's beau, Jeremy, had worked late at his surgery that evening, but before leaving he had pulled up onto his laptop the article in *The Chronicle* which had brought the hounds after Ali's friend the previous week. When he got to Ali's place for supper – only slightly later than he had promised – she was beside the hob putting together the ingredients for a Thai green curry. He read out the relevant passages in which the paper had described how the two wings of the company had conspired together.

'If this is true,' he observed, looking up at Ali, 'and you tell me that Cat is adamant that it is, it really is rather serious; no, very serious. Leaving aside the regulatory consequences for the company, both financial and clinical, what it means is that every product emanating from any part of the group, whether pharmaceutical or food-related, is now potentially suspect. And we're talking about one of the giants of the industry.'

'I imagine that it's just the start of it,' she replied. 'I get the point about creating a new kind of sweetener that accelerates diabetes, but surely they ran a huge risk in doing that? I'm not a scientist, but I should have thought that the odds of the defect — is that the right term for that sort of trickery? — of the defect being discovered by some bright chemist at some point in the future would be relatively high. That would kick off a class-action lawsuit in the States, and the awards that those juries hand out would make any fines they get hit with look insignificant. Look at the awards over that weedkiller. The one that sank the GM crop seller. And what happens over there always ends up here.'

'I agree, Ali. But that's only half of it. For me, the really serious aspect of this is the charge that the company, along with or to the knowledge of others, rigged the supposedly independent tests and the resulting reports relating to the effects of the types of sweeteners that now permeate the food industry. They're in all kinds of artificially low fat products — there's a contradiction in terms that you and I have discussed before. And they're in endless other foods that have been messed about with. And if the public has been the innocent victim of one big con, then this is potentially massive.'

'But will the paper be able to prove it?' she asked.

'I thought you told me that Cat had dug up a load of documents that she had stashed down on Jamie's estate is Dorset.'

'No, that's not quite right. I told you that I had persuaded Jamie to look for them, and that if he finds them he has to send them to Cat's lawyers. I think he's already done that with some of them, and the lawyers have started to look at them.'

'Well, it's a good start.'

'Anyway, I've tried to persuade Jamie to come and stay on Saturday and Sunday. There's another old schoolmate who's back on the shelf, and ... well, you never know. So I left a couple of messages with him yesterday, but he's not got back to me yet.'

'You've been reading too much Jane Austen! Don't forget that it was you who encouraged Cat and Jamie.' He quickly checked himself. 'No, sorry. That was out of order. Anyway, you say that Cat's got a hearing tomorrow in connection with all this? I presume it's all to do with the injunction that the company got against the paper?'

'It was, so I had understood from her. But now Cat isn't entirely sure what the hearing is going to be about, except that she is required to be there.'

'Ah well, she'll tell us over dinner tomorrow evening. Is that still on?'

'She's not rung me yet to say that it's not, so let's hope so. She or Tomo can tell us anything that they want us to know, but I reckon that this is just the start of it. I don't know very much about the law, except that these cases seem to drag on for ever.'

At that point her mobile rang.

'Well, speak of the devil,' she remarked, picking it up. 'Can you sort those?' she asked Jezza, gesturing towards the red pepper and onion that had still to be sliced.

'Hey, bro, what's up?' she began, and then went silent as she listened, interjecting occasionally with a pertinent question. Eventually they changed the subject, and each tried to persuade the other to join them for the weekend, and each recited their excuses as to why accepting the other's invitation was not feasible, his excuse rather lamer than hers. They left matters on the basis that they would speak the next day.

Jezza sensed her concern as she hung up.

'Everything all right down south?'

'I think it's a yes and no answer. He's spoken to one of the lads that works for him, and he's now pretty sure that he missed some of Cat's stuff first time around. He's had a call from her lawyer asking him if he would be willing to give a statement explaining where Cat's stuff has been all this time, and how he managed to miss this new lot the last time he searched for her stuff. As you can imagine, he's apprehensive about getting involved in all of it, and I think he's right to be.'

'By "give a statement", I assume they mean testify as well?'

'Almost certainly, if it gets to trial – which of course is precisely what the media moguls will want, because it will make brilliant copy.'

'So, was that the "no" bit of the answer?'

'Not quite all of it. He's also worried about tomorrow. He thought he would just be acting as a docking station for the courier service, and that all the arrangements had been made by the lawyers for the collection tomorrow morning. But now the lawyers want him to supervise the actual handover of the material.'

'Why can't they send one of their team to do that?'

'Beats me, but apparently there's more of Cat's stuff down there than he'd first supposed. He's going to have to do another search for it in the morning with the lad who helped him before, and her lawyers want him to be able to explain it all. Something about being able to prove the chain of possession?'

'Yes, I'm familiar with that term. But one assumes that the material simply comprises more documents, and if the other side don't know where they are nor where they're being handed over, nor one assumes what's actually in them, then I don't follow what his concern is.'

'Nor do I, but that's Jamie. Always fussing over something.'

'No, wait,' he said mid-slice, 'that's it. The other side have probably taken a very good guess at what's in this stuff. Hence the extra precaution by the lawyers. Speaking of which, what precautions is Jamie taking?'

Now Ali was herself starting to look worried.

'I don't know. It hadn't occurred to me until you asked. Should I call him back and tell him to get some backup?'

'I would, Ali. Far better to be safe than sorry, as my granny used to say. Can he get some of his men to provide muscle?'

'Well, as you never cease to tell me, your granny was never wrong, because grannies always know best. I'll call Jamie now.'

She left Jezza to continue preparing their supper, and picked up her phone as she walked into the next room to speak with Jamie. She returned a few minutes later, looking relieved.

'He's going to call his keepers and his estate manager to act as his escorts, so that will make four of them at least, if not more.'

'Well done. Time for a glass of something?'

She walked over to the fridge.

'Anyway,' he continued, 'judging from what I overheard, your attempts to persuade him to come up to town for the weekend were still-born?'

'Yes, that's no surprise. He came up with all manner of excuses to avoid that. And you're right, I think he suspects another of my attempts at matchmaking, and – no, there's no need to apologise,' she said halting his intervention. 'We both know that my track record in that department is not exactly impressive.'

'But we've spoken about that, Ali. I thought that I had persuaded you that you cannot blame yourself for what happened.'

'You have, and you're right. And thanks to you, I don't. No, I think that I've probably tried to rush him when he's lost all his former self-confidence, and if I'm honest his trust in women, perhaps with the sole exception of myself. But he did repeat his invitation to us to join him for the weekend with him. You probably heard me explaining that you're now on call on Saturday.'

'Yep, sorry about that.'

'It comes with the territory, as they say. We both knew that when we got together.'

There was no sensible response to that. He changed the subject.

'But, look on the bright side, there is a positive that has come out of this. For months there's been this great elephant in the room regarding Jamie in the form of anything to do with Cat. At last that beast has been removed on account of her current predicament. For my money, that is a definite win.'

She gave him a hug.

'There you go at last with them *positive* waves!'

'Someone has to! And you never know, before long he might even agree to see Cat again – with a suitable chaperone, of course.'

'Now who's being Jane Austen-like!'

*

On the other side of London, Tomo muttered incredulously under his breath. He had just opened up an email from Rosalyn. It attached the claimants' witness statement in reply to her own statement in support of Cat's application for disclosure against the claimants. It was one of the more feeble pieces of forensic gymnastics that he had read in his decade or so of practice.

Cat had tied her hair into a knot at the back of her head, and was midway through her preparation of their evening meal. She looked over her shoulder towards the table where he was working.

'What was that?'

He continued reading, oblivious to her question. In other circumstances she might have been piqued that he had ignored her, but not these. She recognised that look, so she went back to the task in hand.

After a few more minutes, Tomo looked up from his laptop, and flicked the pages on his hearing bundle until he found what he was looking for.

He began to prepare an email to Andrew, who he was fairly sure would also be at his desk either at home or in chambers. A part of his subconscious made him look up at Cat.

'I'm sorry, did you say something a moment ago, Cat?'

'I did, babe, but just to ask what y'all had just said.'

'Oh dear, yes, I suspect that I was speaking to myself again. The men in white coats will be here in the morning, so you can rest easy.'

That brought a smile to her face.

'I could hear you mumbling but couldn't make hide nor tail of it. I assume it's to do with this hearing tomorrow, but is it good or bad?'

'Well, since you ask, it's certainly not bad, and I'll know if it's good or really, really good once I've spoken with Andrew.'

'That's *The Chronicle*'s attorney, or is it "silk" – is that right?'

'Right on both counts. I'm going to ping this across to him in a moment with my suggested line of submission, but unless I am very much mistaken the oppo have made a blunder. Well, I think it's potentially a major blunder, but Andrew may put me back in my box. Sorry, I'm being rather cryptic. Let me explain.'

'No hurry, babe, but should I slow this meal down?'

'I'll just be another twenty minutes or so. This is important, because the oppo have just sent us their witness statement in answer to your application.'

'That's the one y'all were expecting, right?'

'That's the badger.'

She knew what twenty minutes meant in legal parlance.

'I reckon I'll slow this right down.'

Tomo only half heard her. He had already begun to set out his draft submission in an email to Andrew. Three quarters of an hour later, he pushed his laptop across the table and walked over to the sofa. Cat was kneeling on the floor beside it in what might have been a perfect yoga position were it not for the fact that she had her own device propped on a cushion balanced across her thighs.

He sat down beside her and gently ran the back of his forefinger down the side of her cheek, wishing she had chosen to wear a longer skirt that evening, as she responded by nuzzling her cheek against his hand.

'You should never trust a lawyer,' he said, only now realising how hungry he was after such a long day.

'I didn't, babe. So, is this deputation a plea from your stomach, or somewhere lower?' she teased in her best Virginian drawl.

'I think we agreed to restrict activities to the former this evening, and I'm expecting a response from Andrew any moment. But yes, very much the former. Can I help with supper? I'm famished.'

'Well now, we can't starve that brain of yours, can we? We are going to need that organ in full working order in the morning.'

She put her device onto the sofa, and rose up from her sitting position to straddle him in one fluid movement.

'And speaking of organs, if I put the chicken breasts in now, supper will be ready in about fifteen minutes.'

She pulled up her tee-shirt, and fed a nipple towards his lips, taking him by surprise. He hadn't realised that she had removed her underwear.

'So, babe, it would be a darn shame to waste that time, when we could be putting it to good use, don't y'all think?'

She leant down, her lips stifling what would have been his admittedly half-hearted protest.

'It's just a little R&R,' she teased, ever so innocently, wriggling on his lap and feeding him her other nipple, and then said, 'Just give me a moment.'

With that, she peeled herself away, fully aware that she had prevailed.

Half an hour later, over supper, he began to explain the latest development to her.

'So,' he began, 'you remember our discussion earlier about the basis of the claimant's case.' It was a statement not a question. 'And you remember that we reminded you that the premise of their case is that you and *The Chronicle* are in possession of confidential and commercially sensitive material that belongs to the company. And they have since queried the provenance and authenticity of the material that you claim to have produced.'

'Sure, I got all that earlier.'

'I never doubted it for a minute,' he said, reassuringly. 'So, their evidence starts with the usual whinge about only having a brief chance to consider the defence that you and your co-defendants have been advised to advance. They rightly acknowledge these as being in essence ones of justification and public interest, which they naturally refute. No surprises there. Now here's the interesting bit.' He paused to slice a piece of chicken on his plate. 'First, they argue that your disclosure request is wrong in principle – I'll come back to that because it's important. Then they protest that your request is too extensive in scope, but that is really only an issue of logistics and dates, which the court can easily sort once it comprehends the scale of the task.'

'Rather like what we've been doing with my disclosure?'

'Exactly. But thirdly,' he emphasised, gesturing with the piece of chicken on his fork, 'they now accuse you and *The Chronicle* of being on a "fishing expedition". By that they mean we are hoping to build our case on the basis of documents that we hope to find as a result of their disclosure, because we would otherwise be unable to make good our defence as matters currently stand. Does that make sense?'

'Okay, I guess,' she acknowledged uncertainly.

'Sorry, that might have been an unnecessary confusion.'

'Just a little,' she replied with a smile.

'Sorry. So, ignore that. There's also a related fourth point, which I'll come to in a second, but they both take us back to the issue of principle, which is really the key to this whole thing.'

She pushed the fork gently towards his mouth, urging him to eat it. He did, greedily.

After a few more mouthfuls, accompanied by all the right facial expressions and sounds of appreciation from Tomo, and seeing him pause to take a sip of wine, she said, 'So, the principle . . .?'

'Exactly. And that's what's so strange about this. They've danced around this issue like a foursome of ballet dancers performing a sword dance.'

'I'm sorry, a sword dance?'

'Ah yes, I've yet to introduce you to Scottish dancing. Now that is something that, knowing you as I now do, you really would enjoy.'

'Is that a glove that you've just thrown at my feet?'

'It's known as a gauntlet, actually, but yes.'

'Well, consider it, what would y'all say . . . retrieved?'

'Touche!' he replied, raising his glass. She followed suit.

'So,' he continued, 'on the issue of principle, they neither admit nor deny that the material that you and the paper have requested is relevant to the issues. They haven't mentioned admissibility, which I take as a concession. So, they have allowed us to demonstrate to the court that this material will need to be disclosed at some point.'

'So, that's good? I am reading that right?'

'It is. No, it's more than good. But here's the thing, and it's the fourth point that I told you they have raised. What they argue, in opposition to your disclosure request, is that their business would be at risk of revealing its trade secrets in public, and thus expose itself to unfair competition from other companies in the same field. But what's key is that they say that this will arise in particular with regard to the manner in which they have commissioned and then published their research material in the past.'

Cat stared at him for a moment in silence. This time it was she who suspended part of her own supper on the end of her fork. After a while, she said, almost in a whisper, replacing her knife and fork on her plate, 'Well, lordy, lordy, ain't that just the Holy Grail.'

'I thought you'd be pleased,' he echoed, raising a finger to restrain further intervention from her. 'But what is both predictable and frustrating is that they don't say – or rather they won't say, probably because they dare not risk it – whether they commissioned their research in common with or at variance with other pharmaceutical companies. The article in the paper of course alleged that it was the former, but their evidence is entirely silent on the point.'

She took a moment to absorb the implications of that.

'But will it work? I mean, will the judge buy it?'

'That's the very question that I posed to Andrew, but not before drawing his attention to the basis on which your former employers applied for and obtained their orders against you. That can be easy for a claimant to overlook when under pressure, and I think that is precisely what they have done.'

'That's the blunder you were talking about?'

'The very same. So, let's take a step back before we continue forwards. You don't need reminding that one of the themes in that explosive article in *The Chronicle* was that the company had *departed* from its normal procurement practice when it commissioned, or according to the paper, rigged its research into artificial sweeteners. The article also exposed what it called the deceit in what later emerged as the report relating to the medium to long-term effects of the types of sweeteners that are widely used in the food industry. So, here's the key thing. In their sworn evidence before the court when they applied for their orders against you, the company assured the court that that both those assertions were untrue. Are you with me so far?'

'Right there, babe.'

'Therefore, in order to prove that what was in the article was untrue, the company will have to explain to the court what its normal procurement practice was. Now, I very much doubt that, when they applied for the orders, it occurred to the company's lawyers that the company would object to providing disclosure of its normal methods of procurement of research. Why should they have done, when their clients had told them that the allegations in the article were completely untrue?'

'In the note of the hearing, that's what their barrister told the judge.'

'Precisely. And the judge will assume, and indeed you alleged, that such a procurement process was recorded in writing, since that would be a common, if not universal, practice within the industry.'

'Well, the guys in CD told me that it had something to do with compliance with European procurement rules.'

'That would make sense, because if challenged the company would need to be able to show that there had been a fair tender process.'

'That's sounds about right.'

'Well, it just so happens that it is that class of documents that you and the paper are seeking to have disclosed now.'

She thought about that for a moment.

'So how come your, what do you call them, your oppo?'

'Schoolboy terminology!'

She grinned at that.

'So how come your *oppo* didn't think of that?'

Tomo had asked himself the same question. 'That's why I've asked Andrew whether he considers their latest move to be a high-risk roll of the dice, or a cunning wheeze.'

As if on cue, Tomo's mobile announced an incoming message. He was about to get up to retrieve it, but Cat put a restraining hand on his arm.

'Babe, finish your meal first,' she commended. 'You've barely touched it, and you'll need all your energy for what lies ahead.'

He affected, unsuccessfully, to ignore her *double entendre*.

'Don't even think about it,' was the best he could do.

Chapter 29

CT's bags were packed, and seemed to beckon to him from the hallway. It would be so, so easy, he thought, to head off to the airport right now, and catch the first flight out in the morning. He could leave this shitstorm behind him. That was surely the sensible thing to do, especially as he had been placed in the frame personally by the harassment claim.

But, ever the gambler, he wagered that he and the chief could still wriggle their way out of this if they could get hold of that material. Having said that, the chief was cutting it fine on that front, since the heavy mob had yet to contact him.

He looked at his watch. It was almost 11.00 pm.

He had transferred all the data from his company sim card onto his spare laptop, and had switched to a new mobile. He had given the number to McBride over the phone, although he was now worried that the guy had written down the number incorrectly. He sent McBride a text urging him to contact him, or at least to get one of his heavies to call him on the new phone.

He inspected his passports, both the real one and the fake, and checked his wallet. He then made another unnecessary tour of the house in order to satisfy himself that he would not leave behind any incriminating material.

At last, his mobile came to life, and from a withheld number, which was what he had expected. Having confirmed his identity, he listened carefully to his instructions, and then proceeded to pack the car.

Chapter 30

Charlie Poore checked his watch. There was less than half an hour to go before the rendezvous time that Jamie had given him last night. It couldn't be earlier than 10.00, Jamie had said, and it could be even later, because they needed to give Joey time to finish up at the dairy. When Charlie had asked why, Jamie had explained that they were going to be reliant on Joey, not least because he had the keys to the barn, and he knew what they were looking for.

Well, there's a thing, Charlie had thought to himself, but had the sense not to express that opinion.

Despite the late rendezvous, Charlie had been at his self-appointed sentry point since just after dawn, watching the approaches to the lane up to the barn from his vantage point high up on the other side of the valley.

The school bus and rush hour, such as it was in this valley, had been long gone, and there'd been nothing stirring down in the valley apart from the odd red deer. Bloody pests they were, especially around this time of year when the roses began to show. The animals were out of season right now, but if this had been the autumn and if he didn't have the priorities that he had that morning, then, as his late father used to say, 'one of they could've fell over easy'.

He'd seen the lights come on at the manor house before 7.00, and imagined that Jamie would have been at his desk for well over an hour already after walking the dog. But not without a strong coffee, he hoped. He might need it today.

He realised that he'd not turned his phone on yet. He so seldom had any use for it these days, mainly because he and his underkeepers kept in touch via their handsets when they went about the estate. He had been listening out for any radio traffic on his own set, and had left it with the volume turned up in the Landy, which was hidden beyond the hedgerow behind him, but there had been silence so far.

He'd left it to the captain to decide whether to alert the local police in the Dorchester HQ about the morning's events. Jamie had originally sounded confident that there ought to be no need to involve the police in all this, but now that Charlie knew what was at stake he wasn't at all sure about that.

*

And so, we find ourselves back where this tale began, within the sparsely lit, muggy atrium outside Court 37 within the High Court in The Strand, London. Cat, reassured by Tomo's presence, had watched as he had gone over to talk with the lawyers acting for *The Chronicle*, although he had spent over an hour and a half the night before discussing tactics with their silk – Andrew was it? – and had then gone back to work on his laptop. She had been asleep when he had come to bed, and barely woke in time to kiss him goodbye at dawn. But he had given her a warm and encouraging embrace when she had met him at his chambers, which was all she needed.

What a difference seven days can make, she thought. Events had moved so quickly since she had opened her door to those lawyers brandishing the orders obtained against her by her former employers. Two of those same lawyers were here now, but their demeanour displayed none of the confidence that had been evident that morning. Instead, they seemed uncomfortable, apprehensive even, as they watched their opponents confer in a huddle in the far corner.

Amongst that huddle was Tomo, who was here to argue her corner. He was deep in discussion with the paper's lawyers over on the other side of the atrium – at least, she assumed they were lawyers. She found herself searching for a collective noun for a group of lawyers. Would it be a 'school of lawyers'? No, that was too respectful, and was insulting to dolphins. Perhaps 'an apology'? No, too neutral. What about 'a plague'? That was more like it; except, she thought, that would only apply to the oppo – she had now embraced that word within her dictionary. Tomo and Rosalyn were certainly not in that category. What about a 'calamity' of lawyers. Well, this was certainly started out as a calamity, and the company's lawyers had done their best to make this one of the worst weeks of her life.

But that was still not right. She tried again. What about 'a conspiracy of lawyers'? That seemed more than appropriate, especially in the current circumstances. Then, oddly, she remembered a word that Tomo had used to describe a squabble between neighbours.

He'd called it 'a right barnie'.

Now that would work, she thought. And between them she could see that the lawyers were indeed engaged in a 'right barnie'. So, she settled on that.

She looked across again at this particular 'barnie' on the other side of the atrium. When she had first seen them, she had thought that they might act for AlphaOm, such was the swagger with which they had made their entrance. But on closer inspection she could not recognise any of the team that had invaded her flat last week. So, she deduced that the guys with whom Tomo was conferring must act for the paper, in which case they would be 'the good guys,' not the enemy. Tomo would no doubt confirm this for her.

In fact, sooner than she realised, as 'the barnie' appeared to be breaking up after much nods amongst the assembled throng, followed by friendly smiles and knowing glances at the oppo, whom she now recognised beside the oak doors.

She watched Tomo stride across the gloomy atrium to stand by her side, accompanied by another, whom she took to be their silk.

'Cat, let me introduce Andrew Sutherland. He's the silk for *The Chronicle* with whom I was speaking last night.'

Andrew gave her a beaming smile, taking her hand in both of his.

'Hello, Cat, if I may, how very nice to meet you at last. And just let me say how heroically brave I think you are for doing this. It took true guts to blow the whistle on your employers in the way that you did. The nation will be truly grateful to you.'

'Why thank you, Andrew. I do truly appreciate you saying that,' she replied in her softly accented tone. 'And I am mighty obliged to make your acquaintance, and to thank you in person for what you are doing to help.'

'Not at all, Cat. It is the least that we could do. But let me assure you that Tom here has played more than his fair share so far. Anyway, I think we are about to be called in any minute, so I shall just have a brief word with the claimants' counsel about this morning's business.'

He smiled again, and left her with Tomo.

'Why, I do declare, Mr Butler. That is as fine a gentleman as a country girl like me could hope to meet.'

'Yep, he can charm the judges all right. Anyway, to business, whilst we have a minute. We are pressing ahead with our application, despite surprisingly vigorous protests from the company's solicitors.'

'But you expected that, surely?'

'Indeed, but they want to object to the comparative lateness of our application, but they've got their own problems on that score. The judge seems likely to ask them for a proper explanation as to why their evidence was filed so late.'

'Is that, like, a black mark?'

'Very much so, and as the claimants that is the last thing they need. Anyway, we intend to push ahead with our application. Andrew will take the lead in our submissions, and I shall pick up any threads relevant to your own disclosure. On which note, I gather we've not heard anything from Dorset, but that's to be expected. It's still early days, and Rosalyn has the contact details for the couriers.'

Cat remained nervous on that account.

'Tomo,' she asked him, lowering her voice. 'Can you ask her to be sure to tell me as soon as the stuff is on its way from Jamie's?'

'Absolutely. In fact, I'll do that now.'

*

Charlie Poore checked his watch again. On the captain's advice, he had stationed Sid, his underkeeper, at the top of the valley so that, between them, they could monitor the arrival of any vehicles they didn't recognise and alert Jamie and the captain. He was a good lad to have on one's side. Well, he was a grown man now was Sid, and had served two tours out in Iraq as a sniper. Word was that he'd earned a gong or two, though he seldom spoke of it. But he was just the sort of muscle that you might want as backup if things turned sour. He'd seen him drop a fox on the estate at a thousand yards.

The captain had Sid under his wing, and the two of them were in contact.

The sun had long ago risen away to his left, and had burnt off most of the morning's dew. It had swung around a fair bit, but not enough to create any risk of a reflection from his binoculars so as to alert anyone to his presence as they drove along the valley road. As a result, that left him free to monitor the road from his vantage point halfway up the hill.

The herd had been grazing on the meadow this past hour, which told Charlie that Joey had been alert to his duties that morning, and was well on schedule. He could still see his truck up by the diary, which meant that Joey should soon finish off his chores.

Time passed slowly. Charlie looked at his watch again. There was less than ten minutes to go.

'Mind, but they're cutting it fine, this courier lot,' he thought, but then so too was Jamie. He looked across at the dairy, and at last saw Joey beginning to lock up.

Just then, something caught his eye over at the top of the valley.

Hello, what's this, he asked himself, reaching for his phone, as he brought his binoculars to bear on what looked like a courier van which had just come into the valley away off to his left. It was driving in the direction of the manor house.

Just then, he heard Sid's call-sign come over the handset in the Landy behind him. Knowing that Sid would have a far better view from where he lay concealed, Charlie went to answer it.

'Go ahead, Sid,' he said into the mouthpiece.

'Charlie, do you have eyes on that courier?'

'I did but I've lost it now that it's driving through the woods.'

'Roger. Any sign of the gaffer yet from where you are?'

Charlie trained his binoculars back onto the manor, but there was no movement from Jamie or of his car.

'No, Sid, but I reckon that'll be because Joey hasn't finished up yet.'

'Hold up, Charlie. I have eyes on a black four-by-four, Rangie by the looks of it, and with those blacked-out windows. It's just driven into the valley from the east, and it's coming down the lane slowly, just hanging back from the courier van.'

'Is it following it, Sid?'

'Difficult to be sure ... it's pulled up a way back by the side of the road now ... Hold up, so has the courier.'

'Where's he to, Sid?'

'It's not far from the end of the drive up to the manor.'

There followed a few seconds of tense silence. It was broken by Sid's voice.

'Charlie, there's a fellow just got out of the Rangie, and ... well, I'm buggered if he's not putting on a combat hood.'

'Don't like the sound of that, Sid.'

'He's up to no good, that's for sure, Charlie.'

'Stay with it, Sid, for now. Let's see what they're playing at.'

'On it, Charlie. No, wait a second, Charlie, the Rangie has just pulled up in front of the van, and the guy with the hood is walking over to it.'

'This sure ain't right, Sid.'

'Hold up, Charlie. I think he's just pulled something out from behind his back and shown it to the van man.'

'Can you tell what it is, Sid?'

'Can't swear to it, Charlie, but it could be a shooter. Any roads, he's bundling the van man into the Rangie. Given him a thumper by the looks of it too.'

'Don't like this one bit, Sid.'

'No wait. He's walking back to the van. Well, bugger me if he's not going to drive it.'

'Crafty devils. I'll get right onto the captain.'

Charlie took out his phone. And then cursed, as it failed to switch on.

'Sid, I forgot to charge the ruddy thing.'

'Try him on the handset, Charlie. He might have it with him.'

Charlie tried the captain, but without success.

'No luck, Sid. Anything your end?'

'Nothing yet, Charlie. The courier is just sat at the bottom of the drive up to the manor for now. You reckon he's waiting for the gaffer?'

'Most like, Sid. You let me know as soon as anything else happens. I'll drive down there and warn Jamie. You get hold of the captain.'

'Too late, Charlie. The gaffer's just left the manor, and he's heading down the drive. Oh yeah, and the courier's still got its motor running.'

'Bugger! They'll be headed for that old barn, I'll wager, Sid. Can you see it from where you're hid?'

'Clear as daylight, Charlie. If I switch to the rifle scope, I reckon I could count the hinges on those old doors.'

*

Over a hundred miles away, another set of old doors were being watched. They were the double doors to Court 37. As they swung open, a careworn usher appeared, clutching in one hand a board holding the list of the cases due to be heard by the surrounding courts that day; with the other he held open the swinging doors.

'AlphaOm plc *versus* Chronicle Newspapers and others,' he announced in a weary and slightly croaking voice.

The grey suits came to attention, and picked up their files.

'Are you all ready?' asked the usher.

There were nods from all the grey suits, but rather more polite responses from Andrew and from Tomo. And in they filed. Tomo ushered Cat into a seat in the row behind him, where she was joined by Ken Baxter and the deputy editor of *The Chronicle*, and then took his seat in front of them.

There followed a subdued bustle as counsel sorted out their various files and prepared water glasses, note pads, and pens, before an eerie calm descended as they waited for the judge.

Cat looked about her in awed silence. She had not been sure what to expect, but these plain and austere surroundings were far removed from her wild imaginings. It all looked so, well, so functional and even ordinary. Nothing like the courtroom dramas that she used to watch on her TV or laptop. She clocked that the judge would be up there on the raised dais, and they would be down here. But, somehow, she had anticipated something more dramatic. This all looked so businesslike.

Tomo turned around to give Cat a warm smile.

'All rise,' called the usher, and the judge entered the courtroom, and strode across to his chair on the raised dais.

The court clerk nodded to the judge to signal that the recording had started, whereupon he read out the same introduction: 'AlphaOm plc *versus* Chronicle Newspapers and others.'

'Yes, Mr Gaitsland,' began the judge in a businesslike way. He looked first at counsel in attendance before him, to whom he gave a nod of recognition, and then the lay attendees, lingering perhaps a little longer than he should have done on Cat, who duly blushed and looked down at her lap.

In accordance with formalities, Gaitsland introduced first Andrew and then Tomo, before informing the judge that Andrew also appeared for Mr Baxter.

'Yes, thank you Mr Gaitsland. Now then: this morning was listed as the return hearing in respect of the various orders that I made a week ago. However, I was informed, late yesterday afternoon – and I'll have a thing or two to say about that in a moment – that the claimants have requested that the hearing in respect of those orders should be adjourned. Now, first of all, Mr Gaitsland, is that correct?'

'It is, my lord, and may I say ...'

'If you'll let me finish, Mr Gaitsland,' interrupted the judge. 'Instead, there is before me an application by the defendants, filed in plenty of time, for a disclosure order against the claimants, which I understand is being resisted. Is that correct?'

'It is, my lord.' This time, Gaitsland had the sense not to say anything further. His instincts told him what was coming.

'Thank you. As I said, the application was filed in good time by the defendants. However, as of close of business yesterday, the court had received neither a witness statement nor any written submissions from the claimants that might vouchsafe to the court the basis on which the application is being resisted.'

He let that admonishment hang in the air for a moment.

'As I say, I had prepared for this hearing yesterday after court, and again this morning. However, shortly before nine o'clock this morning, my clerk handed to me copies of a witness statement and a skeleton argument that were, so I was told, in the course of being filed on behalf of the claimants. I was also handed what I learnt was a cross-application, which again the claimants were in the course of filing, to adjourn the hearing of the defendants' application.'

Again, he allowed a pause to signal his dissatisfaction.

'Now, Mr Gaitsland, leaving aside the discourtesy shown towards the court in filing these papers at such late notice, can you tell me when those instructing you provided copies of these documents to the defendants' solicitors and counsel?'

So focussed had Gaitsland been on other matters that he was not prepared for such a question. He turned around first to his junior, and then to Mary Fellowes behind him, who began to explain to him what had occurred the previous afternoon.

*

When Jamie had heard his mobile ping, he had flicked it open, and read a message informing him that the courier van organised by Cat's lawyers had pulled up at the bottom of his drive, as arranged. He'd replied to confirm that he would meet the driver there shortly, assuming, again as arranged, that it would be the same person who had collected Cat's boxes on the previous occasion. He'd then called Joey to confirm that he was on his way, finished his glass of water and picked up his keys.

His emotions were all over the place that morning. Part of him felt enormous relief that he was finally taking steps to put the past behind him, to overcome the agony of betrayal and the attendant misery of isolation. Yet, curiously, another part of him felt reluctant to let go of what few possessions of hers remained on the estate. And yet perhaps, more than anything else, the biggest part of him knew that, whatever they were able to find that day, he was doing the right thing for Cat.

His distrust of the big pharma companies, not least because of their domination of the medical world, was matched only by his loathing of scientifically modified products that the large multinationals were seeking to peddle. So, if his actions today helped to bring down, or at least to check, one of the pharma giants, then he could take pride in the part that he would have played.

Such were his meanderings that he reached the end of the drive and almost forgot to greet the courier driver who was waiting for him at the agreed spot. He had to refocus himself, and reversed back a few yards.

The driver was wearing dark glasses and a cap, which was not surprising given the bright sunshine, and raised his hand and stepped out of his van.

'Mr Henderson?' he enquired politely.

Jamie raised his thumb.

'Yep, this way if you please,' he replied, beckoning to the courier driver to follow him, then began to drive along the lane towards the gate leading up to the barn, checking in his mirror that the courier was following him. When he got there, he noted that the padlocks had already been opened, which suggested that either Joey was ahead of him, or that he had unlocked them earlier that morning.

Jamie pulled up just before the open gates, and went to speak to the driver, who duly stepped out of the van. Jamie was slightly surprised to see that he was not the same person as he had met here the previous day. When he'd spoken to Cat's lawyer, he'd been led to believe that the courier company would stick with the same driver in order to avoid any confusion over the rendezvous that he'd agreed with her. On the other hand, the driver had found the right place, so maybe all was in order, after all.

'Are you Mr Henderson, sir?' said the driver, effecting to check his job-sheet. Jamie thought he detected an Eastern European accent.

'Yes, that's me. But tell me: is there any particular reason why your company has switched drivers without informing me?'

'Sorry, sir. They just gave me this job yesterday evening, and didn't tell me that you would be expecting someone else. They just sent me your address, and phone number and told me to call when I reached your driveway.'

Jamie weighed that up, and then asked the driver for his ID, which he inspected once the driver had fished it out of his jacket. Satisfied, Jamie told the driver that he was going to collect the materials which the driver had been instructed to collect and deliver to the lawyers in London. On Jamie's request, the driver confirmed the delivery address.

Jamie was about to make his way back to his car when he heard the distinctive sound of Charlie's Land Rover, which seemed to be coming along the lane towards the gate, and at a fair old pace, if he was not mistaken.

He turned to the driver.

'Would you wait here please?' he said to him, as Charlie pulled into the entrance of the track by the gates.

The driver acknowledged, and waited by his van. As he did so, Jamie noticed for the first time that a black Range Rover had just pulled up further up the lane.

Jamie walked over to the Land Rover. Even though both its windows were already open, Charlie leant across and opened the passenger door.

'I need a word, Jamie. Something's come up, urgent like.'

He looked at Jamie, as he used to do as his mentor many years back. It was a look that Jamie knew would brook no dissent. He immediately recognised it, and understood.

He was about to suggest that he collect his own car when he clocked that the black Range Rover had begun to move towards them.

'Jamie, get in,' urged Charlie. 'NOW.'

Jamie knew that voice, and quickly made a dash for the passenger seat. Charlie had the vehicle moving before Jamie had even sat down, and they headed up the bumpy track towards the barn at some speed.

'Crickey, Charlie! This is a bit dramatic.'

'Bloody right it's a drama, Jamie. Those fellows in that black car are up to no good. They've hijacked that courier.'

'What? How the hell did they find us?'

'Never mind that now, Jamie. Have you got your phone with you?'

Jamie nodded.

'Best get on to Captain McGowan sharpish, Jamie, and tell him to call the police. And we could do with some help from the farm lads.'

Jamie saw the obvious sense in that. He took his phone out, and pulled up Sandy's number.

'Jamie?' answered the captain.

'Sandy, we have a problem. I'm with Charlie. There's a black car that's appeared from nowhere that's been parked up in the lane below the old barn. We've driving up to it now, but the other car is following us, so we're going to need some help.'

Charlie had just checked his rear-view mirror.

'The car's still following us, Jamie, and Sid tells me he saw at least one of them take out one of them combat hoods. And he's got a weapon.'

'Bloody hell! Did you hear that, Sandy?'

'I did. I'll get on to Dorchester HQ now. I'll call you back.'

Chapter 31

Andrew Sutherland had been watching the whispered exchange between his opponent and Mary Fellowes with rare amusement. It was not often that, as defence counsel, one was afforded the luxury of seeing the claimants in disarray. Ever the seasoned warrior, he seized that moment to get to his feet in order to address the judge.

'If I may assist, my lord, and perhaps save some of your lordship's time.'

'Of course, Mr Sutherland,' said the judge.

'My lord, I can confirm that my learnt friends provided both to myself and my learnt friend, Mr Butler, copies of the claimants' skeleton argument at around eight o'clock last night. We received the claimants' evidence shortly thereafter, but not the exhibits. Those arrived some time later, but we did our best to interrogate them, since it is our joint application. Thereafter, Mr Butler and I spent what was left of yesterday evening and some of the small hours discussing these over the phone – we had both left chambers by then.'

'Quite,' observed the judge.

'And, my lord,' continued Andrew, 'so as to assist the court, we prepared a short submission in response to the claimant's application. I sent a copy through early this morning. If your lordship has had a chance to read it, then I was proposing to take your lordship through this when convenient.'

All's fair in love and war, he thought to himself, noting his opponent wince visibly as that intelligence was conveyed.

'Thank you, Mr Sutherland. Duly noted, and yes, thank you, I did receive it and have read it,' the judge replied, offering him an understanding smile, before casting a disapproving eye at Gaitsland.

'And, despite the late provision of the claimants' evidence and their skeleton, are all the respondents nevertheless content to proceed this morning with their application?'

'Indeed, they are, my lord.'

Tomo rose briefly and nodded to the judge.

'Very well, Mr Sutherland, but I'll have some more to say about that in a moment after you have presented the defendants' application,' he continued.

Andrew nodded and sat down.

'Let us first deal with the adjournment, if you will, Mr Gaitsland. So, first, are you able to enlighten the court as to the reasons for this late application to adjourn this hearing? I merely ask because when you appeared before me last week, you went to considerable pains to emphasise the urgency of the remedies that the claimants were seeking, and indeed which they obtained.'

'Indeed, my lord . . .'

'And you must forgive me for observing,' he continued, ignoring the interruption, 'that it is not every day in this court that the party seeking to adjourn the return date hearing for a restraining order is the claimant.'

Mary Fellowes had really hoped that the judge would have let them off the hook on this, but it was clearly not to be. She braced herself, dreading the judicial reprimand that would inevitably be forthcoming. If she was hoping for salvation from Gaitsland, she was about to be disappointed. He was not about to take one for the team.

'My lord, my instructions are as follows. In response to this court's disclosure orders, each of the defendants provided to the independent solicitor an initial tranche of hard copy and electronic documents. At the same time, in her affidavit to the court pursuant to the orders against her, Miss Symonds informed the court that she did once have in her possession and control, but does no longer, other documents that she claimed she had originally obtained from the claimants.'

'Yes, I saw that, and I've also read the interim report from the independent solicitor. Mr Peter Langer, I believe?'

'Yes, m'lord.'

'Good. Please go on.'

'I'm obliged, my lord. Subsequently, Miss Symonds produced, from a location belonging to an undisclosed third party, a substantial number of further documents that her solicitors, on her instructions, informed the independent solicitor were the documents that she had obtained from the claimants whilst in their employ. Now . . .'

'Mr Gaitsland, as I said, I have read the report from Mr Langer, and he sets all that out very clearly. He also informs the court that some of those documents, but by no means all, amounting in aggregate to over four hundred pages, were released by him to the claimants earlier this week.'

'My lord, yes, that's right,' replied Gaitsland. 'And it is that tranche of documents that my clients are currently subjecting to forensic analysis in order to determine their authenticity, or potentially and more significantly, the absence thereof, and also any provenance within my clients' IT and other filing systems.'

The judge eyed Gaitsland sceptically.

'Forgive me, Mr Gaitsland, I am not an IT expert by any means, but I should have thought that, given the claimants' substantial resources, the authenticity of these documents and their contents could surely be verified in relatively short order. I am tempted to deploy that much over-used phrase "by the click of a mouse"?'

Whilst the question was far from welcome, Gaitsland had been briefed carefully by Mary on how to answer it.

'Apparently not, my lord. I am instructed that any document created within the claimants' systems that is intended for distribution at board level is coded in a way that permits any individual document to be scanned line by line, and word by word. That scan will do two things. First, it will detect whether the document is genuine, or not, as the case may be, and I am instructed that my clients have yet to be satisfied that the former is the case. Furthermore ...'

The judge raised a finger. 'Just a second, Mr Gaitsland, I may have missed it, but I did not see any allegation of libel in your clients' draft statement of case. Are you telling me that your clients intend to amend their claim so as to allege that?'

'My lord, not until the scanning process has been completed by my clients. On which note, your lordship may have picked up that there is a suggestion that further documents may be about to be disclosed by Miss Symonds either today or early next week. If that proves to be the case, then clearly my clients' scanning process will become more extensive, and thus be further delayed.'

Tomo turned around to catch Rosalyn's eye, holding an imaginary phone to his ear and looking inquisitively at her. Rosalyn checked her phone and, seeing that there was no message from the couriers, shook her head.

'Very well,' said the judge, his meaning intentionally ambiguous. 'I'm sorry, you were telling me that the scan serves *two* purposes.'

'My lord, yes. The second purpose is that it also enables any one document to be traced to its intended recipient within the claimants' offices. As a result, the provenance of any such document can be traced to its source. I am instructed that it is that twin process that has taken and is taking the time, my lord.'

Another sceptical look from the judge.

'But surely, if your clients had installed a *mole-trap* – I think that is the common term for such a facility – does that not speed up the process?'

'I can only repeat my instructions, my lord,' said Gaitsland feebly.

'And, just so that I am clear, Mr Gaitsland, your clients are telling me that their technicians need more than three days to scan some four hundred documents?'

'Those are my instructions, my lord,' was again the best that Gaitsland could manage in response, much to the concealed amusement of Andrew and Tomo.

The judge allowed that answer to hang in the ensuing silence for a short while, looking briefly at Tomo and Andrew, before returning his stare to Gaitsland.

'You see, the reason that I ask is that one of the other documents that I read yesterday in preparation for this morning's hearing was Mr Langer's initial report. It was prepared by him following his supervision of the search of Miss Symonds' flat. I believe you will find it in the bundle ...'

'It is, my lord, and if you give me a second I can give you the reference ...'

'Thank you, Mr Gaitsland, but I don't need to be taken to it right now. No, I was merely going to observe that there was one particular exchange in it that caught my eye. That exchange was between Miss Symonds and Mrs Fellowes, who I believe is the lead partner in the claimants' solicitors, but it was overheard by Mr Langer. Would it be fair for me to assume that you know what I am referring to?'

Gaitsland knew exactly what he was referring to. 'I believe I can hazard a guess, my lord.'

'Well, for the benefit of the defendants, allow me to elucidate,' continued the judge, who was plainly enjoying this.

Tomo passed Andrew a note giving him the reference in the bundle.

'I noted,' continued the judge, 'that in his report, Mr Langer records Miss Symonds as having spoken to Mrs Fellowes words to the effect that everything that had been written by *The Chronicle* was true. I presumed, as no doubt did Mrs Fellowes, that Miss Symonds was referring to the article that had been published by *The Chronicle* a day or so before which gave rise to these proceedings.' He paused for dramatic effect. 'Now, I presume that Miss Symonds did not have the benefit of legal advice at the time that she spoke those words. Therefore, can I just be reassured that there is no objection from those acting on behalf of Miss Symonds, nor indeed from any other defendant, to that statement being included in the bundle.'

The judge had directed his question to Tomo, who immediately rose to his feet.

'None at all, my lord, from Miss Symonds,' he said, and then to inject a bit of mischief, added, 'and, so far as I know, none has been raised by the claimants.'

The judge resisted a smile at that, then continued, 'Thank you, Mr Butler. You see, Mr Gaitsland, the reason why that statement stuck in my mind is that it is one that you so rarely hear from a defendant in this sort of case, wouldn't you agree?'

Gaitsland hesitated.

'Well,' continued the judge, 'I shall let you think about that for a moment. But you see, it got me wondering whether there might be any connection between that exchange and the present application for an adjournment?'

That was delivered as an observation, but it could so very easily have been interpreted as a question. Which was indeed how Gaitsland treated it.

'Well, my lord, my instructions are ...'

'My apologies, Mr Gaitsland, I did not expect an answer. That was merely idle musing on my part. Forgive me – I digress. Let us return to the business in hand.'

So saying, he switched his gaze to his left to focus on the respondents' bench.

'First, I should like to hear from Mr Sutherland and Mr Butler on the matter of the proposed adjournment, and in particular any terms that their clients may wish the court to attach to any further order of the court.'

Gaitsland took that as an instruction to sit down, whereupon, in response to a smile from the judge, Andrew got up.

'Yes, Mr Sutherland ...'

Chapter 32

Jamie scrolled through his phone and fumbled for the mobile number that he'd been given for Cat's lawyer. He found it, and put a call through. To his frustration, his call was diverted to her messaging service. Hardly surprising, thought Jamie, since they were meant to be in court this morning. He rang again, and this time left a brief but urgent message to tell her what was going on, and insisting that she call him back as soon as she got the message.

He switched to his emails, and opened the message from Cat's lawyer. He tapped the number at the bottom of her email and was connected to what he assumed was her PA or receptionist.

As soon as it answered, he spoke swiftly, 'This is Jamie Henderson, from whom your firm is collecting some important documents this morning. Please get a message to Rosalyn that our attempt to enable Cat to comply with the court's orders are about to be compromised. We are being followed by persons unknown, but who I have cause to believe are likely to be very hostile. I need urgent assistance, and the court needs to be informed right now.'

A pause.

'Did you get that?'

'Yes sir, I did. I shall message her at once, although the hearing has probably already started so her phone may be switched off.'

'Just keep trying. Now, can you record what you hear on this phone?'

'Yes I can.'

'Then please do so now.'

Then he slipped his phone into his kerchief pocket and turned to Charlie.

'Why have we come up here, Charlie? The only way out is back down that track.'

'Same goes for him. But up 'ere Sid will have us covered.'

Jamie looked at him, wide-eyed.

'You mean . . .'

'Best you don't know, Jamie. And I've never lied to you since you were a lad, but believe me when I say that we're far better off up 'ere than down there,' said Charlie, pointing his thumb back at the road.

Jamie realised then that Charlie had taken Ali's warning far more seriously than he had hitherto. Perhaps that was no bad thing, he thought.

As they approached the barn, Jamie could see Joey's truck parked up beside it. The barn doors were still shut, so he presumed that Joey must be waiting inside in his truck. Either way, there'd now be three of them. His mind worked fast.

'Charlie, we need to warn Joey. He'll have to pretend that he's forgotten the keys to the barn. Can you do that while I buy us some time?'

'Will do.'

'If at all possible, we need to maintain that pretence for as long as we can, because the longer we can slow things down, the greater the chance that the cavalry will come riding over the hill.'

'That'll be handy, aye.'

On reaching the barn, Charlie swung the Land Rover around so that it was facing downhill beside Joey's truck. He left the engine running as they watched the approaching Range Rover, its black windows advertising its menace.

'I'll just get on to Sid and check for an update.'

Charlie reached over to his handset. 'Sid, you receiving?'

'Right enough, Charlie. And I see you and Joey have got company.'

'We have. Do you know how many there are of 'em?'

'Difficult to tell with those windows. I reckon there must be at least two, but I only saw the one wearing a combat mask, and he's now got back into that car.'

'Odds are just about even then,' remarked Charlie.

'I reckon. And it looks like you found Mr Henderson?'

'Sat right here, Sid.'

'Morning, Sid,' said Jamie. 'Glad to have you with us, so to speak.'

'Wouldn't miss it, sir. Just like being back in the sandpit, sir.'

'Hope it don't come to that, Sid,' said Charlie, apprehensively. 'But keep a close eye on this lot. They're up to no good, for sure.'

'Steady on, chaps, let's not make this like the OK Corral,' Jamie said to Charlie.

As he said that, the car came to a halt a few yards from them.

'Well,' he said to Charlie as he began to exit the Land Rover, 'I reckon they've worked out they've been rumbled.'

'I reckon so.'

As Joey got out of his truck, Charlie walked over to him. A few brief words were all it took, and Joey had the full picture. Joey immediately cursed and blamed himself, of course, thinking that if he'd only told the boss when they were last here that there was another box, none of this would be happening.

Just then, they heard Sandy's voice over the handset. Charlie answered it.

'It's Charlie here, sir. Jamie's with me.'

'Okay. Can you tell Jamie that the police are on their way. There's a patrol car coming from the other side of Bere Regis, and another on its way from Wareham. Ten minutes maximum they reckon, but no mention of any armed response team. I'm going to meet them in the lane. And I've asked Jack to block the gate with a tractor.'

'Thanks, Sandy. And one other thing, Sid reckons he has eyes on us. Can you keep in contact with him. He's got his handset, and his mobile.'

'Roger, and out.'

Jamie then followed Charlie's example and stood beside the Land Rover.

'Well, Charlie, let's see what these fellows have to say.'

Jamie watched as first the driver and then another, larger man slid out from behind the black-tinted doors of the Range Rover. Both men were now wearing dark glasses and peaked caps, and neither had shaved recently.

Jamie saw the larger man, whom he took to be the leader, say something to whoever remained in the car. At the same time, he noticed that Charlie had leant into the Land Rover, and had retrieved the handset.

'Excuse me,' said Jamie tersely to the driver, 'but what exactly do you think you're doing trespassing on my property?'

Neither thug displayed any reaction to Jamie's question, other than to continue to walk towards the Land Rover. When they were a few yards short of Jamie, they halted, arms braced by their sides.

'So, if this is your land, that makes you James Henderson, right?' asked the larger of the two thugs, in a combination of East End and Central European accents.

'The very same. And you are?'

The thug waved away the question.

'You can call me Boris,' he said with a forced smile. 'We've come to collect from you the documents you're holding here. They don't belong to you.'

Jamie frowned in response, but said nothing.

The thug then added, with deliberate menace: 'And we'd like to do it without any trouble, if it's all the same to you.'

He emphasised the word 'trouble', pronouncing it as if it was spelt with a 'bull'.

Jamie opted to try the hastily prepared strategy.

'Well now, Boris, there are two problems with your demand …' he began.

'I'm not fucking concerned about your fucking problems,' retorted the thug.

Jamie had expected that. 'Ah, but you see, there're not my problems. They are your problems, and now I come to think of it, there are three of them.'

'Bollocks!'

'Can I suggest that you let me explain before you pass judgment?'

That rather threw the other man, so Jamie continued.

'First, I am not aware that I do possess any documents or that, if there are any, they may not belong to me. Indeed, I do not even know if they exist. Secondly, even if such documents do exist and they are in my possession, I have been served with an order of the High Court. I have a copy in my car, if it helps.'

He pointed down the lane to his car so as to emphasise the point.

'That order,' he continued, 'requires me to take immediate steps to ensure that any such documents, if they exist and are in my possession, are delivered forthwith to a solicitor who has been appointed by the High Court to collect them. Disobedience of that order, or prevention of its execution, either by myself or others – that's you, Boris – carries severe penal sanctions, including my or rather our imprisonment, which is not a prospect that I especially look forward to.' Then he added, for good measure: 'Nor should you, Boris.'

He then gestured to Charlie and Joey.

'Moreover, I have witnesses here whose purpose is to observe and thus testify, if it becomes necessary, that I have complied with the court's order.'

'As I said, bollocks to that,' replied the thug. 'I've come here to collect what don't belong to you, and that's what I'm about to do.'

Jamie had half expected the man to continue in that vein, and so decided to play along with him for a while. 'Yes, so you tell me. Meanwhile, before we come on the our third problem, or rather *your* third problem, my very clear instructions are that we are only to hand over whatever material that might be found – and I stress the word "might" – to the person presenting the correct ID and password. So, do you have those on your person?'

Silence.

'Well, since you appear to have neither on you, I regret that you will have to return to your employers empty-handed.'

Boris waved away that objection.

'Look, I don't give a fuck about any password, or ID. So, you can forget about all that. Just give me the documents – *now*.'

The last word was almost shouted.

But Jamie remained calmly resolute. 'Well, you see, Boris,' he began in a steady voice, 'the fourth problem is your biggest, because it is a logistical one. In short, none of us have the keys to this barn, which is where we think we are supposed to look. So, we were just saying to each other that we'll have to go back to our respective houses to look for them.'

Then, just to complicate matters, he added, 'Come to think of it, Boris, there's a fifth problem. You see, Charlie here and I were just saying that even if we manage to find the keys, which is doubtful, none of us knows what it is we are supposed to be looking for.' He held out his hands, palms up, and gave an apologetic shrug. 'So, I'm sorry that you've had a wasted journey, but at least the weather's been kind, and you've seen something of Dorset.'

Jamie could sense the mood blacken behind the dark glasses, and realised that, despite his more emollient tone, his bluff was about to be called.

The large thug gave him a thin smile, laced with evil. 'Did you think that we would not bring the tools needed to access that barn, or the person who can find what we came for?'

It was Jamie's turn to be thrown by his opponent's words, as Boris nudged his partner in crime, and jerked his head in the direction of the black vehicle parked behind him, its engine still idling.

The second man, his short legs giving him something of a comic waddle on the uneven terrain, made his way to the rear of the car.

Having opened the boot, he proceeded to remove some bolt-cutters and a small chainsaw.

Meanwhile, Boris stepped back towards the car, and gave two hard raps on the bonnet, whereupon the rear passenger door slowly opened.

Jamie and Charlie were obliged to spectate as, after a theatrical pause, another figure emerged, sporting the same cap and dark glasses and walked towards the front of the car, but in a manner that Jamie sensed was rather apprehensive.

'So, which is it to be, Mr James?' Boris continued. 'Either we break into this barn, or you unlock it for us.'

Well, thought Jamie, it was worth a punt. Little else for it now but to try to even the odds by playing the element of surprise.

He lent into the Land Rover and said to Charlie, *sotto voce*, 'Does Sid know what to do if things start to turn ugly? I've got my eyes on those tyres, if you follow my drift.'

Charlie nodded, and spoke softly into the handset to Sid.

Jamie stroked his chin, as if he was contemplating his choices – of which in reality there were few – and held what he took to be his opponent's icy glare behind the impenetrable dark glasses.

At the same time Joey, sensing that his added presence might come in handy, walked up to stand beside the Land Rover.

*

Andrew Sutherland began to draw his submissions to a close.

'So, in summary, my lord, it hardly lies in the mouths of the claimants, having expressly urged this court to deal with their restraining orders as a matter of urgency, to complain that they have only had a brief chance to consider the gist of the case that the defendants have been advised to advance. They are a multibillion-dollar company, with ample resources, and have engaged one of the largest law firms in London. Not that they need all those resources, because it would not have taken the claimants' lawyers very long to explain to their clients that the defendants are asserting in their defence that every word of the article is true, and that even if the documents cited were confidential, there is a strong public interest defence.'

He paused to let the judge make a note.

'With regard to my clients' application, the claimants argue first that the disclosure request is wrong in principle – and I'll say a bit more about that in a moment if I may – but then they object that the request is too extensive in scope. However, we submit that what this boils down to is really only an issue of logistics, which this court is more than capable of sorting, although your lordship will note that the claimants have not vouchsafed to you what is the likely scale of the task.'

'Yes, so I noticed.'

'We then have what I shall describe as the usual bleat from a recalcitrant party that the defendants are on a fishing expedition. In response to that, we submit that a proper defence cannot properly be advanced in the absence of this disclosure, because it goes to the very essence of the allegations that were made by the defendants in *The Daily Chronicle* which gave rise to these proceedings.'

He kept his eye on the judge's pen, allowing him time to note his submissions.

'Now, your lordship will have no doubt observed that, in their evidence, the claimants neither admit nor deny that the material which the defendants have requested is relevant to the issues in dispute. Likewise, their evidence does not even address the issue of admissibility, which I invite this court to record as a concession. So, in short, my lord, if the claimants have declined the opportunity to address those issues, this court is entitled to conclude, and we would urge you to do so, that this material will need to be disclosed at some point in order that this court can ensure that this case is dealt with justly, and in particular so that the defendants are on an equal footing with the claimants.'

He detected a nod from the judge.

'Finally, my lord, the claimants oppose this disclosure application on the ground that their business would be at risk of revealing its trade secrets in public, and thus expose itself to unfair competition from other companies in the same field. Pausing there, my lord, that is surely a matter that the claimants must have considered, and no doubt been advised on, before they instigated these high-profile proceedings.'

He glanced across at Gaitsland, who was trying hard to conceal a grimace.

'But here's the thing, my lord. The claimants tell you in their evidence that the issue of unfair competition will arise in particular with regard to the manner in which they have habitually commissioned and then published their research material in the past. But they leave that tantalising little nugget, dangling from its fragile branch, without telling this court whether their practice was implemented in common with or at variance with other pharmaceutical companies, either currently or in the past.'

The judge finished his note, then remarked, 'And if I am not mistaken, Mr Sutherland, the article by the first defendant alleged that it was the former? In other words, rather like the characters in *Cossi Fan Tutte*, the article asserted that all pharmaceutical companies had followed the same practice for a number of years.'

Andrew politely smiled at the judge's wit.

'Indeed it did, my lord, which is why it is so bizarre that, when given the opportunity to address the point, the claimants' evidence is entirely silent upon it. And their silence is especially acute when one has regard to the fact that one of the central themes of the article was that it alleged that the claimants had *departed* from their normal procurement practice in this instance. Specifically, that is, when they commissioned, or rather "rigged", as the article stated, their research into artificial sweeteners. So, this court was surely entitled to expect the claimants to address that very serious assertion head on.'

The judge briefly inclined his head as he noted Andrew's submission.

'But, my lord, the article went even further. It also exposed what the defendants say was the "deceit" in the report relating to the medium to long-term effects of the types of sweeteners that are widely used in the food industry.'

'Yes, I have already made a note of that.'

'So, given those allegations, and the fact that in their sworn evidence before you when applying for the orders made by this court, the claimants assured you that all those assertions were untrue, it is all the more extraordinary that the claimants' evidence before you now fails to vouchsafe what *was* their "normal procurement practice". That issue is key to this dispute, my lord, and it forms the basis of the defendants' disclosure application. Which is why, my lord, the defendants say that the claimants should not be permitted to advance their case without producing that disclosure.'

The judge considered this for a moment.

'So, if I understand you correctly, Mr Sutherland,' he observed, 'in the coat-tails of your submission lies a suggestion that the claimants must have approached these proceedings in the belief that they would not be required to disclose any material recording their normal procurement process as regards clinical research.'

Andrew saw Tomo give him a satisfied wink.

'Either that, my lord or, having recognised the risk, they dismissed it because they were confident that they could prove the allegations in the article were untrue on other grounds. However, as I have observed, my lord, they have declined to inform the court in their evidence what those other grounds might be.'

The judge nodded. 'Thank you, Mr Sutherland. Let me hear from the claimants on those points.'

*

'So, which is it to be, James?' said Boris, placing a sarcastic accent on the name. 'Do we open it, or will you?'

Jamie gave what he intended to be a nonchalant shrug.

'Well, it's not as if I have a great deal of choice,' he replied, 'but I think it would be preferable if you were to commit an act of criminal damage. Otherwise, the court might think that I went along with your heist.' Then he added, 'Oh, and whilst we're on the subject, I ought to tell you that the police are on their way. We called them a while back. And another thing, if you look behind you, you will notice that your exit out of this field has been blocked.'

Another icy smile from 'Boris,' but his mood had already changed. 'Nice try,' was his cold response.

'No, I mean that. You're trapped. So, even if you get hold of what you came for, you're not going anywhere.'

Boris continued to stare at him, but the third figure turned to look down the hill, only to realise that Jamie was not bluffing. He moved to warn Boris, but was waved away with an impatient gesture from the larger man.

'So, as I said, we don't want any trouble. And first, I'll take your phone, and yours too,' he said looking at Joey, then added, 'And you there,' pointing at Charlie, 'come away from that car.'

Jamie had half expected that, and hoped that his phone was still transmitting this bizarre exchange to the lawyer's PA.

'Give me that,' Boris shouted at Jamie.

Charlie took advantage of the distraction to remove the keys to his car and hide them under the seat, and then lingered by his Land Rover.

Joey was about to follow Jamie, but then hesitated, sensing instinctively that matters were about to take an ugly turn. He was right.

Boris was used to getting his own way, and was not about to be defied – especially after such a long journey.

'I won't ask you again,' he shouted at Jamie, reaching behind his back with his right hand, 'I mean it.'

When Jamie ignored him and instead began to speak into his phone, Boris pulled out a gun, and raised it towards him.

On seeing that, the third man spoke for the first time, directing his words at 'Boris' in a panicked voice: 'No, Olaf, not that,' he said in a fierce hiss. 'You know the boss said that we were not to use any violence!'

'Boris', or rather 'Olaf', seemed not to hear him, but the interruption was enough to allow Joey to place himself between Jamie and the gun.

He opened his mouth to speak, as did Olaf. Neither did so.

Instead, they both flinched as first the front, and then the rear tyres of the Range Rover exploded with a large hiss, followed by distinct reports of rifle shots fired from what was obviously a considerable distance.

Charlie used the distraction to move slowly backwards to open the rear door of his Land Rover, keeping an eye all the time on the gunman.

For a few moments, none of them spoke. Unexpectedly, it was Jamie who broke the silence.

'So, Olaf,' he said, placing a sarcastic emphasis on the name, 'that'll be Sid, I'll wager.' He slipped his mobile phone back into his top pocket. 'He's an ex-SAS sniper, you know,' he added, in his best impression of nonchalance. 'And I should tell you that there's nothing he loves better on a sunny morning than a spot of target practice.'

Olaf continued to point the gun, so Jamie continued, 'And it's only fair to warn you that he does have a strong preference for a bit of vermin control, if you catch my drift.'

Such unnecessary provocation, in the circumstances, was probably not the most prudent course for Jamie to have taken, as evidenced by the snarl and what Jamie suspected was a narrowing of eyes on Olaf's features. But Jamie ploughed on notwithstanding. 'So, I strongly suggest that you put that gun down, unless of course you want to make Sid's day. He tends not to miss, as you've just witnessed.'

He watched Olaf assess his change in fortune, now that the odds had been evened by the presence of a concealed marksman.

'And best of luck using that as your getaway,' he added, nodding at the crippled car. 'You'd not get further than the gate, even if it hadn't been blocked – which as I told you it has, if you'd care to look.'

Olaf again declined the invitation, but continued to point his gun towards Jamie, although to what end now was less than clear. Jamie waited for him to make another threat, but oddly none was forthcoming, at least not from Olaf.

To Jamie's surprise, it was the third man who spoke to him.

'Look, James. This doesn't need to be like this. If you'll just let us have those documents, we can be out of your hair and away.'

Sudden realisation struck Jamie like a hammer. It was him! It was that loathsome snake!

That voice was enough for Jamie. In a flash it brought instant recognition, and with it all that seething anger and hatred that he'd tried so hard to contain. It swelled up within him, causing his fists and his jaw to clench, boiling into a raging fury.

'Why, you fucking little toad,' he began, oblivious to the danger posed by the handgun, advancing on Thompson – for it was indubitably he. 'How dare you come to my home with these thugs to wash your thieving employers' laundry.'

Joey was slow to react, and Jamie was almost past him when he did. He reached out with both arms and grabbed Jamie, but struggled to restrain him.

'No, sir, please,' he entreated, trying to get a firmer grip on Jamie. Jamie ignored him. 'No, it's not safe, sir, and you've already won.'

If he hoped that such reason would prevail, he was much mistaken. Jamie's blood was up, and he was set upon avenging himself.

Joey continued the struggle. 'Whatever it is, sir, it can wait. Please, sir.'

However, such was Jamie's fury and determination to launch himself at Thompson, cursing all the while, that Joey was failing to keep him away from the other man.

'Leave him, Jamie,' cried Charlie in that split second.

But Jamie and Joey's wrestling match had forced them ever closer to the Range Rover and Thompson, who now tried to step behind Olaf.

The tussling pair looked certain to collide with Olaf, who mistook their actions as a precursor to an attack on him.

'Stop,' cried Olaf, cocking his gun, 'go back!'

But the two of them collided into him.

*

As Tomo listened to Gaitsland's now forlorn attempt to move the judge away from the points that Andrew had made so forcefully, Rosalyn tapped him on the shoulder, holding up her phone.

'I need to step outside for a moment,' she whispered. 'I've got a series of missed calls. Some of them look as though they've come from Dorset. And another two from my PA, plus a long text.'

'Should we be worried?' he asked.

'We'll know soon enough.'

With that, after exchanging a few quiet words with Cat, she bowed to the judge, and slipped out of the court.

Tomo continued to make a note of Gaitsland's submissions, pausing only to pass a scribbled message to Andrew. He continued to listen to their opponent for another couple of minutes or so, until he heard one of the doors to the court swing open behind him. He turned to see an ashen-faced Rosalyn walk unsteadily towards him.

He knew instantly that this was bad news. He got up, and helped her into a seat besides Cat, who likewise sensed that something very bad had just happened.

Tomo sat down beside them.

'What is it?' he asked Rosalyn.

Her hands were shaking, but she tried to remain calm and professional.

'Can ... can you ask the judge for a short adjournment,' she said eventually, doing her best to retain her poise.

'But why, Rosalyn?' asked Cat agitatedly, 'What's happened?'

When Rosalyn remained silent, Cat persisted, now genuinely concerned: 'Please, tell me!'

Rosalyn turned towards her, all colour drained from her face.

'I'm so sorry, Cat. I don't know how this could have happened.'

'How what could have happened?'

'Cat, I'm really sorry ...'

'Sure, you just said that, but about what?'

'Cat, I've just been told that there has been an attack – an armed attack – down on the estate in Dorset this morning, and ...'

'And what, Rosalyn? What is it?' demanded Cat, talking her arm.

Rosalyn took a deep breath. 'I just spoke to someone who says he is the gamekeeper on the estate ...'

'Charlie?'

'Yes ... that's him, I think.'

'And what did he say?'

'Cat, he ... he told me that ... that two men have been shot.'

'What?' asked Cat incredulously.

Cat stared at her in disbelief.

'Which men?' she demanded, squeezing her arm

Rosalyn took another deep breath.

'I'm so sorry, Cat, but ... but, he told me that one of them ...'

'Go on, tell me!'

'Cat, one of them is Jamie.'

Cat reeled back in shock.

'No!'

Her scream brought the proceedings to a halt. Gaitsland stopped in mid-sentence, while everyone else in the court turned towards the source of such distress.

The judge looked down at her with a look initially of irritation, and then of concern, as he beheld the young woman rocking on her seat with her face in her hands.

'No! No! No!' she wailed

Tomo got to his feet and walked quickly back beside Andrew, whence he addressed the judge.

'My lord, I apologise for this,' he told the judge, 'but I regret to inform you that my client has just learnt that there has been a shooting incident at the location where my client's disclosure was in the process of being retrieved.' He let the words hang in the air for their full impact. 'In the course of that incident, a close personal friend of my client appears to have been shot, along with, we understand, another person.'

Those words were greeted with silence.

He overheard a muttered 'oh fuck' behind him to his left from the claimants' side.

As he spoke, Rosalyn had taken Cat's arm. 'Cat,' she said softly but urgently, 'the gamekeeper said that the police had just arrived, and the air ambulance is on the way.'

Cat barely heard the words.

She stood and turned to stare at Mary Fellowes. She pointed her finger at her.

'You promised us,' she said, her soft accent hanging in the air.

'You promised us,' she repeated, louder this time. 'You promised us that you would guarantee that no one else would be allowed to know the address if we told.'

She moved closer.

'Cat,' whispered Tomo, 'not now.'

But his words were lost on her.

'Cat,' Tomo repeated, more urgently this time. She ignored him.

Mary put her hands up in protest, 'I swear to you,' she replied, 'I told no one else.'

Cat scoffed at that.

The judge intervened, 'Miss Symonds?' he said calmly.

But Cat was not finished. She continued to point her finger at Mary.

'If Jamie dies,' she retorted at Mary coldly, 'you will be forever cursed!'

It was Mary's turn to reel backwards in her seat as Cat's words struck home, the shock numbing her. Bizarrely, the image that replayed in her mind was that of the hunchback in that opera as he received his fabled curse.

Cat turned and bowed her apology to the judge, then sat down, putting her head in her hands and letting out a muffled, 'Jamie.'

The judge acknowledged the courtesy, but had already decided on the course of action that he intended to follow.

'Gentlemen,' he said, addressing the three counsel who, in accordance with the etiquette at the Bar, immediately rose to their feat.

'I suggest that a short adjournment is in order. It has just gone eleven, so I shall therefore rise for now, but should like to resume promptly at two o'clock this afternoon. I trust that is convenient to everyone?'

The three barristers each nodded in agreement.

'And between you all,' he said looking at counsel, 'I wish to have an agreed report on my desk by 1.45 today telling me, so far as you are collectively able to ascertain, what exactly has occurred that has caused such evident distress to Miss Symonds. And, if you cannot agree on a single joint report, then I shall expect to have separate reports from the parties by that appointed time, together with an agreed list of points on which you are agreed, and those in dispute. Is that clear?'

All three counsel nodded in confirmation.

'Good. Two o'clock then,' said the judge, rising from his seat.

'All rise,' declared the usher.

*

'Sid, you receiving?' said Charlie into his handset, not taking his eyes off the two thugs in front of him.

'Loud and clear, Charlie.'

'Right, if any of these 'ere "gentlemen" tries to make a move, you be sure to take them down. Meantimes, I'm going to count to three, and if the two fellows holding pistols have not thrown them onto the ground, then I want you to take them out. You got that?'

'Loud and clear again.'

Charlie looked at each of the men in turn, before saying, 'Right, you heard me. I am going to count to three, nice and slow like, so that no one's in any doubt. I want those guns chucked onto the ground.'

He let his words sink in for a full two seconds.

'If you're still holding them when I get to three, Sid will drop you.'

Again, another short pause.

'You get that, Sid?'

'Clear as a bell.'

Charlie looked at the three men opposite him. 'Right then. One ... Two ...'

The second thug looked nervously at Olaf, whose hard features had lost their restrained menace, and who now glanced back uncertainly. Without further thought, first one and then both weapons were thrown towards Charlie, and landed a few feet in front of him.

'That was the first sensible thing that you gentlemen have done.'

Charlie next spoke into his handset again.

'Sid, you tell the captain that we need the air ambulance here five minutes back. And ask him to call Weymouth Coastguard to send their chopper as well if it's still there. And tell me when you've done that.'

After several seconds, Sid's voice gave the required confirmation, then added, 'Don't you worry about those two, Charlie. I've still got them in my sights. You just see to Joey and the gaffer. You've got to stop the bleeding. Get those two fellows to give you their shirts so you can use them as bandages.'

'Good thinking, Sid. Right, gentlemen, you heard that. I'd be obliged if you would both give me your shirts.'

They both stared at him blankly.

'You heard. Take your bloody shirts off now, and tear them into strips for bandages. If you let Mr Henderson and Joey here die, then you'll be facing a murder charge as well as whatever else is coming your way.'

This time, there was no hesitation. Under Charlie's watchful eye, their jackets were removed, followed by their shirts, Meanwhile, down by the gates, the first police car had arrived. Charlie could see that he had stepped out of his vehicle to speak with Jack, whom he assumed must have seen Jamie and Joey fall.

'Sid, can you get a message to Jack to say that the two with the pistols have surrendered them, so it's safe for the police to come up here. And ask him to check that the helicopter is on its way.'

Then he added, 'But don't say a word about your tele.'

After a moment, Sid told him that his message had been delivered.

Charlie heard the tractor's engine start, and glanced down the hill briefly to see it roll back from the gateway to afford access for the police car. Another glance saw the car driving up towards them. He assumed that the officer was calling his station, no doubt reporting the incident and calling for backup.

He waited until the vehicle had stopped a few yards short of the others, and had heard a door open, not taking his eyes off the two in front of him.

'I'm making a citizen's arrest,' he shouted by way of an improvised introduction to the policeman.

Charlie glanced briefly across and recognised Brinley Watkins, who was one of the regular beat constables from Dorchester. He recalled that the two of them had spoken together after the recent briefing on land security.

'These fellows come 'ere, armed, to steel whatever Jamie was ordered by the court to give to that there judge up in town. And the fellow in the middle there has just shot my Jamie and young Joey 'ere. They're in a bad way just now, and could do with a doctor right enough and quick, like.'

The constable assessed the situation, then looked at Charlie, noting that he was holding a handset. 'It's Mr Poore, sir, if I'm not mistaken. I believe we've met. Now sir, I've heard mention of some weapons?'

Charlie pointed to the ground in front of him. 'Them's been sorted. Have you called an ambulance, Brinley?'

Just them, Sid's voice came over the speakers. 'Charlie, Jack has just flagged down one of the GPs from Puddletown who was passing. Talk about a stroke of luck! She's coming up the lane to you now.'

'Thanks Sid. Glad to hear someone's brain is working. Brinley. You need to put some cuffs on the one in the middle here. He's the one that did the shooting.'

Another siren sounded in the distance, becoming louder by the second. The police officer hesitated.

'Brinley, that one's the danger. Do it now, lad.'

At that, the officer walked briskly behind the big man, surprised that he did not offer any resistance, and applied handcuffs against his back.

'Thank you, Brinley,' said Charlie.

Shortly thereafter, a modern-looking Subaru pulled up beside the police car. A concerned looking woman stepped out of the vehicle, and retrieved what Charlie presumed was her medical bag from the rear seat before walking briskly to join their group.

'Thank the Lord, Doctor. Now, Jamie and Joey 'ere were both shot with a single shot. If you need bandages, might I suggest that you use the shirts that these two gentlemen have just kindly donated.'

Then he turned to Brinley: 'Look up, Brinley. Those two pistols on the ground there'll be evidence. But take care, the safety's not on, so them's live.'

The doctor knelt beside the two prone figures.

To Charlie's surprise and relief, Jamie spoke, albeit in gasps.

'Help ... Joey ... first. He ... took ... ahh ... the slug ... first.'

Chapter 33

The three of them had stopped in one of the many corridors in that judicial labyrinth. Tomo had come to stand in front of Cat.

'Cat, please. Just listen to Rosalyn, yes? Please, just let her speak.'

Such was the cauldron of emotions tearing within her, that it was hardly surprising that patience and reason were not foremost in her conscious thoughts.

'There's a bench just here, Cat,' suggested Rosalyn. 'Let's just take stock before we rush into any confrontation with the other side.'

'Take stock!' Cat almost screamed. 'A man that I deceived not once, but twice has now been deceived by me again! That's how he'll see it. If he lives, that is! How in fuck's sake am I supposed to take stock of that?!'

Rosalyn took hold of her hand, resisting Cat's attempt to withdraw it.

'Cat. Can we start from the fact, the absolute, truthful fact that nothing was leaked by any of us or by my office?'

When Cat glared past her, Rosalyn persisted.

'Cat, can we take that as a given?'

'Sure, you go ahead and do that. But just how the fuck do you propose to prove that those bastards did this?'

Rosalyn again prevented Cat from removing her arm. 'Cat, please listen to me. This is important, because I'm going to answer your question if you just let me explain.'

'She's right, Cat. You need to listen to her,' said Tomo.

Cat looked at them both in turn. Her heart was still pounding, and such was her fury that it took a moment for his words to sink in.

'Please, Cat,' urged Rosalyn.

Relaxing a fraction, Cat merely nodded.

'Thank you,' continued Rosalyn. 'So, in a few minutes, Cat, we're going to hear a recording of what just happened down on Jamie's estate. And I'm going to need to you concentrate, really, really hard, and to listen to a voice of a man that Jenny, that's my office PA, heard speaking earlier to one of the men involved. She thinks that you might recognise it.'

'What recording?'

'So, I'll explain,' continued Rosalyn, now letting go of Cat's hand. 'Jamie had called my office when the incident first began. He spoke to Jenny ...'

'Sorry, Jenny?' asked Cat not quite keeping track.

'She's my PA back at the office,' repeated Rosalyn.

'Oh yeah, sorry. You just said that.'

'Don't apologise, Cat, you're in shock,' Rosalyn reassured her. 'I should apologise for going too fast. I'll slow down.'

Cat could merely nod her acquiescence.

'So,' continued Rosalyn now helping Cat to sit down, 'when Jamie rang my office, he spoke to my PA. He warned her that some uninvited visitors had made an appearance at – well, it sounded as though they were outside somewhere. What's important is that he told Jenny to record all that she that was going on, which he was transmitting on his mobile phone this morning. He also told her to call the police.'

Speechless for a moment, Cat looked at Rosalyn in amazement.

'That's right, Cat. We've got it all on tape. Which means that, at the right time, we can play the tape to the judge.'

It took a while for this new intelligence to sink in.

'So, who's on the tape?'

'That,' replied Rosalyn, making as if to rise to her feet, 'is what Tomo and I are hoping that you can tell us – once you've had a glass of water, and some of your arnica – isn't that the remedy for shock?'

Cat nodded, and began looking in her bag.

'But I'll tell you why I believe it to be important, Cat,' Rosalyn continued.

'Okay. Go on.'

'Well, Jenny says that from what she heard, Jamie appeared to recognise the voice of a man, and that's what caused him to lose control.'

Cat looked at Tomo, and then back at Rosalyn.

'What do you mean, lose control?'

'Apparently it led to some sort of struggle, and what she assumes must have led to a gun being discharged.'

Cat looked at her in stunned silence for a few seconds.

Then realisation struck. She shook her head slowly, before saying to both of them, 'There's only one man who could have made Jamie lose control. I think I can be pretty sure who the voice belongs to.'

With that, Cat rose to leave with Rosalyn and Tomo, and together they began the short journey back to Tomo's chambers across the Strand.

Suddenly Cat stopped.

'No, wait. I can't. I've got to tell Ali about Jamie. She can't hear this from the police, or worse still on the news.'

This time Tomo took her arm.

'You can do both, Cat. We have good wi-fi in my chambers, and the guys on the ground down there will be able to tell us where they are taking Jamie. Ali will need to know that, as will you. And the tape should take less than ten minutes to play.'

'Tom's right, Cat,' agreed Rosalyn. 'And the sooner we start, then the sooner you'll be on your way to speak to your friend.'

When Cat still hesitated, Tomo said, 'Please Cat. There're both as important as each other.'

Finally, Cat relented, and they continued towards Tomo's chambers.

*

Mary Fellowes had been unable to rise. Instead, she remained seated, her leg muscles seemingly paralysed as she digested the full import of what had just transpired in court. That an innocent person's life – no, two innocent persons' lives – should have been put at risk as a result of this litigation was unthinkable to her. She had vowed never to allow that to happen on her watch after that terrible experience earlier in her career.

And yet, if what she had just heard was correct, it just had. And her firm – possibly even she herself – was somehow mixed up in it all.

But how could it have happened, she asked herself. Surely the security breach could not have occurred at her end.

She tried to marshal the few facts of which she was certain. The only people who knew of the location for the collection on their side were herself, Tim, and the two counsel who were packing up their papers in front of her. All of them were professionals.

She would vouch for all of them, and none of them – including herself – would ever break their oaths; nor had they anything to gain from breaching their undertakings to the court. Rather, they had everything to lose. But then, even as she had begun to posit in her mind who could possibly stand to gain from such a violent interruption of the proper legal process, the horrible, blindingly obvious, answer screamed at her.

The only people who would want to prevent Cat Symonds from complying with the court's order were her own clients. No one else.

And she knew then that the case was lost.

But first, she had to find out how her clients had become privy to the knowledge of where the documents were being collected. She took a deep breath, and began to struggle to her feet, and was aided in so doing by her assistant, Tim.

Gaitsland caught her eye. 'I think we need to speak, Mary,' he said gravely, 'but not here.'

She tried to reply in the affirmative, but her facial muscles were not responding to any command from her brain. She looked to Tim, who nodded in the direction of the doors, and began to replace her papers in the cases beside her.

A glance showed that Miss Symonds and her lawyers had already left the court.

*

Tomo poured a hot mug of fresh ginger tea for Cat while Rosalyn synchronised her phone with the Bose player in the meeting room at Tomo's chambers. The homeopathic remedy had calmed the initial effects of her shock, yet she cradled the mug in two hands as Rosalyn engaged the recording. It kicked in as Tomo was speaking to Jenny, and they listened in silence as if entranced by an audio thriller.

The exchange between Jamie and a man with the Eastern European accent, whom they assumed to be one of the attackers, was clearly audible. As it moved inexorably towards what they all expected to be its denouement, they were almost taken by surprise when the third voice intervened.

'Look, James. This doesn't need to be like this. If you'll just let us have those documents, we can be out of your hair and away.'

Cat froze. 'Stop,' she said quickly. 'Stop it there and rewind.'

Rosalyn duly obliged. They all listened even more carefully to the replay. Rosalyn paused the recording, and she and Tomo looked inquisitively at Cat. But she stared at the Bose player incredulously.

'Cat?' prompted Tomo after a pause. When she failed to respond, he tried again. 'Cat, do you recognise that voice?'

This time Tomo touched her hand gently, whereupon she looked up at his face. She nodded.

'It's him,' she said softly.

'Who, Cat?' said Rosalyn. 'You need to tell us.'

In the ensuing silence, Tomo squeezed her hand again.

'Thompson. Yes, it's Thompson,' said Cat softly. 'But, I don't understand ...' she began, but her voice trailed off.

'How he got to be there, you mean,' Rosalyn suggested.

Cat took a while before nodding at her.

'Yes, how did he come to know where, on the whole of that big estate, that box was going to be collected by Jamie and his helpers?'

Tomo and Rosalyn looked knowingly at each other. Tomo said what they were all thinking.

'So, that is question number one. How did he find out about the location of the exchange? And that's very likely to be the first question that the judge will want answered, because find out they clearly did.'

'Exactly,' Rosalyn agreed. 'And if the leak didn't come from this end, which it most certainly did not, then it can only have come from their end.'

'Agreed. But that leads on to question number two, which is where matters will become, how shall I put it, delicate for us.'

Rosalyn was the first to follow his thinking. 'Ah, I get it. You're thinking that the judge will next ask how Jamie knew that it had been Thompson who addressed those words to him.'

'I am indeed.'

'As did I. And we know that the logical answer will be that Jamie must have recognised the voice from ... from the stuff that Thompson sent him. But we're agreed that we don't want to introduce those details into these proceedings under these circumstances.'

'Quite so. Which means that we'll have to give that question careful thought before we formulate our response.'

They fell silent for a moment. But then Tomo remembered what he'd promised Cat.

'Right. Let's get your PA on to Dorset Police and find out where they've taken Jamie. Cat, you get over to his sister's office – she'll need to hear the news from you in person. You can't do this over the phone.'

Cat took a large gulp from her cup, and then began to ready herself.

'Next, I'll call Andrew's chambers, and tell him about the recording – which, by the way Rosalyn, we'll need to tell the police about. Can you ask your PA to make digital copies of it and then send one over to Dorset Police. She needs to tell them that they can collect the original from your offices any time today. And ask her to send another copy to me on my chambers email. I can then forward the email to Andrew. Meanwhile, can you arrange for a copy to be sent to the paper's solicitors and another copy directly to Ken Baxter? He'll want to follow this story himself.'

'Will do. What about Gaitsland and the claimants' solicitors?' asked Rosalyn.

Tomo thought for a few seconds. 'No, let's keep them in suspense until we're ready to send them our proposed note to the judge – which we can be pretty sure they will not want to agree with for the purposes of this afternoon's hearing. Anyway, I'd better get on with the draft while you sort out the logistical stuff.'

Cat began to pack her bags.

'Just a minute, Cat,' said Rosalyn. 'When you're on your travels, can you get a message to Ken Baxter at *The Chronicle* to say that you've identified Thompson's voice on the recording of what went on in Dorset. He's bound to have contacts in the police who can provide off the record confirmation that they've arrested him at the crime scene along with the two others who were involved.'

'That's smart thinking,' agreed Tom. 'And the sooner you tell him, Cat, the more chance we shall have of being able to tell the judge. He won't accept the fact on the basis of our say-so alone, but it will provide our side with some very helpful prejudice for what I have in mind.'

'Aha,' said Rosalyn, 'I sense a cunning plan?'

'Actually, I think it's rather an obvious plan. If Ken can get a story out in his rag that one of the claimants' directors was involved in the attempt to prevent Cat from complying with the court's orders, that may force the cops' hand into confirming that publicly. And, if they do, then that would tee up a joint application by all the respondents for the orders to be set aside on the basis that the claimants were in breach of them, and therefore no longer have clean hands – which is a basic requirement of a claimant seeking to engage the court's equitable powers.'

He turned and gave Cat a hug, and a brief kiss, before reaching into his pocket for a handful of notes.

'Here, take this for the cabs and train fares. God's speed to you.'

Chapter 34

Shortly before the hearing in London was due to resume that same afternoon, following the arrests of Thompson and his accomplices, crime scene investigators and firearms officers attached to Dorset Police completed their search of the barn and the crippled Range Rover.

Ironically, the keys to the padlocks on the barn had travelled in Joey's pocket by air ambulance to the hospital. As a result, the investigators had little alternative other than to use industrial bolt-cutters in order to gain access to the barn before the CSI team could conduct their search inside.

Amongst the exhibits that had been removed from the barn was a hay-covered box of documents. The senior investigating officer had been alerted to the likely presence of this exhibit by Charlie initially, and subsequently by Rosalyn. She had managed to speak to him, and had explained its importance. At the same time, she had drawn his attention to the fact that it was possible, likely even, that a judge in the High Court would cause a formal request to be made later that day to his chief constable that copies of any documents found in such an exhibit should be made available, as soon as was reasonably convenient, to Peter Langar, whose status she had explained.

Once the box had been photographed *in situ*, the forensic team confirmed that it was unsealed, and having opened it, that it contained numerous documents. That came as no surprise to him in light of Rosalyn's call.

'There's a fair few in here, guv,' reported the specialist.

'That's to be expected, from what I've read,' said Detective Chief Inspector Harry Brymer, 'but thank you for that intelligence. Can you get these back to your offices and have each document finger-printed and then scanned quick as you can and emailed over to me? I'll authorise the overtime with the chief super.'

'Right you are, guv,' she replied, replacing the lid on the box.

'And I'll need a witness statement from you recording the chain of possession from here to your offices, plus records of the scanning process.'

'Already on it, guv,' she said, carrying the box off towards their waiting van.

Then another thought occurred to him. He turned to his sergeant. 'Dave, are the armed response guys still here?'

'Aye boss, just packing up now.'

'Right, well I want that van escorted back to the forensics unit, and an armed guard placed on the unit until further notice. If these people have tried to grab this stuff once, there's no saying they won't try again.'

'Right, guv. On it.'

'And have armed guards placed around those two victims. If, God forbid, either of them dies, then we'll have a right circus here.'

'On it, guv.'

The DCI looked at his notebook. 'And another thing, Dave. Did you or any of the CSI team see a mobile phone on the ground when they swept the area?'

'Not that I'm aware, guv, but I'll check right away.'

'I'd be grateful, thanks. So, if it's not here, it must still be with Mr Henderson. According to the solicitor who called me earlier, he was using it to transmit a recording of the events that took place here. Can you get one of our lads to bag up his belongings and take them to the forensics lab? And let me know sharpish if the phone is amongst them.'

'Will do, guv,' replied the sergeant, then added before his DCI spoke again, 'and yes, I'll make sure that they all wear gloves, and provide us with signed witness statements by close, reporting on the procedure.'

That earned him an appreciative nod from his boss, who looked at his notebook again before he next spoke.

'Any word as to when we can speak to ... let me see ... Mr Poore?'

'The keeper, aye guv. That's him. No, he's still with the doctor. Took a nasty turn when they placed his boss in the air ambulance, apparently. I reckon the odds are that she'll want him taken to Dorchester General for the usual tests, so it could be a fair while before we're allowed to interview him.'

'Hmm, thought you'd say that. I want to ask him what happened to the tyres on that Range Rover. If I was a betting man, which as you know I'm not, I'd put odds on those not going flat all by themselves.'

'Reckon so, guv.'

The DCI took one last look around the scene.

'Right, I reckon that's all we can do here. Let's get down to the station and make a start on those fellows.'

*

'All rise,' announced the usher.

The assembled lawyers resumed their seats.

'My thanks to you all for your helpful notes within the last hour. You may take it that I have read and digested their contents. Are there any amendments or observations that any party wishes me to record?'

Heads were shaken by those that mattered.

'Very well. So, this court has been informed – albeit that such information has yet to be confirmed by the relevant authorities – that at least two men are believed to have received gunshot wounds at a location in South Dorset where Ms Symonds, who is the third respondent ...'

He paused to look at the claimants.

'Mr Gaitsland, she is still a respondent rather than a defendant, I take it?'

'Yes, m'lord. The claim form has not yet been formally issued or served.'

'Thank you, that is duly noted for the record. I shall therefore refer to your clients as "the intended claimants". So, to resume, the shooting or shootings occurred in circumstances, which I shall describe in a moment, where Miss Symonds, who is the third respondent to these *intended* proceedings against her – he laid particular emphasis on the first word – had caused certain steps to be put in place in order to enable her to comply with an order made by this court last week. Specifically, I am told that Miss Symonds was seeking to retrieve or cause to be retrieved some unspecified documents and other material that she had reasonable cause to believe were or had been the property, confidential or otherwise, of the *intended* claimants,' again he laid heavy emphasis on that phrase. 'That much is common ground.'

The judge checked his note.

'The two wounded men have been identified. The first of them is believed by the respondents to be someone with whom some months ago Miss Symonds had a previous romantic connection. As yet, no particulars have been supplied in that respect whilst attempts are made by the authorities to notify the victim's family. The second is believed to be a farm worker on the first victim's estate. Both of these men are currently believed to be either at or in transit to one of the major trauma hospitals in the south west. Given that the incident occurred in Dorset, I am advised that the victims' likely destination will be Southmead Hospital near Bristol. Initial reports from the scene suggested that the conditions of both men are critical.'

This time he looked across at Andrew and Tomo.

'In consequence of these matters, with the consent of all counsel, I have excused Miss Symonds from further attendance before me at this hearing.' The judge allowed himself a theatrical pause. 'I am told by the respondents that these two men, assisted by a gamekeeper on the first victim's estate, which is in South Dorset, were endeavouring to retrieve the material, to which I have just referred, that may or may not belong to the *intended* claimants. Again, for the record, I am told on behalf of Miss Symonds that this was material that she believed or was advised should properly be produced to the independent solicitor who has been and is charged with supervising the enforcement of the orders which this court made last week. I should add that it was those orders that were the subject of the hearing before me this morning, which hearing I felt obliged to adjourn on account of the developments to which I have just referred.'

Another pause, as he glared briefly at Gaitsland.

'It is alleged by the respondents that, whilst that process was ongoing, the two victims and the gamekeeper were interrupted by initially two other men, who were subsequently joined by a third man. None of these men have yet been formally identified by the relevant authorities. However, the third man is believed by the respondents to be or to have been a main board director of the *intended* claimants. Thereafter, in circumstances which are currently being investigated by South Dorset Police, a bullet was fired from a weapon that had been brought to the scene. It is alleged by the respondents that this bullet caused the two victims to be critically wounded.'

The judge took a sip of water.

'At the scene, a number of men are believed to have been arrested. These include the man who is alleged by all three respondents to be a director of the *intended* claimants. How he and his accomplices, if such they were – and that is a matter for trial – had come to be there will be the subject of the police investigation that has been commenced. That issue will also be investigated in detail by this court, irrespective of the outcome of these *intended* proceedings. Either way, I am assured that this court can be confident that it will be apprised of all the relevant facts as and when they emerge, which I am informed by the first respondent is likely to be tomorrow morning.'

Another dramatic pause.

'Does any party wish to correct my summary?'

Andrew Sutherland was first to stand. 'M'lord, no.'

Tomo rose and concurred, but added, 'My lord, may I add just one point that was brought to my attention just before this hearing resumed?'

'Of course, Mr Butler.'

'My lord, we had hoped that we – the respondents, that is – would be in a position to furnish the court with details of what was contained within the material that was in the course of being retrieved on behalf of Miss Symonds in the circumstances that you have just described. However, I have now been informed that the police are treating that very material as forming part of a crime scene. Consequently, unless and until those instructing me and the supervising solicitor can reach an accommodation with the chief investigating officer or his superintendent, Miss Symonds will not be in a position to continue to comply with this court's orders as regards such material.'

The judge finished taking a note of Tomo's observation.

'Duly noted for the record, Mr Butler, although my experience in this kind of case is that Miss Symonds' temporary incapacity – and let us hope it is only temporary – is likely to prove the least of our problems.'

Tomo bowed and turned to consult Rosalyn.

'Before you sit down, Mr Butler, do those instructing you believe that a direction from this court on the point might be of assistance?'

'Very much so, my lord.'

'Thank you. That is duly noted. No doubt you will remind me if I overlook the point when giving the court's further directions.'

Tomo bowed, and this time sat down.

The judge turned to look at Gaitsland.

'Anything to add on behalf of the *intended* claimants?'

Gaitsland got to his feet with barely disguised reluctance, and looked behind him one last time as if to seek inspiration.

When none was forthcoming, he said, 'No, m'lord.'

'That is most helpful, and it is so recorded. Very well. So, given that these shootings and the attempt by the third respondent to comply with the orders of this court appear to me to be connected, if not intimately so, this court has no alternative other than to ask itself – and the point has already been raised by the respondents in their joint submission to me – a difficult question. Leaving aside for the moment the issue of motive and intent, that question is whether, if the *intended* claimants were in any way responsible for today's events, the court should take due cognisance of that fact in deciding whether or not to maintain the interim orders that it had made in favour of the *intended* claimants.'

He looked sternly at Gaitsland before resuming.

'Whilst recognising that an investigation into today's events has only just been instigated by Dorset Police, the respondents assert that it would be unjust if they were to remain bound by the terms of this court's orders if in fact the intended claimants had themselves sought to frustrate the respondents' compliance with those orders. *Prima facie*, that would seem to me to a reasonable objection for the respondents to take having regard to the rules of equity by which this court and the parties are bound. However, I have yet to hear argument on the point.'

He paused again to look at both teams of counsel.

'My initial view is that this is a genuinely triable matter that cannot be decided on paper. That being the case, then subject to hearing counsel, I shall need to give directions for the hearing of the respondent's submission before any of the substantive issues in these intended – and I stress the word *intended* – proceedings can properly be heard.'

He paused again, looking principally at Gaitsland, and then only briefly at Tomo and Andrew Sutherland. None of them demurred.

'Very well. So, I take it that all the parties and the court are all on the same page, for now at least.'

If there had been a time to speak, this was it. But neither Gaitsland nor Mary considered that any objection at this stage was prudent.

'Very well,' said the judge, maintaining his severe tone. 'Let us hope that such a *status quo* continues.'

There being no dissent from that remark, he continued, 'So, given this present state of concord, I shall invite first the respondents to articulate their submission and then ask the – intended – claimants to respond. As to that, Mr Gaitsland, should I assume that are you not yet in a position to do so today, and that you require more time in which to prepare your response?'

Gaitsland shot to his feet with uncharacteristic alacrity. 'My lord, I regret that we shall need further time, not least to assemble our own evidence in answer to the respondents application.'

'As I suspected. Very well, gentlemen. Given that it is now getting late on a Friday afternoon, I shall adjourn the respondents' application until ten-thirty on Monday morning. However, I should make it clear that I shall be less than sympathetic to any further request to adjourn the hearing in the absence of compelling evidence.'

He looked briefly at Andrew and Tomo.

'Apologies, gentlemen, did you wish to add anything?'

They had both expected this development, but nevertheless effected to consult with their respective solicitors, before Andrew rose.

'Nothing further to add at this stage, my lord.'

The judge nodded. 'Very well, then I shall make the following directions for the hearing on Monday morning. And fear not, Mr Butler, I am alert to your point. So, first ...'

*

Once she had given herself a chance to recover from the shock of the morning's interrupted proceedings, Mary Fellows had tried to elicit instructions from her clients, but to no avail. Her colleagues had fared no better with their counterparts further down the clients' hierarchy.

This only compounded her worst fears.

She and her team had then spent several fruitless hours following that afternoon's hearing trying to set up either a teleconference or a video meeting, but again without success. She had even tried McBride's direct line and his mobile. Both her calls had gone through to voicemail.

Her assistant Tim had informed her that he had only had limited success, in that he had been able to speak with Ted, but only to find that he had been frozen out of the loop so far as matters legal, logistical and strategic were concerned. Ted had communicated to Tim both his outright frustration and his increasing irritation, and regretted that he was in no position to provide any helpful instructions.

And that had been the sum total of her team's communications with the clients. She had to assume that this was deliberate on their part.

However, given the importance of Monday's hearing, her clients' conduct was outrageous. She could not recall any situation in her career in which, following such a dramatic turn of events in a case, her clients had persistently thwarted her team's efforts to make contact within what had hitherto been the established lines of communication between them.

She was left with no alternative other than to obtain confirmation from her counsel that he and his junior both agreed with her conclusion that the clients' only option was to abandon the proceedings – or the 'intended' proceedings as the judge had reminded them on numerous occasions. She would have preferred to have met with counsel that evening, but had thought better of it for two reasons. First, her firm's public relations manager had called to tell her that Dorset Police had arranged to make a statement to the media over the weekend. Secondly, given the hour – it was already gone 6.30 – she and her team were all exhausted, both mentally and physically.

Therefore, the best that she had been able to manage was to arrange a videoconference with counsel on Sunday. Meanwhile, she intended to give the clients a pretty fierce insight into her state of mind.

Chapter 35

The relatives' and friends' suite, such as it is, that is annexed to the A&E wing within Southmead Hospital on the outskirts of Bristol was no doubt intended to convey an atmosphere of intimacy and privacy, insofar as any institutional and functional building can seek to achieve that. However, no designer can assuage the trauma of the intended visitors whose shock-induced vigil such a facility must afford. Each of them awaits news of a loved-one who was currently undergoing emergency surgery in the theatres several floors below them or who had been taken to the Intensive Care Unit housed beyond the double doors at the far end of that suite.

Few of the members of the disparate families, some with and some without their friends, who are assembled here in their various states of spontaneous attire, can have anticipated their presence here today. But here they sit, stand, or shuffle nervously, each of them casting nervous glances from time to time at the double doors.

Cat had been dreading her encounter with Ali, but she knew that she had to be the one who told Ali. Cat had realised that her relationship with Ali would not survive this final betrayal. In the event, however, Ali had been surprisingly understanding, sympathetic even, and rather than display a flurry of emotions she had reverted to her head girl mode which seemed to come so naturally to her.

So, following a series of phone calls and emails to Ali's colleagues at her workplace, she and Cat had caught the mid-afternoon train from Paddington to Bristol Parkway. A short taxi ride had brought them to the hospital.

Neither of them had been expecting the level of security in evidence, including two armed police officers at the entrance to the ICU.

When they had arrived at the suite, all that Ali had been told as Jamie's next-of-kin was that he had been operated on, that the surgeons had successfully removed the bullet, and that he was able to receive post-operative treatment. She had subsequently been told that he was currently in a critical condition and under close medical supervision. She had not been given any indication, despite her and Cat's earlier requests, as to when she might be able to see him.

Subsequent enquiry had revealed that he had been placed into an induced coma, such that he was likely to remain unconscious for 'a few hours yet,' and very likely until the next morning 'at the earliest'.

That intelligence probably made their presence here at this late hour somewhat futile, yet neither of them had wanted to leave the hospital suite. And so, what had been left of the afternoon had slipped into late evening and beyond.

Now, as the first hint of dawn advertised itself in what had hitherto been a clear night sky outside, they continued to wait.

Eventually, Ali had fallen asleep against Cat's shoulder.

Some hours earlier, Cat had become aware of the presence of what she assumed must be the family of the other victim. They had asked the same distraught questions as had she and Ali, but evidently had received the same answers: not exactly evasive, but there was only so much assurance to be gained from being told that the medics were doing all they could in order to preserve life.

'What else could they say?' thought Cat. They would be damned if they raised false hopes only to see them dashed.

Her phone had run out of juice some hours earlier, as had Ali's, and neither of them had brought a charger with them, so there was no way to contact Tomo and at least talk to him to pass the time. There was no news that she could pass on to him in any event.

And so it was that their combined vigil had continued throughout the night, and into the following day.

Cat had just begun to doze off again when the double doors to the ICU were pushed open by a man in a blue gown that she had come to recognise as that of a surgeon. He carried a pad, and was accompanied by one of the nurses that Cat had spoken to earlier that afternoon.

Cat held her breath. The surgeon and the nurse consulted each other briefly, before the taller man appeared to walk towards Cat and Ali.

Even if she had been able to move without waking Ali, her legs would not have obeyed any command that her terrified brain might have attempted to issue.

Chapter 36

Shortly after 10.30 on Sunday morning, a group of journalists huddled into a room used by Dorset Police in Bournemouth for press statements and releases. Several of them were accompanied by camera crews linked to live transmissions via their respective TV and online channels. The room was filled with the usual muffled cacophony as those attending spoke into their handsets in preparation for the imminent statement.

After a few minutes, a hushed silence descended as a number of police officers, some in uniform, entered the room and sat themselves down behind a table on a raised platform. One of the uniformed officers, obviously the most senior judging by his dress, introduced a plain-clothed detective at his side as Detective Chief Inspector Harry Brymer. He then proceeded to inform those present that the DCI was the senior investigating officer in charge of their ongoing enquiries.

The DCI duly tapped on the microphone in front of him, as he had no doubt done on numerous previous occasions, to bring the assembled journalists to order.

'Good morning, ladies and gentlemen. Thank you for your patience. I intend to provide you with a short statement today in order to clarify certain facts concerning an incident in South Dorset on Friday morning. Given that I and my officers are in the early stages of our investigation, and for other reasons that I shall explain in a moment, I do not intend to take any questions at this time. I shall, however, make a brief statement.'

He opened some sheets of paper which he had placed on the table in front of him.

'On Friday morning, officers stationed in Dorchester were called to a rural location in South Dorset following reports that an incident was in the course of developing there. Upon arrival, the officers found two men on the ground who appeared to have received gunshot wounds, and were being attended to by a third man pending the arrival of an air ambulance.

'Also at the scene were three other men who had arrived in a black Range Rover, the details of which I shall provide to you shortly. All three men were arrested at the scene. Two of these men, who speak with Eastern European accents, have so far refused to give their names. However, the third man, who speaks with a clear English accent, has been identified as Mr Charles Thompson. He is believed to be a director of a large pharmaceutical company with headquarters in London. His connection to this case is and will be the subject of further detailed enquiries by my officers as a matter of priority.

'At the scene, two firearms were discovered. They have been transferred to the forensic laboratory in Bournemouth for ballistic and fingerprint checks. However, the officers who initially attended the crime scene have reason to believe that one of these weapons had been responsible for the wounding of the two victims earlier that morning.

'Subsequently, forensic crime scene investigators attached to Dorset Police removed certain evidence from a building that my officers had reason to believe formed part of the crime scene. That evidence was also sent to the forensic laboratory in Bournemouth. However, it seems likely that this material is connected to civil proceedings that were recently commenced in the High Court by the pharmaceutical company of which Mr Thompson is a director. This evidence will also form part of our ongoing investigation.

'The two victims wounded were both treated at the crime scene by a local doctor who happened to be passing, later assisted by paramedics. They were flown by air ambulance to Southmead Hospital outside Bristol. Both were immediately treated by surgeons skilled in the treatment of gunshot trauma, and then moved to the Intensive Care Unit at that hospital, where they were then placed into an induced coma in order to aid their recovery.

'However, I very much regret to report that, at approximately five o'clock this morning, one of the victims was pronounced dead by the medical team at Southmead. His details will not be released until his family and relatives have been informed, and I ask all journalists to respect their privacy. Accordingly, given this development, this case is now being treated by Dorset Police as a murder investigation.'

A buzz of interest filled the room, and a number of journalists made for the exits clutching their mobile phones.

'A further announcement will be made once I and my officers attached to Dorset Police are in a position to do so. My colleagues will hand out details of the vehicle in which the three arrested men had arrived at the crime scene. If anyone has any information concerning the ownership of this vehicle, will they please contact Dorset Police as a matter of urgency. That is all for now. Thank you.'

As the police team rose and began to leave, a barrage of questions followed them out of the room.

*

Mary Fellowes sat before her laptop in her London home. She had been told by one of her team that Dorset Police were due to release the statement at about that time, and that it would be transmitted live.

Mary barely registered the commotion that pursued the departing officers as they left the room. Instead, having pressed the pause button on her laptop, she simply stared at it in a state of stunned silence for what seemed like an eternity, but was probably less than a minute. Such was the extent of her shock that it took her several seconds for her to realise that her mobile phone – which she had switched to silent – had been vibrating on the table beside her. She picked it up and saw that it was Tim calling. She could guess why.

She cleared her throat before answering. 'Hi Tim,' her voice sounding unnaturally thin.

'Hi Mary. Did you catch that press statement?'

'Regrettably, yes, and I can barely believe what I've just heard.'

'I know. I can't believe that the clients can have been that stupid. I mean, sending a team of armed thugs down there ...!'

'I know, my thinking precisely. But you say "clients", when in fact it could be just a rogue element of which Thompson is just one of the players.'

'True, but either way, Mary, there's no way back for them as regards our case, although from what we've just heard I reckon that this is just the beginning of their problems.'

'Very likely, but we are going to have to focus on the fallout as regards the case that we were instructed to present to the court. I think we probably both agree that we can forget about the injunction, but ...'

'Actually Mary, that's really why I called. It's times like these that your bag-carrier gets to say his piece. And it's because I know you well enough that I can anticipate the guilt and responsibility that you will inevitably want to place on your own shoulders. But I wanted to tell you that you cannot take the hit for this, and certainly not on your own, and certainly not before you've taken advice.'

She was moved to hear Tim say this. 'But Tim, we have to find out where and how the leak occurred. It's all I've been able to think about since Friday.'

'There'll be time enough for that inquest, Mary, but I'm not about to watch you fall on your sword for something that was plainly outside your control. And to that end, I wanted you to know that after the hearings on Friday, I went to see the managing partner and put him in the picture. I spent about ... '

'Sorry, you did what?'

'Please don't interrupt me, Mary, because this is important for both of us. As I was saying, I spent a fair amount of time with him to bring him up to speed. Earlier this morning, he rang to tell me that he has arranged for each of us to have separate, independent legal advice from specialist counsel. He's also notified our insurers. He either has sent or is about to send you an instruction that you should not speak to anyone outside the firm in connection with the case before you've sat down with your brief.'

Mary did not know how to respond. 'Sorry, just run that past me again ...'

'Mary, I watched you after that exchange with Miss Symonds. You were in shock, and incapable of speech. I could see that you were in no state to think objectively, both about the clients' position but also about your own. I figured that the last thing that was on your mind was the firm's "adverse events protocol".'

'Sorry, what ...'

'Exactly, I doubt you've even read it. Which is why I decided that I had to take the initiative and take this upstairs.'

She knew he was right. She'd never even heard of such a protocol.

When she failed to respond, he continued: 'Trust me, Mary, I've done the right thing. The lawyers will be in touch with us shortly, I'm told. Meanwhile, he's getting hold of the firm's compliance officer, who also chairs the ethics committee, in order to obtain advice as to whether or not the firm can continue to remain on the record. And that was before this morning's police statement, so I'd imagine that it will now be a fairly short conversation.'

Mary could now see the sense in taking that path.

'Yes, I can see that. The last thing that the board will want is for the firm to be seen as acting for companies who bump off their opponents.'

'Couldn't have put it better myself. But that's not all, Mary.'

'So, there's more?'

'Quite a lot, actually. Are you okay to talk for a while longer?'

'No particular place to go, as the song goes.'

'Fine. So, the boss called in a favour from one of the top silks, who sits on the bench a fair bit. He asked the brief, straight up, can we stay on the record, and even if we can, do we have to tell the judge that the clients unlawfully obtained access to Miss Symonds own personal data on her private email account.'

He sensed May about to intervene.

'No, Mary, as I said, this is important. So, the brief stated in categoric terms that, if we as a firm are privy to the clients' unlawful conduct, then we have a higher duty as officers of the court to act on that knowledge. So, cutting to the chase, the brief says that our duty to the court overrides that which we owe to the clients pursuant to our retainer. So, in short, Mary, we have no option other than to tell the judge.'

Following the ensuing silence, he added: 'And yes, to make your life easier, he opined that, whilst the matter was of course one for us to resolve internally, he could not personally see any circumstances in which we as a firm could properly continue to act.'

He let Mary digest that.

After a while she responded. 'So, what you're telling me, if I've heard you right, is that not only must we cease to act for these clients, but I have to shop them to the judge as well.'

'You know counsel, Mary. They never couch their opinion in black and white. They always bounce the issue back to their client, which in this case is us. So, when counsel says he's speaking personally, what he really means is that in his long experience he's never seen a judge take the opposite view.'

'So, in short, my hands are tied?'

'Pretty much, I reckon. So, shall we focus on the con with Gaitsland later this morning? Also, can I have the luxury of preparing the first draft of our letter to the clients telling them that they are, to quote the Bard, royally fucked, and that they need to find new solicitors to act for them?'

When she failed to reply, he added: 'Come to think of it, I'm rather looking forward to it!'

*

At about the same time, Tomo found his way into the relatives' suite at Southmead Hospital, clutching a shoulder bag full of organic goodies plus a handful of phone-charging packs, guessing correctly that the absence of any overnight calls from Cat meant that both her and Ali's phones needed power. He had spent most of Saturday working with Andrew Sutherland on their submissions ahead of Monday's hearing, but his calls to each of them had gone straight to voicemail. Hence the chargers.

He quickly patrolled the suite searching for Cat and her friend, but he could see neither of them. He undertook a further sweep, but with the same result, so he looked for someone who might be able to assist him, but to no avail.

This was not promising, he told himself, as he placed his bag on the floor and took a seat, looking around him properly for the first time. What struck him immediately was that there were two armed police officers standing beside some double doors at the far end of the suite. He noticed one of them speaking into his mouthpiece whilst looking at him, and immediately clocked that his presence was being reported. Whilst he scarcely answered the description of someone 'acting suspiciously,' he thought that the sensible thing to do would be to identify himself to the officers.

He got up and began to walk towards them, but was intercepted by another man who brandished his warrant card before him.

'Excuse me sir, Detective Sergeant Probert. I'm with Dorset Police. Would you mind stepping this way, sir,' said the plain-clothed officer, whom Tomo at once assumed must be a detective.'

'By all means, officer. You'll be wanting some ID, I assume?'

'That would be helpful, sir, yes,' replied the detective, registering the well-clipped accent of this unknown person.'

Tomo fished out his wallet.

'My name is Tom Butler,' he said, handing the officer his driving licence. 'I am a barrister. I represent one of the parties involved in the matter which no doubt pertains to the reason why you are here.'

The officer turned away from Tomo and spoke into his phone, reading out Tom's details to one of his colleagues.

'Thank you, sir,' he said returning Tomo's licence. 'And who might that party be, if I might ask, sir?'

'She is Miss Catriona Symonds,' replied Tomo, registering the recognition of the name in the detective's face. 'Would you happen to know whether she is still in this part of the hospital, or whether she has already left? She'll probably be accompanied by Miss Alison Henderson, the sister of one of the victims.'

'I can make an enquiry for you, sir, but before I do, are you able to confirm that the *matter*,' laying particular emphasis on that word, 'to which you referred is the one that led directly or indirectly to Friday's events?'

'The very same, officer,' he confirmed, scanning the room again briefly. 'Tell me, is your colleagues' presence over there, and indeed your own, also connected to that same *matter*?'

'I'm afraid that I cannot discuss operational matters with you, sir, as I'm sure you will understand. But can I take it that you caught this morning's press statement given by the senior investigating officer on the case?'

Tomo frowned at the question. 'I confess that I did not. Would you care to elucidate?'

'Certainly, sir. Shall we take a seat over here,' said the detective, pointing to some empty chairs nearby.

Once they were seated, he continued: 'Well, sir, I'll come straight to the point. I regret to inform you that one of the two victims of last Friday's events sadly passed away earlier this morning in the Intensive Care Unit. His relatives are being informed as we speak, so I am not at liberty to disclose his identity to you just yet.'

'How terrible,' exclaimed Tomo, 'and of course I understand. My colleagues and I feared that this might happen.'

'Indeed, sir. However, as a result of this development, and also on account of the use of a firearm, Dorset Police are now treating this matter as a murder investigation.'

Tomo absorbed that information. 'I see,' he said, thoughtfully, 'but can you tell me whether you and your colleagues consider Miss Symonds to be at personal risk of physical harm so as to justify these additional security measures?'

As he said that he looked across towards the doors guarded by the armed police.

'Again, sir, I am not at liberty to discuss operational matters. But, if you give me a moment, I'll just make that phone call for you.'

The detective rose and moved a few metres away, speaking into his phone before returning to Tomo's side.

'There'll be someone out to see you in a minute or two, sir.'

'Thank you, I'm very grateful.'

'It's my pleasure, sir,' replied the detective courteously and left to join another colleague on the far side of the suite.

An eternity seemed to pass before Tomo discerned movement by the double doors. He looked up to see a nurse speak briefly to one of the armed officers, who nodded his head in Tomo's direction.

Tomo rose and walked across the suite to introduce himself, but before he could speak she asked him, 'Hello. I'm Lorna Hashim, one of the nurses on duty in the ICU through there. Would you be Mr Tom Butler, by any chance?'

'Indeed, I am, but everyone calls me Tomo.'

'How lovely. Now, I'm told that you're looking for your client, Miss Symonds, who I believe is a friend of Miss Henderson.'

'That's right, I am.'

He was about to ask whether they were both here when he realised that the nurse might not be permitted to tell him without revealing which of the two victims had died earlier that morning. So, he hit upon a compromise.

'I think that both their mobiles have probably run out of power. So, if I were to give you these charging packs, then could I possibly ask that, if you did happen to, how shall I put it, *bump into* either of them, you might give these to them?'

Lorna gave him a knowing smile as if to congratulate him on his ingenious solution.

'I'd be only too happy to, Tomo,' and then added, 'that is, of course, if I do happen to *bump* into them, as you put it.'

'Naturally, and thank you,' he replied.

She left, and he watched as the police officers checked the contents of the bag before opening the double doors for her.

Another eternity seemed to pass, and the longer it did the more Tomo began to suspect the worst. Such was his state of apprehension that, when his phone did eventually vibrate, he almost dropped it. He saw that it was Cat's number.

'Hey Cat, I've been so worried. How are you both doing?'

'Oh, babe. It's been the worst two nights of our lives, Tomo. We're both so tired that we're way past crying. We had hours and hours of waiting and not knowing how Jamie was doing. And then we saw them ...'

'Saw who, Cat? You're not making any sense. Just take it slowly, all right? All you need to tell me is whether or not Jamie was the one who's died.'

'My heart almost stopped when I saw the surgeon walking towards us. He was coming straight for us, Tomo, until ...' She stifled a sob.

'Until what, Cat? All I know is what the detective here just told me. He said that one of them had died this morning. Who was it, Cat?'

'That's what I'm trying to tell you, Tomo. The surgeon was coming straight for us until the nurse steered him towards Joey's family. I could hardly bare to watch, Tomo, as his mother shrieked her denial. It was awful, Tomo, just too awful to behold, just ...'

The rest of her sentence was swallowed by a series of raking sobs. Tomo waited for these to subside, and then said softly, 'And Jamie, Cat, what about Jamie?'

'Those bastards, Tomo. They've killed an innocent young man ...'

Cat seemed not to have heard his question, so Tomo repeated it. She heard it the second time.

'Ali's speaking to him. The doctors said that it helps. Even when the patient is in a coma, because they reckon that the patient can still hear.'

'So Jamie's alive, then?'

'What? Oh, sorry, yes. That's what I was trying to tell you. But only just. That's why he's been put into a coma – at least that's what they told Ali this morning.'

'So, we must be grateful for small mercies,' said Tomo soothingly, 'and meanwhile keep our fingers and toes tightly crossed.'

After a moment, he added, 'Have you eaten anything, Cat? More importantly, have you drunk any water? There's some in the bag that I asked the nurse to give you.'

'What? Oh, I wondered why it was so heavy.'

'Have something to eat and drink, Cat, then call me back.'

'Okay, babe, and thanks.'

*

Shortly before noon on that Sunday morning, Mary and her team waited patiently for Allain Gaitsland to connect into the videoconference from one of the many meeting rooms in his chambers. Mary was conscious that this was probably the last occasion that they would get time to spend with her counsel on this case.

Gaitsland eventually greeted them with an unnecessarily stiff formality. They all knew why they were they, and what would be the likely outcome. However, they also knew how the rules of the game worked. They needed to bank counsel's formal advice on the feasibility or otherwise of continuing with the case in light of recent events both inside and outside court.

She gritted her teeth as Gaitsland checked the perfect symmetry of his papers on the table before him, and waited for him to begin. After an agonising pause, he addressed Mary.

'So, I take it that we have no further intelligence from the clients that would negate the thrust of this morning's press conference?' he began.

'None whatsoever, I'm afraid, Allain. In fact, we've not received anything helpful yet from the clients. If they're making their own independent enquiries, they've kept that a secret from their lawyers. Therefore,' she added quickly, so as to avoid the papers being re-ordered yet again, and anticipating the inevitable question, 'we are none the wiser as to how and when Mr Thompson became involved.'

She was rewarded with a 'Hmm.'

'So, the answer to your question is no, but I have left messages with the people in both their Legal and Internal Affairs Departments, yet none of them have returned my calls, nor those of my team here. And, in case you ask, I decided that it would not be prudent to contact Dorset Police directly, lest it might draw unnecessary attention to our, or rather our clients' predicament.'

Gaitsland nodded approvingly, before returning to the perfectly arranged sheets in front of him, which he duly re-ordered.

But Mary was not finished. 'However, using an outside agency, whose details need not concern you, my colleagues have been able to obtain confirmation that the three men were indeed arrested at what the police are describing as a crime scene.'

She had the room.

'Our source, who by the way is described as reliable, has revealed that the police, or rather their forensic investigators, removed evidence from an agricultural building that is believed to have formed part of the crime scene. That evidence was later sent to the forensic laboratory in Bournemouth under an armed escort, which the source described as highly unusual.'

'I'm not surprised,' Gaitsland interjected.

'The source is currently ignorant of the precise nature of that evidence, but we can reasonably assume that, whatever it was, it was likely to be connected to this case. I say this because we are told that the senior investigating officer had issued instructions to the forensic investigators attending the scene that copies of the contents of whatever evidence had been retrieved should be provided without delay to the supervising solicitor in accordance with the judge's request in his directions last week.'

Gaitsland did not like what he was hearing.

'So, do I deduce from what you have just said, Mary, that you think that this evidence must be the additional disclosure that Miss Symonds was intending to provide to the court via Mr Langar?'

She held his inquisitorial look. 'That is what I fear, yes,' she replied.

Gaitsland failed to disguise a wince, as he made an entry in his counsel's notepad, before realigning it with his other papers. Even his junior had come to dread this habit.

'So,' Gaitsland resumed, 'we have no alternative other than to address the grave reality of the circumstances in which our clients find themselves. Specifically, it appears that your worst fears have proven to be well founded, such that we need to consider very carefully how we should advise our clients on two points, both of which are interlinked.'

He paused momentarily, but mercifully for everyone else in the room his papers remained untouched.

'The first is whether we can still advise the clients that their prospects of success in the substantive proceedings remain good, or are borderline, or something considerably less. The second comes on top of the judge's obvious scepticism at the clients' failure, it might even be seen as a refusal, to concede that the copious disclosure produced by Miss Symonds is genuine. That issue is whether or not, having regard to recent events, there remains any realistic prospect that the judge will maintain the injunctions granted in favour of our clients when the hearing resumes tomorrow morning.'

He ticked off a note on his pad.

'The key to both of these issues lies in the role played by our clients in the events in South Dorset. As far as I can see, there is no best case. Whether or not our clients acted alone or in conjunction with a third party to protect their common interests, it makes little or no difference. And there is no evidence to suggest that the owners of *The Chronicle* were in any way involved. So, the finger points directly at our clients.'

He allowed another dramatic pause.

'Therefore, we need to focus on what is plainly a worst-case scenario. We have to assume that the police will prove that our clients, possibly a rogue element therein but that matters not a bit, procured sinister agents to prevent whatever is now with Dorset Police from being presented before the court. Given that likelihood, the consequences for our clients, and indeed for all of us, will be profound.'

Mary knew what was coming.

'First, the fundamental premise of the case that we were instructed to present to the court will have been compromised, if not fatally undermined. The obvious consequence of that will be that the injunctions will be set aside. It is one of the founding principles of equity that "those who come to equity must come with clean hands". That principle has been extended over the past century to provide that *those who come to equity must keep their hands clean*.

'So, the second consequence of our clients' actions will be that our clients will no longer be able to prevent the publication of the articles that the owners of *The Chronicle* were ordered to take down. Nor will they be able to prevent the wider media, both here and abroad, from running the story.'

No one dissented.

'However, that would not be the end of the clients' problems – no, not by a long stretch. I shall deal first with the fallout from the likely collapse of these proceedings. It is by no means unlikely that the clients will be found to have been in contempt of the very orders that they had obtained from the court. The penalties, both personally for the directors and corporately for the organisation, will be severe. Next, it is by no means unlikely that either the court of its own volition, or the defendants, will cause proceedings to be instigated for perjury against the clients and the relevant witnesses in respect of the evidence that the clients adduced before the court. Again, the penalties are serious, and include terms of imprisonment.'

His words hung in the air.

'But now I come to what could potentially be the more serious criminal liabilities that may follow, again both personally for the directors and corporately for the organisation. Dorset Police have disclosed that one of the two victims of last Friday's shooting has died. It appears beyond reasonable doubt that the victim was seriously injured as a result of gunshot wounds received at the crime scene. The consequences of this for our clients could not get much worse. As a corporate entity, the clients and those responsible within their organisation will likely now face a criminal prosecution on one or more charges of manslaughter. If convicted, the individuals responsible within the clients will face severe penalties, which will almost certainly include terms of imprisonment, as well as unlimited fines. As far as the company is concerned, if, as in my view seems likely, it is convicted on charges of corporate manslaughter, the financial consequences will be unlimited. There may also follow civil claims for compensation which may well have a wider impact on their business, and I dare say on the entire industry.'

No one spoke.

'So, given the clients' recalcitrance to engage with their own lawyers – despite the manifest urgency – I can only assume that they either know or fear the worst. However, it is our duty, for the time being at least, to convey the thrust of this advice to our clients. To that end, I have prepared a note of advice which I shall email to you shortly. This includes my advice that our clients should forthwith discontinue the proceedings. At the very least, they should not resist the respondents' application tomorrow morning to discharge the injunctions.'

He allowed a further pause, looking around the room inviting dissent. When none was forthcoming, he continued.

'Very well. Can I leave you and your team, Mary, to convey my advice to the clients. I have had a message from Andrew Sutherland asking me when I shall be in a position to exchange skeleton arguments for tomorrow's hearing. The deadline is four pm today, and we cannot afford to incur the judge's wrath again by further delay. That will just compound our problems.'

'Duly noted, Alain,' confirmed Mary.

'Right,' continued Gaitsland, 'it is now approaching midday. Can I ask you to inform the clients that I shall need their confirmation in writing by three pm today that they have accepted my advice. Absent such confirmation, I shall have to decide whether for professional reasons I can continue to represent them in these proceedings, as no doubt will your firm, if it has not already done so.'

Mary was expecting that.

'Duly noted, Alain. Thank you.'

Chapter 37

The following morning saw Andrew and Tomo sitting alone on the bench reserved for counsel in Court 37. They had filed their joint submissions to the judge the previous afternoon in readiness for the hearing of their imminent application, but were still unsure whether it would be opposed. Tomo turned to Rosalyn and asked her if she had received any last-minute communication from the claimants. As he had half expected, there had remained a deafening silence from them overnight, and Rosalyn made one final check in her inbox before shaking her head.

'Still nothing from the oppo,' Tomo said to Andrew. 'But it's gone ten-thirty, so perhaps the judge is in communication with them.'

'Possibly, but following Adrian's message yesterday, we know that he will not be here to represent his erstwhile clients,' replied Andrew.

They were interrupted by the familiar command, 'All rise.'

The judge strode into the court clutching his notebook, which he placed on the bench in front of him, but remained standing, as did the court staff.

'Gentlemen,' he announced, 'before we turn on the recording equipment, I believe that it would be fitting for us to observe a minute's silence in recognition of the death of a young man in connection with the matter before us.'

Both Andrew and Tomo bowed to acknowledge this instruction, and an unfamiliar silence filled the courtroom.

'Thank you,' said the judge, taking his seat after what had seemed a silence of several minutes.

'Now,' he continued, 'you appear to be unopposed, Mr Sutherland.'

'I do indeed, my lord. Mr Gaitsland did me and Mr Butler the courtesy of informing us that he would not be representing AlphaOm today. However, those instructing me and Mr Butler have not heard from his solicitors.'

'I think I can help you there, gentlemen. I received a similar message from Mr Gaitsland yesterday. But where I am ahead of you is that my clerk has just shown me a copy of an application by that firm to come off the record. He has also been informed by them that they will not be attending this hearing.'

Andrew remained silent as he watched the judge retrieve a separate document from his file, and then replace it.

'I am also in receipt of a letter from the partner in that firm to which I shall need to respond in a timely manner. However, gentlemen, the import of this missive would of itself suffice – sorry, I must add the obvious caveat, *subject to hearing submissions* – it would very likely suffice on its own to justify the discharge of the orders made by this court last week. Indeed, it might even have further consequences.'

Andrew and Tomo exchanged appreciative glances.

'But, I digress, Mr Sutherland, with apologies. The point is that your applications would have been granted without this latest intelligence.'

'I understand, my lord.'

'So, for the record, as far as this court is concerned this morning, you and Mr Butler are both unopposed, and it shall be so recorded on the court file.'

'That is duly noted, my lord.'

'So, for today's purposes, unless you have any additional submissions to make to me ...?'

'None, my lord.'

'Indeed, as I expected. So, your clients' joint and unopposed applications are granted. And I shall reserve costs.'

'Thank you, my lord.'

Tomo rose.

'My lord, if I may, could I invite you to note the position with regard to the disclosure that was in the course of being obtained from Miss Symonds pursuant to this court's orders? That disclosure is to be distinguished from the disclosure that the claimants will hitherto have obtained as a result of your previous orders, so far as the same was recommended by the independent solicitor. Your order today pursuant to our applications will require the claimants' former solicitors, their counsel and clients to cause all such disclosure to be returned to the defendants. The same will apply to the independent solicitor.'

'Indeed.'

'As regards the disclosure that is currently in the possession of Dorset Police, I invite you to record that, as a result of your helpful *steer* on Friday afternoon, those instructing me have received what are now believed to be copies of the disclosure seized at the crime scene.'

'Thank you, Mr Butler. That is duly noted. So, it would appear that between them, the defendants have everything they need to start the presses rolling.'

'Your lordship might think so, but I couldn't possibly comment,' quipped Tomo in reply.

'Touché,' the judge responded with a mischievous smile. 'Well, assuming that AlphaOm do not intend to make a fresh application for a restraining order, which I am not trying to encourage them to do, I shall be intrigued to read what your respective clients decide to print over the coming weeks.'

Tomo nodded and sat down, assuming that the hearing was about to end. But, to his surprise, the judge continued, 'And I would just observe that, in my professional, and now judicial, experience, I should record that I have never encountered such a bizarre reversal of fortunes in such a short period of time. But, there it is.'

This time it was Andrew who rose. 'I rather think that Mr Butler and I would like to second that, my lord.'

'Indeed. Well, good day to you both.'

Epilogue

Ten weeks later

Charlie had not touched this gate since that awful day. No, more than that, he hadn't even found the courage to stand at the foot of the rugged lane that ran up to the old stone barn. But now here he was, on this splendid July morning, looking up at it as if it were a foreign land.

Part of him was seething, but a bigger part of him was trembling, lacking the fortitude to walk the two or three hundred yards up that rugged track. The terrain somehow now looked more menacing and forbidding than it had ever done in his mind. So much so that, in other circumstances, he would have taken the easy option and walked away.

And he might well have done, had he not felt the soft hand clasp his own. He sensed at once the same conflicts of emotion, and turned to look at the nervous features of the beautiful young woman who had placed her confidence in him.

He knew then that he could not let her down.

Before he could speak, he caught sight of the sad-faced PC Brinley, who now held the blue police tape in his hand and gave him a reassuring nod, before repeating the same gesture to Cat.

She carried a large bouquet of fresh flowers, their scent almost overwhelming to the point that she felt she might attract the attention of the nearby bees. Her sense of serenity seemed to fortify Charlie.

'Are you ready, ma'am?' he asked in his soft Dorset accent.

In response, Cat looked first at the state of the lane and then at her shoes.

'How ditsy am I, Charlie. I forgot to bring any sensible footwear.'

Before Charlie could reply, she handed him the flowers and bent down and removed her shoes, preparing to make the ascent barefoot. He acknowledged the act in admiration.

'Just take note of those thistles, ma'am. They're a damnable nuisance and can give you no end of discomfort.'

Her hand gave his a squeeze.

'Oh, after what happened here, Charlie, I reckon that a dose of physical pain might be just what my grandma would approve of right now.'

'Aye, ma'am. Can't argue with that, but mind where you tread just the same. There'll be a fair bit of standing about after the service.'

Other things being equal, Cat might have responded, but they had already dealt with the issue of her attendance today. It had been Charlie who had approached Joey's parents to ascertain whether they would permit Cat to pay her respects. Their response had been to send her a personal invitation, with an implied admonishment that she was not to assume any responsibility for Joey's death.

'Can I hold your arm, Charlie?'

'Why, ma'am, that would truly be an honour.'

Her face brightened. And so, on that note, they advanced in silence up the slope, both now absorbed in their own thoughts, with Charlie navigating a route that avoided the worst of the prickly weeds.

After a while, Charlie spoke. 'So, the wife and I were listening to the wireless yesterday evening, and we heard the news lass say that the police had caught the head of that big chemist. You know, the one that you used to stop at?'

Cat halted abruptly, and looked up at Charlie.

'Sorry Charlie, but did you just say that they've caught McBride?'

'That sounds about right, ma'am. I didn't quite catch the name, but I think that might be the one that the lass used.'

Cat gingerly tip-toed around a thistle.

'Did they say where, Charlie?'

He rubbed his cap over his scalp, as he was wont to do when he was thinking. After a while he replied, 'Well, truth be told, Ma'am, I can't now recall. But it was the English police that took him; trying to board some boat or ferry, they said.'

Cat leant her head into his shoulder. A few moments later, she was able to speak.

'Oh Charlie, that will bring proper justice for that young man.'

She sensed Charlie stiffen, and take some deep breaths. She turned into him, and gave him a proper hug.

'Look at us, Charlie. What a pair we make. Let's go up there and say what we both need to say to Joey.'

By way of assent, Charlie released her and slowly helped her to resume their progress up the hill.

On their arrival, the faint but visible brown patch on the ground provided all the evidence that they needed to reveal the location of the shrine they had come to consecrate. Cat turned into their hug once again.

'Oh Charlie, what a trauma you must have been through ...'

He held her embrace, and after a while she became conscious of his shoulders heaving against her, as his own emotions were released.

It might have been minutes. It might have been an hour, but gradually Cat withdrew from their embrace, handing him the flowers and gracefully dropped to her knees.

She placed both hands on the brown sullied soil.

'Joey. I never knew you. But I never intended that you should be placed in harm's way, least of all at the hands of those monsters. Believe me, please, when I tell you that I am so very, very sorry. But, your death will not be in vain. I intend to fight for justice not only for you, but for the thousands, millions perhaps, who have been damaged by their deceit. What I call their *sweet deceit*. And with these flowers, Joey, I give you my word.'

She took the proffered bunch from Charlie, and laid them reverently upon the barren ground before her.

She remained still, her attempt at a prayer murmured through trembling lips, whilst Charlie chaperoned the proceedings.

After a minute or so, she held up her hand, which Charlie dutifully caught in his and helped her to her feet. Before he could begin to wipe his eyes, Cat stopped him, holding both his hands in hers as she pressed herself to him.

'This is how we begin to grieve, Charlie. Hiding from our pain can only make things worse. And besides, there's no one else to see us here.'

Charlie made to protest, but his attempt possessed no intent. Until that moment, he had thought that he had been passing this endurance test for Cat's benefit. But now he realised that she was doing this equally for him, and that this was part of her silent magic. And so he began to cry, releasing both his trauma and his grief, and as he did so felt such a sense of relief that it took him a while to appreciate that his embrace had morphed into something of a bear-hug.

Cat's muffled pleas gradually brought him back to reality.

'Oh ma'am, I'm so sorry. I didn't mean...'

Several heaving, choking breaths later, and Cat attempted to speak.

When that failed, she smiled, then giggled, and then began a full-on laugh. Charlie's features turned from concern to relief, before joining Cat in her laughter. They folded into their former embrace, but this time united by a new determination at last to confront what had befallen their slain confederate.

And so, a minute or two later, they turned their tear-stained faces back to the road and began to descend the rough lane towards Charlie's weather-worn Landy.

Brinley knew better than to catch their eyes, and looked dutifully at the ground as Cat stooped to retrieve her shoes. He watched them drive away, slightly misty-eyed himself, and repositioned the police tape.

As they drove down the road towards the church, Cat pulled out a tissue.

'Could you just let me off here, Charlie.'

He was about to object until he saw her brandish the tissue, and dutifully complied just in time to receive her ministrations. She slowly wiped his face, and then turned the mirror towards her so that she could examine herself.

After a while, Charlie spoke, 'Thank you, ma'am. And I really mean, thank you.'

She patted his hand on the gear stick.

'Well, Charlie, let's just agree that the gratitude probably flows both ways. Please will you grant me that?'

He smiled at her in acknowledgement.

A few moments later, parked as they were a way back from the church, she reached across and kissed his cheek.

'Now, Charlie, you have a sombre duty to attend to. And I'll be just fine here for a minute or two if you'll just let me be.' She then added: 'But not before I have attended to some repairs'

He demurely looked away, and after wrestling with a response, he merely said, 'Ma'am,' and pulled on the hand-brake, having now tumbled why she had asked him to pull up on to the grass verge a few hundred yards short of the church.

He waited as she used the Landy's mirror to redo her make-up. He sensed that it amused her that such decorum seemed so out of place in his antique chariot. But this being Britain, folk in this valley had become used to muddling along, as they had done through two world wars.

So, half blushing, he allowed himself the occasional glance to watch her duly *muddle*, which she proceeded to do with serene calmness.

A minute or so later, she once again resembled the *summer blossom* that he had collected from the mid-morning train, albeit perched atop of her mourning attire, from which she skilfully brushed all traces of the dried earth on which she had knelt a few minutes earlier further down the valley.

Seemingly satisfied with her repairs, she gave him a pat on his hand, and climbed out of the Landy and waved him on his way. They exchanged knowing smiles, and he duly drove away.

Taking her time, she walked along the grassy lane until she reached the lychgate at the entrance to the church, or the *kirk* as her grandma would have described it if she had been here. Then, having checked that no one nearby would recognise her, she walked up to the entrance to the church and discretely found a place at the corner of the last pew at the rear, where she hoped she could remain incognito.

After a while, before the congregation began to arrive, she opened the service sheet that she had liberated from the church entrance, But she was unprepared for the choir's practice of Mozart's *Ave Verum Corpus*. It cut through her soul like a warm knife through butter, and the first tears appeared.

More followed.

Then more, and she allowed them to fall.

And they fell not just for young Joey, but for the hurt she had caused Jamie. But perhaps even more for her own mistakes. Because, had it not been for them, none of this would ever have happened. And that would have been her take-home from this service, but for the fervent hug that interrupted her self-indulgence.

'Cat?'

When she didn't respond, the voice continued: 'Hey, Cat, babe. It's me, Ali ...'

It seemed to take an age for Cat to respond. She made to protest when Ali began to wipe her face.

'Cat. Babe. This is not your fault.'

Cat looked blankly back at her.

'It's not your fault, babe.'

When Cat shook her head, Ali turned her so that they were facing each other.

'Well, if you won't take that from me, babe, then maybe you'll take it from someone who is hurting even more than you.'

With that, she withdrew, leaving Cat, confused and alone in the pew, trying to dry her tears with an increasingly soggy tissue.

She remained sitting there, until she became conscious of another body, another scent, beside her, and then another arm around her.

'Cat?'

She gave a feeble nod.

'Cat, I'm Janie. I'm Joey's mum.'

As Cat made to speak, Janie gave her back a soothing rub.

'Oh, my dear, I don't suppose you've heard the news just now, have you?'

As Janie had expected, this sideways maternal injection stifled Cat's emotions, as Cat looked at her with a revived eagerness.

'I didn't think so, my dear. Well now, we just heard them say on the wireless that the regulators and the police are all over that there chemist who Ali tells us treated you and Jamie so badly these past years.'

When Cat looked at her uncomprehending, Janie continued, 'My dear, none of us really understand what *suspending shares* means, but Ali told us that it's the bit that comes after the rabbit's been shot, and before it's about to be skinned, as we say in these parts. Oh, and apologies if you're a vegetarian.'

Cat shook her head. As Janie had expected after years of motherhood, her intervention had achieved precisely what she had intended. Cat looked at her with a vigour that had been absent only just moments earlier. Janie renewed her hug.

'My dear, you have toppled the Goliath. It's all over the news. How you overcame that court business I've no idea, nor do any of us. Nor can we guess what sling or stone you used to fell that giant.'

When Cat looked at her, uncomprehending, Janie continued, 'All I can say is that our Joey would have been so proud to have been able to play his part in that fight.'

She gave Cat another hug.

'We are all so proud of you. Now, I have to go, my darling. God bless you.'

With that, she kissed away one of the remaining tears on Cat's cheek, then slid down the pew before walking sedately down the aisle.

Meanwhile, underneath the lychgate, having trained Joey's comrades in the village hall with a makeshift substitute, Charlie began to process with them to the church door with Joey's coffin. Mercifully they completed their journey without incident to the altar, where Charlie had prepared the trestles. On Charlie's command they lowered the coffin and gave a discreet bow, then retreated to their designated pews.

Cat was barely aware of these logistics, and the service proceeded in an emotional mist, with varying words and harmonies subliminally registering on her antennae. Afterwards, she watched mutely as Joey's mother, accompanied by a man and two younger women whom she presumed to be her family, followed the coffin towards the churchyard.

Having allowed the congregation to process behind them, she deliberately stayed until she felt sure that she was alone in the church, save for the organist who continued to play a retiring anthem that Cat did not recognise.

Once silence descended, Cat crept down the side-aisle until she could approach the altar.

She had never done this before, but now she knelt before it. She did not know why, but she longed for her granny's faith. It had seemed then so simple back then, and so comforting.

Yet now it was so elusive.

She resented her education, which had exploded so much of the myths on which the Bible had been constructed. Aided by the clergy's *happy-clappy* liturgy, she had been taught to embrace a more humanitarian and agnostic approach to faith. So much so that she had become almost programmed to regard her granny's faith as irrational.

How had Jamie described it? Ah yes: they were part of the 'great unchurched'.

Perhaps not, she pondered.

She remained silent before the altar, not knowing what to say, until she remembered what Granny had taught her. So, she reached for the 1552 Prayer Book that she had brought with her. She found the right page, and then whispered the Lord's Prayer that William Tyndale had incorporated into the first English translation of the Bible, and which Cranmer had so skilfully adopted *verbatim* on behalf of Queen Elizabeth I. Her granny had taught her that this was the only prayer that Jesus had *authorised*, according to the Gospels.

She relished the tranquillity.

After several minutes she wiped her eyes, and rose to her feet. Almost unconsciously, she curtsied in front of the cross. She didn't know why, but it had felt right. Then she took a few steps backwards, before walking slowly down the aisle, with her eyes downcast. She focussed on the stones in front of her, until she raised her eyes towards the main door to the church.

Then she stopped.

And stared.

He was the last person that she had expected to be standing in the aisle.

She stumbled for the support of the nearest pew, and half-whispered, half-spoke his name: 'Jamie.'

She held on to the pew and momentarily closed her eyes. When she opened them again, he was standing in front of her. As he reached towards her, she looked into his eyes in a supplicatory request for atonement, but was unprepared for the gentle hold of Jamie's arms as he slowly pulled her into an embrace.

Neither spoke, nor attempted to. Instead, they both let their tears fall onto each other's shoulders. When they each sensed that the other was ready, they both tried to speak at once, then both paused, before half-laughing.

They resorted to sign language, she telling him to speak first.

When he instinctively shrugged, she reached up her hand, and wiped away the tears on his face with a tenderness that brought first a momentary stiffness to his frame, and then a belated calmness as he accepted her touch.

'I'm so sorry, Jamie,' was the best that she could muster.

As she spoke those words, over Jamie's shoulder she caught sight of Ali standing in the church doorway.

Taking that as an instruction that she was not to be deterred, she continued.

'Jamie, I have hurt you in a way that no woman should. And I am so ashamed of it. It haunts me day and night. In fact, in my every waking moment.'

She looked up at the ornate carvings on the beams.

'Jamie,' she choked, then tried to check herself.

She failed.

'Oh Jamie, I hurt you so badly. I beg you to forgive me.'

She clasped him firmly, unaware that he was weeping so profusely that he had not really heard her. Such a confession in those ecclesiastical surroundings ought to have engendered a fitting response. But instead, there was only the sound of subdued sobs. The encounter might have ended in farce had it not been for Ali, who had silently, and to Jamie's senses, mysteriously, appeared behind him.

She held his shoulder, and spoke softly into his ear. 'Jamie. She is begging for your forgiveness. Jamie, for God's sake, grant it.'

A muffled sob was his response.

'It's your way back, Jamie!'

He tried to speak, but his mouth would not obey his mind. Jamie's silence caused Cat to relinquish their embrace, moaning in regret. Ali grabbed him more firmly, shaking him now.

'Jamie! For God's sake. Forgive her!'

Seconds, minutes, hours even, seemed to pass.

In those precious moments, realisation finally struck Jamie with a force greater than any slap that Ali could have delivered. He became aware first of Cat preparing to slump into the adjacent pew, then of Ali's grasp, and then of his own inaction. And at last, he acted.

He retrieved Cat into his embrace, and when his attempt at words eluded him, Ali's squeeze on his shoulder settled his emotions.

'Cat …' He choked back another sob. 'Cat,' he began, 'please don't do this. None of this is your fault. Cat, none of this is our fault.'

He felt Cat intensify her hug, so he pressed on, at last determined to speak.

'Cat, all this happened because of other people's greed. We just happened to be pawns in a much bigger game.'

Cat hugged him in reply, so he continued.

'So, Cat, there is nothing to forgive. Believe me, I understand now. And I just want to be able to hug you as a friend. That's all we shall be now, Cat. The very best of friends, forever. Yes? Forever?'

Beside him there was initially silence, but then Cat spoke: 'Oh Jamie, do you really mean that?'

He pulled her into an embrace.

'Oh Cat, yes. And before God, and in front of this very altar, I swear it to you. And let me say that, whatever may have happened between us, none of it was your fault. It has taken me time, belatedly I now accept, and mostly due to Ali, to realise that I had got everything upside down.'

She smiled at that, allowing him to continue.

'But then came my dalliance at St Peter's gate, and then this,' indicating the pews either side of them. 'And, if one were looking for lessons in life's perspective, they won't come any clearer than what I've just been through. So, yes, if you really believe that you have done anything that I need to forgive, which by the way I do not, and doubt I ever truly did, then you have my full forgiveness.'

Cat had no tears left, so she just hugged him. As he hugged her.

After a while, each of them silently took one of Ali's arms, and they walked down the aisle into the afternoon sun.

The End

The Author initially practiced at the Bar before becoming a Partner in one of the 'Magic Circle' Law Firms in the City of London. He subsequently returned to the Bar, where he practised in Commercial and Construction disputes. He recently retired to begin a new career as a writer. He now lives in the West Country with his wife, Sophia, and 'Bertie' (Labrador). Their son, Piers, lives and works in London.

Th Portrait is by Nick Bashall.